About the Authors

Award-winning author _____ contemporary romances. _____ books translated into m_____ she is a two-time winn_____ Reviewers' Choice Aw_____ Reviewers' Choice Award _____ _____ she resides with her very patient husband and Writer Kitty. When she's not plotting out her next romance, you can find her with a mug of tea and a book. Learn more at https://jenniferfaye.com/

A. C. Arthur was born and raised in Baltimore, Maryland where she currently resides with her husband and three children. Determined to bring a new edge to romance, she continues to develop intriguing plots, sensual love scenes, racy characters and fresh dialogue, thus keeping the readers on their toes! Artist loves to hear from her readers and can be reached through her contact form or via email at acarthur22@yahoo.com

Award-winning romance author **Kerri Carpenter** writes contemporary romances that are sweet, sexy, and sparkly. When she's not writing, Kerri enjoys reading, cooking, watching movies, taking Zumba classes, rooting for Pittsburgh sports teams, and anything sparkly. Kerri lives in Northern Virginia with her adorable (and mischievous) rescued poodle mix, Harry. Kerri loves chatting with readers. Visit her at kerricarpenter.com or on Facebook, Twitter or Instagram to connect today.

Ever After

COLLECTION

Dreaming Ever After

JENNIFER FAYE

A.C. ARTHUR

KERRI CARPENTER

MIX
Paper from
responsible sources

FSC   FSC® C007454

This book is produced from independently certified FSC™ paper
to ensure responsible forest management.

For more information visit www.harpercollins.co.uk/green

Printed and bound in Spain
by CPI, Barcelona

MILLS & BOON

First Published in Great Britain 2020
By Mills & Boon, an imprint of HarperCollins*Publishers*
1 London Bridge Street, London, SE1 9GF

DREAMING EVER AFTER © 2020 Harlequin Books S.A.

Safe in the Tycoon's Arms © 2014 Jennifer F. Stroka
One Perfect Moment © 2018 Artist Arthur
Bidding on the Bachelor © 2017 Kerri Carpenter

ISBN: 978-0-263-29883-3

SAFE IN THE
TYCOON'S ARMS

JENNIFER FAYE

For Viv.

Thank you for being such a good friend over the years. Your helpful advice and unending support are deeply appreciated. Here's to the future of possibilities.

CHAPTER ONE

A DEAFENING CRACK of thunder rumbled through the darkened house. Kate Whitley pressed a hand to her pounding chest. She'd hated storms since she was a little kid. A brilliant flash of lightning sent shards of light slashing across the hallway while rain pelted the window.

Mother Nature certainly had a wicked sense of humor. Actually, it seemed as though life as a whole was mocking Kate. Absolutely nothing was going according to plan, no matter how hard she fought to put things right.

Her fingers pushed against the cold metallic plate on the swinging hall door. Inside the kitchen, the glare from the overhead light caused her to squint. What in the world was going on? She could have sworn she'd turned everything off before going upstairs. Hadn't she?

She sighed and shook her head. Her mind must be playing tricks on her. The long nights of tossing and turning instead of sleeping were finally catching up to her. And it couldn't have happened at a worse time. In a few more hours, she had to be fully alert. There were decisions only she could make—lifesaving decisions.

If only she could get a little shut-eye, she'd be able to think clearly. But first, Mother Nature had to quiet down. No one could rest with all this ruckus.

It didn't ease her nerves being away from home, even if she was staying in a New York City mansion. This place was nothing like her two-bedroom, ranch-style house in Pennsylvania. Though this oversize house contained some of the most breathtaking architecture, there was something missing—the warmth that made a building more than just a place to hang your coat, the coziness that made it home.

In a big city where she barely knew anyone, she and this house had a couple of things in common—being lonely and forgotten. Somehow it seemed like fate that she'd ended up in this deserted mansion. A warm, loving home had somehow always eluded her, and just when she thought she'd made one of her own, it too was about to be snatched out from under her.

Sadness weighed heavily on her as her bare feet moved silently across the kitchen tiles. The coldness raced up through her pink painted toes to her bare legs and sent goose bumps cascading down her arms. Spring may have brought warmer days, but the nights were still chilly. She rubbed her palms up and down her arms, willing away her discomfort. Perhaps her long T-shirt wasn't the warmest choice for this soggy night, but with her living out of a suitcase, her choices were quite limited.

She yawned and opened the door of the stainless-steel refrigerator. She hadn't had any appetite until now. With so much riding on this upcoming meeting, she'd ended up with a stress headache for most of the day. But back here ensconced between these quiet, peaceful walls, the pain had loosened its vicelike grip.

Now she needed something to ease her hunger pangs. Other than a few meager groceries she'd placed in there earlier, the glass shelves were bare. The friend who'd let her stay here free of charge said the owner was out of town and wouldn't be back anytime soon. From the empty cabinets to the dust-covered bedrooms, Kate deduced no one had lived here in quite a while.

With an apple in hand, she filled a glass of water. She'd

just turned off the faucet when she heard faint but distinct footsteps. The hairs on the back of her neck rose. Either this place had some mighty big rats…or she wasn't alone.

"Stop right there!" boomed a male voice.

So much for the rat theory.

Her heart lodged in her throat, blocking a terrified scream. Who was this man? And what did he want with her? Her lungs started to burn. Was he a thief, a desperate junkie…or worse?

She struggled to suck air past the enormous lump in her throat. A nervous tremor in her hand caused droplets of water to spill over the rim of the glass. Why had she put herself in such peril by making the rash decision to stay in this deserted house alone? After all, what did she know about her newfound friend? Not much. They'd only met a week ago. The older woman had seemed so nice—so understanding in Kate's time of need.

She wondered if a scream would carry to any of the neighboring houses on the block. Probably not. This house came from an era when structures were built with thick, sturdy walls. She was on her own.

"You shouldn't be here." She fought to keep her voice steady. "This place has a burglar alarm. It won't be long until the police show up. I haven't seen your face. You can escape out the back and I won't tell anyone."

"I don't think so. Turn around."

Not about to let this stranger know how much he frightened her, she placed the glass on the counter, leveled her shoulders and took an unsteady breath. When she went to turn, her feet wouldn't move. They were stuck to the floor as though weighted down in concrete.

A crescendo of thunder reverberated through her body. The house plunged into darkness. Kate bit down on her bottom lip to keep a frightened gasp bottled up.

Don't panic. Stay calm.

Could this really be happening? What had she done to piss off Fate and have it turn on her? Hysterical laughter swelled in her throat. With effort, she choked it down. It wouldn't help anything for this man to think she was losing it.

Drawing on every bit of courage she could muster, she forced her feet to move. Once fully turned around, she squinted into the dark shadows but could only make out the man's vague outline. Who was he? What did he want with her?

Then, as though in answer to her prayer, the power blinked back on. When her vision adjusted, she found herself staring at a bare male chest. *What in the world?* Her wide-eyed gaze dropped farther past his trim waist but screeched to a halt upon the discovery of this stranger's only article of clothing—navy boxer shorts.

This night was definitely getting stranger by the second.

She couldn't resist a second glance at her sexy intruder. He definitely wasn't a kid, having filled out in all the right places. She'd only ever seen defined muscles like his in the glossy pages of magazines, and this guy would qualify with his washboard abs. He must be around her age, maybe a little older.

When her gaze rose up over his six feet plus of sexiness, she met a hard glint in his blue-gray eyes. He obviously wasn't any happier about discovering her than she was of stumbling across him.

"What are you doing here?" The stranger's deep voice held a note of authority as though he were used to commanding people's attention.

"Wondering why you're standing in my kitchen."

The frown lines on his face etched even deeper. "This is your place?"

Technically no, but she wasn't about to explain her unusual circumstances to Mr. Oh-So-Sexy. She merely nodded, affirming her right to be there.

His brow arched in disbelief.

Who was he to pass judgment? When she pressed her hands to her hips, she realized he wasn't the only one scantily dressed. With the hem of her worn but comfy shirt pinched between her fingers, she pulled it down as far as the material would allow. Instinct told her to run and put on something more modest. But in order to do that, she'd have to cross his path. Not a great idea.

Her gaze strayed back to the doorway. Sooner or later she'd have to make her move. She wanted to believe he wasn't there to hurt her—wanted to accept the notion that there was some crazy explanation for the nearly naked man standing in front of her, but her mind drew a blank. She glanced back at him, taking in his blondish-brown wavy hair tousled as though he'd just woken up. And his lack of apparel left no room for doubt that he was unarmed.

"Don't look so panicked. I have no intention of hurting you." His deep voice was as smooth and rich as hot fudge. "I just want some answers."

She stuck out her chin. "That makes two of us."

"I guess you should start explaining." He looked at her expectantly.

Kate crossed her arms. He wasn't going to boss her around. She had every right to be here. Then an ominous thought came to her: Who was to say Connie hadn't made a similar offer to this man? But wouldn't it have crossed her friend's mind that this would create an awkward situation to have two strangers—a man and a woman—alone in the house?

As she kept a wary eye on him, she noticed something familiar about him. The thought niggled at her. She couldn't put her finger on where she'd seen him before, probably because the only thing keeping her on her feet right now was adrenaline. She needed sleep. Desperately. But how would she get this man to put on some clothes and go away?

"No more stalling." Lucas Carrington's patience was worn razor thin. Tired of talking in circles, he cut to the chase. "Who are you? And what are you doing here?"

Her lush lips pursed as her eyes narrowed. "My name is Kate Whitley and I have every right to be here—"

"Impossible. More likely you're homeless and broke in here seeking shelter from the storm."

Kate's chin tilted up and her unwavering brown gaze met his. "I'm not homeless. In fact, I'm an interior designer and a darned good one, too."

She did have an innocent girl-next-door look about her, but he knew all too well that things were never quite what they seemed. "Are you trying to tell me you broke in here because you had this overwhelming desire to redecorate the place?"

Her thin shoulders drew back into a firm line. Her threadbare cartoon T-shirt pulled snugly across her pert breasts. He swallowed hard. Okay, so maybe his first assessment of her hadn't been quite right. Gorgeous. Sexy. Curvaceous. Those were much more fitting descriptions.

She continued to glare at him, seemingly oblivious to the fact her demeanor was more alluring than intimidating. And like some hormone-fueled teenager, he found himself unable to turn away from her tempting curves.

"There's no need to sound so condescending." Her voice filled with exasperation.

With effort, his gaze lifted to meet hers. "I'm calling the police. They can deal with you." But there was a wrinkle in his plan—his cell phone was in the other room and the landline in the kitchen had been disconnected ages ago.

"Go right ahead."

Her confident tone surprised him. Did she expect her

beauty to get her out of this mess? Or was she attempting to pull a con job on him? Not that any of it mattered. He didn't have a problem calling her bluff.

"You seem fairly certain you won't get in trouble—"

"I won't."

Lucas was having a hard time focusing on the conversation given that his unexpected visitor was standing in his kitchen with nothing on but a T-shirt, which clung to her shapely curves and exposed her long, long legs. He was definitely beginning to understand why she might rely on her looks. And if he kept staring, this could get embarrassing for both of them.

He forced his gaze to her face, not that it was any less distracting. Was she wearing makeup? Or was her skin naturally that smooth and creamy?

Even more troubling than how beautiful he found her was the way she reminded him too much of the past—a past that had nearly destroyed him. Not so long ago another beautiful woman had stood in that spot. She'd made him promises but ended up breaking each and every one of them. His jaw tightened. The last thing he needed was this stranger's presence to dredge up memories he'd fought so hard to seal inside. He refused to let it happen.

Refocused and clear about his priorities, his gaze returned to her warm brown eyes. She stared directly at him. Pink stained her cheeks, but she didn't glance away. She stepped forward, using the kitchen island as a shield. It was far too late for modesty. Her sexy form was already emblazoned upon his memory.

Stay focused. Soon she'll be gone. One way...or the other.

He cleared his throat. "Okay, you've got my attention. Why won't you get in trouble?"

"I have permission to be here. Temporarily, that is. You know, while the owner is out of town." Kate's eyes narrowed, challenging him. She certainly was confident. He'd give her that. "And now it's your turn to do some explaining. Who are you?"

"My name's Lucas."

"Well, Lucas, I assume you must know Connie, too."

His gaze sought out hers and held it. "Connie? Is that who let you in here?"

Kate nodded as hope sparked in her eyes. "Connie Carrington."

He had liked it better when he thought Kate was a squatter looking for a warm place to sleep. "To be sure, describe Connie."

"Short. Brunette. Sixtyish. Very sweet and generous. She has a friendly smile and volunteers at East Riverview Hospital."

"That's her." It still didn't prove Kate was telling the whole truth, but it was sure looking that way.

"Here's the thing, Connie obviously offered me this place first. And I don't think us sharing the house is going to work."

How dare this woman—this stranger—kick him out of his own house? He opened his mouth to give her a piece of his mind but then closed it. Obviously she didn't recognize him, a small wonder after that ridiculous magazine article earlier in the month had named him Bachelor of the Year. His quiet life hadn't been the same since then.

Kate was a refreshing change from the headline seekers and the husband hunters. Maybe if this were a different time under different circumstances, he'd welcome this beautiful intrusion. But right now all he wanted was to be left alone.

A clap of thunder rattled the windows. Kate jumped. She obviously wasn't as calm as she'd like him to believe. Perhaps they both needed a moment to gather their thoughts. He certainly could use a minute or two to tamp down his unwanted attraction.

"This conversation would be a little less awkward with some more clothes on. I'll be right back." He started out of the room, then as an afterthought he called over his shoulder, "Don't go anywhere."

Lucas strode from the room. His teeth ground together. He didn't want this woman here. He never had company and he preferred it that way. In fact, the less time he spent here, the better he liked it. When he'd asked his aunt to look after the place, he'd never expected her to turn it into a B and B. What in the world had she been thinking?

Maybe his aunt had planned for him to never find out about Kate. After all, he wasn't even supposed to be home for another week. But one untimely setback after another at the future site of Carrington Gems' expansion in San Francisco had ground construction to a halt.

Still, it was more than losing money hand over fist due to bureaucratic red tape that had him cutting his trip short. He put a stop to his thoughts. He wasn't ready to contemplate the devastating situation he'd faced before catching his cross-country flight home.

And the last thing he needed was to return home to find a half-dressed woman making herself comfortable in his house. The image of her bare legs teased his mind, clouding his thoughts.

He cursed under his breath and pulled on the first pair of jeans he laid his hands on. But if he was going to stay focused, his beautiful interloper needed to cover up. He grabbed a heavy robe that should modestly cover her and give him some peace of mind. With a T-shirt in hand for himself, he rushed back to the kitchen clutching both articles of clothing.

"Here." He held out the robe to her. "Put this on."

Her wary gaze moved to his outstretched hand and back. It was then that he got a close-up view of her heart-shaped face and button nose. His thoughts screeched to a halt when he spied the dark shadows beneath her eyes. Sympathy welled up inside his chest. Not so long ago, he'd worn a similar look. It hadn't happened by missing a night or two of sleep. In fact, it'd been the worst time of his life. His gut told him that Kate had a devastating story of her own.

He'd always been good at reading people. It was what helped him run Carrington Gems and hire a reliable staff. So why had he immediately jumped to the wrong conclusion about Kate?

Had his experience with his ex-wife jaded him so badly that he wasn't even willing to give this woman the benefit of the doubt? Or was it the fact she was standing in this house—a place so filled with pain and loss?

Kate's cold fingertips brushed over the back of his hand as she accepted the robe. His instinct was to take her hands in his and rub them until they were warm. But he resisted the temptation. She wasn't his guest...his responsibility.

While she slipped on the robe, he stepped back, giving her some space. He pulled the shirt over his head. Now they could have a reasonable conversation.

Fully clothed, he glanced up, finding Kate's brows furrowed as she stared at him. He followed her line of vision to a large hole in his jeans above his knee as well as the army of white smudges marking up both legs. He really should consider tossing them, but they were just so comfortable. Wait. Why should he care what this woman thought of him or his clothes? After tonight he'd never see her again.

Kate shoved up the sleeves on the robe and crossed her arms. "What do you propose we do?"

In any other situation, he'd show her to the door and wish her well. After all, she wasn't his problem. And being drawn in by her very kissable lips and the memory of how that threadbare shirt hugged her curves was a complication in his life that he just didn't need.

But her pale face with those dark smudges beneath her eyes dug at his resolve.

And he couldn't dismiss the fact his aunt had sent Kate to stay here. Not that his aunt didn't help people on a daily basis, but she knew this house was off-limits to everyone. That meant Kate was someone special. Now he really needed to speak to his aunt, but first he had to make things clear to Kate.

"There's something you should know. This is my house."

CHAPTER TWO

KATE EYED UP Mr. Oh-So-Sexy's faded T-shirt and thread-bare denim. Even her ratty old jeans were in better condition. Did she look gullible enough to swallow his story that he was the owner of this mansion? That would make him wealthy. Very wealthy. And he sure didn't look the part.

"Why should I believe you own this house?"

He frowned. "Because I'm Lucas Carrington. Connie's nephew."

His unwavering tone gave her pause. She studied his aristocratic nose, piercing blue eyes and sensual lips. The wheels in her mind began to spin. No wonder he seemed so familiar. During her many hours at the hospital, she'd ended up thumbing through one magazine after the other. It was within one of those stylish periodicals that she'd skimmed over an article listing this year's most eligible bachelors.

Lucas Carrington had been named Bachelor of the Year. And he had been by far the steamiest candidate on the list. And that had been before she'd garnered a glimpse of his ripped abs. Her mouth grew dry at the memory. She instantly squashed the thought.

The reality of the situation at last sunk in. That man—the hunk from the popular magazine—was standing in front of her in his bare feet. And she was accusing him of being an intruder. This had to be some sort of crazy, mixed-up dream.

"I see my name has rung a bell." Smugness reflected in his captivating eyes. "Perhaps my aunt mentioned me."

The fact he'd been holding that ace up his sleeve the whole time instead of introducing himself up front annoyed her. She wasn't about to fold her hand so quickly—even if she had been beaten already.

She conjured up her best poker face. "Actually, Connie went to great pains not to mention you. She merely said the owner was out of town for an extended period. In fact, when I saw the condition of this place, I didn't think anyone had lived here in years."

A muscle twitched in his cheek as his gaze moved away. "I only need a couple of the rooms. Even when I'm in town, I'm not here much."

"I see." What else could she say? That it was a bit strange to live in a mansion filled with cobwebs and covered in a blanket of dust? But who was she to judge? She was living out of a suitcase, and by the end of the month, she would be technically homeless. The thought of being adrift with no place to call home sent her stomach plummeting. But she could only deal with one problem at a time.

Lucas shifted uncomfortably. "Why do you keep looking at me strangely?"

"I'm trying to decide whether I should believe you. I mean, I wouldn't expect such a wealthy man to wear… umm, that." She pointed at his tattered jeans.

Even though she knew that he was in fact Lucas Carrington, she didn't want to let on just yet. After all, he hadn't readily taken her word that she wasn't a squatter. Why not let him see what it was like not to be believed?

He shrugged. "So they're old jeans. It doesn't mean anything."

"I don't know. This could all be an act. How am I to know that you aren't pretending to be the owner? Maybe I should call the police and let them sort this out."

Instead of the angry response she'd been anticipating, the corners of his mouth lifted. Was that a smile? Her stomach somersaulted.

"I guess I deserve that. Wait here." He set off in the same direction he'd gone to grab his clothes and the robe he'd loaned her.

The scorching hot image of him in those boxer shorts flashed in her mind. Her pulse kicked up a notch or two. If Lucas wasn't already wealthy, he could make a fortune as an underwear model. She'd be first in line to buy the magazine.

Still a bit chilled, she snuggled up in the robe, noticing the fresh scent of aftershave. She lifted the plush material to her nose, unable to resist inhaling even deeper. *Mmm*...

"Is the robe okay?" His smooth, deep voice filled the room.

"Umm...yes." She smoothed the lapel. "I was just admiring its...its softness."

He nodded, but she wondered if he'd caught her getting high off his very masculine scent. No man had a right to smell that good or look that hot with his clothes on...or off.

He skirted around the kitchen island and headed for her. Kate held her ground, all the while wondering what he was up to.

"Here." He flipped open a black wallet. "This should clear things up."

Her fingers slid across the worn smooth leather. She really didn't need to see his driver's license, but she had started this, so she might as well follow through.

She glanced at the photo of a neatly groomed man in a suit and tie. Definitely Lucas, but the spiffed-up version. The funny thing was she liked him in his worn-out jeans and sloppy T-shirt as much if not more than his business persona.

"So now do you believe me?" he asked with a tone of smug satisfaction, as if he'd just one-upped her.

She didn't like him thinking that he'd gotten the best of her.

"I don't know." She held the ID up beside his face, hmming and hah-ing, as though trying to make up her mind. "There's definitely a resemblance, but I'm not sure."

He yanked the card from her hand and stared at it. "Of course it's me! And that's my address…this address."

At last he'd fallen off his cool, confident edge. A smile pulled at her lips. The action felt so foreign to her after the past few stressful months, but the lightness grew, erupting into laughter. The more she laughed, the deeper Lucas frowned. It had been so long since she'd had an occasion to laugh that she didn't want it to end. It felt so good. So liberating. So freeing.

His brow arched. "Have I amused you enough?"

Her cheeks started to ache and she forced herself to calm down. After dabbing both eyes, she gazed up at him. "Sorry about that. But you don't know how much I needed that laugh."

His brows rose higher, but he didn't ask why and it was just as well. She wasn't about to spill her sorrowful tale to this stranger. In fact, she suddenly felt guilty for her outburst. Not because it was at Lucas's expense. He was a big boy who could take a little ribbing. It was the thought of her little girl in the hospital that sobered her mood. Under the circumstances, Kate had no right to smile, much less laugh.

If the hospital staff hadn't invoked their stupid policy, she'd still be there—sitting by Molly's bed or haunting the halls. But the nurses had insisted she needed some rest so she didn't wear herself out.

"Hey, what's the matter?" Lucas stepped closer. His hand reached out as though to touch Kate's shoulder, but then he hesitated.

She blinked back the rush of emotions. "I'm fine. I'll just get my things and get out of your way."

His hand lowered to his side as he glanced around the room. "Where exactly are your things?"

"Upstairs."

"But those rooms aren't fit for anyone. I dismissed the maid service as soon as... It doesn't matter. The only important thing is keeping you out of that mess."

"It isn't so dirty now." At the shocked look on Lucas's face, she continued. "Or at least the room that I'm staying in is mostly clean."

"What room?" His face creased with worry lines.

A crack of thunder sounded, followed by the lights flickering. Kate wrapped her arms around herself. "The one at the end of the hall."

His shoulders drew back in a rigid line as his brows gathered in a dark, intimidating line. "Which end?"

Kate pointed straight overhead.

His shoulders drooped as he let out a sigh. "What in the world was my aunt thinking to send you here?"

Kate had wondered the exact same thing, but she'd come to the conclusion that Connie had only the best intentions... even if they were a little misguided. Now it was time to move on.

Lucas watched as Kate snuggled deeper in his robe. A resigned look etched across her weary features as the dark circles made her eyes appear much too large for her face. She reminded him of a puppy who'd been kicked to the curb and forgotten.

His thoughts rolled back in time to the day when he'd found a stray pup and brought it home. Everyone but his aunt had told him to get rid of the filthy beast. Aunt Connie had been different. She could see what the others couldn't be bothered to look at—the puppy's need to be loved and cared for. More than that she recognized Lucas's need for something calming in the upheaval that was his life.

Lucas brought his thoughts up short. Kate wasn't a stray puppy. She was a grown woman who could care for herself. He had enough problems. He didn't need to be embroiled in someone else's. He should wish her well and be done with it.

A loud boom of thunder shook the very floor they stood on. Kate wrapped her arms around herself as her wide eyes turned toward the window. This storm was showing no signs of letting up. Definitely not a night to be out and about.

If only he knew why his aunt had sent her here....

Kate turned and started down the hall.

"Wait." Unease mounted within him as he realized what he was about to do.

"For what?" Kate asked, stepping back into the kitchen.

He noticed how the rest of her short dark brown hair was tucked behind each ear as though she'd been too busy to worry about what she looked like. The concept of a woman going out in public without taking great pains with her appearance was new to him. This mystery woman intrigued him and that was not good—not good at all.

But more than that, he'd witnessed how every time it thundered, she jumped and the fear reflected in her eyes. He couldn't turn her out into the stormy night—especially when he suspected she had nowhere else to go.

Going against his better judgment, he said, "You don't have to leave tonight."

"Yes, I do."

"Would you quit being so difficult?"

She glowered at him. "But you just got done telling me that you wanted me out of here right away. You're the one being difficult."

He inwardly groaned with frustration. "That was before. Give me a moment to speak with my aunt."

"I don't see how that will change anything. Unless you're still worried that I'm a liar and a thief."

"That isn't what I meant." He jerked his fingers through his hair. "Just wait here for a minute, okay? In fact, sit down. You look dead on your feet."

Her eyes narrowed. Her pale lips drooped into a frown. He'd obviously said the wrong thing…again, but darned if he knew what had upset her. Maybe it was mentioning how tired she looked. In his limited experience with women, they never wanted to look anything less than amazing, no matter the circumstances.

When Kate didn't move, he walked over and pulled out a chair at the table. "Please sit down. I won't be long."

He stepped inside the small bedroom just off the kitchen, which at one point in the house's history had been the domestic help's quarters. Lucas now claimed it as his bedroom—not that he spent much time there. His cell phone was sitting on the nightstand next to the twin bed.

He selected his aunt's name from his frequently called list. His fingers tightened around the phone as he held it to his ear. After only one ring, it switched to voice mail.

"Call me as soon as you get this." His voice was short and clipped.

He couldn't help but wonder where she might be and why she wasn't taking his call. Would she still be at the hospital doing her volunteer work? He glanced at the alarm clock. At this late hour, he highly doubted it.

With his aunt unaccounted for, he'd have to follow his gut. He'd already determined Kate wasn't a criminal. But what would he do with her? Sit and hash out what was bothering her to see if he could help? Certainly not.

He rubbed his hand over his stubbled jaw. He didn't want to get pulled any further into her problems. No matter what her circumstances were, it had nothing to do with him. Come tomorrow, she'd have to find other accommodations.

Still uncomfortable with his decision, he stepped back into the kitchen. Kate was seated at the table. Her arms were crossed on the glass tabletop, cradling her head. He must have made a sound, because she jerked upright in her seat.

Kate blinked before stretching. "Did Connie confirm what I told you?"

"Actually she didn't—"

"What? But I'm not lying."

"No one said you were. But my aunt isn't available. So how about we make a deal?"

A yawn escaped her lips. "What do you have in mind?"

"I'll give you the benefit of the doubt, if you'll do the same for me."

Kate was quiet for a moment as though weighing his words. "I suppose. But what does it matter now?"

"Because you and I are going to be housemates for the night."

"What? But I couldn't—"

"Yes, you can. Have you looked outside lately? It's pouring. And it's late at night."

Her lips pressed into a firm line as she got to her feet and pushed in the chair. "I don't need your charity."

"Who says it's charity? You'd be saving me from a load of trouble with my aunt if she found out I kicked you to the curb on a night like this."

Kate's hand pressed to her hip, which was hidden beneath the folds of the oversize robe. "Are you being on the level?"

She didn't have any idea what it was costing him to ask her to stay, even for one night. This place was a tomb of memories. He didn't want anyone inside here, witnessing his utter failure to keep his family together.

But there was something special about her—more than the way that he was thoroughly drawn to her. There was a vulnerability in her gaze. Something he'd guess she'd

gone to great pains to hide from everyone, but he'd noticed.
Maybe because he'd been vulnerable before, too.

"You don't look too sure about this."

He was usually much better at hiding his thoughts, but
the dismal events of the day combined with the lateness of
the hour were his undoing.

"I'm not. Let's just go to bed." Her drooping eyelids
lifted and he immediately realized how his words could
be misconstrued. "Alone."

CHAPTER THREE

THE SUN HAD yet to flirt with the horizon when Kate awoke to the alarm on her cell phone. Though she'd only snuck in a few hours of sleep, she felt refreshed. Her heart was full of hope that today her most fervent prayer would be answered.

It will all work out. It has to.

As she rushed through the shower, the what-ifs and maybes started to crowd into her mind. Finding a cure to her daughter's brain tumor had been rife with negative diagnoses. That was why they were here in New York City—to see a surgeon who was willing to do the seemingly impossible. But what if—

Don't go there. Not today.

With her resolve to think only positive thoughts, she pulled on a red skirt and a white top from her suitcase. The light tap of the continued rain on the window reminded her of the night before and meeting Lucas Carrington. He definitely presented a distraction from her attack of nerves. She wondered if he'd be just as devastatingly handsome in the daylight. She tried to convince herself that it'd been the exhaustion talking, that no man could look that good. But she'd seen the magazine spread with him shaved and spruced up in a tux. He really was that good-looking. Which raised the question: What was he doing living here in this unkempt, mausoleumlike house?

Kate proceeded down the grand staircase, with her suitcase in one hand and her purse in the other. She hated the fact that she would never learn the history or secrets of this mansion. This would be her last trip down the cinematic steps. She paused to take one last look around.

She was in awe of the house's old-world grandeur. Her gaze skimmed over the cream paint and paused to inspect the various paintings adorning the walls. Her nose curled up. She knew a bit about art from her work as an interior designer and these modern pieces, though not to her liking, would still fetch a hefty chunk of change at auction.

Even though the current decor didn't match the home's old-world elegance, she still saw the beauty lurking in the background. In her experience, she'd never found such charm and detailed work in any of the newer structures. Sure, they were all beautiful in their own unique ways, but this mansion was brimming with personality that only time could provide. She'd be willing to bet that if the walls could talk they'd spin quite a tale. She was certain that given the opportunity to rejuvenate this place, she could learn a considerable amount about its history. But she'd never have that chance.

With a resigned sigh, she set her suitcase by the front door before heading back the hall to the kitchen. She couldn't shake the dismal thought of Lucas turning a blind eye to the house's disintegrating state and letting the place fall into utter disrepair. Who could do such a thing? Was it possible he didn't realize the real damage being done by his neglect?

If the man took the time to walk upstairs once in a while, he'd notice the work that needed to be done. Some of the repairs were blatantly obvious. It was a little hard to miss the *drip-drip-drip* last night as the rain leaked through the ceiling of her bedroom. She'd used a waste basket to collect the water. Maybe she should say something…

No. Don't go there. This house and Lucas are absolutely none of your business.

She paused outside the kitchen door and listened. No sounds came from within. She wasn't so sure she was up to facing him in the light of day after getting caught last night in her nightshirt. Still she refused to just slip away without thanking him for his generosity.

She pushed the door open and tiptoed into the room, hoping not to disturb him since his bedroom was just off the kitchen. Now if only she knew where to find a pen and some paper to write a note.

"You're up early."

Kate jumped. It took a second for her heart to sink back into her chest. She turned to find Mr. Oh-So-Sexy sitting off to the side in the breakfast nook with the morning paper and a cup of coffee. Yep, he looked just as delicious in the morning. Now she'd never get him off her mind.

She moved to a bar stool and draped his robe across it. "I didn't expect you to be up so early."

"I'm a morning person."

His intense stare followed her. What was up with him? She nervously fidgeted with the Lucky Ducky keychain she kept around as a good luck charm.

When she couldn't stand to be the focal point of Lucas's attention any longer, she faced him. "Why do you keep staring?"

"It's just you don't look like the same woman I met last night."

"Is that your attempt at a compliment?"

"Actually it is. You see, my brain doesn't work very well this early in the morning until I finish my first cup of coffee." He held up a large blue mug. "But if you'd like me to spell it out, you look radiant."

Had she heard him correctly? Had a man, a drop-dead gorgeous hunk, just said she was radiant? *Radiant.* The word sounded as sweet as honey and she was eating it all up. Heat swirled in her chest and rushed up to her cheeks, but for that one blissful moment she didn't care.

"Umm, thanks." Her hand tightened around the keychain. "I'm all packed up."

"What's that in your hand?"

She glanced down, realizing she was squeezing the rubber duck to the point of smashing it. "It's just a keychain. No big deal."

He nodded in understanding.

"Do you have any more coffee?"

"I'll get you a cup."

He moved at the same time she did and they nearly collided. Kate froze, but not before she caught a whiff of his intoxicating male scent. He had on a light blue button-up with the sleeves rolled up and the collar unbuttoned. His hair was combed but still slightly damp. And his face was clean-shaven. He looked like a man ready to conquer the world.

Her heart tripped in her chest as she pictured them chatting over a morning cup of coffee and bagel. He'd tell her what he had on tap for the day and she'd tell him about her plans.

Lucas cleared his throat and pointed. "The cups are in the cabinet behind you."

She had to get a grip and quit acting like a high school student with a crush on the star quarterback. The best way to do that was to make a fast exit before she made a complete fool of herself. "On second thought, I don't have time for coffee."

"It's awfully early to be in such a rush. Is something the matter?"

"Nothing's wrong." She crossed her fingers behind her back like she used to do when she was a kid and her father asked her if she'd cleaned her room before allowing her go outside to play with her friends.

Lucas nodded, but his eyes said that he didn't believe her. She never had been good at telling fibs. That's why her father had caught her every time.

A sense of loss settled over her. What had made her think about that man after all this time? She grew angry at herself. As far as she was concerned her father was dead to her. She certainly didn't miss him.

Maybe being alone in a new city had gotten to her more than she thought. It didn't help that she'd witnessed the supportive clusters of families at the hospital while having no one by her side. That must be it.

Stifling the rush of unwanted emotions, she made a point of checking her wristwatch. "If I don't leave now, I'll be late."

"But you haven't even eaten. Don't let me scare you off."

"You haven't. I just have things I must do." She walked over to the doorway and paused. "By the way, did you ever speak to your aunt?"

"No. I think it was too late last night and she had her phone switched off. I'm sure she'll call soon."

"I understand." But Kate still wanted that little bit of vindication. The chance to flash him an I-told-you-so look. "Thank you for letting me spend the night. By the way, there's some food in the fridge. Help yourself to it."

And with that she started down the hallway headed for the front door. She had no idea where she'd find a cheap place to stay tonight. All but one of her credit cards was maxed out since she'd been forced to give up her job to travel with Molly to the long list of specialists. She dismissed the troubling thought. There were other matters that required her attention first.

"Hey, wait!"

Kate sighed and turned. She didn't know what else they

had to say to each other. And she didn't have time to waste. "Surely you aren't going to insist on searching my luggage, are you?"

"Are you always so feisty in the morning? Or are you just grumpy because you skipped your caffeine fix? I know that first cup does wonders for me. See, I'm smiling." His lips bowed into a ridiculous grin.

She rolled her eyes and shook her head. She honestly didn't know what to make of the man. His personal hygiene was impressive, but other than the kitchen his house was a disgrace. And last night he was crankier than an old bear, yet this morning he was smiling. He was one walking contradiction.

Lucas held out his hand. "Let me have your keys and I'll pull your car up to the door so you don't get soaked."

"I don't have one." She'd left her car in Pennsylvania, figuring city driving was not something she wanted to attempt.

"Did you call a taxi?"

"I don't need one." She pulled a red umbrella from her tote. "I'm armed and ready."

"Have you looked outside? It's still pouring. That umbrella isn't going to help much."

"Thanks for caring. But I've been taking care of myself for a long time now. I'll be fine."

When she started to move toward the front door, he reached out and grabbed her upper arm. His touch was firm but gentle. Goose bumps raced down to her wrists, lifting the fine hair on her arms. She glanced down at where his fingers were wrapped around her and immediately his hand pulled away.

"Sorry. I just wanted a chance to offer you a lift. I'll go grab my wallet and keys." He dashed down the hallway without waiting for her to say a word.

This was ridiculous. She couldn't let herself start going

soft. There was only her and Molly and right now, her daughter needed her to be strong for both of them. She would walk to the hospital as planned. It wasn't that many blocks and she'd already done it a number of times.

She quietly let herself out the front door, feeling bad about skipping out on Lucas. For some reason, he was really trying to be a good sport about finding a stranger living in his house. She wondered if she would have been so understanding if the roles had been reversed.

"Kate, I've got them." Lucas called out from the kitchen. "We can go now."

Lucas had never met a woman quite like her. Her tenacity combined with a hint of vulnerability got to him on some level. He sensed she wasn't the type to ask for help and would only take it if it was pressed upon her. Maybe that was why he was going out of his way to be kind to her—because she appeared to be in need of a friend and would never ask for one.

He strode to the foyer with his jacket on and keys in hand. But Kate was gone. He called out to her, but there was no sound. Surely she hadn't skipped out on him.

He stepped outside to look for her. The rain was picking up and so was the wind. But there was no sign of Kate in either direction. This was not a day where an umbrella would do a person much good.

Without taking time to question his next move, he was in his car and driving around the block. She couldn't have gotten far. And then he spotted a perky red umbrella. In the windy weather, Kate struggled to keep a grip on the umbrella with one hand while clutching her suitcase with the other.

He slowed next to her and lowered the window. "Get in."

She ignored him and kept walking. A gust of wind blew hard and practically pulled the umbrella free from her hold.

In the end, she'd held on to it, but the wire skeleton now bowed in the wrong direction, rendering the contraption totally useless.

"Get in the car before you're soaked to the skin."

She stood there for a second as though ready to burst into tears. Then pressing her lips into a firm line, she straightened her shoulders and stepped up to the car. He jumped out to take her things from her.

Once they were stowed away, he climbed back in the driver's seat. "Where are we off to?"

"East Riverview Hospital."

Her face was devoid of any expression, leaving him to wonder about the reason for her visit. She'd mentioned meeting his aunt there, but she hadn't added any details. Was she visiting a sick relative? Or was there something wrong with her? Was that the reason for her drawn cheeks and dark circles under her eyes?

He wanted to know what was going on, but he kept quiet and eased back into traffic. If she wanted him to know, she'd tell him. Otherwise it was none of his business. He assured himself it was best to keep a cordial distance.

Kate settled back against the leather seat. She hated to admit it, but she was thankful for the ride. She hadn't any idea that there would be so much ponding on the sidewalks. Her feet were wet and cold.

As though reading her thoughts, Lucas adjusted the temperature controls and soon warm air was swirling around her. It'd been a long time since someone had worried about her. For just a second, she mused about what it'd be like to date the Bachelor of the Year—he certainly was easy on the eyes and very kind. More than likely, he had his pick of women. The thought left her feeling a bit unsettled.

She couldn't let herself get swept away by Lucas's charms. She had a notorious record with unreliable men.

Why would Lucas be any different? After all, she knew next to nothing about him—other than he was a lousy house-keeper. He'd dismissed his desperately needed maid service. And he went out of his way for strangers he found squatting in his house. Wait. She was supposed to be listing his negative qualities.

She needed to make an important point not only to him but also to herself. "You know, I would have been fine on my own. You didn't have to ride to my rescue."

"I had to go out anyway."

"And you just happened to be going in the same direction."

"Something like that."

The car rolled to a stop at an intersection. Lucas glanced at her. His probing eyes were full of questions. Like what was a small-town girl doing in the Big Apple? And how had she befriended his aunt? And the number one question that was dancing around in his mind: Why was she going to the hospital?

He didn't push or prod. Instead he exuded a quiet strength. And that only made it all the more tempting to open up to him—to dump the details of the most tragic event in her life into his lap. No, she couldn't do that. No matter how nice he was to her, letting him in was just asking for trouble.

Afraid he'd voice his inevitable questions, she decided to ask him a few of her own. "What's the story with the house? Why does it look frozen in time?"

Lucas's facial features visibly hardened. "I haven't had time to deal with it."

"Have you owned the place long?"

"My family has lived there for generations."

Wow. She couldn't even imagine what it would be like to have family roots that went that deep. Her relatives were the here-today-gone-tomorrow type. And they never bothered to leave a forwarding address. Once in a while a postcard would show up from her mother. Her father... Well, he'd been out of the picture since she was young.

She tried not to think about her lack of family or her not-so-happy childhood. It didn't do any good to dwell on things that couldn't be changed. The only thing that mattered now was the future. But there was one thing she could do to help Lucas hold on to a piece of his past.

"You know the house is in desperate need of repairs, especially the upstairs," she said, longing to one day have an opportunity to work on an impressive job such as his historic mansion. "I'm an interior designer and I have some contacts that could help—"

"I'm not interested."

The thought of that stunning architecture disintegrating for no apparent reason spurred her on. "But houses need to be cared for or they start to look and act their age. And it'd be such a travesty to let the place fall down—"

"It's fine as is. End of discussion."

She wanted to warn him about the leaking roof, but he'd cut her off. She doubted anything she said now would even register in his mind.

With a huff, she turned away. Frustration warmed her veins. Here was a problem that could so easily be resolved and yet this man was too stubborn to lift up the phone and ask for help. If only her problems could be fixed as readily.

Her thoughts filled with the possible scenarios for today's meeting with Molly's specialist. This surgeon was their last hope. Kate prayed he wouldn't dismiss the case as quickly as Lucas had dismissed the problem with his house.

She tilted her head against the cool glass. It soothed her heated skin. She stared blindly ahead, noticing how even at this early hour, the city was coming to life. An army of people with umbrellas moved up and down the walks while traffic buzzed by at a steady pace. Her world might be teetering on the edge, but for everyone else, it was business as usual.

Now was not the time for self-pity. As the towering hospital came into view, she straightened her shoulders and inhaled a deep breath, willing away all of her doubts and insecurities.

"Which entrance should I drop you at? Emergency?"

"No. I told you I'm fine. Fit as a fiddle." She forced a smile to her lips before gathering her things.

"You're sure?"

"Absolutely. The main entrance will do."

"You know hospitals aren't a great place to be alone. Is there someone I can call for you?"

He surprised her with his thoughtful offer. How could a man be so frustrating in one breath and sweet in the next?

"No, thanks. I have some people waiting for me."

He pulled the car over to the curb. "Are you sure?"

She nodded. What she failed to tell him was that the people waiting for her consisted of the medical staff. No family. Except for Molly. She was all the family Kate needed.

"Thank you for everything." She jumped out into the rain. "I just have to grab my suitcase."

Lucas swiveled around. "Leave it."

"But I—"

"Obviously you have enough to deal with already. Besides, I'm planning to work from home today. Call me when things are wrapped up here and I'll give you a lift to your hotel."

She had to think fast. Without an umbrella, the rain was soaking her. She really should end this here and now, but she'd feel more confident for the meeting if she wasn't lugging around an old suitcase. Lucas was only offering to keep her possessions for a few hours, not asking her to run off and have a steamy affair or anything. The errant thought warmed her cheeks.

"Thanks for the offer, but I'm not sure how long I'm going to be."

"No problem. Let me give you my number."

In seconds, she had his number saved on her cell phone and was jogging up the steps to the glass doors. Thoughts of Lucas slid to the back of her mind. She was about to have the most important meeting of her life.

She refused to leave until she heard: "Yes. We will help your daughter."

CHAPTER FOUR

"I THINK WE can help your daughter but—"

Kate's heart soared. She'd been waiting so long to hear those words. It took all her self-restraint not to jump for joy. She wasn't sure what the surgeon said after that as the excitement clouded her mind.

For months now, they'd traveled to one hospital after the other. Every time she located a place that offered a possibility of hope, they were there. Now at long last they had come to the right place. The weight of anxiety slipped from her shoulders and left her lighter than she'd been in recent memory.

When a stack of papers was shoved in front of her, she glanced down, spotting her name and a very large dollar figure. Her excitement stuttered.

"What is this?" She couldn't move her gaze from the staggering dollar figure.

"That is the amount you'll need to pay up front if we are to perform the operation."

This couldn't be right. She had health coverage and it wasn't cheap. "But my insurance—"

"Won't cover this procedure." Dr. Hawthorne steepled his fingers and leaned back in his chair. "It doesn't cover experimental procedures. I'm willing to donate my time, but in order for the hospital to book the O.R. and the necessary staff, you'll need to settle this bill with Accounts Receivable." He paused and eyed her up as though checking to see if she fully understood. "You also need to be aware that this is an estimate. A conservative one at that. If there are complications, the bill will escalate quickly."

Kate nodded, but inside her stomach was churning and her head was pounding. Her gaze skimmed over the long list of charges from the anesthesiologist to medications. How in the world was she going to raise this staggering amount of money?

Her daughter's smiling face came to mind. She couldn't… no, she wouldn't let her down. There had to be an answer, because this operation was going to happen no matter what she had to do to make it a reality.

"You should also know that we normally like to treat children on an outpatient basis until surgery but with this tumor's aggressive growth rate and with it already affecting her mobility, I feel it's best to keep her admitted under close observation."

Kate nodded in understanding even though her head was spinning with information. "I understand."

Dr. Hawthorne cleared his throat. "Will you be able to come up with the funding?"

Without hesitation, Kate spoke in a determined voice. "Yes, I will."

The surgeon with graying temples gave her a long, serious stare. She didn't glance away, blink or so much as breathe. She sat there ready to do battle to get her daughter the necessary surgery.

"I believe you will," Dr. Hawthorne said. "I need you to sign these forms and then my team will start working to reduce the tumor's size before surgery."

Kate's lungs burned as she blew out a pent-up breath. She accepted the papers and started to read. Her stomach quivered as she realized the overwhelming challenge set before her.

A half an hour later, with her life signed away to East Riverview Hospital, Kate took comfort in knowing she'd done the right thing. This surgeon had performed miracles before. He could do it again. Kate was spurred on by the thought of Molly healthy once again. She could do this—somehow. She just needed time to think.

The elevator pinged and the doors opened. Kate stepped inside. A man stood in front of the control panel.

"Five, please." She moved to the other side of the elevator and stared down at the paperwork in her hand, wondering how she'd pull off this miracle.

"Kate?" a male voice spoke.

The door slid shut as Kate lifted her head. When her gaze latched on to the man, her breath caught. This couldn't be happening. Not here. Not now.

"Chad, what are you doing here?"

His dark brows scrunched together beneath the brim of a blue baseball cap. "Now, is that the way to greet your husband?"

"Ex-husband." She pressed her hands to her hips. "I tried to reach you months ago. You didn't have time for us then. Why have you suddenly shown up now?"

"My daughter's sick. My family needs me—"

"That's where you're wrong." There was no way she was letting him walk in here and act as if he was their saving grace. "We don't need you. We've been fine all of this time without you."

His gaze hardened. "I've been busy."

After he'd refused to settle down in one place and create a nurturing environment for their daughter, he'd left Kate on her own to have their baby. He'd succeeded in confirming her mistrust of men.

The elevator dinged and the door slipped open. Kate stepped out first and left Chad to follow. They stopped outside Molly's door. Kate didn't want anything to upset her little girl, not after everything she'd been through in the past several months. And certainly not now that she was scheduled for a very delicate procedure.

"How is she?"

"The tumor is causing her some mobility problems."

"Is she in pain?"

Kate shook her head. "Thankfully she feels fine…for now. If they don't do the surgery soon that will change. But…"

"But what?"

"Money has to be raised to cover the surgery. Lots of money." Kate stood between Chad and the doorway to Molly's room. "You should go before she sees you."

He crossed his arms. "I'm not going anywhere." His voice rose. "My Molly girl will be excited to see her daddy."

Before she could utter a word, Molly called out. "Daddy, is that you?"

"Yes, sweetie. I'm here." He leaned over and whispered, "I always was her favorite."

Kate bit back a few unkind words as she followed her ex into the room. She hated how he dropped into their lives whenever it suited him and disappeared just as quickly.

Maybe that was why she'd been initially drawn to him— he was so much like her family, always chasing happiness in the next town. Having a child had been too much for her father, who'd split when she was ten. But her mother had stuck it out until Kate's eighteenth birthday, before skipping town with the current flavor of the month.

But when Kate became pregnant, her priorities changed. She wanted her child to have a real home. She promised herself that her little one would have something she never had—stability.

The same town.

The same house.

The same bed.

She wondered what it'd be like to live in a home like Lucas's, rich with family history. The man didn't know how good he had it. The errant thought brought her up short. Why should she think of him now? And why did just the mere thought of him have her heart going pitty-pat? Maybe because she hadn't anticipated his kindness after finding her, a total stranger, in his house.

"Yay! Daddy's here." Molly's smile filled the room with an undeniable glow.

Chad gave their daughter a kiss and a hug. Kate watched the happy reunion and wondered whether she should be furious at her unreliable ex or grateful he'd made Molly's face light up like Christmas morning. A child's ability to forgive was truly impressive. And right now Molly's happiness was all that mattered.

"How long are you sticking around?" Kate asked, wondering if she had time to grab some much needed coffee and gather her thoughts.

"For a while. Molly and I have some catching up to do."

"Daddy, wanna watch this with me?" Molly pointed to a cartoon on the television anchored to the wall.

All three of them in the same room for an extended period would only lead to problems. Chad had a way of finding her tender spots and poking them. And having Molly witness her parents arguing was certainly not something her little girl needed right now. Kate struggled to come to terms with the fact Chad was suddenly back in their lives.

"I'm just going to step out and get some coffee. I'll be right back." Kate couldn't help thinking that she was a third wheel here, an unfamiliar feeling. "You should know she sleeps a lot."

"No need to rush." Chad used his take-charge tone, which caused every muscle in Kate's body to tense. "How about I stay until this afternoon and then you can spend the evening with our girl. No need for both of us to be here. After all, you have money to raise."

Just the way he said the last part let her know that coming up with the money for the surgery would be solely her responsibility. Her blood pressure rose. What else was new?

She was about to inform him of his responsibilities toward their daughter when common sense dowsed her angry words. An argument between her and Chad was the last thing Molly needed. Still, with all three of them crowded in this small room all day, an argument was inevitable.

"You can leave," Chad said dismissively.

"Yeah, Mommy. Daddy and me are gonna watch TV."

Maybe it was the best way to keep Molly happy. She caught Chad's gaze. "Are you sure you want to stay that long?"

"Absolutely. Molly and I have lots of catching up to do. Is that a stack of board games over there?" He pointed to the corner of the room.

Before Kate could speak, Molly piped up. "Yeah. Wanna play?"

While Chad wasn't reliable for the long haul, when he was with Molly, he was a good father. Kate smiled at her daughter's exuberance. "What time should I be back?"

"Three. I have some things to do then."

"Okay. I'll see you both at three." And to be certain of Chad's intentions, she added, "You will still be here, won't you? Because I can come back earlier."

"I'll be here."

Kate kissed her daughter goodbye and hesitantly walked away. She assured herself Molly would be fine with Chad. In the meantime, she had planning to do. Four weeks wasn't much time to come up with enough cash to cover the bill.

The thought made her chest tighten. She didn't have access to that kind of money. As it was, her house in Pennsylvania was being sold to pay some prior medical bills. What in the world was she going to do?

"Elaina, you have to be reasonable." Lucas struggled to maintain a calm tone with his ex-wife. "All I'm asking is for you to let me see Carrie when I fly back out to San Francisco."

"And I told you it's too confusing for her. She has a dad now—one who doesn't spend his life at the office. Don't come around again. All you'll do is upset her."

"That's not true." His grip on the phone tightened. "You know you could make this easier for her by not yelling at me in front of her."

Elaina sighed. "When you show up without invitation, what do you expect? And I'm only doing what's best for my daughter—"

"Our daughter. And if I waited for an invitation, I'd be an old man. Don't you think her knowing her father is important?"

"No. Don't keep pushing this. Carrie is happy without you."

A loud click resonated through the phone. His teeth ground together at the nerve of his ex-wife hanging up the phone while he was trying to reason with her.

The kitchen chair scraped over the smooth black-and-white tiles as Lucas swore under his breath and jumped to his feet. He paced the length of the kitchen. The sad thing was Elaina meant her threat. She would make his life hell if he didn't play by her rules. She'd done it once by skipping town with their daughter and leaving no forwarding address. This time he didn't even want to think of the lies she'd tell Carrie about him.

This was the reason he'd decided to let his daughter live in peace without the constant shuffle between two warring parents. He wanted a better childhood for Carrie than he'd had.

His thoughts drifted back to his childhood. He'd hated being a pawn between his parents and being forced to play the part of an unwilling spy. Those two were so wrapped up in knowing each other's business and with outdoing the other that, in some twisted way, he figured they never really got over each other.

But if that was love, then he wanted no part of it. That's why he'd decided to marry Elaina. They had a relationship based on friendship and mutual goals, not love. A nice, simple relationship. Boy, had he made a huge miscalculation. Even without love things got complicated quickly. Now he couldn't let his daughter pay the price for his poor decisions.

Lucas stopped next to the table and stared down at the unfinished email. The cursor blinked, prompting him for the next words, but he couldn't even recall what he'd written.

Nothing was going right at the moment. First, his ex-wife declared war if he pursued his right to spend time with his little girl. Then there was the San Francisco expansion, which was hemorrhaging money. His only hope was the launch of his newest line: Fiery Hearts—brilliant rubies set in the most stunning handcrafted settings.

The launch of this line had to be bigger and better than any other he'd done. Fiery Hearts had to start a buzz that would send women flocking to Carrington's, infusing it with income to offset the cost of getting the West Coast showroom up and running. He raked his fingers through his hair, struggling for some innovative, headline-making launch for the line. But he drew a blank.

He closed the laptop and strode over to the counter. He went to refill his coffee cup only to find the pot empty. The thought of brewing more crossed his mind, but he had a better idea—getting away from the house by going to a coffee shop. Between the hum of conversation and his laptop, it'd keep him occupied. And if Kate needed her suitcase, she had his number.

Satisfied with his plan of action, he grabbed his keys and wallet when his cell phone buzzed. A quick glance at the illuminated screen revealed it was his aunt.

"Aunt Connie, I've been trying since last night to get you. Are you okay?"

"Of course. Why wouldn't I be?"

"I'm not used to you being out so late and not taking my calls."

"Sorry. I was at the hospital, sitting with a woman whose husband underwent emergency surgery."

"Did everything go well?" he asked, already having a pretty good guess at the answer. His aunt was too upbeat for things to have gone poorly.

"Yes, the man has a good prognosis. So, dear, how are things going in San Francisco?"

This was his opening to find out what exactly was going on here. "I got back late last night."

There was a quick intake of breath followed by silence. He wasn't going to help his aunt out of this mess. She owed him an explanation of why a stranger was living here in his home without his permission. He might love his aunt dearly, but this time she'd overstepped.

"Oh, dear. Umm…I meant to call you—"

"So you're admitting you invited Kate to stay here without consulting me?"

"Well, yes. But I knew you'd understand." Uncertainty threaded through her voice.

If Connie were an employee, he'd let her have an earful and then some. But this was his aunt, the only family member who'd ever worried more about his happiness than the company's bottom line…or having the Carrington name appear on the society page with some splashy headline. He couldn't stay angry with her, even if he tried.

"It might be best if you ask in the future, instead of assuming." He made sure to use his I'm-not-messing-around voice.

"I'm sorry. She doesn't have any family for support or anywhere to go. And I would have sent her to my place, but you know after the last person I took in, my roommate insisted I never bring home anyone else. How was I to know that woman liked to borrow things?"

"Without permission and without any intention of returning them."

He was so grateful that his aunt had Pauline to look after her. If it weren't for Pauline, he'd never feel comfortable enough to leave town on business. His aunt was too nice, too unassuming. As a result, people tried repeatedly to take advantage of her to get to the Carrington fortune.

"Kate isn't like the others," Connie insisted. "She has a good heart."

"Still, you shouldn't have sent her here. This house... it's off-limits."

"I thought after all of this time you'd have let go of the past."

He'd never let go. How could he? It'd mean letting go of his little girl. A spot inside his chest ached like an open, festering wound every time he thought of how much he missed seeing Carrie's sweet smile or hearing her contagious laughter. But he didn't want to discuss Carrie with his aunt...with anyone.

Hoping to redirect the conversation, he asked, "What do you know about Kate?"

"Didn't she tell you?"

A knock at the back door caught him off guard. He wasn't expecting anyone as he never had visitors. And if it was some sort of salesperson, they'd go to the front door.

"I've got to go. Someone's at the door. I'll call you back later."

"Lucas, be nice to Kate. She has more than enough on her plate. She can use all of the friends she can get."

And with that the line went dead. What in the world had that cryptic message meant? He didn't have time to contemplate it as the knock sounded again.

He let out a frustrated sigh as he set his phone on the center island. So much for getting any answers about Kate. Now all he had were more questions.

The knocking became one long string of beats.

"Okay! I'm coming."

Lucas strode over and yanked open the door. A cold breeze rushed past him. His mouth moved, but words failed him.

There standing in the rain, completely soaked, was Kate. Her teeth chattered and her eyes were red and puffy. This certainly wasn't the same determined woman he'd dropped off at the hospital. Where her hair had once been styled, the wet strands clung to her face. What in the world was going on?

Without thinking he reached out, grabbed her arms and pulled her inside. His mind continued to flood with questions, so many that he didn't know where to start. But finally he drew his thoughts into some semblance of order and decided to start at the beginning.

"Why didn't you call?" He slipped her purse off her shoulder and set it on a kitchen stool. "I'd have picked you up."

Were those tears flowing down her cheeks? Or raindrops? He couldn't be sure. Obviously he'd have to hold off getting to the bottom of this. His first priority was getting Kate warmed up.

"We need to get you in a hot shower." She started to shake her head when he added, "No arguments. You'll be lucky if you don't catch pneumonia. If you hadn't noticed, it's awfully cold to be walking around in the rain."

He helped her out of her jacket, which definitely wasn't waterproof. Next, he removed her waterlogged red heels. When he reached for her hand to lead her to his bathroom, he noticed how small and delicate she was next to him.

She looked so fragile and his instinct was to protect her—to pull her close and let her absorb his body heat. He resisted the urge. It wasn't his place to soothe away her worries. When it came to relationships, he should wear a sign that read Toxic. And that was why he intended to grow old alone.

In his bedroom, he had her wait while he grabbed a towel and heated up the shower. When he returned, she was still standing there with her arms hugging herself, staring at the floor. What in the world had happened? Did she have bad news at the hospital? Had someone died?

Not that it was any of his business. He wasn't a man to lean on. He had no words of wisdom to share to make whatever problem she had go away. If he had, he'd have used it to fix his own messed up life. He'd have gotten his family back. The house would be filled with the sounds of his daughter's laughter. Instead the silence was deafening. He shoved the troubling thoughts away.

"Let's get you in a hot shower." He showed her to his bathroom. "Will you be all right in there alone? Or should I call my aunt?"

In a faint whisper, she said, "I'm fine."

Sure she was. And he had some oceanfront property in New Mexico to sell.

"Just yell, if you need me. I won't be far away."

While she warmed up in the shower, he rushed to the front door and returned with her suitcase. His thumbs hovered over the locks. He stopped. Opening her suitcase would be prying—something he hated when people did it to him, no matter what their intentions. Instead, he retrieved his robe and laid it on the bed, just in case she was still chilled.

Trying not to think of how good she'd looked in his robe, he returned to the kitchen. He grabbed the coffeepot and filled it with water. His idea to step out for a bit was permanently on the back burner. Once he got Kate situated in a hotel, the afternoon would be shot. And so would his patience.

He flung himself down on a kitchen chair, determined to concentrate on something besides his unwanted guest. He opened up his laptop and skimmed over his unfinished email. He had absolutely no desire to work. This realization for a renowned workaholic was unsettling, to say the least. What was wrong with him? Was it the way things had ended in San Francisco with his little girl looking at him with fear in her eyes when he went to pick her up?

He inhaled an unsteady breath. He'd made his choice, not to make his daughter a pawn between him and his ex. It was the right decision...for Carrie. Now he had to get a grip. After all, Carrington Gems was all he had left.

With one ear toward the bathroom and his eyes on the monitor, he started to type. He'd gotten through a handful of emails by the time Kate emerged from the bedroom wearing his robe. Her dark brown hair was wet and brushed back from her face and her cheeks were tinged pink from the shower.

The robe gaped open, revealing a glimpse of her cleavage. His overzealous imagination filled in the obscured details. He should have looked away but he couldn't. He was drawn to her like a starving bear to a picnic basket.

He shifted uncomfortably, fighting back this wave of desire. Sex was not the answer. It only complicated things, even in the simplest of relationships.

The fact he'd never met anyone who was so fiercely independent but at the same time looked worn to the bone only made him more curious about Kate. What was her story? Where had she come from? And what was she doing at the hospital?

He swallowed hard. "Do you feel better?"

She nodded. "I'm sorry to be such a bother."

Was this where he was supposed to step up and comfort her? He hesitated. He never was one of those soft, mushy people. He was a Carrington—strong, proud and unfeeling. Or at least those were the words his ex had thrown at him numerous times and he'd never had a reason to disbelieve her assessment. Until now....

There was something about Kate that bore through his defenses and made him want to fix whatever was broken. But he didn't know anything about comforting people. With each passing moment he grew more uncomfortable, not knowing how he should act around her.

Taking the safe approach, he got up and pulled a chair out for her. "Have a seat while I get you some coffee. Do you take milk or sugar?"

"A little of both, please."

That he could do. It was this talking stuff that had him knotted up inside. He wasn't sure what to say or do. Silence was best. Silence was golden.

Once she finished her coffee, he would see about getting her moved to a hotel. His life would then return to normal. Or whatever qualified as normal these days. And he wasn't going to ask any questions. Her life was none of his affair.

CHAPTER FIVE

KATE SANK DOWN on the black-cushioned chair, mortified that she'd shown up on this man's—this stranger's—doorstep and fallen to pieces. The staggering hospital bill already had her worried beyond belief, but combined with the unexpected appearance of her ex-husband it was just too much. It wasn't often that she let down her guard. And she really wished it hadn't been in front of Lucas.

The steaming shower had helped clear her mind. She'd given in to a moment of fear that she would fail her daughter, but the time for uncertainty had passed. She must be strong now. Besides, she refused to fall to pieces again in front of Lucas. He must already think that she was... what? Pathetic? Weak? Looking for a handout? Or all of the above? She wasn't about to confirm any of his suspicions—not if she could help it.

He pushed a cup of steaming coffee in front of her. "Drink this. It'll warm you up while I run to the deli and get us some lunch."

"Thank you. I'm sorry for imposing again. I...I just started walking and thinking. Eventually I ended up here."

Her hands were clammy and her muscles tense as she clutched the warm ceramic cup. Her gaze strayed to Lucas as he strode over to the center island where his jacket was draped over a stool as though he might have been headed somewhere before she showed up. His strides were long and his dark jeans accentuated his toned legs and cute backside. His collared shirt was unbuttoned just enough for her to catch a glimpse of his firm chest. He'd certainly make some woman a fine catch—except for his lack of housekeeping skills.

He slipped on his jacket. "You can play solitaire on my computer."

"I hate making you go out in the rain—"

"I was going out anyway. I guess one of these days I need to do more than just drive past the grocery store." He flashed her a lighthearted smile. "Do you want anything in particular to eat?"

She shook her head. "I'm not picky."

"I won't be long." He rushed out the door.

Kate was exhausted, but there was no time for sleep. She needed to plan out how to raise the funds for the surgery. Her lengthy walk had given her time to think and she knew there was no way a bank would lend her that kind of money. And she didn't have any rich aunts or uncles lurking in the family tree. That only left a fund-raiser. A big one!

Lucas had said she could use his computer. She pulled up a search engine and began typing. Eventually she stumbled across the fact that the Carringtons used to organize fund-raisers, some even taking place in this very mansion.

Somehow Lucas must have missed the social gene. This house wasn't fit for him to live in much less provide a venue for entertaining. If only the mansion had been better maintained, it'd be ideal for a premium ticket event.

Before she could search for alternate locations that might attract wealthy donors, Lucas returned with a large bag. "Hope you're hungry."

"Looks like enough to feed a football team."

"I wasn't sure what to order. So I got a little of this and a little of that."

They quietly set the table and spread out the food. Kate's

belly rumbled its anticipation. She eagerly munched down her sandwich before Lucas was even halfway done with his. He pushed another foil-wrapped sandwich in front of her.

"That must have been some walk," Lucas said as she unwrapped the food.

"I had a lot of thinking to do."

After she'd left the hospital, she'd tramped around the bustling streets of Manhattan. She'd been surrounded by people from all walks of life and yet she had never felt more alone—more scared that she'd fail as a mother. But thanks to Lucas's kindness the panic had passed and her determination had kicked in. She would see that her little girl got what she needed—one way or the other.

"And did you get everything straight in your head?"

She glanced away, unsure how to answer. She didn't want him to think any less of her for losing complete control of her life, but she hated to lie, too. She took the middle road. "I still have a lot to figure out."

"You know, I find when I have problems at the office that talking them through usually helps. We conduct brainstorming sessions where my key people sit around tossing out ideas, no matter how crazy they might sound. One thing leads to another until we have some potential solutions. Would you like to give it a try?"

She didn't know why he was being so nice to her. A warm shower. His übercomfy robe. A cup of hot coffee. More food than she could ever eat. And now a sympathetic ear. His kindness choked her up and had her blinking repeatedly.

"Hey, it can't be that bad." Lucas squeezed her forearm.

The heat of his touch seeped through the robe, igniting a pulse of awareness. The sensation zinged up her arm and short-circuited her already frazzled mind. Then just as quickly as he'd reached out to her, he pulled back. It was as though he realized he'd crossed some sort of invisible line.

She sniffled. "Actually my life is a nightmare right now."

"The visit to the hospital—was it because you're sick?"

"I wish that was the case."

His brows lifted and his eyes grew round. "You want to be sick?"

The horrified expression on his face made her laugh. She couldn't help it. Maybe this was the beginning of some sort of nervous breakdown, but the look Lucas shot her across the table tickled her funny bone. He probably thought she'd lost control of her senses. But she was perfectly sane and this was deadly serious.

Her laughter was immediately doused by the thought of her daughter. "I don't want to be sick. But if someone must be ill, it should be me. Not my four-year-old daughter."

Lucas sat back in his chair as though her words had knocked him over. "What's the matter with her?"

"Molly needs an operation. That's why we came to New York. No one else was willing to take the risk. But before anything can be done, I have to come up with the money to pay for the surgery."

Lucas's brows scrunched together as though he were processing all of this information. "Excuse me for asking, but don't you have insurance?"

"It doesn't cover experimental procedures. And every cent I have won't make a dent in what I owe."

His blue eyes warmed with sympathy. He nodded as though he understood. That or he ran out of kind words to say. Either way, she'd already said too much.

"I'm sorry. This isn't your problem. I only stopped back to get my things."

"Where will you go?"

"I...I don't know. I hadn't gotten that far yet. But I'll figure out something. I always do."

She got to her feet a little too quickly. The room started

to spin. She grabbed the back of the chair and squeezed her eyes shut, willing the sickening sensation to pass.

The sound of rapid footsteps had her opening her eyes. A worried frown greeted her. "I'm fine."

"You don't look it."

"It's nothing. I just stood up too fast." That combined with three hours of shut-eye the night before and plodding around in the rain on top of the news that she owed the hospital a small fortune had left her drained and off-balance. But she refused to play the sympathy card. She didn't want him thinking any less of her. Then again, was it possible to sink lower in his estimation? She stifled a groan.

"I think this news has taken its toll on you." Lucas stared at her, holding her gaze captive. "Do you have family around to help?"

Did Chad count? Not in her book. "No. My mother is out of town and my father. He's not in the picture. It's just me and Molly."

"I'm sorry to hear that."

An awkward silence ensued. Hoping to fill in the gap so he didn't feel that he had to say anything sympathetic, she added, "We do okay on our own. In fact, I should get back to the hospital soon."

"I'm sure your little girl misses you."

The mention of her daughter had her remembering Lucky Ducky. She pulled the keychain from the pocket of the robe and fidgeted with it.

"I see you have your duck handy. Is it special? Or do you just like to have something to fidget with?"

Kate stared at the trinket. "My daughter gave it to me after winning it at Pizza Pete's Arcade. She said it was to keep me company. I tossed it into my purse and eventually it became sort of a good luck charm."

"He looks like a reliable, no-nonsense duck. No quacking around."

She found herself smiling at his attempt at levity. "He's definitely seen me through some tough times. Now, I should get cleaned up. Molly's dad will be leaving soon and I need to be there when he does so she isn't alone."

His gaze moved to her bare ring finger. "You're married?"

"No. Chad's my ex-husband. And…" She shook her head, fighting to hold back another yawn and…losing the battle. "Never mind. I keep rambling on when I need to get out of your way. I'm sure you have better things to do."

"What time are you expected back at the hospital?"

"Not until three. It's best if my ex and I keep our time together at a minimum. Molly has enough to deal with. She doesn't need to see her parents arguing."

"You still have a couple of hours until you have to be back. Why don't you take a nap and later I'll give you a ride to the hospital?"

His offer filled her with a warmth that she hadn't felt in a long time. "I couldn't ask you to do that. You don't even know me."

"You aren't asking. I'm offering. And after I kept you up late last night, I owe you this."

"But it isn't necessary—

"It's still drizzling outside. You don't need to get wet again. So do we have a deal?"

"How is it a deal? What do you get out of helping me?"

"Let's just say it feels good being able to help someone."

She had a feeling there was more to his statement than he let on. Was he wishing that someone would help him? What could a wealthy, sexy bachelor need help with?

She looked into his blue-gray eyes. "Are you sure?"

"I am. Now do you promise you won't go sneaking off again?"

She was exhausted. And he seemed determined to be a Good Samaritan. What would it hurt to accept his offer?

"I promise."

A ball of sympathy and uneasiness churned in Lucas's gut. He knew all too well the hell a parent went through when they felt as if they'd lost control of their children's safety. When his ex-wife had up and left him, she'd written only a brief note saying she'd take good care of their little girl. Until his private investigator had tracked her down in California, he hadn't been able to function.

This thing with Kate hit too close to home. But how could he turn his back on her when her daughter was in such shaky circumstances?

He needed time to think. In fact, that's all he'd been doing since Kate went upstairs to lie down. But it was almost three and he hadn't seen any sign of her. The memory of her pale face and the dark smudges under her eyes had him thinking she was still asleep. Perhaps she'd forgotten to set the alarm on her phone. Or maybe she was so tired that she'd slept right through it. He couldn't blame her.

He should wake her, but the thought of going upstairs left a sour taste in his mouth. He hadn't been upstairs in a long time. There was nothing up there but gut-wrenching memories of everything he'd lost—his family…his little girl.

Still he had to do something. He'd given his word that he'd get her there on time. The thought of a little girl—the image of his own daughter crystallized in his mind—sick and alone spurred him into action.

He moved to the bottom of the steps. "Kate!" Nothing. "Kate, are you awake? It's time to head to the hospital."

He waited, hoping to hear a response or the echo of footsteps. There were no sounds. Surely she hadn't left again without saying anything. Unease churned in his gut. No.

She'd promised and he sensed that she prided herself on keeping her word.

"Kate, we need to go!"

The seconds ticked by and still nothing. There was only one thing left to do. His gaze skimmed up the staircase. He'd been up and down those stairs countless times throughout his life and he'd never thought anything of it. Then came the day when he'd climbed to the second floor only to find his wife was gone along with his baby girl. The memory slugged him squarely in the chest, knocking the breath from his lungs.

That never-to-be-forgotten night he'd cleared out his personal belongings and moved to the first floor. He'd wanted to avoid the memories...the pain. Now because of Kate and her little girl, he had to climb those steps again.

Putting one foot in front of the other, he started up the stairs. He faltered as he reached the landing with the large stained-glass window, but he didn't turn back. He couldn't. This was too important.

He turned, taking the next set of steps two at a clip. His chest tightened and his hands tensed.

Don't look around. Don't remember. Just keep moving.

His strides were long and fast. He kept his face forward, resisting the instinct to survey his surroundings, to let the memories crowd into his mind—not that they were ever far away.

Lucas stopped in front of her door and blew out a pent-up breath. He rapped his knuckles on the heavy wood door. "Kate, are you awake?"

Nothing.

He knocked again. Still no response.

Was it possible she was sick? Walking around in the cold air while soaking wet certainly couldn't have done her any good. And he wasn't going downstairs until he knew she was all right.

He grasped the handle and pushed the door open. The drapes were drawn, allowing shadows to dance across the spacious room. When his eyes adjusted, he spotted Kate sprawled over the king-sized bed. Her breathing was deep. The stress lines were erased from her beautiful face. And her pink lips were slightly parted and very desirable.

He squashed his line of thought. Now wasn't the time to check her out, no matter how appealing he found her. Relationships weren't in the cards for him. In the end, people just ended up hurting each other. And he wanted no part of that.

"Kate." His voice was soft so as to not scare her. When she didn't stir, he stepped closer. "Kate, wake up."

She rolled over and stretched. The robe fell open, revealing a lace-trimmed pink top that hugged her curves and rode up, exposing her creamy white stomach. The breath caught in his throat. She was so gorgeous. He shouldn't look—he should turn away. But what fun would that be? He was, after all, a man. A little glimpse of her fine figure wouldn't hurt anyone. Right?

Her gaze latched on to him and the moment ended. She bolted upright.

"Lucas. What are you doing here?" She glanced down, cinching the robe closed. "I mean I know it's your house and all…but what are you doing in my room…umm, your guest room." She pressed a hand to her mouth, halting the babbling.

"I tried calling up the steps and even knocked on the door, but you were out to the world."

"What do you want?"

The question was a loaded one and set off one inappropriate response after the other. The first of which was for her to move over in bed. The next thought was for her to kiss him.

He cleared his throat, hoping his voice would sound normal. "It's time to go back to the hospital." He turned for the door. "I'll meet you downstairs."

Drip... Drip... He paused and listened. *Drip...*

Lucas turned on his heels. "Is the faucet in the bathroom leaking?"

"Umm...no."

"But that sound. Something's dripping." He squinted into the shadows. Frustrated, he moved to the light switch. "Can't you hear it?"

"Of course I hear it. I'm not deaf."

He flipped on the overhead light and spotted a wastebasket in the corner. A quick inspection of the ceiling showed water gathering around the bloated section of plaster. Droplets formed and dropped. Bits of fallen plaster littered the floor.

"What the—" He remembered his manners just before cursing. His mother had been the epitome of proper form. Carringtons should never lower themselves with vulgar language, she'd say. Especially not in front of guests.

"It's been like that since the rain started. You need a new roof."

His jaw tightened. "Thanks for pointing out the obvious."

"I told you when we met that I'm an interior designer. I know more about houses than just how to properly hang a painting."

"So you do roofing, too?"

She smiled. "No, I'm not a roofer, but that doesn't mean I can't find someone qualified to do a rush job. Because if you'd look around, you'd realize that isn't your only leak."

This time he didn't care about his manners. "Damn."

He'd turned a blind eye to the house to the point where he had no idea this place was in such bad condition. This went far beyond the mopping and cleaning he'd envisioned.

There was considerable damage to the ceiling that was now bowing, and the crown molding was warped and crumbling.

Kate listed everything she'd noticed that needed repair. Unable to bear the guilt over the devastation he'd let happen to his childhood home…to his daughter's legacy, he turned his gaze away from the ruined plaster. Kate continued talking as though she was in her element. Who knew that fixing up old houses could excite someone so much?

She got to her feet and straightened the bed. "If you want I can make a few phone calls to get people in here to start fixing things up. Maybe they can change things up a little and give this place a makeover—"

"No. I don't want people in here, making changes." He ground out the words.

A frown creased her forehead. "Of course there will have to be changes. Nothing ever stays the same. Life is one long string of changes."

The only changes he'd experienced lately were bad ones that left him struggling to keep putting one foot in front of the other. Like his last visit with his daughter in California—when she'd turned away from him because he was now a stranger to her.

"Listen to me," Kate said, moving to stand right in front of him. "You're going to have to make some decisions about this place. You can already see the neglect is taking its toll. Once it's fixed up, you can move out of that tiny room in the downstairs—"

"I'm happy there."

She frowned at him as though she didn't believe a word he said. "Perhaps then you might consider moving to someplace smaller and selling this house to some lucky family who will appreciate its charms."

He glanced around at the room. This had been his aunt's room, back when he was a kid. In this room, he'd always felt safe and accepted just as he was. This house was a scrapbook of memories, some good, some not so good. He couldn't turn his back on it all.

Ghosts of the past filled his mind. The walls started to close in on him. Each breath grew more difficult. He needed space—air. He headed for the door, ignoring Kate's plea for him to wait. With his gaze straight ahead, he marched down the hall, his breathing becoming more labored. It felt as though the oxygen had been sucked out of the house.

No matter how much he hated to admit it, Kate had a point. This mansion was in worse shape than he'd ever imagined. His shoulders drooped beneath the weight of guilt. His parents and grandparents would be horrified if they were still around to see the neglect he'd let take place. They'd entrusted him with the care of the Carrington mansion and he'd failed. His chest burned as he rushed down the stairs.

Even if he someday won over his little girl—if she no longer looked at him like a scary stranger—he couldn't bring her here. He couldn't show her the numerous portraits of her ancestors that his ex-wife had stashed in the attic. The dust. The peeling and cracking plaster. And most likely mold. It just wasn't fit for a child—or for that matter, an adult.

In the foyer, he yanked open the front door. The cool breeze rushed up and swirled around him. He stood in the doorway as the rain pitter-pattered on the pavement. He breathed in the fresh air—the coolness eased his lungs.

As his heart rate slowed, his jumbled thoughts settled. Kate was right. The house did need more repairs than he'd ever thought possible. And he was way past putting it off until another day. Then a crazy idea struck him. But could it work?

CHAPTER SIX

UPON HEARING KATE'S approaching footsteps, Lucas turned. "You're right."

"I am?" Her pencil-thin brows rose. "Is this your way of apologizing? And perhaps asking me to make those calls for you?"

"Yes, that was an apology." Why did she make him spell everything out? He thought he'd made it clear from the start.

As for having her involved with the repairs, he wasn't sure. Guilt niggled at him. Here she was with so much on her plate and she was worried about him…er, rather his house. This was all so backward. He should be offering Kate a helping hand.

Wouldn't things have gone more smoothly for him when his daughter went missing if he'd let someone in? Instead he'd closed himself off from the world. Lost in his own pain, Carrington Gems had teetered on the brink of disaster. Even today, he was still paying for the poor choices he'd made back then.

Was that the way Kate was feeling now? He glanced into her eyes, seeing pain and something else…could it be determination? Of course it was. She might have had a case of nerves earlier, but he could see by the slight tilt of her chin and her squared shoulders that the moment had passed.

Still, he wasn't quite ready to throw in with a woman

he barely knew…even if his aunt trusted Kate enough to open up his home to her. Still she seemed so excited when she talked about the house. He couldn't make any decisions now. It'd take him some more thought.

He glanced at his watch. "We should go. You don't want to be late."

"But what about the roof?"

"It'll keep for a few more hours. We can talk it over when you're done at the hospital."

He ushered her out the door into the gray, drizzling day. Deep inside he knew that Kate's appearance in his life was about to alter things…for both of them. He didn't know how, but he sensed change in the wind. And after years of trying to keep the status quo, this knowledge left him feeling extremely off-balance.

But no one could understand how hard it would be for him to help this woman with a sick child—a child the same age as his own daughter…who no longer even recognized him. Regret pummeled him. He should have been home more and tried harder to work things out with Elaina, if only for the sake of his little girl. Then it would be him she was calling Daddy—not someone else.

Silence filled the car, giving Lucas too much time to think about what he'd lost and how inadequate he felt as a human. He glanced over at Kate. "What has you so quiet?"

"I was thinking about how to raise money for the surgery."

The streetlight turned green and Lucas eased down on the accelerator. "Do you have any family you can reach out to?"

"No. My family is small and not close-knit. My mother was around when Molly first got sick, but she doesn't have a lot of patience. The longer the tests and hospital visits went on… Well, now she's off in Los Angeles, or was it Las

Vegas, with the new flavor of the month. She calls when she gets a chance."

That was tough. Even though his mother had remarried after his father's death and moved to Europe, he knew if he ever picked up the phone and asked for help that she'd come. She was never a warm and affectionate mother, but she did protect what was hers.

"So without a rich uncle in the family and knowing I won't qualify for a loan, I'll have to organize a fund-raiser. Something that can be arranged quickly and without too much overhead."

He paused, searching for a solution. "I'll help you as much as I can. You just hit me at a bad time as I'm fully invested in expanding Carrington Gems to the West Coast." He didn't bother to add that they'd hit one expensive stumbling block after the other with this project. In comparison to what Kate was facing, his problems paled considerably. "If I think of something that might work, I'll let you know."

"Thanks. And my offer is still open to make those phone calls. I have some contacts in New York who can hook me up with a reliable crew."

The depth of her kindness struck a chord with him. "You'd really do that with everything you have going on?"

"Of course I would. You let me stay at your house for almost a week, rent-free…even if you didn't know it. I owe you so much."

He grew uncomfortable when people started thanking him. He wasn't someone special—definitely not a selfless person like Kate appeared to be. He was a workaholic, who'd lost focus on his priorities and wound up with a house of memories and a business in jeopardy because he'd pushed too hard, too fast to gain the expansion into San Francisco.

"You don't owe me a thing. All I did was let you stay in a leaky bedroom. Not very gallant of me."

She sniffled. "You could have had me thrown in jail. Most other people who find a stranger in their house would call the police first and ask questions later."

Lucas slowed the car as they neared the hospital. Once he maneuvered into a spot in front of the main sliding glass doors, he shifted into Park and turned to her. "Listen, you shouldn't put me up on a pedestal. You barely know a thing about me. Trust me, I have an ex-wife who would vouch for the fact that I'm no saint."

"You're far too modest—"

"Don't let a little kindness fool you. I'm a Carrington. We don't have hearts—instead, there's a rough diamond in its place." His fist beat lightly on his chest. "Harder and colder than any rock you'll ever find."

"I don't believe you."

"It's true. My grandfather told me. I was too young to truly understand what he meant, but now I do—"

"You definitely have a heart or you wouldn't have been so kind to me."

"And you're too sweet for your own good."

The way she stared at him with such assuredness made him want to be that man for her. The kind that was giving and thoughtful instead of focused and driven. For a moment, he was drawn into her dream—drawn to her.

When she lowered her face, he placed a finger beneath her chin. He wasn't willing to lose the connection just yet. Her eyes glinted with... Was it longing? His body tensed at the thought. How could this slip of a woman— a near-stranger—have such an effect on him? And why did he have this overwhelming urge to pull her close and kiss her?

Without thinking of the consequences, he leaned forward. His lips sought hers out. They were soft and smooth. A whispered voice in the back of his mind said he should not be doing this. Not with Kate. Not with anyone.

But when her mouth moved beneath his, logic escaped him. It'd been so long since he felt this alive—this invigorated.

He went to pull her closer, but the seat restraint kept them separated except for his lips moving hungrily over hers. His hand reached out, cupping her face. His thumb stroked her cheek, enjoying her silky, smooth skin. All he could think was that he wanted more—more of her kiss… more of this connection.

A bright flash broke the spell. Lucas pulled back, struggling to catch his breath. His gaze moved to the window. Immediately he spotted a photographer smirking at him. Lucas surmised from past experience that the guy would take the picture and fabricate an eyebrow-raising headline to fit it.

"Wait here. I'll be back." Lucas jumped out of the car and started after the photographer. "Hey, you! Stop!"

The reporter had too much of a head start and slipped into a waiting vehicle. Lucas kicked at a pebble on the side of the road and swore.

What had he gotten himself into this time? Of all the foolish things to do. He'd been so touched by her insistence in believing in him that he'd momentarily let down his guard. He hadn't thought about where they were or what he was about to do. He'd just reached out to her, needing to feel her warmth and kindness.

How was he supposed to know there was a photographer at the hospital? And how could he anticipate that they'd be noticed? Normally it wouldn't have been a big deal, but with Kate involved it was different. She already had so much on her plate. She didn't deserve to have to put up with the press. Those news stories, as they loosely called them, were nine times out of ten malicious pieces of gossip—such as the story his ex-wife had read about him being involved with one of the Carrington models. But it had been only one crack in an already crumbling marriage.

Kate hadn't signed on for any of this media mayhem. She didn't deserve to have her name associated with some trumped-up story. He just wished he could shield her from the public eye. With a frustrated sigh, he climbed back in the car.

"What's going on?" Kate's eyes filled with concern. "Why were you chasing that man?"

"The man was a reporter and he took a picture of us—"

"What?" Her face lost most of its color. "But why? None of this makes any sense. Why would he be interested in me? In us?"

Lucas raked his fingers through his hair. "Normally it wouldn't matter. And any other time the paparazzi wouldn't have given us a second look, but last month there was this magazine article—"

"The one announcing you as Bachelor of the Year."

"You saw it?" His muscles tensed, hating the thought of being played by her. "You knew who I was from the moment we met, didn't you?"

"That's not true." She held up both palms, feigning an innocent expression. "At first, I didn't recognize you in your boxers. I guess I was a bit distracted." Color rushed back into her cheeks. "The more important question is what will this reporter do with the photo?"

He shrugged. "My guess is he'll sell it to the highest bidder—"

"But he can't. If it gets out people will think that you and I are...uh—"

"Involved." He wasn't used to women being repulsed by the idea of being romantically linked with him. "Is the idea of people thinking we're a couple so bad?"

"Yes."

Her snap answer stung. He didn't know what to say, so

he leaned back in the driver's seat. Maybe he should be relieved by her lack of interest, but he wasn't. And that knowledge only aggravated him more.

"I'm sorry." She fidgeted with her purse strap. "I didn't mean for that to sound so harsh. I'm just not used to the paparazzi. And I really don't want my picture in the news."

Now that he could understand. His family had been making headlines longer than he'd been alive and he still wasn't comfortable with it.

"Most likely something more newsworthy will come along and they'll forget about us."

"Oh, good." The stress lines eased on her pretty face.

He didn't really believe it, but there was always a sliver of hope. And right now, Kate looked as if she could use some positive thoughts.

Later that evening, Kate made sure to double-check the dead bolt on the door. She glanced out the window, relieved to find that no one had followed her.

"Anything wrong?"

She jumped at the unexpected sound of Lucas's voice. "Umm…no."

Had she imagined someone had been watching her at the hospital? Definitely not. She might be a lot of things but paranoid wasn't one of them.

"Listen, if you're stressed about what happened between us earlier, don't be." He shuffled his feet and wouldn't look her in the eyes. "It was all my fault and it won't happen again."

Kate didn't know whether to be insulted or relieved. She hadn't been able to forget that kiss either—that mind-numbing, toe-curling kiss. And he was right—there shouldn't be a repeat.

"If you don't make a big deal of it, neither will I."

He looked as if he wanted to say more, but then he turned away and headed for the kitchen. "I ordered pizza, if you're hungry."

She followed him. The aroma of tomato sauce and sausage wafted across the kitchen. "Smells good. Did you by chance order a salad to go with it?"

"Yes, I did." He looked very proud of himself as he pulled a bowl from the fridge.

"Thank you."

She sat down at the counter, still unsettled. She kept going over the memory of that man lurking in the hallway at the hospital. She hadn't thought anything of him at first. But as the evening wore on, she'd noticed him again.

Lucas waved a hand in front of her face. "Kate?"

What had he said? She hadn't been paying attention. "Umm…sure. Whatever."

He placed a slice of the thin-crust pizza on a plate and pushed it in front of her. She didn't make a move as she kept replaying the events from the day.

"I wasn't going to ask," Lucas said, "but you obviously aren't going to eat until you resolve whatever has you so distracted."

"There was a man lurking in the pediatrics unit this evening. At first, I thought he was there to visit someone, but he stayed in the shadows and sort of watched everyone. I wasn't sure about leaving, but when I mentioned him to a nurse, he just sort of vanished."

"I hired him," Lucas said in a low, even tone.

That news had her sitting up straighter. "You hired someone to spy on me?"

"He was there to protect you."

"Protect me?" Her voice rose. "From what?"

"Remember the photographer outside the hospital?" Her hands pressed the countertop as she nodded and he continued. "I didn't want him or any other reporters to bother you with questions, so I sent an off-duty security guard from Carrington to make sure that didn't happen."

"I thought you said the press wouldn't make a big deal of it."

"I just wanted to be sure they left you alone."

"So you do think they'll go ahead with the photo?"

He wanted to assure her that she had nothing to worry about, but he couldn't lie to her. "Probably."

Her eyes lit up. "You can stop them."

"Me? How am I supposed to do that?"

"Pay the guy off. Bid on the photo. I don't know. There has to be a way."

"Even if I wanted to stop him, I don't have the man's name."

"How am I supposed to throw myself on people's mercy and ask for money after my name and face have been tangled up in some tabloid scandal?"

"So you've come up with a plan to raise the money?"

She sat back with a huff. "We're thinking of making it a costume party. Something unique. Your aunt offered to help."

"You've been talking to my aunt?"

"Since I don't know anyone else in this city except you, I approached her to help me organize the fund-raiser. Your aunt seems to know everyone, and if she doesn't know them personally, she knows someone who does. Your aunt loves to talk. We even talked about this house."

His eyes widened. "What exactly did you tell my aunt about the house?"

"Not much. Just that I found this place fascinating. The house is rich in architecture and history. I find it almost as intriguing as its owner."

"You do?" He searched her eyes as she smiled at him.

Was she flirting with him? He gave himself a mental jerk. He didn't need to hook up with her. He just needed her professional expertise. "I have a proposition for you."

CHAPTER SEVEN

LUCAS HAD BEEN considering his plan all day. Kate obviously needed some immediate monetary assistance plus a roof over her head. And he needed someone to oversee the mansion's repairs—someone who appreciated its old-world charms. Kate fit that bill perfectly—if only he could forget how tempting her lush lips were.

She eyed him up tentatively. "What sort of proposition do you have in mind?"

"Since you like this place so much, what would you say if I offered you a job working here?"

Confusion reflected in her brown eyes. "You want me to work for you? Even after the run-in with the photographer?"

"Don't worry. I'll bet the article will be a small, obscure piece. Hardly anyone will notice it." He crossed his arms and rocked back on his heels. "As for the arrangement I'm proposing, it can benefit both of us."

She paused, glancing around the house. He could practically see the wheels in her mind spinning. He'd hired enough people to know when they were eager for a position.

"I...I can't. My daughter is in the hospital and I need to get this fund-raiser off the ground."

She did have a very valid point. But there had to be a compromise. He could see how tempted she was to work on the house, and he knew from his experience with stressful situations that a diversion would do her some good.

He cleared his throat. "The thing is, I have a couple of projects with Carrington Gems that are going to take all of my time." He stopped, realizing his responsibilities paled in comparison to hers. "The real truth is I can run a business, but I don't know how to turn this mess into a home again."

A smile touched her lips and her shoulders straightened. "What makes you think I can turn this place around?"

He didn't want her taking this the wrong way, especially after she thought he'd hired someone to spy on her. He'd have to phrase this carefully. "You got me to really think about this mansion and what my neglect is doing to it. And you mentioned that you have interior design experience. So I checked out some of your prior work. It's good."

Surprise lit up her eyes. "Thank you."

"And I really like your website."

She smiled broadly. "I built it myself."

"You're a woman of many talents. Maybe I should have you consult on Carrington's upcoming web campaign."

Interest sparked in her eyes. "Are you launching a new line of jewelry?"

He nodded, not surprised that she was familiar with his company. His father's lifelong dream had been to make Carrington Gems into a household name. In fact, they still used his father's slogan—*Carrington Gems for the queen of your heart.*

"I'd love to see the new jewelry." Kate's face lit up with excitement. "Your magazine ads already have a distinctive look. I like that they are never overdone and always tasteful."

He stood a little taller. Though he had a team that put together the ad campaigns, he was an active member, adding his input here and there. He was after all a Carrington and he had a vested interest in any images that represented his company.

"I'm also in the middle of an expansion project, which

needs more attention than I'd anticipated. So you can understand that I won't be available to oversee things here. However, I'm more than willing to compensate you for your time."

"My daughter has to be my priority—"

"Of course. We can work around that. Your ex-husband, is he still planning to be at the hospital part of the day?"

Kate nodded. "Actually, I do have a few ideas for the house."

"What would they be?"

Kate began listing off everything she'd like to do to the house, most of which hadn't crossed his mind when he'd offered her the job. Yet she had so much passion in her voice that he didn't want to stop her. The things he'd read about her and her work online didn't live up to the impressive woman standing before him.

As she continued explaining her vision, he couldn't believe someone could be so passionate about working on a house. His ex-wife, Elaina, had only ever been this excited about new clothes or jewels. Kate was definitely a different breed.

She paused and looked at him expectantly. "What do you think?"

"If I do what you suggest, will you take the job?"

"A good contractor can take care of everything."

Lucas shook his head. "I'm not going to let a bunch of people I've never met come in here and take over. You've already displayed your ability to take charge by getting me to see the condition of the house. You'll keep those workers in line and make sure that no changes are done without my authorization."

"I appreciate your faith in my abilities, but I can't be here every minute of the day while my daughter's in the hospital."

He knew he was asking a lot, but he needed to know that

his most treasured memories were handled with the utmost care and respect. "You said so yourself—you can't be there when your ex is with your daughter during the day. I'm offering you a chance to do what you obviously love while earning some money—"

"But what if my ex suddenly decides to skip town, as he's been known to do in the past?"

"We'll deal with that if or when we have to. But this will give you something to do besides sitting around, worrying. There's nothing worse than a day filled with worrisome thoughts and nothing but time on your hands."

"Sounds like you're speaking from experience." When he shrugged but failed to add any details, Kate continued. "And what do I do about the fund-raiser?"

He'd thought about this, too. "I think between my administrative assistant, who is practically a party-planning pro by now, and my aunt, who knows everyone who is anyone, you'll have time to spare. But if you decide to pass on the job, I totally understand. I'm sure I'll find someone to oversee things…eventually."

"This isn't a wait-and-see problem. One more big rain and you'll have untold damage. You need a new roof, and who knows what else, today."

"Does that mean you accept the position?"

Kate was impressed by the speed and ease with which Lucas solved problems. A snap of his fingers and all was right in the world—except for this time.

As tempting as it was to take on this exclusive job and add it as a crowning jewel in her portfolio, she still had a much bigger problem. She needed money for the operation. And though she didn't doubt that Lucas's assistant and aunt could throw together a lavish party, it was still her responsibility. And its success was paramount.

"As much as I'd like to, I can't accept your offer. I have to concentrate on the fund-raiser."

Frown lines creased his forehead. "How is that going?"

She shrugged. "The location is going to be a problem as there are a lot of spring weddings taking up the prime locations, not that I have enough for a deposit on the plush venues anyway. I have some phone messages in to other places—I'm just waiting for them to get back to me."

"I'm sure it'll all work out."

She couldn't help but wonder if he really thought that or if he was just telling her what she wanted to hear. "Connie helped me come up with a theme. It's going to be a vintage costume party. Hopefully people will have a lot of fun dressing up."

"My aunt is a great lady to have around to help plan a party. She's had a lifetime of experience. Between my great-gran, my grandmother and my mother, there was always some sort of social function going on here."

"Really? I've never been to a formal party other than a friend's wedding."

"Not even a work function?"

"By the point where I was in a position to be invited to client parties, I had Molly to consider. I didn't get to spend enough time with her as it was, so I stayed home. We put on an animated movie and ate popcorn."

"You're a very dedicated mother."

Heat flared in her cheeks. "I...uh... Thank you."

"Don't worry, you didn't miss much at those parties."

Her mouth gaped. "Of course I did. It's a girl's dream to get all gussied up and go to the ball. You can say that because you've gone to countless parties. Just once I'd like to check it out for myself."

He chuckled. "Beneath the jeans and T-shirts, I guess you really are a girl."

She frowned. "You actually had doubts about me being a girl?"

"Not at all. You just struck me as being different from the other women I've known."

"I'm not sure if that's good or bad."

"It's neither." He cleared his throat, looking exceedingly uncomfortable. "What if I throw in free room and board if you work for me?"

The man certainly didn't give up easily. "From what I've seen in the kitchen, I'd probably starve to death."

"You've got me there. But I have all of the local take-outs on speed dial. And…maybe I'll entertain some of your design ideas."

She had to admit she was impressed, but she couldn't spread herself too thin. She opened her mouth to turn him down…again.

"No." He held up his hand to silence her. "Don't answer so quickly, because this will be my last offer and I can see the glint of temptation in your eyes."

On second thought, her serious consideration of his offer would give her license to browse around. She'd love to check out the closed-up rooms she hadn't dared explore before. "Do you mind if I look around? To see what I'm getting myself into?"

He waved his hand, granting her free passage. "Help yourself."

She jumped to her feet and hurried down the hallway. She noticed how he trailed her—so close that the scent of his spicy cologne wrapped around her. She paused in front of the double doors just off the foyer and glanced over her shoulder as though making sure he hadn't changed his mind about her nosing around the place.

"Go ahead." His tone was reserved and a bit hesitant.

She turned and pushed the doors open. This was her first glimpse of the living room and she was impressed by its sheer size. Her entire ranch house could fit in this one room with space to spare. And the ceilings were at least twelve feet high, giving the room a wide-open feel.

But there was something not quite right. She scanned the area again, taking in the furniture. Though of high quality, it was too contemporary for the house. And the impressionistic artwork on the walls didn't quite fit. A stately home such as this deserved to be decorated with items that exuded grace and elegance, not flash and fad.

With no throw covers, everything was coated in heavy dust that tickled her nose and made her eyes water. Beneath the filth, the house looked as though the occupants had gotten up one morning, gone about their day but never returned.

Throw pillows were haphazardly strewn about as though people had tossed them aside and forgotten to pick them up. Even a newspaper was spread across the glass coffee table, open to the sports page. Was that why Lucas lived like he did? Was he waiting for someone to return? A lost love?

Kate recalled him mentioning an ex-wife. Was that it? Was he still grieving the loss of his marriage?

A white-and-pink figurine caught her attention. Drawn to it, like a curious feline to a buzzing fly, she couldn't stop herself from picking it up. It was of a mother holding her baby girl. Her fingers stroked over the smooth surface. The mother and child were smiling at each other as if they'd just spent a marvelous day together. It touched something deep inside Kate and had her frowning at the thought of never spending another carefree day with her daughter.

"Put it down."

Kate jumped at the boom of Lucas's voice. Her fingers tightened around the porcelain figurine to keep from dropping it. With the knick-knack safely returned to the dust-covered end table, she faced Lucas. "You know you're going to have to learn to trust me or this will never work."

His expression transformed into one of contrition. "Sorry. I... Oh, never mind."

She noticed a deep sadness in his eyes and wondered what had put it there. But she knew it was none of her business. He probably didn't want to talk about his past any more than she did.

"The good news is from what I've seen of the downstairs, there's no damage. The rooms need a thorough cleaning and a fresh coat of paint. How attached are you to the furniture?" She tried to sound impartial just in case he actually liked the pieces.

"It can go as far as I'm concerned. Does this mean you've accepted the job?"

Oh, she was certainly tempted. "This place is so big. You know you could clear away the furniture and dance in here."

"It's been done before."

"Really?"

He nodded. "My great-grandmother started the tradition of throwing grand parties here at the house. She considered it her duty to entertain clients of Carrington Gems. She'd think up some of the grandest parties. It didn't matter the occasion as long as she could get together the city's movers and shakers to flaunt Carrington's latest creations."

Already Kate could imagine the big-band music, the beautiful dresses and glitzy jewelry. "Oh, how I'd have loved to attend. It must have been something."

"Great-gran was a crafty one. She knew these women were quite wealthy and hated to be outdone by anyone. So my great-grandfather ended up employing the finest craftsmen to design something unique for each of them."

"Those must have been some grand parties."

"They were. In fact, there should be pictures of them around somewhere." He paused as though trying to remember what had happened to them. "Then again, I think they might have been packed away in the attic. Elaina, my ex, didn't like to have antiques and memorabilia around. She called it clutter."

Without thinking, Kate blurted out, "Did Elaina by chance redecorate the house?"

Pain showed in his eyes. "I thought it'd make her happy. She made a mess of the house and…" He pressed his lips together as though realizing he'd said too much. In a blink, the glimpse into this man and his closely guarded feelings was once again hidden behind a wall. "About my offer—are you willing to take me up on it?"

Looking around the place, she was filled with ideas. "How would you feel about making a deal?"

"I thought that's what I'm trying to do. Name your price."

"It isn't your money that interests me." She worried her bottom lip. Should she do this? She had to be crazy, but what did she have to lose?

"What sort of deal do you have in mind?"

"When the work is all said and done, I'd like to borrow your house for an evening." The words poured out of her mouth like a breached dam, but at least they were now out there. "We could hold the fund-raiser here. In honor of your great-grandmother, we could have a 1920s flapper party—"

"What?" He reared back as though slapped.

"Think about it. You could show off your new line of jewelry."

"Impossible. I don't want people parading through my house like it's some sort of museum. You'll have to find another way to advertise your interior design work."

Her hands pressed to her hips. "That's what you think? That I'm planning to line potential clients down the block to have a look-see at your house? Well, you don't have to worry—the thought never crossed my mind."

She had more to say about him misjudging her, but she

bit back her tongue. She couldn't forget how much was riding on her making a successful deal.

He eyed her up as though trying to make up his mind. "Maybe I jumped to the wrong conclusion. But the days of parties being thrown here are over. We'll find you another venue."

"Not one with so much allure or history. We could double or triple the ticket price for people to come to the Carrington mansion." Lucas shook his head, but she couldn't stop. The ideas were coming hard and fast. Her hands waved around as she talked. "Think about it. This could provide publicity for Carrington Gems, too."

She didn't see why they couldn't both benefit from this production, but she could tell he wasn't quite sold. Now how would she nudge him into agreement? She didn't have a clue, but there had to be a way.

"Do you really think people are going to line up to come here?" He glanced around at the dirty surroundings.

"I know it needs a little TLC, but this place will draw in lots of curious folks."

"I don't think so."

Her insides quivered as she stepped up to him. "Please. I'll beg if I have to."

CHAPTER EIGHT

A BALL OF SYMPATHY churned in Lucas's gut. He knew all too well the private hell a parent went through when they felt as if they'd lost control of their child's well-being. But Kate was asking him to open up his home—a piece of himself—to public scrutiny. His life was already disrupted enough by that magazine article. He didn't need people he didn't even know coming in here and whispering behind his back.

He needed time to think. But not here. Not now. He turned on his heels.

"Wait!"

His steps faltered, but he didn't turn back. He couldn't. It would be utter torture to witness the desperation written all over her delicate features. Or the disappointment when he denied her what she so badly wanted.

"I'm not finished." Her voice cracked with emotion. "At least hear me out."

He didn't know what else she had on her mind, but he at least owed her the decency of hearing her out. He stopped in the foyer and turned. The desperation on her face ate at his resolve.

"I'm sorry." She caught up to him. "I don't mean to pester you. I just… I need to do everything to help my daughter."

Lucas shifted his weight from one foot to the other. This

wasn't his problem, no matter how bad he felt for her and the awful situation she was facing. He couldn't let himself get sucked back into the miserable murkiness of helplessness. Yet turning his back on Kate clearly wasn't an option either.

When the silence dragged on, Kate spoke up. "Do you like my idea about planning a party like your grandmother might have done? You know, displaying the new line of jewelry?"

He actually liked her suggestion a lot. "I'd need to find someone to wear the jewelry."

"I'm sure you must have some beautiful models on hand. Any woman would die to wear Carrington Gems."

"But this will have to be done right. The clothes and hair will all have to be choreographed to give the gems the best display possible."

"You make it sound very planned out."

"It will be. Trust me. Only the best for Carrington."

The smile dipped from her face and she suddenly looked quite serious. "Does this mean we have a deal?"

"Not quite." Though a voice inside him said he was crazy to open his home to the public, business sense told him this personalized campaign might make a big difference to the Fiery Hearts jewelry launch. "I want daily progress reports, including any surprises or unexpected delays. If I find at any point you aren't completely forthcoming, the deal is off."

He wasn't the first client to micromanage a project. Having Lucas looking over her shoulder wasn't her preferred way to work, but she'd make do. "Not a problem. I can write up a daily summary of our progress."

"I'd prefer to have these updates in person. Say over dinner each evening."

"You want us to dine every night?" She hadn't counted on that and after the kiss in the car, she wasn't so sure spending time together was a good idea. She wasn't ready for a relationship—she wasn't sure she ever would be again. They hurt way too much when they ended.

"Considering we'll be living here together, I don't see where that will be such a hardship."

"But I'll be at the hospital."

"No problem. I'm used to eating late. I'll have something waiting when you get home." He sent her a don't-argue-with-me look. "I'll let you think it over."

"I don't need to." His eyes lit up with surprise, but the truth was she didn't have any time to waste. This place needed lots of TLC. "It's a deal. Now would you mind if we went upstairs? I'd like to get your input on some things."

His head lowered and he spoke in a strangled voice. "I can't go back up there."

Not *I won't* or some other excuse, but rather *I can't*. What was up with that? She was tempted to ask—tempted to ease his pain. But she reminded herself that this was a business relationship. Nothing more.

"Lucas, thank you…for all of this." When his gaze rose to meet hers, she noticed a poignant sadness in his eyes. "Tell me, what do you plan to do with this house? You know, once it's fixed up?"

He ran a hand over the back of his neck. "Does it matter?"

"Actually it does. If you're planning to sell, then the interior should be more neutral to invite people to envision their family and possessions within these walls. But if you have plans of keeping it and living here then we can tailor everything to your taste."

"It doesn't matter. Use your best judgment."

Frustration bubbled up in Kate. She'd never encountered this problem before. Usually her clients had too many ideas—ideas outside of their budget and she'd have to rein them in. And though she was tempted to run with the utter freedom he suggested, something told her that Lucas wasn't as apathetic to the house's remodel as he wanted her to believe.

She lifted her chin and looked him straight on. "If you would walk through the rooms with me and give me a basic idea of what you have in mind, I could come up with some sketches for you to look over."

"I only have one requirement. There's a room upstairs at the other end of the hallway from yours. I don't want anyone in there. It's locked and it's to remain that way."

"But this place is filthy. You might not want to paint the room, but we'll need to clean it."

"No. I don't want you going in there. Period."

What in the world was his hang-up about that room? Had it been the room he shared with the ex-wife? Was he secretly pining for her? Somehow his reaction still seemed over the top.

Perhaps someone had died in the room. If so, that would explain why he was acting so strange. And it'd be a more reasonable explanation for turning this house into some sort of mausoleum. If she were ever to lose Molly... Her heart stuttered and a cold sweat broke out on the nape of her neck. No. She would not go there.

"I'm sorry. I didn't realize it was important to you."

He rubbed a hand over his jaw. "It's just that it's my... uh, never mind. I just need it left alone."

"I understand."

The man might be a little rough around the edges and have a few peculiarities, but she wanted to reach out to him and find out what he'd been on the verge of saying. Still, a nagging voice in the back of her mind warned her not to let her defenses down around him. In her experience, men were basically the same—unreliable.

She'd thought the moon rose and set around her father—how could she have been so wrong? She wanted to tell herself that it was because she was a child and didn't know any better. But that didn't explain Chad. She'd utterly and completely fallen for his charm and empty promises. She'd even agreed to his spur-of-the-moment proposal and rushed Las-Vegas-style I dos.

She'd convinced herself that he'd eventually settle down—once they found the right town. But no matter how many jobs he had in this place or that place, none of them suited him.

By the time she became pregnant, she couldn't remember the address of her latest apartment. She was certain when she told Chad about the baby that it would give him a reason to plant some roots. She'd been so wrong.

He'd been enraged and was convinced that she'd tricked him into getting her pregnant. He'd left that night, only to play a sporadic part in their daughter's life while he continued to chase his ever-changing dreams.

And now, at this vital juncture in her life, Kate didn't need any complications. Lucas was one walking string of complications. The first and most important was that he was providing her with the means with which to raise the money for her daughter's surgery. If their relationship didn't last—and relationships never did—the price was just too great.

"Did you see this?"

The following morning, Kate couldn't tear her eyes from the photo of her and Lucas in the paper. If she'd ever had any doubts about whether that kiss in the car had been a dream, she now had proof. But this picture made the kiss appear less than innocent. In fact, the clench appeared quite steamy—on both sides.

Her cheeks flamed as she recalled his lips moving over hers. The way her stomach had filled with a fluttering sensation. And the way he'd left her longing for more. But that wasn't going to happen. She wouldn't let it.

With a frown pulling at her face, she glanced at the photo again. Maybe the photo wasn't an exaggeration, but it had been a private moment—a lapse in judgment, never to be repeated.

Lucas didn't say a word as he sipped his coffee, which added to her frustration.

She smacked the paper. "This headline is outrageous. Carrington Heir Snared?" She set aside her steaming mug, feeling the heat of embarrassment rising up her neck and setting her face aflame. "I thought you said if the picture made the paper, it'd be obscure."

"Don't let it get to you. It's not worth getting worked up over."

"Nothing! How can you call my private life splashed in the news nothing?" Her eyes took in each and every innuendo. She couldn't stop reading any more than she could stop breathing. "This is going to be a disaster. How am I supposed to face everyone much less ask people for money when this article implies you and I are...you know."

"Sleeping together." He supplied the answer so smoothly, so casually as though having the whole world contemplating his sex life was the status quo.

"We have to do something." Her mind frantically sought out an answer. "We should sue them."

He shook his head. "First, it would only make this below-the-fold story bigger. And second, they don't actually lie. We are sleeping together under one roof—"

"But in separate beds."

"And we were seen leaving here early in the morning."

"But it wasn't the wee hours of the morning like they said."

"You're splitting hairs. Besides, did you happen to think

about spinning this publicity around and using it to your advantage?"

"But I don't want publicity. I'm happy with my quiet life."

"Ah, but you're forgetting about the fund-raiser. You know what they say—any publicity is good publicity. Well, maybe not any publicity, but you know what I mean."

The scary part was that she did know what he was trying to say. And she didn't know whether to be angry...or excited.

Maybe she'd misunderstood. "Are you saying we should pose as a happy couple?"

"It's out there now. You might as well capitalize on the news coverage."

"And you're okay with this?"

He shrugged. "I know how to work the press when I need to. It's all an act for the sake of the fund-raiser and the launch of Fiery Hearts. Why not let it play out?"

She crossed her arms and pursed her lips. She noticed how he never said that he was comfortable with this plan, but he seemed resigned to do his part to help their mutual cause. Instead of being angry with him for putting her in this position, she found herself liking him a little more.

"Kate, if you're ready to go, I can drop you off at the hospital on my way to the office."

She shook her head. "I'm not ready to put your plan into action."

"Even so, you can't let those reporters dictate how you live your life. And I promise to be a perfect gentleman and keep my hands to myself."

What worried her more was the thought that she wanted him touching her. She found she liked having him close. Her heart thump-thumped at the memory of him next to her. His finger beneath her chin. His deep, hungry gaze. His lips pressed to hers.

Drawing her meandering thoughts up short, she said the first thing that came to mind. "You should come to the hospital with me. Once I take care of the billing department, we could visit Molly."

He shook his head. "I don't think so."

"Molly wants to meet you. I told her you make the most beautiful jewelry. She wants to know if you make tiaras for princesses."

"I'm sorry. I can't meet your daughter today. My schedule is backed up." He started out of the room. "But I'll make it up to you."

"How?"

"You'll be the first to have a preview of the Fiery Hearts collection."

"I can't wait." She loved jewelry, even if it was only to admire it while window-shopping. "Don't forget to let me know when you have some free time. Molly would really enjoy meeting you."

"I won't forget. Let's go."

Five minutes later, Kate settled into the seat of Lucas's expensive sports car. She loved the buttery-soft leather upholstery, the purr of the powerful engine and most of all, the driver. She watched as Lucas grasped the black shifter. His long, lean fingers drew her attention. Her mouth grew increasingly dry. Why was he getting to her? Was it the tempting thought of what it'd be like to once again be held by those hands? The thought of a mere gentle caress had a sigh slipping past her lips.

"Did you hear me?" Lucas's deep voice jarred her from her ambling thoughts.

"I was thinking about the article." It was that darn paper that filled her mind with…things. Bad things.

He slowed to a stop and glanced her way. "Quit worrying. It'll all be fine."

She was drawn in by his mesmerizing stare. After all,

he was very handsome and very available. Her heart beat faster as heat swirled in her chest and spread out to her limbs. Did he have the heater on in here or what? "Mind if I open the window a crack?"

"Go for it." He chanced a quick glance her way. "Are you feeling okay? You look a little flushed."

"I'm fine." She resisted the urge to fan herself. "Honest."

She eased the window down and savored the cool morning air. What in the world was up with her? Article or not, since when did she let a man get to her?

In an effort to act normal, she said, "You wouldn't believe how helpful your aunt has been. When I'm not at the hospital, she checks on Molly for me."

"I thought your ex was with her."

Kate shrugged. "He's supposed to be, but he isn't exactly reliable. And I don't want Molly to feel like everyone has forgotten her. So Connie and a couple of the nurses promised to call if Chad decides that sitting with a sick kid isn't for him."

"My aunt is very outgoing. She'd help anyone in need. No matter what."

Kate's body tensed. Surely he wasn't implying that she was taking advantage of the woman, was he?

"I didn't ask your aunt for anything—"

"I'm sure you didn't. She never had the opportunity to have a family of her own, and since I'm the only relative she has left, she likes to take in strays—"

"Strays! I'm not a stray." Kate glared at him. "I didn't need to be taken in. Molly and I have been doing fine on our own."

He shifted in the driver's seat. "I didn't mean that like it sounded."

"And how did you mean it?" She wasn't letting him off the hook that easily.

"I just worry. My aunt has a history of taking in the

wrong sort of people—people that take advantage of her naïveté. If you hadn't noticed, my aunt goes through life with rose-colored glasses on. She can't or won't see the bad in people."

Actually Kate had noticed that his aunt was surprisingly trusting and friendly. Lucas didn't seem interested in offering more about his aunt, and she didn't want to probe any further.

They pulled up in front of the hospital and Kate noticed Lucas's shoulders tense as he scanned the area, most likely searching for more photographers. She followed his line of vision, but didn't see anyone paying them the least bit of attention.

"I'd better hurry. After I confirm some details about the fund-raiser with the billing department, I'm going to stick my head in and say good-morning to Molly before heading back to the house."

"Won't your ex be with Molly?"

She nodded. "But it isn't like we're mortal enemies."

"You aren't?"

"We'll never be buddies or anything, but we can tolerate each other…at least for a minute or two."

"And you're okay with him spending time with Molly after being gone so much of the time?"

With anyone else, she wouldn't get into this type of conversation, but something told her this was important to Lucas. "Letting Chad back into our lives is the last thing I want. But this isn't about me. This is about Molly. And she wants him, so who am I to stand between them? But it doesn't mean I trust him to stick around. Old dogs don't learn new tricks, no matter how much they might want to at the moment."

Lucas gazed past her, as though lost in his thoughts.

She got the distinct impression that his relationship with his ex wasn't so amicable. But if that was the case, why was he alone in a dusty house of memories, pining for her? There were a lot of missing pieces to Lucas's puzzle. And though she knew better—knew to keep her distance—she was intrigued by him. What was the real story behind New York City's most eligible bachelor?

CHAPTER NINE

LIFE HAD KATE in the fast lane with no signs of things slowing down.

A week had already passed since Lucas agreed to let her manage the repair work on the house. During that time, they'd fallen into a routine of morning coffee together followed by a late dinner when she got home from the hospital. Sometimes they ate in and sometimes he'd take her out. It was never anything fancy, a little off-the-beaten-path pizzeria or a mom-and-pop diner. She actually enjoyed the warm, inviting atmosphere more than if they'd gone to a high-class establishment where the point was more about being seen than having a relaxing dinner.

But when it came to lunch, she was on her own. Today she didn't have much of an appetite as she arrived at the hospital for an upcoming meeting with Molly's surgeon. They were awaiting test results to make sure the procedure was still an option. Kate had prayed long and hard that there wouldn't be any further complications.

"Kate, did you hear me?" Connie Carrington, Lucas's kindhearted aunt, smiled at her from the other side of the table in the Hospitality Shop. "I said Lucas is lucky you happened into his life."

"I didn't exactly stumble into his life. You had a big hand in that."

"I did, didn't I?" The woman smiled broadly. Her bouncy

personality didn't quite jive with her prim and proper appearance. Her short silver hair was swept off to one side. Her smooth, porcelain complexion had just a hint of makeup and a pair of dark-rimmed glasses perched upon her petite nose.

"You sound quite pleased with yourself."

"My nephew needed his eyes opened before that house collapsed around him. Thank you for making him see sense."

"I don't think it was me as much as the dripping rainwater."

Connie reached across the table and patted her hand. "You, my dear, are good for him."

She highly doubted that. There was an undeniable vibe between them—more like a magnetic force. But he didn't seem any more eager to explore their options than she was to get in any deeper. Experience had taught her that once they crossed that line, there would be no going back.

"Regardless, I have a feeling the house is going to be a huge success. I just hope Lucas likes what I've done."

"I'm sure he will. It's about time that boy lets go of the past and starts living again."

This was a prime opportunity to ask about Lucas's history and the story behind that locked room at the end of the hall, but she couldn't bring herself to do it. She and Lucas were forging a friendship of sorts. If she was going to learn about his past, she wanted it to come from him. She didn't want to sneak around behind his back.

Connie sipped at her coffee and returned the cup to its saucer. "I meant to tell you that splashy headline in the paper was just the publicity we needed."

"It was?"

Connie nodded. "Tickets are going fast. A little more of that free exposure and we should be able to sell out."

Kate lowered her voice. "So you think I should go along

with Lucas's idea to play the happy couple in hopes of gaining more publicity?"

Connie reached out and gave her arm a squeeze. "I do. I really do."

"I…I don't know."

"You've already started quite a buzz. People want to meet the mystery woman caught kissing the Bachelor of the Year. Many women have tried to capture my nephew's attention, but few have ever turned his head. And after the divorce, he's closed himself off. But you—you're making a big difference—"

"What difference would that be?" questioned a familiar male voice.

Kate turned. Her face warmed, wondering how much he'd overheard.

When neither of them replied, his searching gaze moved between the two of them. "Is it some big secret you're sharing?"

Kate's heart pounded in her chest. She was a miserable liar. Her best defense was silence.

Unable to look Lucas in the eye, she lowered her gaze. She noticed his sharp navy suit was tailored to show off his broad shoulders and tapered for his trim waist. Talk about fine packages. Even fully clothed he was definitely Mr. Oh-So-Sexy.

Realizing that she was publicly ogling him, she reined in her thoughts. What was she doing lusting over him? He was here to be a supportive friend. If it weren't for him and his aunt, she didn't know where she'd be or how she'd take care of her daughter.

Lucas and Connie made her feel as though she were no longer alone in this world.

"Heavens, no. We don't have any secrets." Connie's voice wobbled just a bit. "I was telling Kate that even though she isn't doing the guest list and ticket sales that she's making the biggest contribution by pulling together the venue."

"I agree. She's doing a fantastic job." Lucas gave her an approving nod. "The downstairs is all cleaned up and the painting has begun." He smiled, causing the ever-present sadness in his blue eyes to disappear. She wished he looked like that all the time.

"Now, if only the upstairs would go just as fast." Kate finished off the last of her coffee.

"I'm sure it'll all come together."

Lucas's belief in her abilities meant a great deal to her. And the fact he'd shown up today to show his support totally caught her off guard.

She flashed him her best smile. "I'm so glad you decided to take me up on my offer to meet Molly. It'll be a nice surprise for her. Wait until she finds out she has a special visitor. And I see the milkshake I ordered for her is waiting at the checkout."

"But I don't have time—"

"I'll hurry."

Embarrassed by the way she'd nervously chattered nonstop, Kate rushed away. Just because he'd shown up didn't mean she should read anything into his presence. Should she?

Before Lucas could explain that he was there to meet his aunt for their regular lunch, Kate was already across the room.

With a resigned sigh, he sat down across from his aunt. "What's going on here?"

"Kate and I were just discussing the fund-raiser. I'm so glad you agreed to do it at the house. I know that must have been a difficult decision for you, but I'm really proud of you for making the right one. Kate hasn't had many breaks. And at this moment in her life, she can use all of the help she can get."

His aunt might be far too trusting of people she barely knew and might always be looking for the good in everyone, but in this instance he thought she might actually be right. He'd observed Kate this past week, and though he'd given her plenty of chances to take advantage of him, whether by sloughing her work off on someone else or by sponging off him or by leaving him with the bulk of the housework, she'd been a stellar employee.

He shifted positions on the hard plastic chair to get a better view of Kate's slim figure as she stood at the checkout. She was a fine-looking woman. The man who'd walked away from her couldn't be very smart. And best of all, she was as sweet on the inside as she was on the outside.

He jerked his gaze back to his aunt. "And from what I understand, you're helping Kate organize this fund-raiser."

Connie glanced at her wristwatch. "Of course. The girl needs someone to steer her in the right direction. Unless you're offering to take over."

Lucas held up both hands. "Count me out. I'm no party planner. Besides, I have urgent matters to deal with at Carrington. The San Francisco project has hit a snag. More like a brick wall."

His aunt's gaze narrowed in on him. "You aren't thinking of skipping town, are you?"

"Would that be so bad? Or don't you trust Kate after all?"

"I trust Kate. It's you that worries me."

"Me. Why me?"

"How long are you going to keep hiding and putting your life on hold? Why aren't you fighting for custody of your little girl—"

His voice lowered. "You know why. And I don't want to discuss it any further."

He thought if anyone would understand his need to do this, his aunt would. She'd saved him from being a pawn between his arguing parents more than once. He wouldn't do that to his daughter.

"But you are missing so much of Carrie's life—"

"Leave it." He fought back his rising temper. "I thought by agreeing to this fund-raiser, it'd make you happy."

His aunt's gaze needled him. "You only get one go-around in this life and it goes by in the blink of an eye. Please don't waste it."

His palm smacked the tabletop. "I'm not."

No matter how much he missed his little girl, he had to put Carrie's happiness above his own, something his parents had never done with him. And right now his ex-wife was hostile on the phone and argumentative in person. If only he could make her see reason.

Connie got to her feet. "Kate's finished checking out. You better hurry and catch up with her since you two have plans—"

"But we don't have plans. The only reason I'm here is because you insist we meet here for lunch once a week— even though I've offered repeatedly to take you anyplace you'd like."

"And you were late today. Now it's time I got back to work." Connie glanced in Kate's direction. "She's waiting for you. You don't want to disappoint her, do you?"

Before he could argue, his aunt walked away. His gaze immediately sought out the door, but Kate stood between him and the exit. He mentally ran through a list of excuses of why he had to leave. Each excuse sounded more pathetic than the last.

He straightened his shoulders. Time to make a confession. He approached Kate, who was holding a tall cup with a lid and a straw. She'd understand everything once he explained about the mix-up. After all, misunderstandings happened all the time.

She glanced up and a smile bloomed on her face. The color in her cheeks and the light in her eyes touched something deep inside him—a place that had felt dead up until now. He didn't want her to stop smiling, not now…not ever.

"Are you ready to go?" Kate motioned toward the door.

He should speak up…explain that he'd only come here to visit with his aunt. That he had no intention of venturing into the pediatrics unit full of tiny humans—little ones like his Carrie. His mouth opened, but when Kate grabbed his hand, giving him a gentle tug, the words balled up in his throat. He glanced over his shoulder at Connie, but she wasn't paying any attention as she took food orders from customers.

His gut churned. He was backed into a corner with no easy way out. Maybe he could just say a fast "Hi" and then be on his way. In and out. Fast as can be.

"I…I can't stay long."

Kate's eyes lit up. Her lips pursed as though a question teetered on the tip of her pink tongue. His breath hitched in his throat. *Please don't ask any probing questions. Not here. Not now.*

Kate's face smoothed. "We can take the steps if you think it'll be faster."

He exhaled a long-held breath. He understood the strain Kate was under…more so than he'd ever want to admit. He shook his head, resigned to wait for one of the four elevators. As though summoned by his thoughts, a chime sounded and the door in front of him slid open.

Like the gentleman his mother raised him to be, he waited for Kate to step inside. His gut churned with anxiety. On stiltlike legs, he followed her.

"Are you okay?" Kate asked, drawing him out of his thoughts.

They were standing alone in the elevator as it slowly climbed to the fifth floor. He kept his eyes on the row of numbers above the door, watching as they lit up one after the other.

"I'm fine."

"Really? Because ever since we got in the elevator, you look stiff and uncomfortable. And the frown on your face will scare the kids in pediatrics."

He hadn't realized his thoughts had transferred to his face. Willing himself to relax, he tried changing his stance and forced his lips into what he hoped was a smile.

Kate turned to him. "You know you don't have to do this. If you've changed your mind about meeting my daughter, just say so."

Apparently he hadn't done a good enough job of putting on a more pleasant expression because right now, Kate's eyes were filled with doubt. He didn't want to add to her list of concerns. After all, this was a quick visit. Soon it'll all be nothing more than a memory.

"How's your daughter doing?" He was truly eager to hear an update on the little girl, hoping things were improving.

"Today we get the results of her latest scan to see if the treatments are shrinking the tumor."

"Will that make the surgery easier?"

Kate straightened her shoulders. "That's what I'm told."

He wondered if Molly was the spitting image of her mother. Did her eyes light up like her mother's when she was excited? Did her cheeks fill with color when paid a compliment? And when she was concentrating while working with her hands, did the tip of her tongue press against her bottom lip?

Lucas drew his thoughts up short. He couldn't believe in the limited time he'd spent with Kate that he'd gotten to know so much about her.

The elevator dinged and the doors opened. Kate exited the elevator and turned back to him, still leaning against the handrail. "Are you coming?"

He swallowed hard and stepped out onto the pediatrics floor. There was no doubt about which unit they were in as a painted yellow giraffe with brown spots covered the wall, stretching from floor to ceiling, followed by a hippo, tiger and zebra. Large, leafy trees and tufts of grass were painted in the background. Someone had spared no expense in giving the tiny patients the feeling they were anywhere but at a hospital.

His thoughts took a sudden turn back to his own daughter. Would she like the painting? Did she like giraffes? What was painted on the walls of her bedroom?

The fact he knew none of these answers angered him. He should know. Any father worth the name Dad should know this about their child. Yet, Elaina had stolen those moments from him. And worse yet, he'd let her.

He used to think it was the sacrifice he had to make, but being around Kate and listening to her talk about her daughter, he had to wonder if there was another choice he could make.

"Molly's room is at the end of this wing." Kate pushed open one of the double doors.

He followed her past the nurses' station in the center of the floor. A collective buzz of children's voices filled his ears. He'd made sure to avoid kids since he'd come back from California—since he'd confronted his ex-wife.

His steps slowed. The distance between him and Kate widened. The giggle of a little girl filled his head. He paused and glanced as the child sat on the edge of her bed. She had curly blond locks like Carrie's and was smiling at someone. His daughter had never smiled at him like that. The knowledge stabbed him in the chest, robbing him of his breath.

"Lucas," called out Kate.

He meant to keep moving, but he was drawn by this little girl. Her sweet smile threw daggers into his heart. Instead of smiles, Carrie had looked at him with tears in her eyes as Elaina raised her voice, shook a finger in his face and insisted he leave.

Pain churned inside him as though someone had reached down his throat and ripped out his heart. A cold, aching spot remained. He closed his eyes and turned away from the little girl. He shouldn't have come here. This was a mistake. He needed to leave. Now.

Kate reached out and touched his arm. "Molly's room is just a few more doors down this hallway."

The heat of her touch seeped through his suit coat. He glanced at Kate. Her eyes pleaded with him. He wanted to do this for her more than he could say, but the trickle of the little girl's laughter was his undoing. He needed to get out of there. He needed to breathe.

"I'm sorry. I can't."

With that he turned, jerking his arm from her touch. He could feel her lethal gaze shooting daggers into his back. He deserved her anger and so much more.

He'd failed Kate and he hadn't even had the nerve to explain it to her. Although it wasn't as if she'd understand. Her daughter loved her. Looked up to her. Trusted her.

He inwardly groaned as the thought drove home the pain and guilt. If he was doing the right thing for Carrie, why did it feel so wrong?

Unwilling to wait for the elevator, he took to the stairs. He raced down them as though the hounds of hell were nipping at his heels.

Kate would think he was a total jerk. And maybe she was right. Perhaps there was something inherently wrong with him that drove away his ex-wife. And now his child.

CHAPTER TEN

KATE SWUNG THE hammer with more force than was necessary, missing the nail and putting a small half-moon indentation in the plaster. Just what she needed, something else to fix. It'd been two days since the incident at the hospital and she was still fuming. It was Lucas's fault. He'd made a point of avoiding her, rushing off to the office early and receiving an urgent phone call and hurrying out the door just as she returned home for dinner. He assured her it was important business, but she didn't know if she believed him.

Her mind warned her that Lucas was a typical man—unreliable. Why in the world had she let herself believe that he'd be any different than the other men who passed through her life? They said what they thought she wanted to hear and yet when it came to following through with their promises, they never did.

Lucas might clean up nice with his tailored suits and polished dress shoes, but beneath all of that varnish, he was just another lying man. She grabbed a nail, positioned it along the new chair rail and swung the hammer. Hard. Once again, she'd let her guard down and thought she could trust him. She swung the hammer again, hitting the nail dead center. When would she ever learn not to trust men?

She took another whack at the nail, shoving it further into the wall. Not about to ruin the chair rail with a ding from the hammerhead, she looked around for a nail set.

Not finding one handy, she grabbed a scrap piece of wood from the floor, positioned it over the nail and swung again.

"What did that piece of wood do to you?"

Lucas. She'd know his deep, rich voice anywhere. Any other time it'd have washed over her like warm maple syrup—sweetening her up. But not today.

She didn't bother to stop and face him. Another couple of taps and the nail was flush with the wood. "It got damaged from the leaky roof and had to be replaced."

"That isn't what I meant. Seems like you're taking your anger out on that nail. Did something go wrong with the renovations?"

"No." The fact that he was acting all Mr. Innocent drove her nuts. "I have everything under control."

"Listen, I know I've been busy, but it couldn't be helped. With the party coming up, we've had to kick up the media blitz for the new jewelry line."

So that was how it was going to be. Act as if nothing happened. She should have predicted this. Her ex swept any trouble under the carpet and pretended as if it never happened. Well, not today. Something had happened and she wasn't about to forget it.

She set aside the hammer and stood. "Don't do this."

"Do what? Ask about the progress on the house?"

"No. Avoid me and then act like there isn't a problem between us."

A muscle twitched in his cheek. "I wasn't avoiding you. Honest. My marketing director went on an early maternity leave and everyone is pitching in to pick up the slack with the upcoming campaign—"

"Stop. This isn't about your business. This is about you skipping out on me at the hospital without so much as an explanation."

"I…I'm sorry." He looked as though he was searching for the right words. "I wanted to meet your daughter but…"

"But what?" He seemed sincere and she really did want to understand. "Talk to me."

"I can't. Not now. Just please believe it had nothing to do with you or Molly. I'll make it up to you. I promise."

The little voice in her head said not to believe him, but her gut said something else entirely. Not sure which to trust, she decided she needed time to think without him clouding her thoughts with the pleading look in his blue-gray eyes.

"Thank you for your apology, but I don't have time to talk now. I need to finish replacing this chair rail."

"It looks like you'll have this place in tip-top shape in no time."

"I wouldn't jump to any conclusions yet. There's a lot to do and if we're going to showcase the tunnel, we'll need every single minute before the party."

"The tunnel?"

Kate made a point of inspecting her handiwork. Finding a nail that wasn't quite flush, she grabbed the hammer and the scrap piece of wood and gave it a whack. "Surely you know about the prohibition tunnel beneath the house."

"Of course I do. But my family liked to pretend it didn't exist. I'm surprised you know about its existence."

Kate cocked a smile. "You really need to read more often. You'd be surprised what you learn."

"I read the *Wall Street Journal* every day."

"Something tells me that prohibition tunnels wouldn't be of interest to that paper."

"Wait. Are you trying to tell me that you read about my house and my family in the paper?"

"Not exactly. Your aunt mentioned that the place had quite a history. And then I did some research online. You'd be amazed at what is put online these days. This house is just teeming with history."

Lucas raked his fingers through his hair, scattering

it in a haphazard fashion. "Great. Isn't anything private anymore?"

"Quit grumbling and come check it out." She started for the door. When she didn't hear Lucas following, she turned back. "You have to see all of the work the men did on the tunnel—from rewiring the lighting to replacing the rotted wood. Although to be honest, it's more like a long skinny room than a tunnel."

Lucas let off an exasperated sigh, but she knew once he explored the hidden tunnel, he'd be as impressed as the rest of them. She led him to the back stairs that was constructed of stained wood. But it was the small landing that was a beautiful maze of inlaid wood.

"Someone was very clever," she said, coming to a stop by a sunset-inspired stained-glass window. "I'm guessing it was your great-grandfather's idea to create such an artistic floor pattern. If I hadn't known to look, I never would have guessed the center section opens up."

Sticking her finger in a discreet thumbhole, she lifted the wood panel. Inside was a rustic wood ladder.

"Don't worry. The ladder is safe. The men just finished the repairs today and I haven't had a chance to look around. You must be familiar with it."

"Actually, I've never been down there. My grandfather had the entrance sealed. I'm surprised the workmen were able to open it up without damaging the wood."

"Believe me, it took a while and lots of care. But I think they did an excellent job. Let me be the first to give you the grand tour." She didn't bother to wait for him to make up his mind. She started her descent.

Entering this rustic area was like stepping back in time. She let her imagination run wild, thinking of the old-timers trying to outsmart the cops. The Roaring Twenties must have been a very interesting era, especially for the Carringtons with their hidden tunnel.

Kate rubbed her bare arms. There was a distinct drop in the temperature down here. She was certain the goose bumps were from the chill in the air and had absolutely nothing to do with her view of Lucas's long legs or toned backside as he descended the ladder.

She gazed around, imagining the wooden racks lined with bottles. "Back here there's a rack with some very old wine. Seems it was shuffled out of the way and forgotten."

"Interesting. Did you uncover anything else?"

"Afraid not."

He moved closer to get a better look. It wasn't until then that she noticed how tight the quarters were down there. Lucas's broad shoulders filled the space between the brick wall and the wooden shelves. There was no getting around him. And there was no room to back up.

Lucas's spicy cologne teased her senses. How could one man look and smell so good? And why did her body so readily respond to him? She knew better than to let her guard down around him. Perhaps inviting him down here was not the best idea.

"That's all there is. We should go."

Lucas glanced up from the bottle of wine he was examining. His gaze met hers. "If I didn't know better, I'd say you were afraid to be so close to me."

The problem was she liked it too much. If they stayed down here much longer, she was afraid she'd abandon her common sense and cave into her body's lusty desires.

"I...I have work to finish."

"I'm going to look around here a little more."

He returned the dusty bottle to the rack and turned, signaling her to pass him. Anxious to make her escape, she moved. By the time she figured out there wasn't enough room for them to modestly pass, her body was sliding over his. Toe to toe. Thigh to thigh. Chest to chest.

The temperature suddenly rose. Her gaze caught his. Did she stop moving? Or had time slowed down?

"Kate." His voice was raw and full of unmistakable desire.

She'd lied to herself. That first kiss was unforgettable. The memories flitted through her mind every night. What would it hurt to let him kiss her again? Just to see if it was as good as she remembered.

Her heart pounded, echoing in her ears. Her breath hitched. She was playing with fire. She should move. Leave. Run. She didn't want to get burned. But she couldn't turn away from his hungry gaze.

His head dipped. Her eyes fluttered shut. Curiosity and desire collided, holding her in place. And then he was there. His touch was warm and gentle as his lips brushed over hers. No kiss had ever felt so heavenly. Her insides melted and pooled in the center. If she weren't pinned between his hard chest and the wall, she was quite certain her legs wouldn't have held her up.

But all too soon reality rumbled through her dream. The memory of how he had walked away from her at the hospital shattered the moment. She couldn't do this. Not with him.

She couldn't trust him.

Ducking her head, she moved to the ladder. With lightning speed, she rushed up the rungs and hurried back to the library, hoping Lucas wouldn't follow. She willed her heart to slow. For her lips to quit pulsating. Most of all, she needed to think clearly. And with Lucas around, her thoughts became a jumbled heap.

What in the world had just happened?

Had he dreamed that one succulent moment? He ran his tongue over his lower lip, tasting the sweetness of Kate's cherry lip balm. A frustrated groan rumbled in his chest.

He'd given his word that he wouldn't let something that foolish happen again. Yet every time Kate came close and he could smell her fruity shampoo and feel the heat of her touch, logic evaded him.

Now that his ill-laid plan had gone awry, he couldn't leave things like this. He started up the ladder, wondering what he should say to her. "I'm sorry" just didn't seem enough, but he had to try. With the wood plank back in place, he headed for the library.

He rolled his shoulders, trying to ease the tension running through them. He was making too much of this. It was barely even a kiss. No big deal.

When he strode into the library, Kate once again had a hammer in one hand and some trim in the other. He waited for her to turn. When she didn't, he cleared his throat.

"About what just happened, I just want you to know that I shouldn't have overstepped—"

"It was nothing." She kept her back to him, shielding her facial expression. "Now you see why I think the tunnel would hold a lot of appeal for people."

She waved off his kiss as if it was nothing—as if it hadn't meant a thing. The thought that this thing—this growing attraction—was all one-sided pricked him. His jaw tightened and his body tensed. Why was she being this way? He wasn't the only one who felt something.

Kate swung around to face him with the hammer still in her hand. "Do you have a problem with the plans?"

Lucas found himself eyeing the business end of the hammer. If she meant to gain his attention, she'd certainly done that. Not that he couldn't easily overpower her. After all, she was inches shorter than him and looked to be as light as a feather. Only feathers didn't have so many delicious curves. Kate's waist dipped in above the flare of her hips, and his fingers itched to wrap around her and pull her close.

He was tempted to remind her that though the kiss had been brief, it'd definitely ignited a flame.

He straightened his shoulders. "And what if I do have a problem with all of this?"

"You're backing out on me now?" Kate's features hardened and he couldn't help but notice how her knuckles turned white as her grip on the hammer tightened. "You can't do that. I won't let you. We have a verbal agreement. If you even think of backing out now, I'll…I'll…"

He smothered a chuckle as her threat lost steam. Not wanting to add fuel to her rising temper, he willed his lips not to lift into an amused grin. She sure was cute when she was worked up. Maybe it wouldn't hurt to egg her on a little more.

"Should I be worried?"

"You already agreed to this party. It's too late to back out now. I already gave my word to the hospital that I'd have the funds for the operation."

Her words hit him with more sting than any blow from a hammer. She was right. How was he supposed to put up an argument now when faced with a little girl's well-being?

As though remembering the hammer was still in her hand, Kate bent over and placed it on the white drop cloth lining the floor. She straightened and tilted her chin upward. "Besides, your aunt thinks the prohibition tunnel will play in nicely with the 1920s flapper theme."

"That's what I'm afraid of," he mumbled.

As though he hadn't spoken a word, Kate continued, "She also said that at last some good would come from the Carrington history."

He didn't like being ganged up on by his aunt and his… What was Kate to him? A friend? She was closer to him than he let anyone get these days. But *friend* didn't seem to fit what they had either. Especially not after that brief but stirring kiss.

Just then Kate leaned toward him. He froze. What was she planning to do? His gaze slipped down to her lips. They were full and rosy, just perfect for another sweet kiss. Anticipation grew. Was it possible she'd enjoyed his touch more than she'd been letting on?

His breath hitched as she moved closer. Her hand reached out to him. What was she going to do? Pull him down to her?

The thought of her being so bold…of her taking control of the situation turned him on. His eyes drifted closed. All semblance of logic fled his brain. He waited for her to make her move, willing her to keep going.

Long-ignored desires roared through his heated veins. After all, they were alone and it was late in the evening. No one would bother them until morning. And it had been so long since he'd let his defenses down—since he'd been close with anyone.

"There. All taken care of."

Lucas's eyes sprang open. What was taken care of? Certainly not his needs—his desires.

"Don't worry." Kate held out a white piece of fuzz for his inspection. "At first, I was worried that it was some spackling, but it's just lint. Your suit has been saved."

His suit? That wasn't what he was concerned about at this moment. His clothes might be fine, but his mind and body were a jumbled mess. He swallowed hard, working hard to control his wayward thoughts.

"Why are you working so late?" His voice came out much harsher than he'd intended.

Kate's brown eyes flashed with surprise. "I had things to do."

"You're supposed to be overseeing the project, not doing all of the work yourself."

Her hands pressed against her slender hips and her eyes

narrowed in on him. "I'm doing what needs to be done. Unlike some people in this room, I keep my word."

Her barbed comment didn't go unnoticed by him. She was still ticked at him about the episode at the hospital. He should explain to her what had happened. But that would only lead to more questions…questions he didn't want to answer.

Not now.

Not ever.

When he didn't respond, she added, "You know, if you didn't want to meet my daughter, all you had to do was say so in the first place."

"But I wanted to—"

Lucas stopped. His jaw tightened, his back teeth grinding together. What was he saying? This wasn't going to make things better for either of them. But the damage had been done.

An inquisitive gleam showed in her eyes. "What do you mean you wanted to? Why'd you change your mind?"

He glanced away and shuffled his feet. His gut told him that she wasn't going to drop the subject until he fessed up. But how could he do that? He didn't talk about his past with anyone…not even his aunt.

"Surely you have something to say for yourself." Her tone was hard and sharp.

He didn't like being pushed around. His ex-wife had known his vulnerabilities and used them for her own benefit. He wouldn't allow someone else to take advantage of him again.

Kate could push and shove as hard as she wanted, but he wouldn't give in…not until he was ready.

"I'm tired. And I still have reports to go over. There's Chinese takeout on the counter if you want some. And just so you know, I am truly sorry."

He turned away from the confused look in her eyes,

telling himself that he didn't care. This woman meant absolutely nothing to him.

Nothing. At. All.

But if that was the case, why as he yanked the door shut behind him did he feel like a total heel? And why did he want a chance to make things right with her?

CHAPTER ELEVEN

HE'D TOTALLY OVERREACTED.

So what if he'd lost his mind for a moment and kissed her again? It didn't mean he was falling for her big brown eyes or her cherry lips. The whole lack of judgment thing could be written off to a few restless nights and the stress of not bringing in enough money to cover the overages regarding the San Francisco expansion.

Days passed and with each day that went by, Lucas noticed that they were falling back into an easy routine. Pretending they hadn't shared yet another even more intense lip-lock seemed to work during the day, but at night, when he should be sleeping, images of Kate and her tempting kisses filled his thoughts.

"Sorry I'm late." She rushed into the kitchen after returning from her visit to the hospital. "You didn't have to wait to eat. In fact, I'm not really hungry."

"I have plans for us tonight. Instead of the food coming to you, you are going to the food."

She shook her head before sinking down onto a kitchen chair. "I'm sorry. I'm too tired to go anywhere."

Dark shadows under her eyes sent up warning flares. Maybe asking her to work on the house was too much for her.

He realized that in his attempt to avoid his unwanted attraction to her, he'd failed to do his duty as her boss—and, dare he admit it, as her friend. He'd let her work herself into the ground while he'd been busy at the office. He had to fix this, but how?

"No problem. When you get your appetite back, I'll get you whatever you want." He sat down next to her. "Your wish is my command."

With her elbows propped on the table, she rested her chin on her upturned palms. Was it exhaustion that had her so down? Or did she have bigger things on her mind? Was it Molly? Had her health taken a turn for the worse? His chest tightened.

"How's Molly today?"

Kate's eyes widened. "How did you know that's what I had on my mind?"

"What else would you be thinking about?" Unlike him, she probably hadn't fantasized the afternoon away, imagining the temptation of another kiss.

"Molly's refusing the surgery."

This news set him back. "What do you mean refusing?"

"Well, she didn't put it in those terms. But she's moody and depressed. She's insisting on going home and I can't blame her. She's been poked, prodded and examined for months now."

He'd have a hard time dealing with that and he was an adult. He didn't know how a child could put up with visiting doctor after doctor. Children were supposed to be outside, running around in the fresh air playing dodgeball or jumping rope, whatever it was that little girls liked to do.

"I'm sorry. That can't be easy for either of you. Did you tell her that it won't be much longer?"

Kate nodded. Her eyes glistened with unshed tears. "What am I going to do? They say with tricky surgeries that the patient's attitude plays a huge role in the recovery."

He didn't have any experience with sick people or surgeries. He'd been a kid when his grandparents passed on.

And his father died of a massive coronary at his desk at the Carrington offices. So all he could do was try to remember what it felt like to be a kid. And his favorite memories were of the times when he'd been with his aunt.

A thought sprang to mind. "Why don't you give Molly something to look forward to?"

Kate narrowed her gaze on him. "Don't you think that's what I've been trying to do?"

"You aren't understanding me. What if you give her something to dream about? A plan for when she gets out of the hospital?"

"I'm running low on brilliant ideas. And by the time Molly is out of the hospital, I won't have two pennies to rub together much less money for a trip to Disneyland."

This was a small way he could help Kate. "You don't have to spend a lot to make your little girl happy. And you don't have to visit Sleeping Beauty Castle either."

Kate jerked upright. "How would a bachelor like yourself know about Sleeping Beauty Castle?"

He wasn't about to tell her that he too had a little girl and when he used to read her bedtime stories, he'd promised to take her there when she got a little older.

"Who doesn't know about the castle?" he bluffed. "It's in almost every Disney commercial. But what I was trying to say is that you don't need that. You could plan a whole vacation right here in New York City."

"You may not notice the cost, but dinners out and show tickets add up quickly."

"But there are other options."

Kate rolled her eyes. "If you are going to tell me to take Molly window-shopping, save your breath. That will never fly. She'll want everything she sees."

"I can assure you that good times don't have to cost a fortune."

"And what would you know about it? You probably grew up with the proverbial silver spoon in your mouth."

"You might be surprised to know that my childhood didn't have as many silver spoons as you'd imagine."

She paused and eyed him up. "There's no way you're going to convince me that your family sent you out into the world to earn bread money."

Her words pricked his good mood, deflating it. "Money isn't everything. Sometimes I think it would have been better to be born into a different family, one who didn't worry so much about money and appearances. Maybe then my parents wouldn't have…"

"Wouldn't have what?"

He glanced up to find genuine concern in her eyes. He hadn't meant to open this door to his past. Some things were best unsaid. But in this one particular case, his past might show Kate just how good she and her daughter have it.

He sighed. This still wasn't going to be easy. "Maybe without Carrington Gems and the status that came with it, my parents wouldn't have gotten divorced. But even after they got divorced, things didn't get much better. They still fought, mostly over me."

"I'm sorry."

Not about to get into how they'd turned him into a spy for each of them, he continued, "It was during this period that my aunt would whisk me away. She could see that I wasn't happy. So she'd take me on day trips around the city."

Kate waved away his idea. "I'm sure it was nice. But if I want to distract Molly and give her something to look forward to, it's got to be better than a walk in the park and a push on the swings. Besides, when she gets out of the hospital, we'll be heading back to Pennsylvania. This job is great, but it'll be over soon. I have to think about either getting my old position back or finding a new one."

He frowned at the thought that one day soon Kate would be gone. He was getting used to having her around. Not that he was getting attached to her or anything. He just liked having someone at home with whom to share a meal and make conversation.

Still, he'd like to see that Kate and her daughter had good memories to take home with them. His idea would take some convincing. However, seeing something with one's own eyes was always more persuasive than a sales pitch.

Yes, that's what he'd do—show Kate a good time.

The next morning, Kate was back working in the library, mulling over how to cheer up Molly. She liked that Lucas had been there pitching helpful ideas. Most of all, she liked that he'd opened up some about his childhood. Things must have been bad if his aunt felt she had to get him out of the house. Her heart went out to that little boy who'd been in such an unhappy situation.

"Let's go."

Her head jerked up at the sound of Lucas's voice. "What are you doing here?"

"I came to pick you up."

She straightened, not recalling that they'd had any plans. Yet he was standing there midmorning in a dark pair of jeans, which accented his athletic legs, and he'd unbuttoned his blue collared shirt and rolled up the sleeves. What in the world had gotten into him? And why did she find herself staring at him like some starstruck high-schooler? Probably because it should be against the law to look that good.

His blue eyes twinkled with mischief. "Well, are you just going to stand there smearing paint everywhere?"

She glanced down, finding the paint stick she'd been using to stir the white paint for the trim dripping all over the drop cloth. She hurried to set it aside and put the lid back on the can. Something told her that she wouldn't be doing any painting until Lucas left, not if she wanted to get the paint on the walls and not the floor.

That was one thing about this project that she really enjoyed, being able to work with her hands. At her old job she'd done the sketches, consulted with the owners and supervised the transformation. But she hadn't rolled up her sleeves and dived in with the detail work. When she finished with this project, it truly would be the crowning accomplishment in her portfolio. First, though, she had to get it finished. Too many things were riding on her bringing this project in on schedule.

"I can't go anywhere. I have work to do." She pressed her hands to her hips.

"You need a break."

"What I need is a few more hours in the day."

"I thought you might say that so I'd like you to meet Hank and Mike." Two men in white overalls stepped into the doorway. "They can paint or whatever it is you need them to do."

"But I can't just leave."

Lucas grabbed her hand and pulled her toward the door. "We have to hurry—"

"Is it Molly? Did something happen—"

"No. Nothing like that. This is all good. I promise." He sent her a reassuring smile that made her stomach dip. "Go get changed while I make a quick phone call. We have someplace to be."

"I need to have a few words with these guys."

Lucas frowned.

"It'll only take a minute."

"Hurry." He turned and strode away.

Minutes later, dressed in fresh jeans and a pink blouse, Kate stepped outside. The bright sunshine warmed her skin. With just a gentle breeze, it was warm enough to venture out without a jacket.

As they made their way down the sidewalk, she couldn't hold back her curiosity. She stepped in front of Lucas and turned. "I'm not going any further until you tell me where we're headed."

"Didn't your mother ever teach you to wait patiently for your surprise?"

"My mother didn't do surprises. Let's just say she had an active social life and kids didn't really fit into the equation."

Lucas's lips pressed into a firm line. "If it makes you feel any better, I know where you're coming from. My mother wasn't big into the parenting scene either, unless it fit some sort of social agenda."

Their conversation dwindled as they started to walk again. Destination unknown. Kate gave up worrying about it and lifted her face up to the sun. The exercise and the sunshine were working wonders on her mood. The tension in her neck and shoulders eased away.

In no time at all, Lucas was taking her by the hand and leading her through Central Park. "Come on."

This was his surprise? A trip to the park? Her good mood dimmed as she thought of how much Molly would enjoy this adventure. "What are we doing here?"

"I'll show you." He led her over to a beautiful white horse-drawn carriage and held out his hand. "We're going for a ride."

"Are you serious? But why?" She hesitated. "I shouldn't be here."

Lucas's dark brows drew together. "Why?"

"Because it isn't right. Not with Molly in the hospital."

He nodded as though he understood. "I guess I didn't think this through. Would you rather go see her?"

"Yes…but I can't. This is Chad's agreed time with her. And she likes having her dad around. And I…I don't do so well with his occasional snide little comments."

"Well, since you can't see Molly yet, consider this a research project."

"Research?"

"Sure. I'm showing you how to have a good time without spending a fortune. You didn't believe me so I decided to show you."

"This can't possibly be that cheap."

"You'd be surprised. It's actually reasonable. Although the price does go up if you reserve a carriage for a specific time or have some extras thrown in."

Kate was impressed as she climbed in the carriage with a plush red interior. The driver, all decked out in white tails and a hat, closed the door for them. Instead of fighting it and thinking of everything she should be doing, she settled back on the seat and enjoyed the moment.

Now, she truly felt like Cinderella. Wait, that would make Lucas her Prince Charming, and she'd already decided that could never be. As the horses' hooves clipped along, she shoved the troubling thought to the back of her mind. Why ruin this one magical moment with reality?

A few minutes later, Lucas leaned over to whisper in her ear. "Are you enjoying your surprise?"

His breath tickled her neck, sending an army of goose bumps down her arms. "I am." The admission rolled easily off her tongue. "But I don't know if Molly would be excited about a carriage ride."

"Sure she would. What little girl wouldn't want to ride in a horse-drawn carriage?"

"Perhaps."

"I guess I'll just have to work a little harder. I'm sure I can come up with an idea or two sure to impress a little girl and a big one, too."

Kate's stomach fluttered. Maybe it wouldn't be so bad to let herself imagine that Lucas was her Prince Charming and this was the carriage taking her to the ball. After all, fairy tales weren't true. Everyone knew that. This would just be pretend.

When Lucas stretched his arm out behind her, she gave in to the dream and leaned back. Her head rested on him and shivers of awareness cascaded down her spine. She closed her eyes, willing this moment to go on and on. They could just keep going, leaving their troubles behind. A smile tugged at the corners of her lips as she envisioned them riding off into the sunset together. If only fairy tales came true...

"And what has you smiling?"

Kate's eyelids fluttered open. She'd been busted. It was almost as if he could read her thoughts, but even if he could, there was no way she'd confirm how she'd been daydreaming about him pulling her closer and pressing his lips to hers.

She crossed her fingers before telling a fib like she'd done as a child. "Just enjoying the day."

All too soon the ride was over. Lucas gave her a hand down. It was then that she realized they hadn't stopped in the same spot where they'd started.

"It's time for lunch and I know the perfect thing to have on our outing."

He treated her to a hot dog with the works. They settled on a park bench and quietly ate while the world went by without any notice of them. When they'd finished, Lucas took her by the hand and they started walking. He smiled, appearing very relaxed. She hadn't seen him in this good of a mood since...well, ever.

After they'd walked a little ways, she couldn't contain her curiosity. "Where are we going now?"

"You'll see in just a moment."

Soon carousel music lilted through the air, giving the day a surreal feeling as though all was right in the world.

"Come on." He pulled her closer to the colorfully painted merry-go-round.

"Why?"

"You'll see."

How could she resist when he looked like an excited child himself? Laughter bubbled up in her throat, and she let him lead her by the hand. But when he paid for her to ride the merry-go-round, she hesitated.

"I can't ride that."

"Why not?"

"It's for kids."

"Are you trying to tell me that you aren't a kid at heart? Besides, you wanted examples of things you can do with Molly on a budget. This is one of them."

"True." She really did like the idea. She'd been to a carnival as a little kid with her father and she'd loved riding the carousel, especially the horses that went up and down. "But that doesn't mean that I have to ride one."

"Give me your phone."

"What? Why don't you use your own?"

"It will be simpler this way."

"What will?" The man certainly wasn't explaining himself very well today.

"I'm going to take some photos for you to show Molly."

"I don't know." What would Molly think? Her mother off playing without her. Guilt riddled her. "What if it upsets her?"

"You have a good point." Then he snapped his fingers. "I've got it. Just don't show her the pictures with you in them. And make sure you promise to bring her here as soon as she's healthy enough."

Kate wasn't so sure. But so far nothing else was helping to cheer up her little girl. Even the surprise of her father showing up had worn off. Kate was getting desperate to give her daughter hope. Maybe Lucas was right. Maybe this outing would give her the ability to paint a picture in her daughter's mind of the fun things they could do...together.

She wouldn't be an absentee parent like her father...or her mother. Even though they had shared the same house, her mother had been so wrapped up in her own world that she'd never had time for Kate.

She glanced over at Lucas. What would he be like as a father? Probably terrific, if today was any indication. Not that she would be sticking around to find out.

While riding the merry-go-round, she noticed a small crowd forming nearby. Cameras were flashing. It took her a couple of passes to realize they were talking to the city's mayor and his young family, who were most likely campaigning.

A niggling thought started to churn in her mind. Something Connie had said about a little more press coverage and they'd have a sold out venue. With all of those reporters, it surely wouldn't be that hard to get coverage, but it would have to be something really good.

When she got off the ride, Lucas was waiting for her with a bouquet of balloons fastened to his hand. One of the reporters sent an inquisitive look in Lucas's direction. So his Bachelor of the Year status was still giving him quite a bit of notoriety, or was Lucas Carrington normally that notable of a figure in the Big Apple? Which left her wondering if she should play upon his fame—after all, it was for a good cause.

He smiled, looking proud of himself. "Admit it. You had fun."

"Yes, I did. You've made this an amazing day. Thank you."

He handed over the bouquet of rainbow-colored balloons. "Does this mean I'm forgiven for being a jerk the other day?"

He had really hurt her, but the more she got to know him, the more she realized he truly was a good guy.

"It depends…" When his gaze dipped to her lips, her thoughts scattered.

"Maybe this will help convince you."

Lucas's hands wrapped around her waist, pulling her closer. She willingly obliged. Her breath locked in her chest as she waited. Hoping. Longing.

It that moment, the world slipped away. It was just the two of them on this enchanted day. His head lowered. Her chin tilted upward.

CHAPTER TWELVE

LUCAS SHRUGGED OFF the glances he kept getting from some of the paparazzi. He wouldn't let them ruin this day. Normally he would have quietly slipped away with Kate. But he'd agreed to play up this relationship in public, so there was no need to deny he was enjoying Kate's company. And there was no need to resist what he'd been dying to do all afternoon...

His lips sought hers. The more he tasted her, the more he desired her. When she kissed him back, he forgot their circumstances, their differences and even where they were. The fact she desired him was a powerful aphrodisiac. Her kisses were even more arousing in person than they were in his dreams. A moan swelled in his throat.

Kate startled him when she pressed her hands to his chest and pushed. She broke free of his hold and stared up at him with rosy cheeks and a questioning stare.

"Lucas, people are staring."

So much for staying calm, cool and collected around her. He should probably apologize...again, but this time he wasn't sorry. He'd enjoyed holding her close and he didn't notice her complaining.

"That guy over there," she pointed to a young man who met Lucas's gaze straight on, "I think he took our picture."

Lucas glanced back but the man had disappeared into the crowd. "Good."

"Good?"

"Yes. Remember you and I are playing the happy couple for the press. So turn that frown upside down."

She smiled, but he could tell it was forced. Was she unhappy about the kiss? Impossible. She'd been an active participant. Maybe it was the fact they'd end up making headlines again. She hadn't been too thrilled with it the first time around. It was best not to say anything.

"How about some ice cream before we head back?" He could really deal with something icy cold about now.

A little bit later, they headed back to the house and Lucas couldn't believe what a wonderful day they'd shared. Thanks to Kate, he'd let loose and laughed. He'd truly enjoyed himself.

Kate's hand was wrapped with the ribbons of six helium balloons. A rainbow of colors. All for Molly. In Kate's other hand, she was holding a strawberry ice cream cone. He couldn't turn away as her tongue darted out and slowly made a trail up the creamy surface. There was no point in continuing to deny the chemistry running between them. And he knew by the way she'd eagerly returned his kiss that she felt it too.

He couldn't wait for later tonight. A little dinner after she got home from the hospital. Some conversation. And then, well, he'd let nature take its course.

"What are you grinning about?" Kate shot him a curious stare.

"I'm just basking in the glow of your happiness."

"Seriously? You really do know how to lay it on thick, don't you?"

"Sometimes it works."

"So what you're saying is that you make a habit of seducing women with horse-drawn carriages and rides on the carousel."

He truly enjoyed this playful side of Kate. "Afraid I've been busted. But in my defense, you did enjoy yourself."

She gave a nonchalant shrug, but he noticed the smile she was fighting to hold back. He liked making her happy. He liked it a lot.

She glanced up at him. "Truthfully I haven't had this much fun since I was a kid."

"Did your parents take you to an amusement park?" He was genuinely interested in learning more about her.

"No. But my dad used to take me to the fire department's summer carnival."

"Sounds like a nice memory. Do you keep in touch with your father?"

She frowned and shook her head. "That's all in my past. I learned long ago to keep looking forward. Nothing good comes from glancing back."

"Memories are important." His thoughts drifted back to the time he'd spent with his little girl. "I don't know what I'd do without them. What was your childhood like?"

Kate picked up her pace. What was it about her past that could change her mood so rapidly? Didn't they say that keeping things bottled up only caused them to fester and the only way to heal was to let it all out?

"Talk to me, Kate."

"You aren't going to drop this, are you?"

"Not until you tell me a little about your past...your father."

She stopped suddenly and glared at Lucas. "My father turned his back on a ten-year-old girl who worshipped the ground he walked on, and he didn't so much as say goodbye."

"Surely he didn't just walk away without a reason?"

Kate huffed and started walking again. "Floyd loved surprises. And his biggest surprise of all was disappearing from my life."

"But before he left, you two were close, what with the memory of the carnival and I'm guessing there must be others."

"What does it matter?" When a large black dog on a much too long leash approached them, Kate dodged in front of Lucas, giving the dog a wide berth. Once they passed the overly friendly four-legged canine, she slowed her pace. "I don't know why we're talking about him. I told you, it's ancient history."

Lucas didn't understand why all of a sudden this had become so important to him, but he couldn't let the subject drop. "Are you saying he was a bad parent?"

She stopped and pressed her hands to her hips. With her shoulders squared, she tilted her chin. "Actually it's the opposite—Floyd was a good father. We had a lot of fun together. He made up for my mother's lack of interest."

"I wish my father had been more like yours. He spent all of his time at the office and left me at home with the nanny, unless my aunt took pity on me, dressed me up and took me out."

"I guess we both came up short in the parenting department."

Lucas looked up, spotting a silver car going much too fast. Kate was too busy talking to him to notice. When she went to step off the curb, he grabbed her arm, pulling her back. She lost her balance and fell against him.

Her body seemed to fit naturally against his. He wanted to keep her safe next to him. But more than that he wondered who she leaned on—who watched out for her. He didn't like thinking of her all alone in the world.

Kate glared at him and moved away. "What did you do that for?"

"You almost stepped in front of that car."

"Oh. I didn't see it."

It was probably his fault. He was pushing her too hard

to open up, but he couldn't stop the flow of questions. He needed to know a little more. "So what happened to your father? Why did he just up and leave?"

She sighed. "He and my mother fought a lot, but it was always behind closed doors so I don't know what they argued about that last night. My mother would never talk about it. When I woke up, he was gone. He never came back. And my mother refused to answer my questions. Finally, I quit asking."

As her words sunk in, Lucas's gut knotted. He realized why this conversation was important. He wondered what his little girl would one day say about him. But Carrie wouldn't even have the benefit of good memories. Then again, she wouldn't have the horrid thoughts of being a pawn between her parents—nor the overwhelming guilt from spying on one parent for the other. When his daughter was old enough to understand, she'd realize he'd made a very difficult decision in order to spare her. It was this knowledge that got him through the long, lonely evenings and the depressing holidays. He was doing what was best for Carrie.

He reached for Kate's hand and gave it a squeeze. "I'm sure there has to be a logical answer to what happened—"

"That makes one of us. There's no excuse for just abandoning your child."

The raw edge in her voice cut him deeply. His fingers released her hand. He struggled to keep walking. Was this animosity the way his daughter would feel about him?

Before he could catch his breath, Kate continued. "The only excuse is that he never loved me. He tossed me aside like yesterday's garbage. Men like him are as low as pond scum. No. Lower."

The ice cream churned in his stomach. All Lucas could muster was a nod.

Not love her? Lucas couldn't imagine anyone being able

to resist Kate's smile or her teasing ways. But the firm set of her jaw and the lines between her gathered brows said she fully believed what she was saying. He wanted to put his arms around her and assure her that she was loved, but he couldn't.

He was the last person she'd want holding her. After all, in her book he was lower than pond scum. What was lower than that?

"I don't want to talk anymore about my father. I'd rather think about the beautiful day we had. Maybe it doesn't have to end yet."

Lucas consulted his watch. "Actually, it's almost time for you to head over to see Molly."

It was for the best. He'd already scrapped his plans for this evening—or any evening for that matter. Kate would hate him when she found out that he was an absentee father. And he couldn't blame her. He wasn't pleased about the situation either. He just wanted what was best for his daughter—and now it was going to cost him the respect and friendship of someone who'd given him the gumption to get on with life.

Then again, what if Kate never found out about Carrie? What if he left out that part of his past? But could he do that? Could he deny his own daughter?

Absolutely not. He was not a liar. And he was proud to be Carrie's father. He'd just have to find the right time to tell Kate. Somehow there had to be a way to make her understand. But how?

The next morning, Kate awoke with a definite crick in her neck. She rolled her shoulders, trying to ease the discomfort. Maybe working into the wee hours of the night hadn't been her brightest idea. She'd meant only to sit down on the floor to take a break and the next thing she knew it was morning.

But after that earth-moving kiss in the park during the romantic—dare she say it—date, she'd been full of energy…that was until she'd sat down. She yawned and pushed aside the drop cloth she'd ended up using as a make-shift blanket. Getting to her feet, she stretched her sore muscles.

Heavy footsteps sounded in the upstairs hallway. She glanced at the time on her phone. It was far too early for the workers.

"Kate?" Lucas's voice rang out.

"In here." She smoothed her hair with her palms.

Lucas appeared in the doorway with his hands full. "I thought we'd have something a little different this morning. I ran out for some of that flavored coffee you're always going on about and a couple of blueberry muffins."

"Is this a special occasion?"

He handed over a coffee. "No. I just thought a change in routine might do us good."

She gratefully took a long, slow swallow, letting the warm, creamy coffee fill her mouth with the most delicious flavor. That first sip of the day was by far the best. "I definitely approve."

"When you didn't show up for breakfast, I decided to check on you."

Since when had he started worrying about her? Surely she'd misunderstood. But the fact he'd noticed her missing and tracked her down was something she just couldn't ignore.

"I wanted to start work early. I need to get this done on schedule."

Lucas peered around. With his height and broad chest, he seemed to fill up the room. Awareness awakened Kate's sluggish body. The fresh scent of his cologne wafted past her nose and wrapped around her. Did the man have to smell so good?

He moved, visually examining the balled-up drop cloth on the floor and then taking in her rumpled appearance. "Starting early? It looks more like you never made it to bed."

She shrugged, hoping he wouldn't make a big deal of it. "This coffee sure hits the spot."

He continued looking around before turning back to her. "You're working too hard. If you need more help, just tell me."

"I will." But right now she had something else on her mind. "You know, I was thinking that the night of the fundraiser would be the perfect time to announce the sale of this place."

He stared at her as if she'd sprouted another head. "Why would I do that?"

"I'm obviously missing something. I know when we discussed it earlier the situation still wasn't clear, but isn't the point of fixing up the house to put it on the market? I mean it isn't like you live here. In fact, you hate being here—"

"I do not." He looked away, studying something on the floor.

"Don't give me that. Every time I turn around, you're running out the door. I get it. This place doesn't hold good memories for you. I have a couple of places like that myself. So why hold on to the house? Let someone else enjoy it."

He ran a hand through his hair, scattering the short strands. "I don't know if I'm ready to make a decision of that magnitude. Lately, I seem to be making one mistake after the other."

"Does that include kissing me?" Kate clamped her lips shut, but it was too late. Her thoughts were out there. Hovering. Waiting.

She should brush aside her careless comment and pretend she was teasing, but she couldn't. She honestly wanted to know how he felt about her.

With every bit of willpower, she lifted her chin and looked at him. Wondering. Hoping.

His Adam's apple bobbed. Their gazes met. And the air around them seemed to crackle with awareness.

"Kissing you is all I've thought about." His voice was deep and thick, sending goose bumps of excitement down her spine. "My only regret is that it ended far too soon."

His intense gaze held hers. She should turn away. She should... She should...

Long suppressed desires swelled inside her and squelched her train of thought. He stepped forward, closing the gap between them. Her stomach fluttered and dipped. The tip of her tongue swished over her now dry lips. He was going to kiss her again, and she wanted him to because for better or worse, she wanted to taste him on her lips.

The breath in her lungs hitched. She'd never anticipated anything this much in her entire life. Her chin tilted upward. And her heart pounded.

Being cautious wasn't all it was cracked up to be. This once she wanted to throw caution to the wind. She wanted to live in the moment.

She shifted her weight to her tiptoes. And then he was there. His warm breath tickled her cheek before his lips pressed to hers. They moved gently at first, tentatively as though questioning her. But that wasn't nearly enough for her. She met his kiss with a hunger that startled her. He tasted like rich, dark coffee and she'd never tasted anything so good.

Mr. Oh-So-Sexy could most certainly kiss. In fact, she'd never enjoyed anything so much in her life. Her needy body leaned into his hard contours. The fact that he wanted her was all too evident and had her insides melting into a liquid pool of desire.

Standing there, wrapped in his arms, her problems and responsibilities temporarily fell away. In that moment, she was the woman desired by the most thoughtful man she'd ever known, who could kiss the common sense from her mind. But one thought came to mind—one very clear and concise thought.

She was in love with Lucas.

She didn't know where or when it had started, but she was falling hard and fast for him. And try as she might, she couldn't stop her heart from spiraling out of control.

Her fingers blindly plucked at his silk tie, pulling it loose. She fumbled with his shirt buttons until enough were undone that her hands could slip over the bare skin of his shoulders and back. Her core temperature climbed with each tantalizing move.

"Tell me now if you want me to go." His voice was raspy as his fingers slipped beneath her shirt.

"Stay. Please."

Her eyes opened for a second, glancing over to the tangle of drop cloths she'd used not so long ago as a makeshift bed. Not exactly the Plaza Hotel, but right now, it didn't matter. His tongue swept inside her mouth, teasing and taunting. Her thoughts scattered.

They stumbled backward, still clinging to each other. Now that she'd found him, she never wanted to let go. She couldn't get enough of him…of his touch. Lucas lowered them to the floor and they landed with a bit of an "oomph" that jarred their lips from each other.

He brushed a few strands of hair from her face. "Sorry about that."

"It's okay. I had a soft landing."

She was half sitting, half lying in his lap while staring into his darkening eyes. They mesmerized her with their ability to change color with his moods. Right now, she was drowning in them.

She was the first to make the move this time. Hungry for more of him, she leaned forward. Her mouth claimed his—needy and anxious. There was no mistaking the passion in his kiss as he followed her lead.

But then he pulled back just enough to start a trail of kisses down over the sensitive skin of her neck. A moan of desire swelled in her throat. She'd never felt such desire by a man. He gave as good as he got and she couldn't wait to find out what else he was good at....

CHAPTER THIRTEEN

THE THUD OF work boots on the steps roused Kate as she savored the way her body still thrummed with utter satisfaction. She lifted her cheek from Lucas's bare shoulder. "Shoot. It's Charlie."

Adrenaline pumped through her veins as she scrambled to grab the edge of the white drop cloth. What had she been thinking to do this here?

Obviously her brain had short-circuited as soon as Lucas's lips had touched hers. Now she didn't know how she'd be able to face the foreman. She pressed her hands to her heated cheeks before combing her fingers through her flyaway hair. One look and Charlie would know what had happened. Soon everyone would know. How in the world would these men ever respect her when they found out she was sharing a bed with the owner?

Lucas jumped to his feet, springing over to the door, pushing it shut. Kate didn't need an invitation. She rushed to locate her discarded clothes.

A knock sounded. "Kate, are you in there?"

She held her breath, hoping Lucas had remembered to catch the lock. The doorknob jiggled. When the door didn't budge, she expelled a pent-up breath. But she still felt the heat on her chest rise up her neck and engulf her entire face.

Lucas was the first to find his voice. "She'll be with you in a couple of minutes."

"Mr. Carrington, is that you?"

"Yes. We are going over some plans."

Is that what he called it? If she'd recalled correctly they'd gone over those "plans" a couple of times…at least she had. A fresh wave of heat rolled over her. She didn't even want to know what was going through Charlie's mind. His imagination was probably painting him a pretty accurate picture of their "meeting."

In a flourish of activity, they dressed. Resigned to the fact she'd done her best to fix herself up without a mirror, she turned to Lucas. She straightened his tie and in turn, he ran his fingers through her hair and tucked a few strands behind her ears.

"Ready?" he whispered.

She wasn't, but she had this feeling Charlie wasn't going anywhere. She nodded and Lucas opened the door.

The foreman ducked his gray head inside. His intense stare took in her not-so-neat appearance, before zeroing in on the scattered drop cloth on the floor next to Lucas's rumpled-up suit jacket.

The man's gaze came back to Kate. "Anything you need?"

She shook her head, not trusting her voice. It took all of her determination to keep from wringing her hands together. She'd never been caught in such a compromising situation. She felt like a teenager, experiencing love for the first time.

A knowing smile pulled at the older man's unshaven face. "Sorry. I didn't know you two were…umm, having a private meeting." He winked. "No biggie. We can go over the discrepancy with the paint order later."

Kate was so hot now that beads of moisture dotted her forehead. She swallowed hard and refused to let on that this thing, this moment of craziness with Lucas, had affected her. There would be time to sort things out later…

much later. First, she had to get her head wrapped around what had happened.

She stepped toward the door. "Charlie, we can go downstairs and go over it now."

"Nah." He waved her off. "You two finish your umm… meeting. I'll go head off the men so they don't disturb you." He started to turn away, then glanced back. "Ya know, the missus was just showing me the picture of you two in the paper this morning. I told her it wasn't any of our business. But thought you should know."

"Thanks." Lucas didn't smile.

Charlie nodded and pulled the door shut. Neither said a word as the foreman whistled a merry tune as he moved down the hallway.

When they were alone again, Kate groaned. "This is awful. I don't know how I missed hearing his approach. The man's footsteps are louder than a stampede of cattle."

"You weren't the only one who was caught off guard. Did you see the unhappy look on his face when he first walked in? I thought for sure I was going to have to defend myself. Looks like you've won him over."

"We're friends. When you work seven days a week with a person, you get to know a lot about them and their family. Just like you and I have gotten to know each other really well. I don't think he'll say anything."

"It won't matter if he does. The whole city thinks we've been doing this all along."

Lucas adjusted his shirtsleeves before slipping on his suit jacket that now had distinct wrinkles. He kept his head lowered as though it took every bit of his concentration to adjust his clothing. But Kate knew differently—knew he had something else weighing on his mind. He was probably just as confused as she was about where they went from here.

No matter what, she couldn't deny that she'd never been kissed quite so thoroughly in her entire life. Nor touched so tenderly and made to feel that her happiness came first. Lucas was a unique man and his ex-wife must have had a few marbles loose to let him slip away. But she couldn't go losing her head over him. She had to keep her focus on Molly and the fund-raiser.

Lucas looked down at the mess of throws on the floor. "I'll just give you a hand straightening up—"

"No. Don't. I've got it."

"Are you sure?"

"Positive."

She licked her dry lips, noticing how they burned a bit. She couldn't remember the last time they'd been kissed raw. But this day—this beautiful day—she wouldn't forget.

With her back to him, she started to fold the cloth. "Besides, I have to hurry. I need to get to the hospital for an update with Molly's doctor."

Lucas slowly moved to the door before turning back. "At least let me give you a lift."

"This," her hand waved around, unsure how to label what had just happened between them, "doesn't change anything. I have a sick daughter and that has to be my focus. Not you and me. Not this moment when we both lost our heads. Just Molly."

His mouth opened as though he wanted to say something, then closed.

When he didn't leave, she added, "As for getting to the hospital, I'll be fine on my own. Always have been. Always will be."

"I never doubted it." There was a strained pause. "But will you have enough time to get cleaned up and walk to the hospital?"

She glanced down at her wrinkled work clothes. Drat. She hated that he'd made a valid point at her expense. "I...I can grab a cab."

"Listen, I'm sorry about what just happened." Another

poignant pause filled the air as she piled the drop cloths in the corner to deal with later. "I lost my head. It won't happen again. You have my word."

He was apologizing? She hadn't seen that one coming. Had their lovemaking been that bad? Was she that out of practice?

Impossible. She knew when a man was into the moment. And Lucas had certainly been into her. So why the regret?

Maybe it had something to do with the ghosts that lurked within these walls? Or more likely he realized that she wouldn't fit into his posh world. She was a nobody from Pennsylvania, who didn't even have enough money to cover her daughter's medical bills.

Certain that she'd be best off keeping as much distance from him as possible, she said, "I've got to go. I'll see you at dinner for your daily update."

Her vision blurred as she walked away. She blinked repeatedly. She'd let herself get caught up in the moment. That had been her mistake. One she didn't intend to repeat—no matter how much her heart said otherwise.

She dashed the moisture from her lashes. Now how were they supposed to continue with their arrangement? Was it possible to move past something this big—this memorable?

Lucas hated that he'd lost control. He'd been a grump all day to the point of scaring his administrative assistant with a snarly response. He'd of course apologized, but she still kept her distance the rest of the day.

Unable to concentrate at the office, he'd come home earlier than normal. He sat at the kitchen table for a long time, staring blindly at the blinking cursor on his computer. His thoughts kept replaying how he'd made love to Kate. What he'd thought would be a chance to scratch an itch had turned into a mind-blowing moment.

From the second he'd laid eyes on Kate that morning,

he'd been a goner. With her hair all tousled and her cheeks rosy, she was a natural beauty. There was nothing phony and artificial about her. He couldn't help but imagine what it'd be like to wake up next to her each morning. That had been his first mistake.

He'd only compounded matters with his second mistake, kissing her. And though he'd savored every delicious moment of their lovemaking—a memory he wasn't likely to forget anytime soon—he couldn't repeat it. For both of their sakes. Once she found out about Carrie, she'd never look at him the same way.

With difficulty, Lucas choked down that last thought. If only there was some way of convincing her that sometimes people made choices they wouldn't normally make in order to spare those they loved.

Lucas's fingers moved over the keyboard, examining the social media campaign planned for the upcoming jewelry launch—Fiery Hearts He wanted the name on every social media outlet. He was monitoring the Fiery Hearts campaign very closely. Nothing could go wrong.

He didn't really understand the allure of these social sites. He avoided them like the plague. But he was all for different strokes for different folks. And as a businessman, these places were invaluable resources for interactive advertising and research.

He opened a window for MyFriends, keyed in his name and pulled up his personal account that he used to help get the word out about Carrington promotions. He was surprised to find that even with infrequent postings, he'd gained a number of friends.

He moved to the Carrington Gems MyFriends page, which he was pleased to find had a larger following than the last report he'd received. He read over the last few postings, happy to find excitement growing over the launch.

Once he shared the information about the Fiery Hearts

reveal from the Carrington Gems page on his personal page, he also decided to share the announcement about Kate's fund-raiser. The posting included a photo of Kate and her daughter. They certainly looked a lot alike—both beautiful. He smiled.

With his work done on the site, he wondered if Kate had an account. It would be one way to keep in contact with her when this fund-raiser was over and she moved on. For her, he just might become more active on social media. He searched for her name but didn't turn up any results. Then for curiosity's sake, he typed his mother's name and when her face appeared on the screen, his mouth gaped. It seemed MyFriends must be a trendy hotspot.

Then on a lark he typed in Floyd Whitley. Immediately he got a listing. There were three candidates. Lucas knew that he should stop there. But what would it hurt to do a little more digging?

He quickly narrowed the list by nationality and he had one candidate. And Kate resembled the man with her dark hair and her big brown eyes. What were the chances this wasn't her father?

But the man's details were hidden because they weren't friends. So Lucas hit the "Be MyFriend" button. As the message sent, Lucas wondered about Floyd's reason for leaving his little girl. No matter what Kate thought, most people just didn't walk away without a reason.

And then without warning a message popped up on his screen. Floyd had accepted his invitation. Now what? Common sense said he should back away. But when a message appeared on the screen, Lucas was drawn in.

Floyd: Do I know you?

What had Lucas been thinking to contact this man? Had he lost his mind? He didn't have any right to be interfering in Kate's private life just to try and make himself look better in her eyes. For all he knew this man could be nothing but trouble.

"Whatcha doing?" Kate came in the back door.

Lucas slammed his laptop closed. If Kate ever found out he'd opened Pandora's box, she would never forgive him. And he couldn't blame her. He'd let his curiosity get out of hand.

"I...I was just doing some work."

"You look like things aren't going well."

He got up, filled his coffee cup to the top and stared at the rising steam. Shoving aside his near misstep with Floyd, he knew there was something much more important he needed to do—tell Kate about his daughter.

Maybe if he'd done this sooner, he wouldn't have gotten the crazy idea to hunt down her father. He wouldn't have gone off on a lark to prove to her that there are legitimate reasons people walk away from their children.

Lucas turned, finding her still smiling at him. "What has you so happy?"

"I talked to your aunt last night and she said since the second photo appeared in the paper, ticket sales have increased to the point where she thinks we'll sell out. You don't know what a relief that is, but of course, your aunt is insisting we keep up the pretense of being a happy couple until the event. Will that be a problem?"

He shook his head. "Not for me."

"By the way, Molly's excited about the idea of vacationing right here in the Big Apple."

"That's great." He was happy to know that he'd done at least that much right.

As the silence dragged on, Kate sent him a quizzical look. "You know, I was showing Molly the pictures of the carriage and the carousel and she got excited. Except she said when we go for a ride, she wants to pet the horses. Do you think that'll be a problem?"

Lucas shook his head. "Shouldn't be."

Before he could say more, Kate rushed on. "And she made me promise to take pictures of some huge toy store. I don't know how she heard about it, but she wants pictures of the giant piano. So since you're good at playing tour director, what do you say? Want to go with me this week?"

What did he say now? He couldn't refuse Kate anything. Not when she looked at him with those hopeful eyes.

"We'll go," he mumbled.

"You promise? I don't want to let Molly down. So if you aren't up for it, I'll go by myself."

"I promise." He stiffened his shoulders and swallowed. He couldn't drag this out any longer. The truth had to come out now. "I have something to tell you."

CHAPTER FOURTEEN

THE HAIRS ON Kate's arms rose. Something was wrong. Tension rippled off Lucas in waves. And no matter how much she tried to sidestep it with a smile and light conversation, he wouldn't let go of whatever was bothering him. It must be something pretty big.

He stepped closer. "I don't know how to say this."

Say what? Had he changed his mind about having the party here? Surely that couldn't be it. There was no way they could change venues at this late date. The party was only a couple of weeks away.

"Whatever it is we'll work it out."

"I wish it was that easy. The thing is—"

"Excuse me." One of the men Lucas had hired to lighten her workload entered the kitchen. He looked a bit uncomfortable and stuffed his hands in his pants pockets. "Ms. Whitley, we're having a problem. You know that room you wanted us to empty? Well, we're having a problem fitting everything into that smaller room."

"It'll fit. There wasn't that much furniture to move."

"That's the thing—it's not the furniture. It's all of the toys and stuffed animals."

"Toys?" The whole time she'd been working here, she hadn't seen any child's items. None at all. Her gaze sought out Lucas. "Do you know what he's talking about?"

"Damn." Lucas's mug slammed down on the counter, causing Kate to jump.

He moved with long, swift strides as if the house was on fire. She practically had to run to keep up with him. What in the world was going on? Toys? In this place?

Once they made it to the top of the staircase, Lucas turned left instead of right. Suddenly things started to make sense. When she'd told James to clear out the room at the end of the hall, he must have gotten her instructions mixed up and gone to the wrong end—the room with the locked door.

Lucas's shoulders were rigid and his hands clenched. The angry vibes reverberated down the hallway. He'd agreed to the fund-raiser under one condition—that this room not be disturbed. How in the world was she going to make him understand it was an accident?

Lucas came to a stop in the open doorway. "Where are the pictures? The crib?"

"We moved them into the spare room down the hall. One of the rooms that doesn't have any damage like Ms. Whitley told us."

"And did she also tell you to break the lock on the door?"

The man's face paled and he shook his head. "We thought the doorknob was jammed. So we removed the handle. Sorry 'bout that."

"Go. Now." Lucas turned his back on the man.

The workman sent Kate an uncertain look. She waved him away. But Lucas had another thing coming if he thought she could be dismissed so easily. Especially when she didn't have a clue what was going on here.

Lucas's large frame practically filled the doorway. She had to peer around him to get a glimpse into the room. It was painted pink with white-and-yellow flowers stenciled about the white chair rail. There was a gigantic stuffed polar bear with a great big red bow. And a wooden rocking horse. This was definitely a baby girl's room.

Before Kate could formulate any questions, Lucas turned an accusative stare her way. "We had an agreement. You promised not to bother this room."

"I didn't. I swear."

Kate pressed her hands into her hips and pulled her shoulders back. She wasn't about to take the blame for a mistake that obviously wasn't hers. Surely Lucas had to understand that sometimes misunderstandings happened.

He raked his fingers through his hair, scattering the short strands. "I never should have agreed to any of this."

Her curious gaze returned to the nursery. This stuff wasn't old. It was actually quite modern and very expensive, which meant that up until recently there had been a child here.

She turned on Lucas. "Is this your daughter's room?"

Lines etched his face, aging him about ten years. "Yes. Her name's Carrie."

This news shocked Kate. After she'd opened up to him about so much of her life, including the ugly stuff she didn't share with anyone, she felt as if their friendship was one-sided.

"Why is this the first I'm hearing of her?"

"What do you want to know?"

"Everything. Who is she? Where is she?" Then a horrible thought struck her. Was it possible something had happened to his daughter? Was that why he'd reacted so strangely in the pediatric ward? "Did…did she die?"

"No." A moment passed before Lucas spoke up. "Carrie is a healthy, active four-year-old."

"But I don't understand. This room is made up for a baby. Where is she?"

He ran his hand over his face. "I changed my mind. I don't want to talk about her."

That answer wasn't good enough, not after he'd pressed her to dredge up the information about Floyd.

"Obviously you've been keeping this to yourself for far too long. Look at this house. You've kept it locked up like some museum. I'm guessing you did this to hold in all of the memories. If you won't talk to me, you should find someone to talk to."

"Fine." He exhaled a long, weary sigh. "If you want to know the truth, my ex-wife left me and took our daughter."

Kate knew she was missing a piece of the puzzle because she couldn't make sense of his anguish, his need to keep this room locked up. "You must miss her terribly."

"More than you know…"

Kate approached him and reached out, touching his arm. "I'm sure when you have her here for visitation, she sees how much you love her. She won't forget you. You're her daddy."

He jerked away from her touch. "Carrie doesn't know me."

Surely she hadn't heard him correctly. "What do you mean she doesn't know you?"

"I mean she lives in California with her mother."

"And?"

"There's no and. That's it. End of story. They have their life and I have mine."

The jagged pieces of this puzzle fell into place. She knew this picture—had lived out a similar experience. Lucas was just like her father, a love 'em and leave 'em type. And like a fool, she'd gone and opened her heart to him.

Anger, frustration and disillusionment bubbled up in her. "You don't see your own child? But why? How can you just forget her, like she never existed?"

He nailed her with a stern look. "I will never forget her. Ever!"

"Then why isn't she here with you? At least part-time?"

"It's better this way."

"Better for whom? You?"

"Of course not. Do you think I like this?" His shoulders drooped and his gaze no longer met hers. "Do you think I enjoy having my daughter run from me because I'm a stranger to her?"

Kate crossed her arms and angled her chin. "It doesn't have to be that way."

He shook his head. "You don't understand."

"Then explain it to me."

He sighed. "My ex-wife has gone to great lengths to keep me from my daughter. And now that she's remarried, she doesn't want me ruining her picture-perfect family. She's threatened to make everyone's life impossible if I push her on this."

"She can't just keep you from seeing your daughter because it suits her. You have rights—"

"And I also know what it's like to be the pawn between two warring parents—how torn you feel when they want you to take sides. If it wasn't for Aunt Connie looking out for me, I don't know what I'd have done to get away from the fighting." A muscle twitched in his jaw as he stared off into space. "I won't put my daughter through that."

"So instead you'll let your daughter wonder the rest of her life why you didn't love her enough to stick around." Kate's voice wobbled. "You ran instead of standing up and doing the right thing for your daughter."

"I'm doing what's best for Carrie—"

"No. You did what was best for you." Her chest ached as though her heart had been ripped out. "You aren't the man I thought you were."

His head lowered. "I suppose I'm not."

"How could you keep this all a secret after I opened up to you about my father? I started to think we might have a future. I was so wrong."

"And I was wrong to let you in this house. You need to leave." He strode away, leaving her to make sense of things.

"What? But the fund-raiser—"

"Can be held elsewhere. I don't care where you hold it as long as it isn't here. I don't want anything else moved or disturbed. Send those men away."

Lucas stormed off down the hallway. He couldn't be serious. After all the work, all the plans, he was canceling everything? The backs of Kate's eyes stung. She blinked repeatedly. One lousy mistake and her chance to raise the money for her daughter went up in a puff of smoke. She told herself that's what the tears were about—not the fact that Lucas had been keeping this big secret from her.

She swiped her cheeks and sucked in a shaky breath. Things couldn't end like this. He had to be reasonable about the party. They had an agreement. She started after him.

By the time she made it downstairs, Lucas was gone. There was only one thing for her to do. Leave. But this wasn't over. Not by a long shot. But first they both needed to cool down.

Lucas stood alone in the elevator. Just him and a fuzzy pink teddy bear that was wearing a pink rhinestone tiara he'd had specially made for Molly. He hadn't seen or heard from Kate since he'd reacted without thinking and fired everyone. And he couldn't just leave things like this. He wouldn't let Kate or her daughter down. He had to do something to remedy things. Something drastic.

He stared down at the wide-eyed stuffed animal and started to think over what Kate had said the other day about Carrie. Was Kate right? Would his daughter believe he didn't love her? Surely when she was older she'd understand his reasoning. Wouldn't she?

He pushed aside the thoughts of his daughter, though

they were never far from reach. But for these next few moments, he needed to be focused.

"This will all work out." When he realized he was talking to a teddy bear, he moved the stuffed animal behind his back.

The elevator door slid open and Lucas took a deep, steadying breath. A painted giraffe and smiling rhino greeted him, but he didn't smile back. Hesitantly putting one foot in front of the other, he started down the long hallway. The sounds of young children echoed between the walls. The voices still dug and poked at his scarred heart, but he refused to turn around. This trip was more important than his own pain and guilt.

On the ride here, he'd debated how to say what needed to be said. He still didn't have a plan. That in and of itself was so unlike him. He was a visionary. He knew where he wanted his business to go and he took the lead. This time he didn't have a clear vision, only the hope that there was some happy solution to this mess.

He paused outside Room 529. The lilt of Kate's voice followed by a giggle filled the air. He took a deep breath and then rapped his knuckles on the propped-open door before stepping inside the dimly lit room.

"Who's that?" The little girl, who was the spitting image of Kate, pointed at him.

Surprise lit up Kate's face. "Well, that's…umm, was—"

"I'm your mommy's friend. You can call me Lucas."

Molly's gaze swung between him and her mother as though trying to make up her mind whether to like him or not. At last, she smiled. "What's behind your back?"

"Who, me? I don't have anything behind me." He turned around in a circle as though to look behind him, all the while holding the pink bear against his back. "See. I told you there was nothing there."

Molly giggled and Kate smiled.

"Silly, it's right there. Behind you."

Once again he turned around. "I'm telling you, I don't see a thing. Maybe they should check your eyes while you're here."

"I saw it. It's a pink bear."

"You saw a pink bear?" Molly nodded and he stepped closer. "Maybe you better point out this bear that's following me around."

He turned slowly this time and just as he predicted, Molly grabbed the bear. "See, here it is. And it has a crown." Molly pulled the tiara off the bear's head and put it on her own. "Lookie, I'm a princess."

"A very pretty one. Just like your mother." Molly giggled and Kate blushed. "You better keep a close eye on that bear. He seems to like getting himself into mischief."

He winked at Kate and noticed how she fought back a smile. She wasn't as easy to win over as Molly. Oh, well, he'd dug his hole and now it was time for him to pull himself out. But if the gleam in her eyes was any indication, he was making progress, even if she wouldn't admit it.

"I hear you liked the pictures your mother took of the horse and carriage and the merry-go-round."

Molly nodded. "I get to ride them as soon as I get outta here."

"Not quite," Kate corrected. "We have to wait for the doctor to say it's okay."

"And I wanna go play on a giant piano. Have you seen it?"

He really liked this pint-size version of Kate. "I haven't. But it sounds exciting."

"Mommy's going to take me pictures."

"She is?" He glanced over at Kate, hoping to see her stern expression lighten into a smile. No such luck. "Maybe she needs help finding it."

Molly's eyes widened. "You know where it is?"

He nodded. Molly chattered some more before she faded off to sleep while watching a cartoon. Since it was the end of visiting hours, Kate left with him.

When they reached the elevator, Lucas broke the silence. "I'll give you a ride."

Kate's brows lifted. "You don't even know where I'm staying."

"At my place."

She made an indignant sound. "As I recall, I am no longer welcome there."

The elevator door opened and they stepped inside with an older woman and her husband. Kate moved toward the back and he followed.

He leaned near her ear. "I didn't mean for you to actually leave for good. I lost my cool."

Kate's brown eyes flared. "If that's your attempt at an apology, you have a lot to learn."

"Come on, Kate. Surely you've overreacted before and done something without thinking."

She crossed her arms and gazed straight ahead as though he wasn't there.

The older woman turned to him. "Sonny, you need to say you're sorry and buy her some flowers. Women always like that."

Her husband gently elbowed her. "Helen, let the kids work this out on their own."

"I was just trying to help." The elevator stopped and the couple got off.

Alone at last, Lucas moved to stand in front of Kate. "I'm sorry. I shouldn't have said what I did. And I'll buy you a whole flower shop if it'll make you happy again."

"You should know that I have a brown thumb." Her eyes met his. "As for the rest, you're right. You shouldn't have said those things."

The fact she was able to joke around a little about her

brown thumb had to be a good sign. "Please, will you come back and finish the project?"

Kate shrugged. "I'll have to think about it."

"Will you at least come back to the house with me?"

"Seeing as my things are still there, I suppose."

Boy, she wasn't going to make it easy. Then again, he hadn't exactly been easy to deal with either the other day. He could only hope that with time she'd give him a second chance.

CHAPTER FIFTEEN

IT CERTAINLY WASN'T easy. Not at all.

But over the course of the following week, Lucas had convinced Kate he was truly sorry for his outburst. In the end, Kate agreed it was best for everyone to go ahead with the fund-raiser. In return, he insisted on keeping his promise to escort her to New York's grandest toy store. He cajoled her into allowing him to buy Molly a dolly with a few accessories. After all, what was a doll without a wardrobe? Even guys like him knew how important clothes were to both big and little girls.

With only a week to go before the sold-out Roaring Twenties fund-raiser, Lucas was surprised by how well things were progressing with the house. Of course, circumstances could still be better between him and Kate. He planned to work on that, starting with a fancy dinner out.

He was just about to ask her out when her phone rang. As she talked to the unknown caller, her happy face morphed into one of an angry mother bear. "Yes…I understand… I'll be there."

He'd never seen her look so cross. His foot tapped the floor as he waited for the phone call to end. "Is Molly all right?"

"Physically she's fine. Emotionally, that's another story. That was Judy, one of Molly's nurses. She called to let me know Chad was just there to say goodbye."

"But how can he leave now? Molly's surgery is next week."

Kate's hands tensed. "He got a business offer in Tucson. Too good to pass up. He'll supposedly be back as soon as he can."

Lucas watched as Kate paced. He wanted to comfort her, to put his arms around her and pull her close, but he wasn't sure that's what she'd want. Reading women was not something he excelled at. So he sat at the counter, waiting and watching.

"This is classic Chad behavior. Worry about himself first. And the hell with everyone else." She paced back and forth. "This is my fault. My gut said he wouldn't stick it out, but I let him get close to Molly anyway. When will I learn not to count on people to hang around?"

An urge came over Lucas to say she could count on him. He wouldn't walk away. The thought caught him off guard. Was that truly how he felt? Or was he merely sympathizing with her?

She stopped and faced Lucas, her eyes round like quarters. "The house. The men. What am I going to do? Molly needs me. The nurse said she was in tears. But there are still things to do here before the party. I…I…"

He appreciated that Kate took her obligations so seriously. Maybe that was his problem—he took his work way too seriously. It'd cost him dearly. He didn't want Kate to make the same mistakes—putting work ahead of family.

But that would mean he'd have to step up and take over the house renovations. When he'd first met Kate, he'd have never dreamed of working upstairs amongst the memories, but now…

He might not be ready to pledge to Kate forever, but this burden with the house, this was something that he could do for her. It was a chance to show her that not all men were like her father and her ex-husband. He wouldn't cut and run when times got tough. He would be her friend as long as she wanted.

Firm in his decisions, he reached for his keys. "Here. Take the car. And don't worry about things here."

"But it's not finished. The paintings and furniture still need to be placed. And the nursery. I never got a chance to put it back together. I'm sorry." Her eyes filled with tears.

Lucas pulled her close. He rubbed her back while resting his head against hers. "Don't worry. Between Charlie and me, we've got it covered."

Kate pulled away and stared up at him. "But you have your work and the Fiery Hearts launch. And you're already short your marketing director."

"I will take care of everything. I promise. Now go. Be with your daughter. And stop worrying. I've got this under control."

With Kate out the door, Lucas phoned his extremely organized assistant. For the first time in almost two years, he told her he would be out of the office. He relayed what needed to be done in terms of the San Francisco project and the launch of the new jewelry line. He also told her that if she needed him, he'd be at home for the next week—words he'd never said to her at such a critical juncture for Carrington Gems. And he knew he'd made the right choice.

Not so long ago, he wouldn't have believed it…but sometimes there were things more important than work. Kate was counting on him. And he vowed not to let her down.

Lucas changed into a pair of comfy jeans and a ratty old T-shirt. He moved swiftly back to the kitchen where he'd left some rough sketches Kate had done up for him to show him how she planned to stage each room. They'd be his saving grace, but when he sorted through the pile of papers and receipts to locate the drawings, they weren't nearly as detailed as he'd thought.

"How hard can it be?" he muttered to himself as he moved through the hallway.

Taking a deep breath, he started up the steps. He took them two at a time and paused at the top when he came face-to-face with a portrait of his great-grandparents on the opposite wall. They were the inspiration for the Roaring Twenties party. He hadn't seen this part of his past in years...ever since Elaina had decided the mansion needed a more modern look.

He smiled as his gaze moved down the hallway, taking in the paintings that had hung in this house as far back as he could remember. Kate had thoroughly disagreed with his ex-wife's decor, going with a more traditional look. He thoroughly approved of Kate's approach and the use of family portraits and heirlooms.

He felt more at peace in these rooms than he had in a very long time. The tension in his neck and shoulders eased. Kate had worked miracles to turn this place into a home. And now it was time he worked one of his own.

His gaze paused on the open doorway to the nursery. He could put the room back to the way it had been before the workers dismantled it. He recalled the room down to its finest details. But this room wasn't his priority. He pulled the door shut and locked it. He would deal with it another day. There was something more important he needed to do.

A week had passed and Kate couldn't wait to see Lucas's attempt at remodeling. He'd been keeping her bedroom off-limits until he finished.

"Close your eyes." When she didn't move, he lifted her hand over her eyes. "And no peeking."

She shook her head. "You're worse than a little kid."

"It'll be worth it. I promise."

She did as he said while letting him guide her down the hallway. "Okay, you can open them."

Kate smiled as she stood at the doorway of the original bedroom she'd been using up until Lucas had taken over finishing the upstairs. "Wow. I didn't expect you to do such an amazing job."

"I had a great incentive."

She turned to see him staring directly at her. Her heart fluttered and heat rushed up her neck, flooding her face. Had he really done all this for her?

The once bright white walls were now a soothing sandy tan. And the crown molding had been repaired and painted a soft, creamy white that matched the ceiling. She couldn't have done better if she'd picked the colors herself. The furnishings were new. The dark wood of the big sleigh bed fit perfectly in the room.

"Seems you have a hidden talent. I guess you don't need my services after all."

Lucas's head ducked. "The truth of the matter is I sort of…umm…hired the woman at the furniture store to help me get the details right. I know you were making a point of using the furniture that has been in my family for years, but I wanted something new for this room."

She was impressed Lucas seemed to be moving forward and letting go of his tight grip on the past. She wanted to turn and throw her arms around him, but she held back, waiting to hear his reasoning for the new furniture and the impressive makeover.

Lucas took her by the hand and drew her inside. It was only then that she noticed a small table off to the side, all done up with a lace tablecloth, tapered candles and a long-stem red rose. China and stemware completed the impressive setup. No one had ever done anything so romantic for her.

Kate's mouth gaped. "Is this for us?"

"Unless you were planning to have a late dinner with someone else."

"Definitely not. I just wasn't expecting you to go to all of this trouble."

Lucas shrugged. "I thought you might like it, but if you don't, we could go back downstairs."

"Oh, no, this is fine." She glanced down at her jeans and blue cotton top, feeling severely underdressed. "Maybe I should get changed."

"Not a chance. You look beautiful just like that."

Her stomach fluttered.

"Would you like some champagne?" He moved to the table and withdrew a bottle from an ice bucket and held it out to her.

Her gaze strayed over to the bed where the beige comforter was already drawn back. Her pulse accelerated. Lucas was attempting to seduce her. They hadn't made love since that one time, both agreeing that it would be best for their working relationship to keep things casual. So what had changed? Or was she reading more into this than he intended?

"Lucas, I don't understand."

Her stomach was aflutter with nerves as she waited and wondered where this night was headed. Where did she want it to go?

Lucas walked up to her. "I'm sorry things between us have been so bumpy. I'm hoping they'll be better from now on."

He wrapped his hands around her waist. The heat of his touch radiated through her clothing. Her heart thumped with anticipation. He was trying to show her that he could change and she wanted nothing more than to give him a second chance.

His head dipped and she leaned into him, enjoying the way his mouth moved over hers. Each time their lips met, it was like the first time. And she never wanted it to end. Because with each kiss, her heart took flight and soared.

But she couldn't lose control now. She couldn't cave into the desire warming her veins just yet. First, she needed some answers.

With every bit of willpower she could muster, she braced her hands on his shoulders and pushed away. She drew in an uneven breath and willed her pulse to slow. She glanced up, seeing the confusion in his eyes.

"We need to talk." She took a deep breath, hoping the extra oxygen would help clear her thoughts. "This is beautiful, but why have you gone to all of this trouble?"

Her fevered wish was for him to say he loved her. That he needed her. And that he was ready to make peace with the past and reach for the future she knew they could have together.

"I thought it was self-explanatory."

She licked her dry lips, searching for the right words. "Is this the beginning of something? Will you still be interested in me…in us next week? Next month?"

"I…I don't know. You're rushing things."

Kate shook her head. "I'm not rushing anything. This—" she waved her hand around "—was your idea. Are you saying there's room here for me and Molly in your life?"

His brows lifted. "You mean here, in this house?"

She nodded. Inside she was begging him to pick her, to choose a future with her.

"I don't know if I can live here with another family."

His lack of certainty hurt her deeply. She loved him. She'd accepted that fact back when they'd made love. Even though she'd been fighting it, it'd only grown stronger.

"And does that include your daughter? Do you not have room for her here either?"

"You don't know what you're asking."

"Yes, I do. I'm asking you to show your daughter how much she is loved. To keep her from ending up like me, with no family around for the good times and the bad."

"But what if she gets hurt in the cross fire between her mother and me?"

"You'll see that it doesn't happen."

He moved closer, reaching out to Kate. "None of this has to stand between us."

"You never said what it is you want for us."

His hands lowered to his sides. "Why do you need it defined? Can't we just take it one day at a time?"

She drew in a breath and leveled her shoulders. "At the beginning, I thought that something casual would be enough. But it isn't. Soon Molly will be getting out of the hospital and she'll be asking questions about you and me. What do I tell her if I don't even know the answers myself?"

Lucas raked his fingers through his hair and moved to the other side of the room. "I don't know if I can make a new start. Commitments haven't exactly worked out for me if you haven't noticed."

"I'm not asking you for a commitment. I'm just asking if you care enough about me to explore a future together. Can you do that?"

Before he could say a word, her phone buzzed. She wanted to ignore it. Lucas's next words were so important, but if it was the hospital, she had to take it. She held up a finger, stemming off his response. She withdrew her phone from her pocket.

After a brief conversation with Nurse Judy, Kate turned to him. "I have to leave."

CHAPTER SIXTEEN

KATE SAT BESIDE Molly's bed and watched her little girl sleep peacefully. The night before, the hospital had called because Molly had woken up from a nightmare, crying inconsolably for her daddy. Inside Kate seethed over the man being so thoughtless about carelessly dropping in and out of his child's life.

At least Lucas didn't put his daughter through that kind of hurt, but he could do so much more. He could be a reliable part of his daughter's life, if he'd get past his worries. Sure, it might not be easy for him to deal with his ex-wife, but she knew how important it was for a child. And she just couldn't be involved with someone who wasn't there for his family through thick and thin.

She watched her daughter take a late-day nap after one of her treatments. In a couple of hours the fund-raiser was due to kick off. She'd been counting on Chad to watch over their daughter while she attended the event and met with donors. Chad hadn't been thrilled about the idea of being left out of the swanky party, as he put it, but she'd pushed how important it was for Molly and he'd grudgingly relented. So much for him being there for them.

"How's she doing?" came a very soft male voice.

Kate jerked around to find Lucas standing just inside the room. His face was drawn and his eyes were bloodshot as though he hadn't gotten any sleep. She hated how she'd had to run out on their conversation the night before. So much had been left unsaid.

"She's doing better." Kate still got angry every time she thought of how Chad had skipped out, leaving Molly disappointed and heartbroken. "I thought you'd be at the house getting ready for the party tonight."

"Between my assistant and Aunt Connie, they have everything under control. What they really need is you."

Kate's gaze strayed to her sleeping daughter. "I can't leave her alone."

"But you are needed for something very important."

The house was complete. The party was under control. She couldn't think of a single thing that needed her attention. "What is it?"

He pulled a black velvet box from behind his back. "I need you to wear this tonight when you meet your guests."

Excitement pulsed in her veins. "Is this from the Fiery Hearts line?"

"Yes, it is. I know how anxious you've been to get the first glimpse. I only have a few of the pieces, but they are the stars."

"Hurray!" She quietly clapped her hands together in excitement. "Show me."

He flipped open the lid and her mouth dropped open at the heart-shaped ruby and pearl choker with a matching bracelet and earrings. She reached out to trace her finger over them.

"They're gorgeous."

"You approve?"

She nodded, still taking in their beauty. Nurse Judy entered the room to check Molly's vitals.

"Look, Judy." Kate pointed at the sparkling jewelry. "Aren't they gorgeous?"

"They're stunning. Someone sure knows how to pick out great gifts."

"This isn't a gift." Kate shook her head. "These are part of Carrington Gems' newest line."

"Actually," Lucas interrupted, "they are for Kate to wear to the party tonight."

"I couldn't." Kate pressed a hand to her chest, feeling a bit flustered. "You were supposed to have some beautiful model show them off."

He smiled and continued holding the jewelry for her to take. Judy moved over to Molly's bed while Kate tried to figure out what this all meant…if anything.

He gazed deep into her eyes as he pressed the box into her hands. "I can't think of anyone more beautiful than you."

"But…but I can't. I have to stay here."

"This is one party you aren't going to miss. And that's why I'm here. I will sit with Molly."

"You? You're the one who should be at the party. It's your house."

"Ah…but this evening is your creation. And you are the infamous woman in the photo that everyone wants to meet. You will be the star."

She hated that he had a point. This was her party—her idea. The thought that people were going to attend with the interest in meeting her made her stomach quiver.

"And," he added, "I need you to be the face of Carrington Gems."

"Me? I couldn't." She worried her bottom lip. "You need someone beautiful—"

"Someone just like you. And if you need anything my aunt and my assistant will be on hand."

Kate cast a hesitant glance at Molly. She really didn't want to leave her, but this fund-raiser was vital for her surgery. Maybe if she just slipped out for an hour or two…

Judy caught her gaze and smiled. "Go. Molly will be fine. There are plenty of people around here who will keep an eye on her. And I promise we will call you if anything comes up."

Kate stood, still feeling so unsure about this arrangement. She looked into Lucas's steady blue gaze and could feel his strength grounding her. He placed the jewelry case in her hand.

"There's a car waiting downstairs to whisk you off to the ball."

"Just like Cinderella."

"Most definitely."

If only her Prince Charming was going to meet her at the party. But this wasn't a fairy tale. This was reality. She'd been on her own before—why should tonight be any different?

Lucas settled back in the chair, leafing through the financial magazine he'd brought along. He couldn't remember the last time he'd been able to sit down and read something besides sales reports and marketing projections. He glanced over at Molly as she cuddled with the pink teddy bear in her sleep. She was so cute—so like her mother.

"Okay, you can go."

He glanced up, finding Judy standing there. "Go where?"

"Cinderella needs her Prince Charming. So off to the ball with you."

"I can't. I promised to watch over Molly."

"I just got off duty and my husband said he'd entertain our little ones with a pizza and movie so I have the evening free. I know you're dying to be with Kate. So go."

"Is it that obvious?"

She nodded.

"Do you think Kate will mind? I mean, I don't know how this works."

"Kate has become a friend. It'll be okay. Remember, I

am a nurse. Molly will be in good hands." She sent him a reassuring smile.

Lucas prayed that Judy was right. He headed out the door and rushed home, finding the mansion all lit up. It'd been so many years since it'd come to life like this. Instead of the dread he thought he'd feel, he was excited to see Kate. He had something to tell her…something very important.

And what could be better than telling her at the party? It would be a night to remember. Anticipation flooded his veins as he moved with lightning speed through the back door, past the servers dressed in old-fashioned police uniforms. He chuckled to himself at the irony of having police officers serving drinks at a prohibition party. Kate certainly had a sense of humor.

He quickly showered and changed into his tux. By then the party was in full swing. He really didn't want to face the people or the questions. But he had to do this for Kate.

He plastered on a smile and worked his way through the milling guests decked out in 1920s attire from fringe dresses to black pinstripe suits and hats. It was like walking back in time. He smiled and shook hands with people he knew. Some patted him on the back, congratulating him on an excellent party and his choice of such a gorgeous hostess. Lucas promised to stop back later to talk and moved onward.

His gaze searched the crowded living room where a few people were dancing to big-band music. But Kate was nowhere to be seen. He scanned the foyer, followed by the dining room but still no luck. Was it possible she was upstairs showing people around? He started for the steps when he spotted his aunt.

"Do you know where Kate is?"

"Aren't you supposed to be with Molly?"

"Judy got off duty and offered to sit with her so I could

be here for Kate. I really need to talk to her, but I haven't been able to catch up with her."

"Finally came to your senses about her, didn't you?"

He nodded. "If she'll give me a chance."

"I think you'll find her showing some interested guests the prohibition tunnel. But Lucas…"

He didn't have time to chat. He'd been waiting too long for this conversation. Actually, instead of words he intended to show her that he could be the man she needed him to be…the man his family needed him to be.

At last he found her on the landing, talking to an older, familiar gentleman, but Lucas couldn't recall his name. He gazed up at her. A cute black hat was settled over her short bobbed hair. She looked adorable. The Fiery Hearts ruby and pearl choker sparkled on her long neck. His pulse picked up its pace as he imagined replacing the necklace with a string of kisses.

His gaze slid down, taking in every breathtaking detail. In a vintage black dress, her creamy arms were bare except for the matching bracelet. A murmur of approval grew in his throat, but he had enough sense about him to stifle it.

The dropped waist on her dress lent itself to a short skirt, which showed off Kate's long legs in black stockings and black heels. He'd never ever get tired of looking at her. She was by far the most beautiful woman and the ideal choice to wear the Carrington Gems. He gave in to an impulse and let off a long, low whistle.

Kate turned and color tinged her cheeks. He ascended the steps and made a hasty apology to the gentleman before taking her hand and guiding her up the steps.

Kate stopped at the top of the stairs, refusing to take another step. "Lucas, you're supposed to be at the hospital."

"Judy is sitting with Molly. She said I couldn't miss being here for you and I have something to show you."

He couldn't wait to show her the nursery that he'd

changed into a little girl's room—a room for Carrie. If it wasn't for Kate, he might not have understood that letting go of his daughter might hurt her more than fighting to have her in his life. He owed Kate a debt of gratitude.

She withdrew her hand. "Can it wait? I have guests to greet."

"It's important. I've done a lot of thinking about what you said about the future. Just give me a minute to show you what I've come up with."

Her eyes lit up and sparkled with interest. "Since you put it that way, lead the way."

He smiled. This night was going to be unforgettable for both of them. It would be a new beginning full of countless possibilities. His chest filled with a strange sensation—dare it be hope.

"Ms. Whitley." One of the young male servers rushed up the stairs. "Umm…Ms. Whitley." The young man's face filled with color. "I'm sorry to disturb you. I…umm… You're needed downstairs."

She flashed a smile, visibly easing the man's discomfort. "What's the problem?"

"There's a gentleman downstairs. He says he needs to speak with you."

"Please tell him I'll be down in a moment."

The young man shook his head. "He isn't an invited guest. At least I don't think he is. He isn't dressed up. The man says he needs to speak with you right away."

"I'm coming." The young man nodded and hustled back down the stairs while Kate turned to Lucas. "It must be Chad. Seems he came to his senses about leaving. Molly will be so happy. But first I need to have a serious talk with him. Can we finish this later? After the guests leave."

Lucas didn't want to wait. He wanted to show her that he was taking strides to be the man she wanted. But part of that meant having patience—after all, he wasn't going anywhere. Their talk could wait. But that didn't mean he had to like it.

He groaned his impatience and nodded his agreement.

She lifted on her tiptoes and went to press a kiss to his cheek, but he turned his head, catching her lips with his own. He'd never ever tire of kissing her. He went to pull her closer—to deepen the kiss, but she braced her hands on his chest and pushed away. The kiss might have been brief, much too brief, but it promised of more to come.

"Later." She flashed him a teasing smile.

He ran his tongue over his lower lip, savoring her cherry lip balm. He stifled a groan of frustration. He wanted more of her sweet kisses now...and later. Forever.

The last word caught him off guard. He never thought he'd ever use that seven-letter word in terms of a relationship again. But Kate had come into his black-and-white world and somewhere along the way had added all the colors of the rainbow. His heart was healed and ready to fight for those he loved.

How it'd taken so long for him to come to terms with how he felt about Kate was beyond him. Now, he couldn't wait to tell her that he loved her. He was dying to know if she felt the same way. But what choice did he have but to wait? Only a little longer and then he'd have her the rest of the night.

"Let's go greet your ex."

They'd just turned the landing when Kate asked, "So what was it you wanted to show me—"

Her words hung there as she came to an abrupt halt.

"Kate, are you all right?"

When she didn't move, didn't say anything, he followed her line of vision to an older man with white hair standing at the foot of the stairs. He was definitely too old to be Chad. And there was something vaguely familiar about him. In a pair of jeans and a plaid shirt, he certainly wasn't here for the party. The man stared back at Kate with tears in his eyes.

Panic clutched Lucas's chest. The face. The age. The look. It all came together at once. This was Kate's father—her estranged father, Floyd—the man he'd connected with on MyFriends.

A hush fell over the crowd as though they sensed the tension in the room and were checking it out. The paparazzi covering the event for all of the major news outlets moved in closer. Their flashes lit up the room, causing even more people to move in for a closer view. Lucas waved them off and the flashes stopped. But it was too late—the press was going to have a field day with this story. Guilt weighed heavily on Lucas's shoulders.

Floyd placed a foot on the bottom step and Kate took a step back.

"Katie, you look so beautiful all grown up. You're the spitting image of your mother—"

"Don't! Don't say that. There's nothing you could say that I want to hear. Just go."

"Katie girl, I'm sorry—"

Her voice shook. "I don't know why you picked now to pass through my life, but just keep going. You're good at walking away, so don't let the door hit you on the way out."

Floyd's gaze moved to Lucas. A light of recognition filled the man's eyes.

Lucas might not have talked to the man online, but looking back now, he realized even seeking him out and sending a friend request had been too much. The man had already been curious about who he was—all he had to do was look on Lucas's MyFriends page to find a picture of Kate. He'd unwittingly laid out a trail of breadcrumbs that anyone could have followed—including Floyd.

Finding his voice, Lucas said, "You should go. Now."

Kate's shocked look turned in Lucas's direction. He

froze. The breath trapped in his lungs. He wanted to wind back time and change things, but he couldn't any more than he could ease her pain.

"You did this." Her voice vibrated with emotion. "You brought him here, didn't you?"

Her pointed words jabbed at his heart. He wanted to explain and make her understand that he hadn't invited Floyd here. He'd never ever orchestrate a public reunion.

"I didn't invite him—"

Her eyes narrowed. "But you contacted him, didn't you? You couldn't leave well enough alone."

Lucas wanted to deny it, but he couldn't. He was losing the woman he loved and there wasn't a damned thing he could do about it. He merely nodded.

"You had to prove me wrong, didn't you? You had to prove to me that...that he—" she pointed at Floyd "—had some excuse for leaving me just so you could feel better about walking out on your own daughter. I should have never trusted you. When will I ever learn not to trust people?"

"You can trust me—"

Her chin lifted and her eyes shimmered with unshed tears. "No, I can't. You just proved me right. Molly and I are better off on our own."

Lucas could feel the curious gazes boring into his back. He wasn't worried about himself as he was used to providing fodder for the press, but Kate didn't need her private life made public knowledge.

"Kate, this isn't the place for this."

Her brows drew together. "Maybe you should have thought about that before you started poking around in my life. I'm not the one who made it possible for Floyd to be here. You did that all on your own. I should have known I couldn't trust you. I won't make that mistake again."

Kate spun around and sailed up the stairs. Even though he hadn't invited her father here, he had opened Pandora's box. Like Cinderella running off into the night, Lucas knew their fairy tale had just ended.

CHAPTER SEVENTEEN

IT HAD TO BE HERE. It just had to be.

But search as she might, Lucky Ducky was missing.

Kate shoved aside her purse. How could this happen? Ducky was always in her purse. And as Molly's surgery dragged on, Kate was starting to feel nervous. She knew it was silly, but that toy made her feel somehow connected to Molly. She could still envision her sweet smile when she'd handed over the trinket—back before Molly had gotten sick.

With a sigh, Kate slouched back in the stiff hospital chair. Two days had passed since she'd left Lucas at the party. She still couldn't believe he'd stepped so far over the line by contacting her father. She glanced over at Floyd. He sent her a reassuring smile. It was good to have family around. And if it hadn't been for Lucas's meddling, Floyd wouldn't be here. But did that excuse Lucas's actions?

"You've got plenty of time before we hear anything about the surgery," her father said. "Why don't you call that young man of yours and let him know how things are going?"

"I don't see the point. Even if we find a way to get around what he's done, he'll eventually leave."

"I know you don't have any reason to believe me of all people, but not everyone walks away."

"The people in my life do."

"If he really loves you, like I suspect he does, he'll stick." Her father sighed and ran a hand over his day-old stubble. "Don't let my poor decisions color the rest of your life. If you quit letting people into your life, you'll end up old and alone. You know Molly isn't going to stay small forever. Why don't you give him a call and see what happens?"

She hated to admit it, but Floyd had a point. Molly would eventually move on with her own life. But the thought of putting herself out there only to have Lucas reject her scared her to bits.

"I doubt he'll want to talk to me."

"You'll never know until you try. From the sounds of it, you both have some apologizing to do. But he appears to be a good guy. Is he?"

She nodded. "But I can't forget that he went behind my back and contacted you."

"Everyone makes mistakes." Her father reached over and grasped her hand, giving it a squeeze. "If it wasn't for him, I might never have gotten up my courage to track you down. I know we still have a long ways to go, but you are willing to give me a second chance and what I did was so much worse than Lucas's misstep."

But it was more than Lucas contacting her father—it was the way he was willing to back quietly out of his daughter's life. Sure, he had his reasons, but none of them were good enough to walk away from someone you loved. A lump formed in the back of her throat. But wasn't that what she was about to do—walk away from the man she loved without giving him a chance to explain?

The realization that she still loved Lucas even after everything that had happened jolted her. What should she do now? Ignore her feelings and hope they went away?

"Call Lucas."

It was as if her father was privy to her thoughts. Was that even possible after their extended separation?

Just yesterday morning, the day after the party, Floyd had caught up with her here at the hospital. At first, she hadn't wanted to hear what he had to say, but eventually she reasoned that if she ever majorly messed up with Molly, she'd want to be given a chance to explain.

Her father had struggled with the words, but at last he admitted how he'd gotten caught up in gambling and put the family in deep debt. Things continued downhill to the point where he got involved with some unsavory loan sharks. A shiver had run over her skin when he'd described how they'd roughed him up when he didn't have the money he owed. Unwilling to make his family targets, he'd left. It'd taken him years to conquer his addiction, but by then he figured it was too late to fix things.

"The difference is you were trying to protect us." Though she still hadn't made peace with her father's choices, she was willing to give him a chance as long as he was upfront and honest with her. But there was something she'd wondered about. "Mom never spoke of you after you left. I never understood why."

"I hurt her deeply." Her father leaned back in his seat and ran a hand over his aged face. "Things were so messed up back then. I loved her, but love doesn't mean that two people are good for each other. Your mother and I, we were too different. You and Lucas, do you have things in common?"

She thought of the man who could make her heart skip a beat with just a look. They were different, but not to extremes. They liked the same sorts of food. They both enjoyed quiet evenings at home. And they both thought family was important. Secretly she was missing Lucas and wishing he could be here with her now. When he held her close she felt safe and protected—as if nothing could go wrong.

The push-pull emotions raged inside her. But when it came down to the bottom line, she loved him. Nothing had changed that.

And there was something he'd intended to show her. If she didn't talk to him, she would always wonder what it had been. Would it have made a difference?

Oh, what would it hurt to let him know that thanks to his help, Molly was having her surgery? And she would thank him for bringing her father back into her life. She owed him that much.

"I'm going to step out into the hall." Kate got to her feet. "Can you let me know if there's any news?"

"Sure. Go ahead. I'll be right here."

"You don't know how many years I've waited to hear those words." She started to lean down to kiss his weathered cheek but hesitated. They had a long way to go before they'd be that close. "Thanks."

"Things will be different from here on out. I promise." His voice cracked with emotion. "Now go patch things up with Lucas."

"I'll try." But she wasn't getting her hopes up too high. She already missed Lucas terribly. To set herself up for another fall would be devastating.

Lucas waited as the hospital elevator stopped at each floor, allowing people to get on and off. Every muscle in his body was tense. Logic said he shouldn't be here. He didn't want to do anything to upset Kate on such an intense day. But he had something important to give her. He stared down at Lucky Ducky in his hand. He ran his thumb over the toy and prayed some of that luck would rub off on him.

His cell phone vibrated and he retrieved it from his pocket. He was surprised to see Kate's name flash across the screen. "Hello."

"Lucas, it's Kate. I…I needed to talk to you."

"Where are you?"

"At the hospital. Today's Molly's surgery."

"Hang on a sec." He worked his way through the throng

of people and stepped off the elevator into the hallway. "Any word on how she's doing?"

"Nothing yet. We should hear something soon."

He heard the echo of Kate's voice. He took a few steps and peered down the hallway, finding her leaning against the wall with her back to him. He hesitated, not knowing what sort of greeting to expect. He reconciled himself to the fact that he deserved whatever she dished up.

He continued down the hallway. "Kate, turn around."

When she did, surprise lit up her eyes. She looked bone-tired and he wanted nothing more than to wrap his arms around her. But he couldn't. It wouldn't be what she wanted after the way things had played out with her father. If only he'd thought it through and realized how easy it'd be for the man to track them down via the party announcement on his MyFriends account.

But it all came down to the fact that he shouldn't have been meddling. He'd totally messed things up. And the only thing he could think to do was apologize and hope she'd forgive him.

They stared at each other, but he was unable to read her thoughts. Her face was devoid of emotion.

"I'm sorry," they said in unison.

"You are?" Again they spoke over each other.

Kate laughed. Her sweet tones washed over him, easing the tension in his neck and shoulders. Maybe there was a chance she didn't hate him. Maybe it wasn't too late to fix things. But he knew he was getting ahead of himself. First things first.

"Kate, I'm sorry about contacting your father. I just thought… Oh, heck, I don't know what I was thinking." He ran a hand over his tense neck. "Maybe I thought if I could show you that your father was a better man than you thought that I'd have a better chance with you."

"You were that serious about me that you thought you had to go to such lengths to win me over?"

He nodded, fighting back the urge to pull her close and do away with the talking. But something still needed to be said. "Remember how I wanted to show you something at the party?"

She nodded.

"I was wondering how you feel about yellow gingham? At least I think that's what the woman at the store called them—"

"Called what?" Kate's brows drew together as she stared up at him.

"The new curtains I put in the nursery. Well, it isn't a nursery anymore. It's a little girl's room."

Kate's eyes widened. "What are you saying?"

He cleared his throat. "If it wasn't for you, I wouldn't have realized that even though I was working so hard to shield Carrie from seeing her parents fight, she might just be as hurt by the knowledge that I didn't go the extra mile for her. I had a very interesting conversation with my ex-wife's new husband. It seems he's a lot more reasonable since he has kids and an ex-wife. Anyway, he's going to talk to Elaina, and I have my attorney working on a formal visitation schedule. It will be a gradual process until Carrie knows me, but someday I plan to bring her to New York."

"That's wonderful. I'm so happy for you and your daughter."

"And you? Will you be happy, too?"

"That's one of the reasons I was calling you. I wanted to tell you, or I mean, I wanted to thank you for bridging the gap with Floyd. You were right, too. He did have a reason for what he did. As for why he never contacted me later, well, we're working on it."

"Still, I'm sorry I overstepped."

"Is that why you're here? To apologize?"

Then he recalled the trinket in his hand. "Actually, I came to drop off Lucky Ducky. I found him on the floor next to the dresser in your room. I figured today of all days you wouldn't want to be without him."

Kate immediately reached for the keychain and held it close. "Thank you. I was searching for this earlier and I was really upset when I thought I'd lost it. I know it's silly to be so emotional over a cheap toy, but Molly gave it to me and that makes it very special."

And now he had one more important thing to ask her. His gut churned. "I was thinking maybe of starting over and selling the mansion. I'd like to have my new family start in a new home and make new memories." He could see the surprise light up her eyes, but he kept going. He had one chance at getting this right. "Kate, would you consider staying with me and being part of that new future?"

Had she heard Lucas correctly? He wanted a future with her?

Before her brain had a chance to formulate an answer, her father's voice called out to her. She turned and saw Dr. Hawthorne enter the surgical waiting room. Her heart raced. *Please let it be good news.*

"It's the surgeon. Come on," she called over her shoulder to Lucas.

They rushed down the hallway and joined her father. The surgeon sat down and pulled off his scrub cap. "The surgery was a success."

Tears of joy sprang to Kate's eyes. Her baby had made it. She swiped at her cheeks while Lucas gave her a reassuring smile that made her insides flutter.

The doctor continued going over the results of the surgery. "Lastly you should know that there is no guarantee the tumor won't come back. She'll need to be monitored on a regular basis."

His words rang loud and clear in Kate's mind. A guarantee. That's what she'd been looking for with Lucas. She'd been hoping for the impossible—a man who wouldn't ever fail her. And that was asking the impossible.

Life didn't come with guarantees. You simply had to make the best of the good…and the bad times. A step-by-step process. And she couldn't think of anyone that she wanted to be by her side during that journey more than Lucas.

She reached out to Lucas and slipped her hand in his. His touch was warm and strong. Her heart surged with love.

When her father walked with the surgeon into the hallway, she turned to Lucas and wrapped her arms over his broad shoulders and held on tight. She never wanted to let go.

At last, she'd found what she'd been searching for…her home. It wasn't a building with marble stairs and spacious rooms—it was right here in Lucas's arms…in his heart.

She pulled back just enough to gaze up at him. "I love you."

"I love you, too."

She swiped away more tears of joy. "This has been a day of miracles."

"Does this mean that you'd be willing to face the future together?"

She nodded. "And I think the perfect place to start a whole new life is the Carrington mansion."

"You do? You're not just saying that?"

With her fingertip, she crossed her heart. "I love it and I love you."

EPILOGUE

One year later...

"IT'S GORGEOUS. I don't think there's a single cloud in the sky."

Lucas's gaze never left Kate's face. "Definitely gorgeous."

She glanced over at him and rolled her eyes. "I was talking about this spring day. It's so warm and sunny. Makes me feel like I could conquer anything I set my mind to."

The hum of happy voices filled the air as they stood side by side in Central Park. Lucas smiled. He just couldn't help it. Life was good and he was doing his best to savor every moment.

He wrapped an arm around his wife's shoulders, pulling her close. "You know when I brought you here for the first time, I never dreamed this was possible."

"Well, you better believe it, because those are our daughters over there petting that horse. Looks like they'll be wanting a carriage ride next."

His mind tripped back in time. "I remember a certain carriage ride and how it earned me a kiss—"

"And a photo in the paper of us in quite a steamy liplock."

"I couldn't help myself. I had to see if your kisses were

as sweet as I remembered. But they ended up being even sweeter. Want to give it a try now?"

She smiled and shook her head. "Do you have spring fever or something?"

"Just a guy in love with the prettiest girl around."

The past year hadn't been the easiest, not by a long shot. But thanks to Kate, he had opened his eyes and realized that caving in to his ex-wife wasn't in the best interest of their daughter. Carrie was very much a part of him and he felt whole with his family around him. And though it'd been tough at first, he hadn't given up. This was Carrie's first visit to New York and she couldn't have been happier having a sister and another family.

"You seem awfully chipper for a workaholic who has been away from the office all week. Admit it, this staycation isn't so bad."

"Maybe you have a thing or two to teach me after all." He still loved his work, but he'd learned to delegate things when his workload became too heavy. Because he'd found something he loved even more than Carrington Gems— his family.

Kate glanced lovingly up at her husband. How was it possible for him to grow more handsome with each passing day? A smile pulled at her lips.

This past Christmas, they'd had a small ceremony with Molly standing tall by her side. The event had taken place at the Carrington mansion with just a few friends and family invited, including his aunt and her father, who hit it off quite well. It was great having people in their lives to create such precious memories.

Kate's gaze moved from her husband to Molly's glowing face as she ran a hand down the horse's side while her grandfather talked with the horse's owner. "It's hard to believe a year ago Molly was in the hospital. Now, she's a smiling, healthy little girl. I know there's still a possibility that the tumor will return, but with lots of hope and prayers, it's gone for good."

Lucas drew her closer to his side and kissed the top of her head. "Molly is going to have a long, happy life."

"I believe you're right. And now I have one more thing to tell you that will make this day even better."

He gazed down at her. "I don't think that's possible."

She pulled away from him so she could look him in the eyes. "Is that a challenge, Mr. Carrington?"

"Yes, it is, Mrs. Carrington."

She smiled victoriously because she already knew that she'd won. "How would you feel about having a baby?"

The color drained from his face. Not quite the reaction she was expecting. Then his eyes grew round like quarters. And she couldn't be certain, but she'd hazard a guess that he'd stopped breathing.

"Lucas, do you need to sit down?"

"A baby?"

"Yes, a baby. You are happy about this? Aren't you?"

"Woohoo!" He scooped her up in his arms and swung her around in a circle. "We're having a baby!"

His lips pressed to hers. Her heart swelled with love for the most amazing man she'd ever known. Their life might not come with a preordained path, but she knew as long as Lucas was by her side, they'd get through the twists and turns—together.

* * * * *

ONE PERFECT MOMENT

A.C. ARTHUR

Prologue

"Just this one time," Ava Cannon whispered as his hands cupped her butt.

"Once is enough," Gage Taylor murmured while moving them farther into her trailer.

He kicked the door closed with his foot, pausing a second to reach back and lock it. Then his hands were on her once more, his mouth crashing down over hers. The kiss took her breath away, every stroke of his tongue sending searing bolts of desire through her system until her fingers were gripping his shirt. The feel of his strong biceps through the cotton material, coupled with the hardness of his body, now pressed closely against hers, caused Ava's knees to tremble.

This was what she'd been fighting for over the last couple of months. Each day she'd stepped onto the set of *Doctor's Orders*, knowing that he would be there. The strong hands that she'd seen holding her script as he'd checked the words she'd written, monitoring them for medical accuracy, now touched her body.

"It will be enough," Ava whispered when he tore his mouth away from hers and she could take a breath.

He tugged the hem of her shirt from her pants. She lifted her arms up over her head, and he pulled the shirt off. His hands immediately went around her to the clasp of her bra, which he quickly unhooked before removing and tossing it somewhere on the trailer floor.

"Enough," he mumbled as he dipped his head. "More than enough."

His lips were on her breast then, teeth holding a turgid nipple before he sucked her in deep. Ava arched her back, her hands going to his shoulders as she tried to hold on to him. When he moved to the other breast she let her head lull back, her eyes closing to the delicious sensations rippling throughout her body.

Dr. Gage Taylor was a brilliant obstetrician and researcher. He'd come highly recommended when she'd asked who in the New York area would be a good consultant for her show. And when he arrived in her office that first day, she'd been rewarded with how jaw-dropping handsome the guy was. Ava should have known then that she was in trouble.

Now, she was pulling at his shirt until the buttons popped off. He grunted and hurried to unsnap his pants while she did the same, toed off her flats and pushed her pants and panties down her legs. His shirt was on the floor, his pants undone, his hands moving quickly to pull a condom packet from his wallet. She pushed his pants and his boxers down as he ripped the condom packet open and then smoothed the latex over his length. He wore leather loafers that he kicked off his feet before stepping out of his pants.

Ava sat on the couch. She scooted back on the wide pillows and looked up at all of the heavenly goodness that was Gage Taylor. Six feet one inch of golden honey-hued skin, ripped abs, muscled limbs and a thick, long erection. She swallowed as her gaze rested there.

"Just this once," he said, his voice deep and husky in the confined space of the trailer.

Ava licked her lips and nodded. "Yes, just this once."

He was over her by then, his lips on hers, his knee spreading her legs apart. She opened her mouth to his persistence, clasped her hands to the back of his head to hold him there. He pushed them both back to a lying position on the couch, arranging himself between her legs. He said something, but Ava couldn't hear him over the pounding of her heart and the rush of desire.

Her legs were already trembling by the time the crest of his erection touched her entrance. He pressed harder.

She moaned deeper, and their "one time" began.

Chapter 1

New York City
Three Weeks Later

Gage stepped out onto the sidewalk on a warm September morning, three weeks after they'd wrapped up shooting on *Doctor's Orders*. Despite the strange hours he'd been keeping during the seven weeks he served as an on-site consultant for the network medical drama, this morning he was expected at the hospital by nine. That meant he was taking his usual four-block walk to the Nancy Links Medical Center, where he'd worked as an obstetrician for the last four years.

He held his briefcase in one hand, cell phone in the other as he walked away from the thirty-story condo building, his Italian leather dress shoes clicking on the sidewalk. This afternoon he was seeing patients, but this morning was relatively free, he noted as he looked at his mobile calendar.

Gage had discovered early in life that being organized was a necessity. Growing up in a household with five siblings meant he had to know what was his and where his personal belongings were at all times. He'd learned a lot growing up as one of the infamous Taylor sextuplets, enough to make not repeating past mistakes one of his main priorities in life.

He looked up in time to see the light changing and then crossed the street just before his phone rang.

"Dr. Taylor," he answered because he could see from the caller ID that it was the hospital calling.

"Good morning," his assistant, Carrie, replied.

Carrie had been with him for the last six months. For his first two years at the medical center he'd been in residency, and then his inaugural research paper on infertility and the strides that had been made in the field had been published. That had propelled his career forward, and Gage became a staff obstetrician as well as a grant recipient in the following weeks to continue his research. With those dual titles, he'd been given a corner office on the hospital's fourth floor, an administrative assistant and, just recently, a lab assistant. His first admin had gone on maternity leave just weeks before his father's death last September. Since then, he'd gone through three more assistants, who had been sent to him via an employment agency.

Who would have thought that after all this time out of the spotlight, there would still be someone—actually three someones, all female—who not only knew who he was, but were also ready to claim their place in the spotlight by either working for him, or possibly sleeping with him.

Gage blamed his father's death a year ago for the renewed interest in the first African American sextuplets to be born in Temptation, Virginia, thirty years ago. After leaving his wife and seven-year-old children, Theodor Taylor had gone on to become the CEO of Taylor Manufacturing, building an empire that designed engines for a Japanese automotive company. Stock in the company had soared at the time of Theodor's death, and when it was announced that the estate would be handled by the children, Gage recalled fielding calls from newspaper reporters to investors asking about their plans for the international company. That was until Gray, the oldest Taylor sextuplet, brokered a deal to sell Taylor Manufacturing and divided the proceeds evenly among the siblings.

"Dr. Gogenheim wants to see you as soon as you get in this morning," Carrie was saying as Gage shook his head to rid himself of the memories of his father.

"Really? I didn't see anything on my calendar," he replied. "I planned to reach out to that research facility in Paris before their offices close for the day when I get in."

"I recall you mentioning that yesterday when we spoke. However, Dr. Gogenheim's assistant just called to see if you were in yet. I told her you were on your way."

"I am," Gage said just before a driver slammed on

the brakes, subsequently causing the cars behind him to do the same.

Those were the glorious sounds of a morning during rush-hour traffic. When the noise subsided, he continued. "Fine, I'll go right up to his office, but please have the number and the name of a contact person at the facility in Paris on my desk for when I return."

"Yes, sir. I'll get that information now."

"Thank you, and, Carrie?"

"Yes, sir, I hadn't gone down to get your Caffè Americano yet. I'll wait about half an hour. It will be on your desk when you finish with Dr. Gogenheim."

Gage smiled. "Thanks, Carrie."

He'd never been a morning person. To survive undergrad, med school and residency required the strongest coffee possible. Luckily for him, there was a Starbucks on the ground floor of the medical center. Gage showed his appreciation for Carrie going the extra mile to get his coffee by opening a credit account with the barista and paying them monthly for all drinks and any other items that he and Carrie ordered.

After disconnecting the call, Gage scrolled through some of the emails he'd missed in the last couple of days because he'd spent the weekend at a colleague's house in the Hamptons. He had been attending, of all things, a baby shower.

Gage approached the hospital minutes later and walked through the revolving glass doors. His honey-colored burnished leather wingtip lace-up Tom Ford shoes clicked against the polished floors as he made his way through the lobby and down the hall toward the elevators that would lead to the obstetrics and gynecology floors. He slipped his phone into his suit jacket pocket just before stepping into the elevator. When he heard someone yelling, "Hold the elevator!" he extended his arm so that his briefcase kept the door from closing.

"Thanks," the woman, dressed in light blue scrubs, said as she made her way into the compartment and pressed the floor she needed.

"No problem," Gage said and returned the smile she was so eagerly offering.

As the elevator began to move, he thought of how pretty she was, with her dark brown hair pulled back from her face and green eyes twinkling each time she looked up at him. He could ask her out, but he'd decided a long time ago that the quick, no-commitment type of interaction he preferred to have with women didn't bode well in the workplace.

The elevator stopped on her floor, and before she stepped off, she turned back to look at him. "Have a great day, Dr. Taylor."

Her arm extended, and Gage looked down at the business card she held in her hand. He immediately accepted the card and wished her a great day, as well. When the doors closed and he was alone, Gage looked down at the card, a smile ghosting his face.

"Miranda," he said and continued to read the words on the card as the elevator moved again.

She was a radiologist on the third floor. And she was hot. He tucked the card into the side of his briefcase and stepped off the elevator when it opened on his floor. He wasn't going to call her, Gage told himself.

Regardless of how good she looked. He had rules, and he had learned the hard way that it was best to stick to them, always.

"Good morning, Dr. Taylor. Dr. Gogenheim is waiting for you," the receptionist said when he stopped in front of her. "Just go on back to his office."

"Thank you," Gage replied with a nod.

He was known throughout the hospital, a fact that should have bothered him considering he despised his family's notoriety. But this was different. Gage's recognition at the hospital came primarily from being a talented doctor who brought huge research grants to the facility and added to their already stellar reputation. The Taylors of Temptation, on the other hand, had commercialized a serious health condition for thousands of couples, and topped that off with a very public betrayal of marriage vows and desertion of a family. It had been the beginning of the worst years of Gage's life.

Thankfully, that was then and this was now.

He gave a quick knock and then entered the office. Mortimer Gogenheim sat behind his desk, his thinning black hair brushed neatly to one side of his head, thick framed glasses perched on his nose.

"Good morning, Gage. Take a seat," he said.

Gage nodded and moved to sit in one of the guest chairs across from the sleek, dark wood desk. "Good morning," Gage replied. "I was surprised you wanted to see me so early. I thought the board meeting was scheduled for this morning."

Which was why he hadn't scheduled anything on his personal or business calendar. Gage wanted to be available the moment the board of directors decided he would become the youngest chief of obstetrics at the medical center. With all the research work he'd done this year, coupled with the latest grant that would fund the department's research labs for the next three years, he was a shoo-in for the position. At least that's what Mortimer had told him a couple of months ago. After that conversation, Gage was elated that his dream was about to become a reality, much sooner than he had ever anticipated.

"We had the meeting last night over dinner. My son-in-law received a job offer in Europe, so my daughter announced two weeks ago that they were moving over there. My wife was beside herself with worry at not being able to see the grandkids. So I'm stepping down sooner than I'd planned because we're going to move over there with them," Mortimer said as he sat forward, letting his arms rest on the desk.

Gage nodded. "Family first," he said. "I understand."

He did understand that concept, even if he didn't have a wife and kids of his own. Outside of his job, Gage only had his family. His five siblings—Gray, Garrek, Gemma, Genevieve "Gen" and Gia—who lived in different areas of the United States. They'd grown up in a tight-knit household, and even though distance separated them, they'd tried to remain as close as their mother always wanted.

"Good," Mortimer told him with a nod. "So I'll get right to the point."

Gage sat up straighter in the chair and thought about how his sisters were going to react when they heard the news. His oldest brother, Gray, was an overachiever himself, becoming one of the first African American billionaires to own and operate his own electronics company before he turned thirty. And Garrek was an exceptional navy pilot who was steadily moving up in the ranks. They were both tenacious and goal-oriented, just like Gage. His sisters each had stellar careers, as well. Gemma owned an upscale beauty salon in Washington, DC, while Gen ran her own software development company, and Gia worked as an executive chef at one of Chicago's swankiest restaurants.

He'd call Gemma first, he decided as he nodded and stared expectantly at Mortimer. She would never let him live it down if he didn't.

"The chief position is going to Edgar Rodenstein. He's been in this field for more than thirty years, and he's worked with the medical director before. In fact, Bart was the one who recommended Edgar for the job. So we're confident that the transition will be smooth. You, on the other hand, well, we're extremely happy with the work you've been doing in infertility and multiple birth research. We'd like you to continue in that vein, and we will possibly entertain a chief researcher position for you in the future."

Gage was stunned. The calm and relaxed feeling he'd had only moments ago as he'd stepped off the elevator had dissipated. It was now replaced with a sick feeling that had him shaking his head.

"Bart—" he began and then corrected himself "—the medical director hand-selected who would work with him?" he asked, and then answered his own question. "Of course he did."

Because that's what men like Bart Thomas did when faced with a younger, smarter and more innovative candidate. He selected the guy he knew best, the one he could control under the guise of training, no doubt. Gage was livid.

"I guess that makes sense," he continued because he had no intention of showing Mortimer how truly upset he was about this development.

Mortimer nodded and cleared his throat. "It makes perfect sense. The board agreed. The transition will begin immediately. We'll need you to be on hand in case further press conferences or other media appearances are required."

"I'm not sure that will be possible, Mortimer," he said before he could completely work through his thoughts. "These past few months have been a little hectic with my research and patient list, combined with the work on the television show. I was actually considering taking some time off."

Mortimer sat back in his burgundy leather chair, setting his elbows on the arms and clasping his hands. "Really?" he asked and arched a bushy gray-haired brow.

"Yes," Gage replied, his tone smooth and even, as if this was what he'd planned to say from the moment he walked into the office. "My brother and his wife have just welcomed twins, and I've been meaning to get down to Virginia to see them."

"Well, the arrival of babies is always a festive occasion," Mortimer said. "Especially in our business."

Gage chuckled along with him. "Definitely. So I'll be completing the proper paperwork this morning and briefing the other doctors in my department on my patient statuses."

"How long do you plan to be away?" Mortimer asked. "The department agreed to work around the shooting schedule for that show because it was good exposure for us to have your name and the hospital's name running in the credits of a nationally viewed program every week. New-patient visits at the clinic have grown by thirty percent in that time."

Gage nodded. He didn't need Mortimer to tell him that he'd been an asset to the medical center. He already knew that. Which was why being passed over for this promotion was a bunch of good-ole-boy crap that Gage did not appreciate.

"I'm aware," he replied. "Which is why I believe that a three-week vacation is not only warranted, but justified."

While Gage had adjusted his hours at the medical center during the shooting of *Doctor's Orders*, he hadn't missed a beat with his own patients and had even been on call most of the time while on set, rushing to the medical center to deliver three babies for other doctors who were on vacation. He would wait to see if Mortimer pressed this issue to play that card.

Instead Mortimer nodded, his cool gaze resting on Gage. "You're right," he said. "I'd hoped, however, that you would be available to represent the hospital to the media."

"I'd rather stay out of the media, if at all possible,

Mortimer. I'm sure you understand my reasons," Gage told him.

While he'd been more than excited to have his research paper published and enjoyed the accolades that came his way in the medical industry, Gage did not do media. He never granted interviews and did not appear for photo opportunities or press conferences. Up until this point, Mortimer had been happy to stand with his chest poked out, speaking on behalf of their department.

This was why Gage had been more than surprised when a production assistant from the television network had contacted him with regard to working on a show they were developing. He'd immediately turned them down, thinking they were asking him to star in the show. Gage never wanted to be in front of a camera again. But when he found out the position was simply as a consultant where he could lend his expertise and still stay in the background, he'd agreed.

"Yes," Mortimer replied. "I do understand."

"Well, then," Gage said as he stood. "I'll head down to congratulate Ed and then take care of the arrangements for my vacation."

Mortimer stood. "How are you going to adjust for three weeks without being at the hospital?" he asked. "You are your career, Gage."

Gage nodded because just fifteen minutes ago he'd been telling himself that, as well.

"I'm going to be with my family, Mortimer," was all he said before walking out of the office.

Gage squared his shoulders and walked as proudly as if he'd just received the best news of his life, down the hall and back to the elevator. As far as his career went, he wasn't sure what his next step was going to be, but didn't doubt that he would figure it out. He always did. For now, Gage was going to see Gray and his new nieces and nephews. He was going back to family, the only people he could ever trust and depend on.

Los Angeles

Ava wanted to scream at her mother.

It wasn't the first time, and she was fairly certain it wouldn't be the last. But instead of screaming, she used the fact that she was running late for a meeting to get off the phone with Eleanor Cannon. That was only a temporary reprieve, but Ava would take what she could get.

Coffee spilled onto the marble floor as she stepped into the hallway of the Yearling Broadcast Network. Two years ago, when Ava was just twenty-five years old, she'd walked down this same hallway with her heart pounding wildly, her entire life bound in sixty-three typed pages. The TV script for *Doctor's Orders* was the result of a year and a half's work, researching and developing her idea for the new medical drama. She was young and unknown at that time, but had landed the face-to-face meeting with Carroll Fleming through the showrunner for another show where she'd worked as a staff writer. Now Carroll was her current executive at the network after helping her to develop and launch *Doctor's Orders*.

Today's meeting was with Carroll and Jenner Reisling, a development executive at the same network. Ava was going to pitch her new series idea to them and prayed that the success of *Doctor's Orders*, currently the network's number one show on Thursday nights, would add weight to the new pilot following the lives of African American law students navigating their way through school, the professional world and, of course, love.

She was only a few minutes late but hated that just the same. Ava prided herself on being professional at all times. She'd always had to be. As a woman in the television industry, she knew she had to be on her game, no matter what her credentials were.

"I apologize for being late," she said immediately upon entering the conference room. "I know your time is valuable, so I'm ready to get started."

Carroll, with his shiny bald head and long, bushy red beard, sat forward in the chair he'd been lounging in.

"Don't speak of it," he said, pulling some papers that had been spread across the conference room table into a neat pile. "We were just talking about the ratings for the season finale of *Doctor's Orders*."

"Phenomenal," Jenner, a slim man with dirty-blond hair and dark brown-framed glasses, said. "As a first year procedural in a really competitive time slot, you knocked it out of the box with this one."

Ava beamed. That was the praise she'd wanted to hear for the last year. Actually, the last five years, since she'd decided that writing was her niche. She didn't believe it was conceited at all to like hearing that she'd done a good—no, a *great*—job with her first network show. Especially after all the critical words she received from her mother in her lifetime. If she'd listened to anything Eleanor Cannon said, Ava doubted she'd be where she was today.

"I'm elated at the show's success," she said and pulled three copies of her newest screenplay out of her bag.

The bag was huge and just a little worn around the straps. It was her favorite because it easily accommodated all the necessities she carried with her daily. Today, in addition to the script, she'd added her handheld recorder so she would be sure not to miss anything that was said in this meeting, a second spiral notebook that would be solely dedicated to this screenplay and any additional work she needed to do on it, and her newest pair of reading glasses because she'd accidentally stepped on the old pair when they'd fallen off the desk in her apartment.

"We are, too," Carroll continued and folded his hands over his stack of papers.

Jenner sat right next to him, smiling across the table at Ava.

"Yes, that's great," she continued as she pushed copies of the bound pages toward each of them. When they were both looking down at the cover page, Ava took a deep breath and let it out slowly.

"That brings me to this new pitch. Two young African American women spend their weekdays attending competing law schools, drinking and partying on weekends and navigating the murky waters of dating 24/7. This new, vibrant, urban take on sex and young professionals in the city will cater to the twenty- to thirtysomething crowd. A prime time slot would be

Sunday evenings. This would be an hour-long show, with a huge draw to advertisers geared toward the female consumer."

Jenner flipped through the pages of the script and glanced down at them. Carroll did neither. Instead, Ava found him staring at her as he drummed his fingers over his stack of papers.

"We have another idea in mind," Carroll told her.

Ava was about to open her mouth to speak, but she thought better of it. She always tried to evaluate her words carefully. Something else she'd learned from her mother, or rather because of her mother. Eleanor Cannon said whatever she wanted to say, whenever she wanted to say it. Even if it ended with hurt feelings or offense. Her mother believed that because she was a millionaire, she was entitled to speak her mind and never apologized for doing so. But Ava believed in giving people respect and demanded the same in return.

"I don't understand," she replied finally.

"Not that this wouldn't be great," Jenner began. "You've already proven that you have your finger on the pulse of what viewers want. And your pitch was quite intriguing. But I'm looking for something specific to boost our reality television programming."

"I see," Ava said. "I don't write reality TV shows."

She rarely even watched them. While they were extremely profitable and most brought in huge ratings and large sums of advertising dollars, they didn't exhibit the creativity and originality Ava liked to pour into her shows.

"You haven't yet," Carroll said, his excited smile spreading widely across his face.

The last time Ava had seen that smile was the day he'd shown up in her trailer on the set in New York to tell her they'd been renewed for a second season. That had been just six hours before she'd returned to her trailer with another man—the man who continued to creep into her thoughts on a daily basis.

"These are notes on the previous show of this kind," Carroll continued. "We want you to look at these to get a feel for the subject matter."

"You'll still have creative freedom to work this out in the way you see fit, but we're really aiming for the family reunion angle. If you can have a preliminary outline of the show in three months, we'll be ready to shoot the first pilot right after the first of the year. We already have the time slot selected. It will air at eight o'clock Thursday evening, with its debut on Thanksgiving Day. This will give us time to put a vigorous promotional plan in effect," Jenner told her.

Carroll was nodding now as he pushed that pile of papers across the table to her.

"*Doctor's Orders* is number one in the Thursday at eight slot," she said slowly, not liking where she felt like this was going.

"We know! We know," Carroll continued with glee. "That's why this is so perfect. That's why you are the perfect one to write this new script."

"I thought reality shows were supposed to be unscripted," Ava told him. "If you already have the idea and time slot locked in, you don't need me."

Besides, Marcelle, her agent, hadn't said anything to her about the network wanting her to work on a different project. She'd spoken to her late last night, and they were both pumped about the new pilot idea. Ava wasn't interested in a reality television show.

"Oh, but we do need you," Jenner said. "I believe you can bring a fresh slant to this idea and the execution of the show."

Carroll nodded enthusiastically. "We both believe you can do this, Ava. Especially since you already have a foot in the door with one of the stars of the show," Carroll continued.

"What are you talking about?" Ava asked. "This is the first I've heard of this show at all. How do I know who is starring in it?"

Carroll rubbed his thick fingers together, and Ava could swear his cool gray eyes glowed with excitement.

"His name is Gage Taylor. He just worked on *Doctor's Orders* with you," Carroll said.

Gage Taylor, as in the gorgeous doctor whom she'd spent the last two and a half months acting as if she weren't attracted to? The man whom she'd finally decided to have once and for all as a celebratory prize for the second season renewal? The guy whom she hadn't seen since that night, yet had thought about at least once each day in the past two weeks?

"He's a doctor," she said after taking a deep breath and releasing it slowly. "Is this show about doctors? Because I really don't want to work in the same area. That's why my new show idea is so different from *Doc-*

tor's Orders. One is a procedural drama, while the other will be mostly drama, with lots of sex thrown in."

"No," Jenner replied. "This show is not about doctors. It has its own fantastic and totally original idea we're trying to bring across!" Jenner told her. "It's a reality television family coming back together thirty years after their original story aired. We're going to call it *The Taylors of Temptation: Remember the Times*."

Ava sat back in her chair and stared at them.

"Thirty years ago, Olivia and Theodor Taylor had the first sextuplets born in the town of Temptation, Virginia. The parents are dead now, but we want to bring the sextuplets together again, in Temptation, to see how their lives have changed," Jenner told her. "The network is already on board with the concept and you writing it. All you have to do is grab your computer and head out to Temptation to get started."

She had never heard of *The Taylors of Temptation*. Probably because she was only twenty-seven, and this show would have originally aired before she was born. Gage Taylor had come to her via recommendation from Daniel, her production assistant, whose wife, Leslie, was one of Gage's patients. Ava had known they'd need a consultant to make sure the story lines surrounding the doctors and the clinic where they worked was as authentic as possible. So she'd taken Daniel's and Leslie's word for how good Gage was and ended up enjoying working with him. A lot.

She folded her hands in her lap and shook her head once more. "I do not write reality television," she told them again.

This time Carroll's smile disappeared, and the cold edge of those gray eyes rested solely on her.

"Then you don't write another show for this network," he said with finality.

Ava couldn't breathe. She wanted to curse or kick something…possibly Carroll. Instead she kept her lips tightly clamped.

"Look, Ava, we like you," Jenner began. "*Doctor's Orders* is doing very well, and we'd love to continue working with you. To possibly develop other shows with you in the future. But for right now, this is the show we want. Do you understand?"

She absolutely did. They were giving her an ultimatum. One Ava didn't know if she could walk away from.

Chapter 2

Temptation, Virginia

One week after the tumultuous meeting at the network, Ava drove a rented fuel-efficient car into the town of Temptation, Virginia.

For the last thirty minutes, her speed had slowed. After passing the large heart-shaped sign with "Welcome to Temptation" written in bright turquoise letters, she'd felt a bit of calm take over. The drive from the airport took a few hours, and she'd hurried at first, driving as if she was on her way to an emergency. She wanted to get this over with.

Except Ava knew it wasn't going to be that easy. She hated that Jenner and Carroll had given her no choice in this matter. Or rather, she despised that their choice meant she would either have to shop her new idea to another network—and risk news traveling that she was difficult to work with—or do what she was told to do, something she'd sworn she was beyond doing.

Ava was not difficult to work with. Not on the set of the first network series she'd written for, or as the executive producer and writer of her own show. But that didn't mean Carroll wouldn't put that rumor out there, just to keep her from working anywhere else in television. That's how the industry worked. There were lots of intimidation tactics used by those in controlling positions, and Ava was glad that hers had, thankfully, only included a delayed green light of her new show idea. She knew of too many women who had suffered in other ways.

Ava was going to write the treatment for this show. Taking the next step in her career meant that much to her. And while she was sure she could use her family's influence to work with another network or even to produce her own movie if she wanted to, Ava chose not to do that. She wanted to do this on her own merit, and she would, even if it meant approaching a family who—she'd learned from the research she'd done in the last few days—had done all that they could to stay out of the spotlight.

Mature trees ushered her along the road, standing thick and tall on both sides. The sky was a perfect blue, accompanied by the fluffiest white clouds and shimmers of golden sunlight. She'd cut off the air-conditioning and rolled down the front windows, inhaling deeply the warm, fresh air. In the rearview mirror, looking as if they were somehow following her, were the peaks of the Blue Ridge Mountains. Ava figured they were just as majestic and beautiful up close as they were from this distance.

She wished this excursion would allow time for a hiking trip along some of the famous trails she'd read about during her research of the town. But she was on a tight schedule. Jenner wanted a thirteen-episode outline by Halloween—six weeks from now—and final consent contracts signed by each of the Taylor sextuplets no later than Thanksgiving. This would keep them on schedule for shooting to begin in January. Ava tightened her grip on the steering wheel and focused her mind once more on the plan she'd come up with.

Grayson Taylor was the CEO of Taylor Electronics and had recently returned to Temptation, found a wife with twins and renovated the old Victorian house where the original Taylor family had lived thirty years ago. Just three weeks ago, Grayson and his wife, Morgan, had welcomed a second set of twins, giving them a total of four children. Ava couldn't imagine taking care of anyone but herself—four kids would definitely be out of her league. Grayson and his family would be the key to getting all the siblings on board. She'd concluded that because, as the oldest, he also seemed to be the spokesperson for the Taylor sextuplets.

She made a right turn that landed her on a dirt road and was just about to check her GPS when her phone rang. It was on the console, connected to the charger, and she pressed the button to answer without looking at the screen. She was more concerned with whether or not she'd taken a wrong turn.

"You said you were going to call me back. You didn't. I despise lies, Ava. You know that."

Ava rolled her eyes and silently chastised herself for not checking her caller ID before answering.

"Hi, Mom. I'm in the car," Ava replied because she knew her mother hated her talking on the phone while driving—even if Ava used a Bluetooth.

"Then why are you answering the phone?" Eleanor immediately asked.

Ava smiled.

"I didn't want to ignore your call. Listen, I should be at the bed-and-breakfast in about twenty minutes. I'll give you a call as soon as I get settled in."

"Bed-and-breakfast? Where are you? And who stays in a bed-and-breakfast when there are perfectly acceptable hotels throughout the world?"

Not Eleanor Cannon, that was for sure. Her mother would only stay in the best hotels, drive the fanciest cars, pay a small fortune for the most stylish clothes, and buy whatever else her inherited fortune would allow. Everything her mother did was done with style and grace, while Ava had adopted a more frugal lifestyle that drove Eleanor insane.

"I'm on a research assignment. I'll give you a call with more details once I'm settled."

Her mother would want the name of the bed-and-breakfast and a landline number to reach Ava in case cell service suddenly went down worldwide. Being an only child hadn't been easy for Ava. In the past six years since Ava's father's unexpected death Eleanor had become even more overbearing.

"That will be fine. I'll wait for your call. Drive safely," Eleanor said before disconnecting.

Ava took that to mean she'd better call her mother back, or Eleanor might send out the cavalry to look for her.

Tossing the headset onto the seat, Ava returned her attention to the GPS. The directions took her down a long cobblestoned street. Hearty mums stuffed in big black pots circled each lamppost. Cute little storefronts had twinkle lights or harvest baskets, pumpkins and gourds decorating their slice of the sidewalk. People moved about, walking slowly and staring at the decorations or what the store had advertised in their front windows, Ava couldn't tell which. What she saw on their faces, however, was, without a doubt, contentment.

She drove the remaining ten minutes until making the final turn to her destination. The Sunnydale Bed-and-Breakfast was a stately white colonial house with black shutters, nestled in the center of a cul-de-sac and surrounded by a number of beautifully mature trees. It looked like something straight out of *Leave It to Beaver* or one of those other old black-and-white family shows. Ava favored nostalgic television over today's modern reality. But while recognizing the need to grow and accept change, she still tried to bring a sense of those old-time family values and simplicity into her writing. A fact, she hated to admit, that would come in handy for this project.

She parked the car and reached over to grab her

phone and purse before stepping out. She traveled light, with only one huge duffel bag and her laptop, which she retrieved from the back seat before locking the car and heading up the brick walkway toward the house.

The bed-and-breakfast looked exactly as it had in the brochure, including the chubby shrubs lined up along the perimeter with picture-perfect precision. Ava smiled at the pair of stone bulldog statues guarding the premises as she stepped up onto the porch. Opening the door, she walked inside and was further warmed by the historic charm that continued. Scuffed wood-planked floors, and emerald-green-and-white textured wallpaper stretched throughout the front foyer and along the wall next to a winding glossy cherrywood railing.

She liked it here. Liked the ambience and was glad she'd selected this brochure from the three Saraya, her assistant, had given her. The research trip had been quickly planned once she'd decided to go through with the project. And once that decision was made, Ava had known exactly how she wanted to approach it—straight through the heart.

The Taylors had loved this town and the people who lived here. If Ava were going to write this show, she had to get to know the people here. What they liked, how they lived, what they feared, all of it. Then she'd tackle the Taylor sextuplets.

"Well, hello, ma'am. Welcome to Sunnydale," an older gentleman said.

He stood behind the front desk—a continuation of the cherrywood, with a black marble top. There was a large fresh flower arrangement toward the end of the desk, closest to the wall, along with a shiny gold bell and a placard on the other end that explained all the forms of payment accepted.

"Hello," Ava replied. "I have a reservation. My name is Ava Cannon."

The man never even looked at the computer sitting on the part of the desk that faced a bay window. Instead he stood and came around until he was directly in front of her. He extended his hand and gave a toothy grin.

"I'm Otis," he said. "Welcome to Sunnydale and to Temptation."

"Ah, thank you," Ava said and shook his hand.

He was still holding her hand seconds later when a younger man entered the lobby area.

"The paint's still wet, but the job's done, Mr. Otis. I have to head back out to Harper's place, but just let Nana Lou know we'll be sending her an invoice in the mail," the second man said.

There was a big contrast between the two men, and Ava, always one to pay attention to the details, picked up on it immediately. The first man, the older one who had just been called Mr. Otis, wore dark gray pants that were baggy on his slim frame. Black suspenders helped to keep the pants from falling down, and his short-sleeved light blue dress shirt was wrinkled, with a floral trimmed handkerchief in his breast pocket. His skin was a very weathered almond complexion, and his hair—what was left of it—was short, gray and curled close to his scalp.

The second man was much younger, probably in his early to mid-twenties. He was at least six feet tall with a short bush of brown hair, and he wore faded jeans and a plaid shirt with drops of paint all over it.

"Pardon me," the younger guy said. "I didn't mean to interrupt your check-in."

They would know instantly that she wasn't from Temptation, and it had nothing to do with the cream-colored pantsuit she was wearing. Ava had left the jacket to the suit on the back seat of the rental car so that her arms were bare in the peach tank top she wore. Her shoes were comfortable leather flats, and the flashiest piece of jewelry she wore was the diamond tennis bracelet her father had given her as an eighteenth birthday present.

No, they knew she wasn't from here because they knew everybody in this town. She could see it by the way they were assessing her.

"Hi. I'm Ava Cannon," she said and was finally able to ease her hand away from Mr. Otis's grip. She extended it to the young man, who smiled as he shook it.

"I'm Craig Presley," he said. "Welcome to Temptation."

"Thank you," Ava said. Both of them were actually very welcoming and genuine.

"No thanks necessary. In fact, since you're new to town, I would like to personally offer my services to show you around," he said.

Craig Presley had a nice smile and warm, happy eyes. He was cute and friendly, but he wasn't her type. Nor was hooking up with a guy in this town on her agenda.

"Presley? Are you any relation to a Harper Presley?"

"Yes," Craig replied. "Harper's my cousin. Are you looking to have a house renovated or built? Presley Construction can definitely take care of that for you. We're the best in town. Here, let me get you a card."

He was digging into his back pocket now, pulling out his wallet as he hunted for a card.

Mr. Otis scratched the side of his head. "If you're thinking about planting roots here in Temptation, you should talk to Fred Randall about purchasing some land or a house. Then you get in contact with Harper. She's a wisp of a pretty gal, and she's mighty talented, too," Mr. Otis stated.

"I'm just visiting," Ava said and then thought quickly of something else. "But I like what I've seen of this town so far." She shrugged. "Would be nice to maybe have a vacation home here."

Craig handed her a card. "Then Presley Construction is definitely here to work with you. Phone numbers, email and address are on the card. Harper does all the intake for new clients. I can introduce you to her. I just need to make a quick trip back to the warehouse and clean up a bit. Then I would love to take you to dinner to tell you more about Temptation."

Ava looked down at the card and nodded. Harper may be the head of Presley Construction, but she was also the fiancée of Garrek Taylor, the navy pilot. How lucky was she to have made this connection to the Taylor family so quickly?

"Or she can just take a little walk down Sycamore Lane. Three blocks past the traffic light and to the left—

you'll probably bump right into Harper at Gray Taylor's house. They're having a barbecue tonight."

And the luck just continued to flow, Ava thought with a smile.

"Oh no, I wouldn't want to intrude on a family gathering. I can just call tomorrow to schedule an appointment."

"Nonsense," Mr. Otis said. "Nana Lou baked some cookies for Jack and Lily. I told her I'd run them over there, but you can deliver them in my place. Gives you the perfect opportunity to meet up with Harper."

It certainly did. Almost too perfect, but Ava decided she would take it. This wasn't LA or New York; people here were just friendly, she reminded herself. Nobody was going to be suspicious if a stranger just showed up with a plate of cookies. At least she hoped not.

"Tell Harper I sent you to her," Craig added. "I'll take a rain check for dinner."

Ava found herself liking Craig Presley because she could definitely relate to his tenacity.

"I sure will," she said. "Thanks, Craig, and you, too, Mr. Otis."

Craig headed out, leaving Ava and Otis alone.

"Like Craig said before, no thanks necessary, ma'am," Otis replied with a shake of his head. "I'll just run out to the kitchen to get those cookies for you. Then I'll take your bags up to your room."

"That would be great," Ava told him. "Oh, wait, don't you need to swipe my credit card, get my ID or have me sign something?"

Otis chuckled. "I can get all that when you come

back. If you're thinking of getting a place here, we definitely don't want to put that off."

No, Ava did not want to put off the beginning of her second phase of research. She smiled and thanked Otis once more. She hadn't been in Temptation for more than an hour, and already she was on her way to getting this story done.

Gage had been in Temptation for two days and he was already dressed down in basketball shorts, a T-shirt and tennis shoes. Garrek's fiancée, Harper, hit the volleyball with a force Gage wasn't expecting, and he ran backward in order to save the shot. He tripped over something and fell back instead.

And then she was there.

"Hello, Dr. Taylor," she said with that smile that never failed to take his breath away.

She stared down at him, dark hair framing her pretty face, a light pink gloss on her soft lips. And Gage thought he must be dreaming.

"Ava?"

He moved quickly, coming to stand in front of her.

"I think you were trying to catch this," she said and gave a light kick to the ball he'd been after.

Gage put his foot on the ball to stop it from rolling, but did not take his eyes off her. She looked amazing, her long legs clad in cream-colored pants, the formfitting peach blouse and all that thick hair hanging past her shoulders. He'd forgotten how sexy she was.

"Yeah, thanks," he said and then asked, "What are you doing here?"

"Delivering cookies," she replied and held up a plate covered in foil.

"All the way from New York or LA or wherever you live?" he asked.

It may have seemed like an odd statement since this was the last woman he'd had sex with. In a perfect world, he would have known more about her besides her last name and professional occupation. But in Gage's world, it was the norm. He didn't need to know much about the women he slept with, because he never intended there to be anything beyond the physical. It was easier that way.

"I'm ah…on a kind of retreat," she replied. "A writing retreat."

He nodded, noting the plausibility of her response, but still wondering how, of all the places in the world, Ava Cannon would turn up in Temptation.

"And a cookie delivery service?"

She looked down at the plate and then up to him again.

"They're from someone named Nana Lou. Mr. Otis at the B and B said she promised to make them for Jack and Lily."

Gage frowned. "Who?"

He'd come to Temptation to be with his family and so hadn't met many people living in the town.

"Nana Lou is like our grandmother, but not really. She bakes the best double chocolate chip cookies ever," Lily said.

The precocious seven-year-old girl appeared, leaning against Gage's leg.

"You're hogging the ball, Uncle Gage," she continued before bending down to take the ball he still had under his foot.

"You must be Lily," Ava said, her attention shifting to the little girl Gage had been thoroughly enchanted by in the last couple of days.

He'd come back to Temptation to meet Gray's new family and had been amazed at how much he adored the children. Sure, he delivered babies for a living, and he studied ways to help every woman wishing to have a baby fulfill her dream. But Gage didn't think of becoming a father himself. Still, not even the smiling faces of youth, or the pure sweetness of babies, had been able to erase the thoughts of his one night with Ava. In fact, it had been all those things combined that kept Gage from thinking about his career situation.

"I am Lily, and this is my Uncle Gage. I have another uncle— his name's Garrek—but he's away flying planes right now."

"Oh, that sounds cool. These cookies smell amazing, Lily. Do you think I could try one?" Ava asked.

"Sure. Mommy won't let me and Jack have more than one for dessert. But Jack doesn't like to share, so you should take yours now."

"Hey, guys, Morgan is calling us in for dinner," Harper said as she joined them. "Oh. Hi," she added to Ava.

"Hello," Ava replied. "I'm Ava Cannon. I'm in town for a writing retreat and was told to deliver these cookies."

"And she's Uncle Gage's friend," Lily added.

Gage didn't know what to say. Hence the reason he'd

been standing there watching the exchange between his niece and his ex-boss-slash-one-night-stand.

"Hi, Ava. I'm Harper Presley."

"Oh, it's a pleasure to meet you, Harper. I met your cousin Craig when I was checking in to the B and B. He gave me your card."

"Really?" Harper asked. "Do you have a house that needs to be renovated?"

"No," Gage replied quickly. "She's just here to write."

Harper, with her sandy-brown hair pulled back from her face, arched a brow as she looked at him.

"You two know each other?" she asked.

Before Gage could answer, his legs almost buckled once more as a laughing seven-year-old ran into him.

"Come on, Uncle Gage, you're gonna make us lose," Jack said.

"You already lost. He fell, and the lady got the ball. That means the girls win. Right, Aunt Harper?" Lily asked.

"I'm calling interference," Gage told Jack. "We'll need a rematch."

Lily pouted, and to Gage's chagrin, Ava knelt down until she was face-to-face with his niece.

"Boys always try to cheat. I think he fell on purpose so he could ask for a rematch," she said.

A mutinous Lily nodded her agreement. "I think so, too."

Harper chuckled. "Okay, we'll have a rematch, but Morgan has dinner ready. You two run along and wash your face and hands so we can eat."

Thankful to Harper for getting rid of the children,

Gage turned his attention back to Ava. It was close to six o'clock in the evening, and the sun was beginning to set; still, the last fading rays cast Ava's creamed-coffee-toned skin in a golden hue that looked surreal. Or maybe it was because this was the first time he'd seen her outside of the sultry dreams that plagued him each night in the last few weeks.

"Why don't you join us for dinner, Ava? Gray and Morgan always cook a ton, and since you're a friend of Gage's, you should definitely be here to help us celebrate his homecoming," Harper said.

The gratitude Gage had just felt toward his soon-to-be sister-in-law dissipated as he turned from Ava to look at Harper with a frown.

"I'd love to," Ava happily replied.

"Great, Gage will bring you up to the house," Harper said. "I'll just go and tell Gray and Morgan to set another place at the table."

When Harper was about to walk away, Ava spoke again. "I really appreciate the offer. I've been traveling all day, and I don't even know if my room at the bed-and-breakfast is ready yet. I just dropped my bags off and came straight here."

Gage touched her elbow to stop her from following behind Harper.

"Why would you come here? How did you know where here was?" he asked, because no matter how his body was reacting to seeing her again, his mind was still suspicious.

Old habits were hard to break.

A breeze swept by, and Ava eased her arm from his

grasp. She pushed her blowing hair behind her ears. And Gage thought he'd never seen anyone as pretty as she was at this moment.

"Small towns are great for writing retreats. Meeting Craig at the B and B and Mr. Otis having cookies that needed to be delivered were coincidences," she said.

Gage watched her lips moving as she spoke and listened to the slightly husky timbre of her voice. Not only did he listen, but he felt as if that voice, her words, somehow touched a part of him. It was ridiculous, he knew, yet…he decided to believe her. It wasn't that big of a deal. She could go wherever she wanted without needing his permission. Just because she ended up here, at the same time he was, didn't mean anything. He needed to stop being so suspicious all the time.

"I would have never expected you to be here," he replied.

"It's work," she said. "Everything I do is about my work."

Gage could definitely relate to that. In contrast to her writing retreat, however, he had been taking the last couple of days to think about things other than his career. She was one of those things, even though he'd called himself a thousand fools for thinking about a one-time fling weeks later.

"But I can go if it's weird for you," she continued.

Was it weird for him?

Considering he hadn't expected to see her again until it was time to start shooting the second season of the show, maybe. Realizing that his body had already begun reacting to seeing her—via the beginning of an erection as his gaze dipped from her big brown eyes to the unmistakable curve of her full breasts in that tight blouse—hell no, this wasn't weird at all.

"It's cool," he replied. "But we'd better get going. From what I understand, my sister-in-law, Morgan, does everything based on a schedule these days. Something about having a set of twins in elementary school in addition to a set of newborn twins and coveting any sleep she can get."

"Two sets of twins?" Ava asked with an incredulous look on her face.

Gage nodded and smiled. He ignored the burst of pride that spread throughout his chest as he looked toward the house and the back porch, where his family had begun to assemble at the table to eat the celebratory meal. Gage never talked about his family to anyone because he liked to believe they belonged to only him. Not a part of the world, the way his father had tried to make the sextuplets.

"Yes," he continued and began walking toward the house. "My older brother Gray is married to Morgan, an elementary school teacher. They have a boy and a girl, Jack and Lily, who you just met. Ryan and Emma are the new babies. Do you like babies, Ava?"

She shrugged as she walked beside him.

"I never thought about it," she said and then looked at him with a sinfully delicious smile. "I like how babies are made, though."

The semi-erection that Gage had been trying to ignore grew instantly as he recalled her smiling up at him that night he'd moved between her legs and thrust his length deep inside of her. She'd told him how much she liked it that night, and Gage would swear that the smile she was giving him now was meant as a reminder.

"Yeah," he said grinning back at her. "So do I."

Chapter 3

"Gage was working on a television show," Gray said for the second time as they all sat around the light oak dining table on the covered back porch.

His incredulous tone was not lost on Gage, or anyone else at the table, for that matter. Gage sat back in his chair trying not to address the unspoken questions that loomed over them.

"He was a great help to the show," Ava answered. "I'm certain we wouldn't have been renewed for a second season without his expertise. Comments about the show's authenticity were constantly in the reviews."

Gage hadn't read any of the reviews for the show. He enjoyed looking over the scripts and meeting with the writers—that part made him feel useful.

"I've seen the show," Morgan said as she returned to the table.

Ryan had been fussing while they ate dinner, so Morgan excused herself the minute Jack and Lily were finished. She took the older twins into the house with her while she tended to the new baby. In the days since he'd been here, Gage had concluded that Morgan was a good mother who adored her children. She also loved his brother, almost as much as Gage suspected Gray loved her. That realization had been a shock to Gage. His brother had found love and happiness, two things Gage knew would never surface in his own life.

"I love to watch procedurals," Morgan continued once she was seated. "And I thought the idea of one being set in an OB-GYN clinic on Staten Island was a fresh take compared to most of the drama series on television these days."

"I don't watch a lot of current television shows, but Corbin Yancy also has a show on the home improvement network. He and his wife are redecorating their house in Palm Beach," Harper added.

Ava nodded. She'd just finished taking a sip from her glass of lemonade. Gage watched her small hand with the neatly trimmed nails as it slipped from the glass and rested on the table.

"Corbin is great and his wife's a sweetheart," Ava told them. "He loves the show and worked really well with Gage to make the character he played come to life on screen."

"Wow," Morgan said. "So Corbin Yancy as Dr. Steven Renfield is actually Gage Taylor, my brother-in-law. I feel like I'm related to a celebrity now."

"I'm not a celebrity," Gage quickly replied.

The comment came in a sharper tone than he'd anticipated. The questioning and concerned looks coming from Harper and Morgan irritated him. For the two days that he'd been here, Gage had been successful in simply enjoying these new members of his family, and not thinking too much about the other family members who had let him down.

"I know some things that can help make the show work, but that's all I do," he said, trying for a lighter tone this time.

"Never thought my brother would be in show business," Gray said blandly.

Gage knew what Gray was thinking. From the moment he'd walked up onto the porch and introduced Ava, he'd been sure what Gray's reaction to who she was, and how Gage knew her, was going to be. Which was precisely why, when he'd first arrived in Temptation and Gray had asked what he'd been doing with himself, Gage had left out the part where he was working on a successful television show.

"Why is that? If you don't mind my asking," Ava said.

In addition to being a very good-looking woman, Ava Cannon was candid and real. Traits Gage hadn't thought Hollywood types could have. He'd watched her on the set with the crew and the cast, and each time he'd noted how sincere she was in whatever she was saying or doing. Whether correcting something in the script, or expressing her concerns to the director, or simply accepting a meal from one of the vendors, she always made eye contact and made everyone feel as if they were on the same level. Gage had admired that about her.

"Our family doesn't have a good history in the television business," Gray answered.

"But we don't need to talk about that right now," Morgan hurried to say. "It's just so nice to have Gage here visiting, and then for you to show up, too, Ava, is wonderful. I feel like we're celebrating so much these days."

"Almost too much," Gage said quietly.

When he looked up to see that Ava was now staring at him, Gage thought it was time to shift gears.

"So, Harper, when does Garrek think he'll be back for a visit?" he asked. "It would be great to see him while I'm here."

"Not until Christmas," Harper replied.

She was a nice woman—intelligent and talented, as he'd seen by the work she'd done on the old Victorian. She was not at all the type he'd thought Garrek would settle down with, but after talking to her and meeting her family, Gage could see the appeal. In fact, he was surprised at how it made him feel that his brothers had found really nice women. The Taylors didn't believe in happy-ever-after, because that wasn't how it had worked out for their family. All the happiness they'd once known had come crumbling down, and in the aftermath, each of the sextuplets had been left to figure out not only their place in the world, but what type of life they would have as a result.

Gage opted for work and family. Seeking emotional ties with anyone else was futile and doomed to end disastrously. It was that simple.

"That's too bad," Morgan replied with a frown.

"Still, it's enough time for you to visit the hospital with me to check on the progress of the new wing," Gray reminded Gage.

Gray was working on the Taylor Generational Wing at All Saints Hospital in Temptation. He wanted Gage's input on the obstetrics and gynecology department and research program that was set up in their mother's name. Even though he'd vowed not to think about work while he was here, there was no way Gage was going to refuse to help his brother.

"Absolutely," Gage replied to Gray. He needed to meet with both his brothers, but for now, Gray would have to do.

"How long are you planning to stay, Gage?" Morgan asked. "With the holidays coming up, I was hoping to get all the Taylors to come for dinner. I know it's been a long time since all of you were together, but that needs to change."

Morgan was petite, friendly and just a little bit bossy, which Gage concluded was exactly what Gray needed in a woman.

"That's a great idea," Harper added.

"I should have a few more rooms at the house completed by Thanksgiving, so whoever doesn't stay here can come out there with Garrek and me."

"Oh, a big family Christmas sounds amazing," Ava said.

She looked at Morgan and Harper with an expression that matched the women's excitement.

Unsure what to make of that, Gage replied, "I don't know if I'll be able to get away again that soon. And I only have three weeks to stay this time."

Silence fell around him, and Gage felt uncomfortable with the thought that he was spoiling their plans. He was even more uncomfortable about Ava being here, with his family, making plans for the holidays.

"Well, I think I should be going now," Ava said and pushed her chair back from the table. "I apologize for interrupting your family celebration. But I do thank you so much for your hospitality, Morgan and Gray."

"Don't mention it," Morgan said before leaning over to nudge her husband.

"Ah, she's right. It was a pleasure having you, Ava," Gray told her.

"We're all set for our meeting tomorrow," Harper added.

Ava nodded. "That's right, we are. I'm really looking forward to hearing your ideas about tiny homes. I've been thinking about having one built for a while, just haven't had the time."

"Well, you're in Temptation now," Morgan continued. "We take life at a slower pace here than in Los Angeles. I hope you get lots of writing done while you're here. And please feel free to stop by whenever you get tired of sitting at your computer. You're welcome here anytime."

Gage tried not to frown at that statement. He'd taken Harper's offer to stay at the house she was renovating for her and Garrek.

"Thanks. I'm just going to head back now. I'll be seeing you all soon, I suppose," Ava said as she stood this time.

Gage stood, too. He didn't know why, but he did.

"I'm going to head out, as well. I'll see Ava back to the B and B," he said.

"That's an excellent idea," Morgan added with a smile.

"I'll meet you for breakfast at the hospital in the morning," Gray said.

"I'll be there," he replied.

Gage moved around the table to hug and kiss Morgan and Harper good-night. He shook Gray's hand and then went to stand beside Ava. She was looking at him with a smile, and Gage wondered what she was thinking. He wondered what she'd thought about that night after they'd been together in her trailer. And he wondered if she'd thought about him at all since that time.

That thought stuck with him as he followed her back to the B and B in his car. And when he stepped onto the sidewalk and walked with her up to the front door, he continued to tell himself that the one night of great sex had been just that—one night.

Until now.

"Come inside with me," Ava said to him.

"Sure," he replied without hesitation.

* * *

"This isn't New York," Gage said after closing and locking the door to her room.

Otis hadn't been at the front desk when they'd walked into Sunnydale. A woman with long braids and a quick smile gave Ava the key and told her where her room was located. It had only taken Ava a couple seconds to realize the woman's quick smile was directed at Gage. That, for some insane reason, turned her on.

Gage Taylor turned her on. He had since the first day she'd watched him walk onto the set. Dressed in a black suit, white shirt and purple tie, he'd stolen the breath of every other female on the set. And he wasn't even a movie star. It was his swagger, Ava later surmised. The way his slightly bowed legs moved and the expertly cut suit hung on his broad shoulders. How his goatee was cut so precisely and his skin tone resembled the most decadent caramel. The husky and confident tone of his voice and the candid and intense way he had of looking a person straight in the eye when they talked. All of that combined with his quick wit and easy humor was nothing short of perfect. Perfectly, mouth-wateringly sexy. Period.

"No," she replied and turned to face him. "This is Temptation."

It was a place she'd arrived at only hours before. She'd come here to work on a project she wasn't one hundred percent on board with. She had not come here to have sex with Gage again. But she wanted to. There was no point denying that.

He crossed his arms over his chest. The chest she'd

known, from the way his dress shirts molded to him when they were on the set, would be deliciously muscled.

"That it is," he continued, his voice lowering slightly.

His gaze pinning her to where she stood.

"And I'm tempted," he said.

Ava tilted her head and once again replayed all the reasons why this was foolish. While they were currently in the off-season of *Doctor's Orders*, Gage had already signed a contract to work on the second season with her. Which made him an employee or coworker. In addition, he was one of the Taylors of Temptation, the family that her new project centered around. Her job here was to get each of the sextuplets to sign a contract that would allow cameras into their lives for three months. From her research, she had a feeling that wasn't going to be an easy feat.

So sleeping with Gage...again...wasn't a good idea.

"I am," she replied, "very tempted."

"I don't do relationships," he told her, but moved from where he stood, until he stopped only inches away from her.

"We've already had this conversation," she said and took the last step to close the distance between them. "You don't do relationships. You like your privacy. I'm focused on my career and will let nothing interfere with achieving my goals. You're attracted to me, and I'm attracted to you."

"For this one time," he said and used a finger to trace the line of her bottom lip.

Heat spread quickly throughout her body, her fingers clenching and releasing at her side as she tried to remain still for just a moment longer.

"Again," she whispered and gave in.

Coming up on the tip of her toes, Ava wrapped her arms around Gage's neck and pulled his head down so that her lips could touch his. That simple connection set off an explosion of heat that soared through her body. The memory of their night in the trailer had never dimmed in her mind; still, this touch sent her reeling in pleasure. He was a master at kissing, touching, seducing, and unlike in any other area of her life, Ava let go, let him take charge.

He slid his hand around her waist and down to grip her bottom. Ava sucked in a breath and moaned as he licked first her top and then her bottom lip. His fingers tightened on her, and in the next second he was lifting her off the floor. She wrapped her legs around him and eagerly delved back into the kiss.

"Bed," he mumbled between sucking on her tongue and gasping for air. "This time, the bed."

"Right," she replied as she realized he was carrying her to where he wanted her.

Ava couldn't think. She'd never been in this room before, so she wouldn't have been able to direct him to the bed anyway. Still, all her mind could absorb was the instant need that being near him sparked. She'd been afflicted with this situation for the past months as they'd worked closely together. And that night in her trailer, she'd perhaps foolishly thought that it would be cured. But it hadn't. She'd continued to want Gage long after that night. Only the thousands of miles that she'd put between them by returning to LA had kept her from showing up at his apartment and begging him to take her once more.

When he laid her down on the bed, Ava stared up into the face that had haunted her dreams too many times to count. He was possibly one of the most handsome men she'd ever seen. Certainly he was the best lover she'd ever had. But there was something else—she'd noticed it just now for the first time. Gage's dark brown eyes held a hint of wariness, even at this moment, a fact that shocked her.

"This is not why I came here," she said on impulse. "I didn't follow you so that we could do this again."

"Did you hear that?" he asked as he stared down at her.

"Hear what?"

"The sound of my ego deflating," he replied and then gave her that cocky grin she'd seen a few times before.

"I'm serious," she said, but found herself smiling, as well.

He shrugged and lifted the T-shirt he was wearing up and over his head. "I never pegged you for a stalker," he told her after tossing his shirt onto the floor.

She sat up on the bed and removed her shirt. "I definitely do not stalk," she said.

"But you stare," he added.

Ava's gaze snapped back to his face, as she'd been caught staring at his bare chest. He looked like he'd been sculpted instead of being a flesh-and-blood man. There was no other body like this, she was certain.

"Only when it's something I like," she admitted and kicked off the flats she'd been wearing.

Gage had removed more of his clothes during their banter, so that now he stood naked in front of her. She still had on her bra and panties, but he quickly rid her of them.

"So let's be clear," he said as he eased off the bed once more and found his wallet in the side pocket of his shorts.

"You're here to write and I'm on vacation."

Ava watched as he moved, loving the unfettered view of his butt and, when he turned toward her once more, his beautiful erection.

He handed her the condom packet and continued, "So this is just…"

She nodded as she ripped the foil and slid the latex out. "Is just one time. Right. Agreed."

Her hand moved slowly as she smoothed the condom over his thick length. She loved how he felt: hot, heavy, potent. She resisted the urge to moan, and he pushed her legs apart before coming over her on the bed.

"I'm going to enjoy this agreement," he whispered as he grinned down at her.

Biting on her bottom lip, Ava wrapped her arms around his shoulders and lifted her legs until they were around his waist. "Me, too," she said when the tip of his erection tapped her entrance, as if asking permission.

He rotated his hips. She lifted her bottom a bit off the bed until they were joined. He pushed inside her slowly. She dug her fingers into the skin of his back. He moaned until he was completely embedded inside her and her legs trembled. Tossing her head back against the bed, she gasped because there had never been a moment when she wanted anything as badly as she did right now. There'd never been another man to drive her to this point of desperation.

When he moved again it was to pull out of her slowly, and Ava thought she would scream. This was madness. It was torture. It was…intimate. It wasn't what she wanted, or rather, what she'd had in mind when she invited him up here. Her thought had been of him pounding into her with the same hungry ferocity that was roaring through her at this moment. She wanted to hear the sound of their bodies clapping together as they stroked and pushed to get to that delicious pinnacle. She did not want lovemaking because this had nothing to do with love.

As Ava had always done in her life, she took control. This way she was assured to get what she wanted. She moved quickly, catching him off guard and twisting their bodies until she came out on top. They both heaved out a breath as her hair draped down, the tips touching his cheeks as she grinned.

"I'll take it from here," she said and pushed back until she was straddled over him, his length still buried deep inside.

He gave her that smirk once more and lifted his arms so that his hands could cup her bare breasts.

"Do your thing," he replied.

And she did.

Ava rode him until they were both panting. His hands had gripped her hips, holding on to her tightly as she circled, lifted and sank down, taking everything he dished out and giving him all she had.

Minutes later, after they'd both moaned with their release, he wrapped his arms around her back, holding her against his chest. She felt his heart beating a quick rhythm, slowing only as time passed. She didn't move because she needed to catch her breath, as well. But the moment he lifted a hand and stroked the back of her head, once and then twice, as if he were enjoying the feel of her hair or something equally intimate, Ava pulled back.

"Bathroom," she whispered when he stared up at her, a quizzical look on his face.

He waited a beat before replying. "Yeah. Okay."

He released her, and Ava moved quickly, sliding off him and off the bed. "I have an early morning tomorrow," she began. "I want to get some work done before I'm scheduled to meet with Harper at her office. And I've been traveling all day so—"

He sat up, and Ava took another step back toward where she'd noticed a door, which she assumed led to the bathroom.

"Got it," he told her. "I'll get going."

"Ah, good night," she said and almost cringed at how crazy she must sound to him. *Good night. Thanks for the great sex. Now be gone.* Yes, definitely crazy.

Gage looked at her then, his gaze holding her to that spot. "A very good night, Ava."

When she couldn't decide whether he wanted her to say or do something else, or if she even wanted to say or do something else, Ave decided to cut her losses. She smiled and then turned before closing herself in the bathroom, leaving Gage—and the feeling that maybe they shouldn't have done this one more time—behind.

Chapter 4

"You're not listening."

"I am," Gage replied. He moved away from the windows where he'd been looking out at the town of Temptation.

He liked the view of thick trees, leaves already the rich orange, green and yellow of autumn and the rooftops of homes built in the colonial and Victorian style. Just beyond those homes was a field of grass that gave way to a thicker copse of trees. Farther east was the Lemil Mountain Lake, a popular tourist destination for Washington, DC, and Raleigh, North Carolina, residents, because of its less-than-five-hour drive. Feeding into the Potomac River, a tributary to the Chesapeake Bay, the lake area held fond memories for Gage.

Gray frowned before continuing. "This wing of the

hospital is dedicated to our mother. It's built to house the new obstetrics and gynecology department. As well as a spacious research facility to be dedicated to the study of—"

"Infertility and multiple births," Gage finished Gray's speech.

He turned away from the window to face his brother, who was standing a few feet away from him, dressed in black slacks, gray dress shirt and tie. Gage opted for a more casual look this morning, with jeans and a polo shirt. With one hand stuffed in his front pocket, he dragged the other down the back of his head.

"I'd like your hand in this," Gray said. "Dad wanted us to do this together."

Gage gave a wry laugh. "I'm still trying to wrap my head around you actually wanting to carry out Dad's wishes."

"We're not kids anymore, Gage," his brother told him.

Gray moved to stand closer to the alcove in the wall. Six feet tall, broad shouldered, intimidating glare—that was Grayson Taylor. He was always in control of his emotions, the situation around him, the people in his care, everything. Gray was born to be a leader. Gage, as the next youngest sextuplet, had always been carefree, fun-loving and easy to get along with. That's what Gemma would say. He wasn't the one in charge, nor was he the one the siblings thought would ever stay focused long enough to become successful. But he had, and now Gray was asking for his help. Pride swelled in Gage's chest at that thought, even though standing in this hospital talking about their father still managed to irritate him.

"I'm well aware of the fact that we're adults now. I mean, look at you with your lovely wife and four kids all settled in the house where we were born," he said.

Gray smiled. Happiness looked just as good on Gray as his expensive tailored suits.

"I love them more than I ever thought possible," Gray said.

Gage nodded.

"The way Mom loved us."

"Dad loved us, too," Gray said.

When Gage only raised a brow, Gray continued, "Look, I know about the past. We all know, Gage, we lived it. And we can't go back and change it. What we do now is what counts. It's the only thing we have control over, and it's all we have to leave our children."

"Unless you don't have children, like me," Gage countered as he fingered the keys in his pocket.

Touching that one key in particular had his mind circling back to the day he'd found out he didn't get the promotion. As disappointed as he'd been, Gage stayed at work that day. But instead of making the call to the foundation in Paris, he spent the day preparing for his time off. He drafted memos for Carrie to send to the other doctors in his department with notes about his patients with specific health concerns and tests that could not be rescheduled, and at the end of the day he returned to his apartment to pack for his trip.

The envelope that Gray had sent earlier this year was still unopened, sitting on the edge of Gage's desk in his home office. After their father's death, Gray had found envelopes marked for each of the sextuplets and a bank account under the name of Taylors of Temptation LLC. Each of the siblings were named as owners of the account holding a balance of 6.8 million dollars. In death, Theodor Taylor had been more than generous with the children he'd left for a production assistant all those years ago.

For endless moments Gage had simply stared at the envelope, knowing that now was the time. When he'd first received the envelope, he'd wanted to ignore it and whatever was inside of it, because it had come from his father. But since he was planning a return to his childhood home, Gage figured the time for ignoring the envelope had passed.

There were six sonogram pictures inside. They were lettered, so Gage put them in order from A to F. He was "Taylor Baby E" and he stared at that picture for some time before moving on to the only photograph from the envelope. It was of Theodor and Olivia holding their six little babies while sitting on the couch in the old Victorian house like one big happy family. On a ragged sigh, Gage had set all the pictures aside and checked the envelope one last time before tossing it into the trash. There was a key inside.

"Hey, you still with me?" Gray asked, interrupting Gage's memory.

Gage cleared his throat and pulled his hand out of his pocket.

"Ah, yeah. I'm good," Gage said. "It's cool. I'm on board. Do you have a plan for this wing? I mean, something in writing I can review and then add to if necessary?"

For a few seconds Gray just stared at Gage, then he took a few steps, his dress shoes quiet on the beige carpet.

"I do. They're in my home office. Is everything all right, Gage?"

"Of course everything's all right. Why would you ask me that?"

"Oh, because about five months ago Garrek suddenly appeared in town under the pretense of just stopping by for a visit. Turns out he had been reported as AWOL and needed an attorney to get his military career straight. So I'm asking you again, is everything all right?"

Gage had heard—via Gemma—of Garrek's troubles in the navy, and he'd reached out to his brother about six weeks ago to make sure that he was doing well in his new position.

"I should have come for a visit sooner," he told Gray. "I just didn't have time, or I didn't make time, if I listen to what Gemma has to say. I didn't get a promotion I was looking forward to at work, so I figured now was as good a time as any to take a step back and reevaluate things. And I opened that envelope you sent me."

Now Gray nodded. He folded his arms over his chest.

"What was in it?" Gray asked.

Gage shrugged. "Just some sonogram pictures of us and a picture of Mom and Dad."

"Speaking of that, we haven't had any success in figuring out who transferred that money into the Grand Cayman accounts."

"Garrek said they'd come from an address here in Temptation," Gage said.

"They did. But the house was used as a rehabilitation center at that time. There were at least twelve adults living there during the month the deposits were made."

Gage shook his head. "Is it really that important that we find out who put the money into those accounts? I mean, Dad is gone and whoever made the deposits is likely gone, too, so why shouldn't we just move on?"

"You don't want to know?"

"I don't want to live in the past," Gage told him. "My whole purpose in being here right now is to look forward to the future."

It had taken Gage a long time to be able to say that. He only wished that he totally meant it.

"And Ava Cannon is your future?"

Gage immediately tensed. He inhaled slowly, determined to keep his body and expressions as normal as possible.

"Ava Cannon is a television producer and writer. I have a professional relationship with her."

When Gray tossed his head back and laughed, Gage frowned.

His brother clapped a hand on his shoulder and said, "You keep telling yourself that."

Gage didn't reply to that comment because he hadn't come here to talk about Ava.

"Why don't you just tell me more about this facility?" he said instead.

And when Gray kindly obliged, Gage walked through the hallways of the hospital, listening to his brother talk about the town, the doctors and the additions he had made. He did not think about the vixen who had once again brought his body to a fierce release last night.

Or the fact that despite their declarations to the contrary, and what he knew he should do, Gage wanted her again.

Ava finished the last bite of the best meat lover's omelet she'd ever had while scrolling through pictures of tiny houses on her iPad.

"Presley Construction has never built a tiny house," Harper said from across the table where they sat in Ms. Pearl's Diner. "But one of my new interns is fascinated by them and has shown me some drafts she made of a couple. If you're really interested, I can set up a time for us to meet with Fred Randall. He's the best real estate agent in town. Actually, he's the only agent in town," she added with a chuckle.

Ava looked up as she reached for a napkin. Wiping her mouth, she chuckled, as well.

"Small town, I get it," she said. "I don't know if I'm ready for that step just yet. I only wanted to get your thoughts about the idea."

That was partially true. Looking at tiny houses had become one of Ava's guilty pleasures in the last couple of years. With work and warding off the blind dates her mother routinely sent her way occupying most of her time, there was rarely time to do the things she loved.

Harper sat back against the red vinyl-covered booth. Her sandy-brown hair was pulled back, hanging down in a straight ponytail. She had inquisitive brown eyes and a pretty freckled face.

"Are you sure you want to build a tiny house in Temptation? I mean, you're a producer and a writer. Why would you want to live here as opposed to in some luxury condo or mansion in LA?" Harper asked.

"I have a condo in LA. My mother is only twenty minutes away and drops by whenever she feels like it. My agent also drops by a lot instead of calling to discuss whatever business she has with me. So sometimes the condo can be a little too busy for writing. I'm always looking for a quiet place to get work done."

Harper chewed the last piece of her blueberry muffin. "I see. So this would be like a vacation home?"

"Something like that," Ava replied. "Your family has lived here for years, correct? Did the Presleys always know the Taylors?"

Ava had been up all night thinking of how she would start the conversation with Harper. She'd also been thinking about Gage and how they'd ended up in each other's arms once more. The last thought had given her much more trouble than the first.

"My father knew Theodor Taylor pretty well, and my grandfather knew Olivia Taylor's family. They both said the two seemed to be revitalized by the birth of the sextuplets. And there are people around here who still talk about having television crews here all the time, boosting revenue for local shops and B and Bs that housed them. It was a pretty exciting time."

"And now? I mean, in the years since they've been

gone, it seems like the town is still bustling without the added attention," Ava stated.

"You're right." Harper finished off her glass of water with lemon. "The town has come a long way and we've thrived over the years. But I have to admit that when Gray came back last year and saved the hospital and community center from going into a stranger's hands, the people here were relieved. It's like they've always wanted a Taylor to live here again."

Ava smiled as she digested that tidbit of hopeful information. "I'm sure you're happy they came back. Especially Garrek."

Harper's smile was quick and brilliant. It touched every part of her face from the rise of her high cheekbones to the little light that appeared in her eyes.

"I wasn't looking for love," she told Ava. "I was just trying to do a good job for Gray and Morgan, and then he appeared. It's been a roller-coaster ride, believe me, but one I'd take over and over again."

Ava tilted her head and resisted the urge to say, "Awww." She wasn't a romantic—far from it, if truth be told. Grand gestures like candlelit dinners, flowers and frilly words didn't mean much to her. Maybe because her parents didn't have that type of relationship. Or it could be that she'd watched too many girls in high school and college falling for one guy after another who gave them the words, the gestures, even the gifts, only to have the relationship ultimately break apart in the end. Either way, Ava had known all along that happy-ever-after was not for her. Tops on her agenda was professional success. After that, well, she'd settle at some point with a happy-for-now ending.

"I wish I could have met him," she said instead. "Gray seems like a nice man. He's definitely devoted to Morgan and the children."

"Oh, there's no doubt about that. They all have his heart and soul completely. I love being with them at the house because that love just radiates throughout the walls. And I'm glad that Gray's move back here seems to be bringing the other siblings back to Temptation one by one."

"Really? Do you expect the sisters to return to town soon?" Ava asked.

That would be perfect for her.

Harper had just begun to shake her head when her gaze drifted over Ava's shoulder and her smile spread once more.

"I'm not sure," she said. "Morgan's definitely trying for that big Christmas gathering. But for now, I think the whole town is just curious about his return," Harper said.

Before Ava could ask who she was referring to, or even turn to look in the direction of Harper's gaze, he was there. Standing at the table, staring down at them with dark brown eyes and that sexy-as-hell smile.

"Good morning, ladies," Gage said.

"Good morning," Harper said. "I thought you and Gray were having breakfast at the hospital this morning."

"We were," he answered. "But trust me, I've had

enough hospital cafeteria food. Thought I'd try to find some real sustenance here."

Harper and Ava both chuckled.

"Well, Ms. Pearl makes the best waffles. I can't eat them on mornings when I have to work because I get so full and they put me right to sleep. But you should definitely try them."

Gage was nodding his agreement when Harper began to stand.

"I have to get going to another site now, but, Ava, if you want to continue talking about the tiny house, just give me a call."

"I will," Ava answered while ignoring the questioning rise of Gage's brow. "Thanks so much for taking the time to talk to me about it."

"No problem. I'd love to work with you on the project. Just keep me posted. And, you, I guess I'll see around," Harper said to Gage. "Maybe tonight at the wine festival?"

"There's a wine festival tonight?" Ava asked.

Harper smiled as she moved out of the booth and Gage took her seat. "There's always a festival or celebration or some type of event going on in Temptation. We're heading into our fall festivities now. So tonight's the wine festival, and then in a few weeks we'll have the fall festival and pumpkin-carving contest. After that we're full swing into the holidays, and believe me you haven't seen anything until you've seen Temptation all lit up and ready to celebrate Thanksgiving and Christmas."

Again, Ava wanted to sigh with contentment. She'd

never lived in a small town and so had never experienced festivals or pumpkin-carving contests. Her childhood had consisted of boarding schools, summer camps, etiquette classes, ballet lessons and formal dinner parties.

"Well, I love wine, so I'm definitely there," she immediately replied.

"Then I guess I'm going, too," Gage said cheerfully.

"Great!" Harper said, excitement clear in her voice. "See you both later."

It was that excitement that put Ava on edge. Who was she kidding? Gage was putting her on edge. Again.

"So you love wine," Gage said immediately when they were alone.

Ava was saved from providing an answer when the waitress came over to ask what he wanted. He ordered the waffles and orange juice, and Ava thought the woman's face might actually crack, she was grinning at him so broadly. She shook her head at the obvious infatuation and wondered if Gage dealt with this all the time. And if he liked it.

"I need to get back to my writing," she said, suddenly irritated.

Gage reached a hand out quickly to touch her wrist. "Keep me company while I have breakfast," he said. "Otherwise that waitress is going to keep coming back, and I'm really not in the mood for that type of attention right now."

"So that not-so-subtle flirtation happens to you all the time?"

He shrugged. "Sometimes."

"And you normally like it, but not today. I see. Well, what makes today so different?"

Damn. She sounded testy and hated it.

Gage sat back, resting his hands in his lap now. "I don't know what's different," he told her. "I'm still trying to figure it out. But, maybe it's you."

No. It couldn't be her.

"That's ridiculous. We're not committed to each other in any way," she stated. But inside she wondered if that should actually be a question.

The thought was totally foolish. This was Gage Taylor, an employee and the subject of her new project.

"No. We're not," he told her. "But we are sleeping together."

"It was just for one ni—" she started to say.

Gage arched a brow again as her lips snapped shut.

"Look, I'm not in the market for a relationship any more than you are. But I like honesty. So I try to be as honest with myself as possible."

Ava tried to ignore the sting she felt when he said "honesty."

When he continued, she took a sip from her glass.

"We've been together twice now. That doesn't make us a couple, but it certainly classifies us as sleeping together."

She couldn't argue the logic.

He nodded and thanked the waitress when his food and juice were delivered.

The offer to get him anything he wanted and yet another bright smile had Ava's fingers fisting at her sides.

She forced herself to breathe and relax because she was being ridiculous.

"Well, I can work while you eat," she said and then looked down to her iPad once more.

"Or you can tell me why you're talking about building a house here in Temptation if you just came for a writing retreat," he said.

Right, Ava thought as she took another drink from her glass. She could tell Gage why she was lying about her real reason for being here. That was sure to go over well.

Chapter 5

"I'm still waiting for a call back on that rain check."

Ava turned at the statement and found herself staring up at Craig Presley.

It was a little after seven in the evening, and since daylight saving time hadn't occurred yet, the sun was just waning in preparation to set. The Fall Wine Festival was being held at Treetop Park, which was just down the street from Temptation's town hall.

After spending her day walking around the town and talking to the wide array of citizens, Ava had headed back to the B and B, where she'd showered, checked emails and dressed for the festival. When she'd stepped outside again, it was to learn that the evening weather had shifted to a more comfortable temperature than earlier, so her decision to wear the navy blue ankle pants and beige sleeveless blouse with nude-colored sandals was a smart one. She'd driven the fuel-efficient hybrid rental car and parked on the street across from the park. The one with all the colorful houses.

"Oh, hi, Craig. I'm sorry. I've just been busy writing and stuff."

He smiled, a really nice smile. Craig was a good-looking guy who probably had women smiling at him the same way Gage did. She shook her head in an attempt to get Gage out of her mind.

"It's cool," he said. "I understand. We just finished up a big project, so I'm glad to have the festival to unwind a little."

"It looks like a good crowd," she said turning her attention toward the stalls and tents where people were lined up.

"Come on, let's start tasting," Craig told her and took her hand before she could respond.

They walked past two stalls with super long lines and when Craig joked about people in Temptation not being afraid to get drunk in public, Ava laughed.

"What's so funny?" a woman who had just stepped in front of them asked.

She wore gray dress pants with a purple blouse. Her hair was feathered back from her carefully made-up face, and her lips pursed as her eyes assessed every part of Ava.

"Hi, Ms. Millie," Craig said, gripping Ava's hand a little tighter.

"Craig," the woman—Millie—replied. "You have

manners, son, I know your daddy taught them to you. So make the introductions."

Rude didn't quite seem to describe this woman.

"I'm Ava Cannon," she said because she was a grown woman and did not need Craig to make introductions for her. "I'm visiting Temptation on a writing retreat."

She was losing track of how many times she told that lie, but didn't want to think about that at the moment.

"Ava Cannon," Millie said and continued to look as if Ava had body odor or food stuck in her teeth.

"I'm Millie Randall. Chairperson of the chamber of commerce. We usually like to welcome the visitors to Temptation personally. But I didn't know you were here. Not until this morning at least when I saw you coming out of the diner with Gage Taylor."

"Yes. I had a breakfast meeting with Harper this morning, and then Gage showed up." For whatever reason, Ava felt like she needed to explain.

"And now you're here with Craig. Well, it seems you're certainly getting around. Are you writing about the men of Temptation?" Millie asked.

"I hope not," Gage said from behind Ava.

Her heart skipped a beat at the sound of his voice, but she did not turn to look at him. This situation had gone from strange to uncomfortable in record time.

"Hey, Gage," Craig said. "Glad you could make it to your first wine festival in Temptation."

Gage had come to stand next to Millie, across from Craig and Ava.

"I thought Ava and I would enjoy our first festival together," Gage said.

"Hmmmm." Millie made the sound and looked skeptically from Gage to Ava, letting her gaze linger there.

Ava wanted to scream. Or turn and run back to her car and drive all the way back to LA. Anything to not be in the middle of something she didn't even understand herself.

This was silly. She wasn't doing anything wrong. Gage had said so himself—they weren't a couple.

"I just got here and ran into Craig," she said.

"And then we ran into Ms. Millie," Craig said.

Millie nodded. "And now we're all here together."

Ava remained silent.

"Why don't you come with me, Craig? I have something in my car for your father. You can take it to him."

Craig looked at Ava.

"She'll be fine with me," Gage said in a stiff voice.

"Come, Craig," Millie commanded and turned around to start walking away.

With an audible sigh, Craig released Ava's hand. "I'll be back," he said to her.

"Oh, don't worry about it," she told him. "I'll probably leave in a few minutes anyway. I still have work to do."

He gave her a quick smile as he back-walked in the direction Millie was heading. "That's fine, but my rain check still holds."

Ava smiled. "No problem."

But there was a problem. When they were alone, Ava felt it. She couldn't explain it, but she felt it in the way Gage was staring at her.

"So," she said finally because she was tired of standing there feeling ridiculous. "I'm going to just grab one drink, and then I'll be going."

He wasn't frowning, but he didn't look happy either. "I think we both need a drink."

That was an understatement, and the first booth they made it to, Ava eagerly accepted one of the red wines they were offering. It went down smooth and had a sweet taste, so she took another. She didn't know if Gage was trying the white or the red wine, but she finished her second and was just swallowing the third, when he stopped her.

"Slow down there. You have to pace yourself when you come to these things. Otherwise I'll have to carry you back to the B and B."

Gage's voice was deep, and rubbed against all of her nerve endings with quick and potent efficiency. The fact that she was still undeniably attracted to him after their two hookups was not nearly as surprising as the low hum of guilt she'd been carrying with her since answering his question about her tiny house quest this morning.

"Oh, no worries about that," she replied. "I can hold my liquor."

"Really? Spending your evenings in bars putting back a few is how you roll?"

His tone was lighter than just moments ago, but Ava didn't feel like laughing.

She shrugged. "Boarding school wasn't nearly as prim and proper as my mother thought it would be."

He nodded. "So you were that girl, huh? Boarding schools, fancy cars, Ivy League college."

"You attended Columbia for undergrad and medical school," she said.

"Checked up on me, did you?"

"I did my research," she said. "As I do with all the people I work with."

"That makes sense," he replied.

He took the empty glass from her, their fingers brushing with the action. She was just about to pull her hand away when Gage reached for it.

"I'm not a holding-hand type of guy," he said, staring down at her fingers.

Ava was about to say that she wasn't either, but that would have been silly since Craig had been holding her hand when Gage joined them.

After a few seconds more, he released her hand and returned her cup to the stall.

Okay, she was being foolish, there was no reason this should feel awkward. She wasn't committed to Gage, and she hadn't been doing anything wrong with Craig.

So when Gage turned to her again she started to walk, and he joined her.

"I know this is your first wine tasting in Temptation, but have you been to one of these before?" she asked after they'd passed a few stalls decorated with plastic vines and grapes.

"I've been to wine and cheese receptions in the city, and I have a friend who lives in the Hamptons who has an annual get-together to showcase his family's vineyard, but this is different."

"I agree," Ava replied. "This is different."

He may have thought she was referring to the wine

festival, but she wasn't. Her thoughts were circling more around the fact that she was actually thinking about everything she'd said to Gage in the last two days, versus the two times they'd spent in each other's arms, and the truth of why she was here. It was complicated, and while she could simply tell him everything right here and right now, she didn't.

What Ava did do, however—and to her utter embarrassment—was trip over some power cords that had been stretched across the grass from one booth to another. With her arms flailing forward, she prayed she wouldn't fall flat on her face, but her feet were already doing some type of clumsy dance that almost assured that fate.

"Whoa, there," Gage said.

His arms went around her waist, and pulled her back against him as his words whispered into her ear.

A few choice curse words and a deep breath later, Ava's feet were once again solidly on the ground while her cheeks fused with heat. "These cords should probably be stretched behind the tents. Instead of across the path where people have to walk."

"That's very true," Gage replied.

His lips were close to her ear so that his words were warm and…oddly sexy. The arm he still had wrapped around her waist felt almost possessive, and her blouse rode up her back at their close proximity.

"I'm okay now," Ava said nervously and attempted to move out of his grasp. But he held on.

"You sure? How many glasses of wine did you have before I showed up?" he asked with a chuckle.

Ava managed a smile even though she was beginning to feel pretty warm in the cool autumn evening air.

"I'm not drunk, Gage. Just a little clumsy, I guess."

Even though she'd never been known to be clumsy
before. Nor had she considered herself easily flustered
by some guy.

Pulling down her shirt, she looked at Gage and tried
to keep her smile in place. "The cords are a hazard and
could incite a lawsuit."

"Say that a little louder, and I'm sure by night's end,
everyone in town will fall over themselves trying to
make your visit here as safe and enjoyable as possible.
That's how threats tend to work here," Gage said.

"I didn't," she replied. "I mean, I wouldn't. I was just
saying that someone else might. And how do you even
know how people here would act? This is your first time
back in Temptation since you were a kid."

For a few seconds Gage looked at her oddly, like
maybe she shouldn't know that about him. Or maybe
he just didn't like hearing that little bit of truth.

"And besides, different people have different reac-
tions," she said after clearing her throat.

They were standing in the middle of the walking path
and a woman bumped into Ava, mumbling a quick "excuse me" as she moved to another booth.

"Let's get out of the way," Gage said, touching her
elbow.

They walked past the row of tents to an open area
where lawn chairs and blankets were spread out around
the gazebo.

"Morgan and Gray are trying to get a babysitter so

they can come out tonight. So I was sent down here early with blankets and instructions to get a good spot facing the stage."

"I didn't know there would be music," Ava said and turned to look at the men setting up instruments in the large gazebo.

This was a perfect location to view a concert. There were two large screens set up on either side of the gazebo for those in the back to see.

"Yeah, I hear they do this twice a year," he told her. "Have a seat."

Ava looked at Gage and then down to the blankets before taking him up on his offer and sitting down. He followed, but he leaned back so that he was propped up on one elbow right beside her. If she lowered her hand, she could touch the small mole just beneath his right eye.

She didn't, of course. That would have been... intimate.

"I don't remember anything like this when I lived here. I was only seven when we left, so most of my memories consist of riding bikes up and down our street and going to the lake for picnics," he said abruptly.

Ava waited a beat before following his lead.

"Did you like living here?" she asked.

He reached out and touched the tips of the belt knotted at her waist.

"It was a house in a town," he replied. "At the time, I didn't know anything else."

"But it must have been fun in that big house, and being celebrities." The last word was spoken quietly.

His fingers paused on the material as he slowly looked up at her.

"It wasn't a choice," he said. "We never had a choice in the matter."

This time they would, Ava thought. She would lay it all out for them, and she would offer them the opportunity to say what they would like their show to be.

"I know a few child stars, and they're ecstatic about being on television. Mostly they're happy when the workday is over for them and they can play with whatever new and not-yet-on-the-market toy their agent has acquired for them."

She chuckled lightly, but Gage did not crack a smile.

"When you build your tiny house, you should look for a space like this," he said after a brief pause. "A wide-open area with a killer view."

So they were back to her lie…or rather, her omission.

"A view of a stage?" she asked jokingly.

"No," he replied with a shake of his head. "Look beyond the stage, Ava. Look at what nature has for you."

She did as he said. She shouldn't have. The moment she saw the mountaintops pressing into the fading purple and blush sky, she sighed and silently agreed. This was a view she could wake up to each morning. If she were actually moving to Temptation.

"It's a great view," she said. "Do you recall waking up to it when you lived here?"

"As I said before, I left when I was seven," he replied. "My mother packed us up and moved us to Florida. We lived in a house on Pensacola Bay, so my view there was of the water. I've loved the water ever since."

"I don't know how to swim," she said absently. "I grew up in Beverly Hills. We had a pool, but I never learned how to swim."

It sounded strange. Everybody knew how to swim. Right? It wasn't her fault that she had piano lessons during summer camp when other children were swimming in lakes and sleeping in tents. And when her parents had pool parties, Ava wasn't invited. When her parents weren't having a pool party, the pool was gated off because Eleanor didn't want Ava to fall in and drown, since she didn't know how to swim.

"I can teach you," Gage stated evenly.

"What?"

"I can teach you how to swim," he repeated.

Ava looked down at him again, just as the music began. More people had joined them on the grass, some standing, others sitting on their own blankets. Gage pushed himself up to a sitting position and scooted closer to her. After the first few melodic strands were played by the jazz quartet, she replied, "I'd like that."

She'd always wanted to learn how to swim, and what better way to learn than in Gage Taylor's arms?

Gage had reserved the indoor pool at the community center for a few hours. He was going to teach Ava how to swim. And that was all. He could do that.

What he couldn't seem to do, to his dismay, was forget how he'd felt seeing her holding hands with Craig Presley. It didn't matter. Gage had spent the last two days telling himself that. Ava Cannon was not his to feel possessive over. Yet, he'd wanted to snatch her hand away from Craig's that night. He'd wanted to let Craig and any other guy in this town know that she was with him. But she wasn't, at least not in that way.

She was, however, walking toward him wearing a simple yellow bikini that looked like sunshine against her golden brown skin, beneath a sheer white shirt that brushed over her knees. Her hair was piled atop her head in a way that reminded him of how she looked in the moments after they'd both reached their climax. Her face was free of makeup and as lovely as he'd ever seen it.

"Hi," she said when they were standing just a few feet away from each other.

"Hi yourself," he said over a tongue that had grown thick with lust. "Glad you could join me."

Gage was lounging in the hot tub while he'd waited for her to arrive. The way his body instantly reacted to seeing her made him grateful for the warm rolling bubbles around him.

"Are we swimming or soaking?" she asked after a few seconds of silence.

"Swimming, of course." He resisted the urge to frown as he turned his back to her and walked up the three steps to exit the hot tub. His black swim trunks were baggy enough—he hoped—so that when he turned to face her, he didn't embarrass himself and possibly her at the same time.

"I did tell you that I've never had a swim lesson before," she was saying as she moved to one of the lounge chairs and dropped the large bag she'd been carrying. "Right?"

"You did. So we'll take this slow."

But the moment she grabbed the hem of that shirt and pulled it up over her head, all thoughts of slow vanished from his mind. He wanted to take her, hard and fast, right there on the lounge chair, or in the pool.

"Great," she said as she turned to him. "I appreciate you taking the time to do this."

Yeah, he was doing a great deed here. Teaching her how to swim. And thinking of how quickly he could get her out of that skimpy bikini and on top of him.

"It's no problem. Everyone should know how to swim."

Gage cleared his throat and mentally kicked himself for being a horny cad. She was serious about learning, so he needed to get serious about teaching. Which would probably involve touching.

With a shake of his head, he led them to the side of the pool that was five feet deep.

"Come on in," he told her after stepping into the chilly water. He immediately bent his knees so that he was submerged up to his neck, acclimating himself to the new temperature.

"Oh!" she said with a shiver after sitting on the side of the pool and putting her feet in first. "Cold."

"Yeah," he replied with a nod and a smile.

Gage walked over to where she sat, touching her ankles and then smoothing his hands up and down her legs, introducing the cold water to her skin.

"You have beautiful eyes," he said while his hands continued to move. "That's one of the first things I noticed about you."

"They're just brown," she said and tilted her head while staring at him.

"They're expressive," he replied. "Whatever you don't say with words is mirrored in your eyes."

She looked away, and Gage moved in closer until his shoulders were between her knees. He moved a hand from her leg and cupped her cheek, turning her gently until she faced him again.

"That's how I knew you wanted the same thing I did. In the studio, each time we looked at each other, I knew," he said, his voice gruff with growing arousal, and just a hint of something more.

"There's a professional code of conduct," she replied before her tongue snaked out to lick her bottom lip quickly. "I like to follow my own rules. Especially on set. And sleeping with my consultant wasn't a good idea."

His hand slipped down to the smooth column of her neck. "The idea may not have been good, at first," he said. "But damn if we weren't great together, Ava. Both times."

Gage watched as she tried to deny it. She opened her mouth, snapped her lips closed and thought about what to say. But her eyes were already telling him—and his body—what he wanted to know.

"I don't know how to explain it either," he said. "I'm not usually so taken by one woman."

She nodded. "Right. You're like the rolling stone," she said.

Gage froze, the lyrics to The Temptations' famous song playing in his mind. "No. That was my father."

"I—" Ava began, but Gage touched a finger to her lips.

"I can't think of anyone but you. Since the first day on set, it's been you in my mind day and night. I've given up trying to explain it," he told her.

In fact, he'd decided that maybe it was best not to overanalyze this. They were attracted to each other, and that was that.

"Besides," he said, bringing his other arm up to wrap around her waist, pulling her closer to the edge of the pool, "we're not technically working together right now. The second season doesn't start taping until next year."

The slight tilt of her lips had his chest tightening.

"You've thought of everything, haven't you?"

"No," Gage said. "I've only thought of you, Ava. Only you."

In the next instant Gage was pulling her into the water with him, wrapping her legs around his waist as his lips met hers. Her arms were twined around his neck, and their tongues joined together in a delicious duel.

That tightening in Gage's chest simmered to a warm glow that spread throughout his body, even as they stood in the cold pool water. Her breasts pressed into his bare chest as she licked hungrily over his lips. His fingers splayed over her back before moving down to grip the plump globes of her bottom. She tightened her legs around him, pressing her center into him. Gage groaned with the deep pangs of sexual hunger that pierced through him.

He moved his fingers down farther, beneath the rim

of her bikini bottom until he could feel the crease of her backside. *Farther*, Gage thought. He needed to go farther, to touch more, to feel… The second he pushed through the warm folds of her center, the pounding of his heart grew louder, echoing in his ears.

Ava arched her back, her hands moving to his shoulders, blunt-tipped nails digging into his skin. Through partially opened eyes, Gage watched as passion played over the delicate features of her face with his touch. Tracing his fingers back and forth through her arousal-coated folds had her eyes closing, lips parting as she moaned.

She felt like heaven, like the finest silk beneath his fingers. When she whispered his name and Gage pressed one finger deep inside her entrance, Ava bucked over him, and Gage eased in another finger. Her hips began to move, pumping against his fingers as he thrust them in and out of her. Water sloshed around them, creating a cool reprieve from the fiery passion rolling over them at this moment. She pulled her bottom lip between her teeth, in a look that was as enticing as any *Playboy* centerfold Gage had ever seen. Her head was tilted back, breasts cupped in the yellow material jutting forward. Her nipples were hard, and Gage ran his tongue over his bottom lip as he imagined taking them in his mouth.

Pumping furiously in and out of her now, he felt his arousal stretching to painful proportions behind the material of his trunks. Her arms had begun to shake; hair that had been pulled up into a messy bun had escaped and now flowed freely down her back. She moaned again, this time long and loud as her legs tightened around him and her nails pressed hard into the skin of his shoulders. Gage moved his fingers faster inside her, feeling her muscles tighten in an attempt to constrict the motion. Her release came strong and hot over his fingers as she moaned his name before leaning forward and dropping her forehead to his chest.

Seconds later and with his fingers still inside her, Gage heard her whisper, "If I'd known this was what a swim lesson consisted of, I may have signed up sooner."

Gage chuckled. He pulled his fingers from her and gripped her hips, letting her legs fall from his waist. When he was sure her feet touched the bottom of the pool, he looked down at her and then hugged her close on impulse.

"I would have offered sooner," he told her.

Much sooner. If he'd known what it would feel like to be with a woman more than once, Gage was certain he would have tried it.

But something told him that it wasn't the number of times that was making the difference. It was Ava.

Chapter 6

Ava felt both at home and out of place at the same time. Morgan's kitchen was homey and welcoming. The soft white cabinets and sage-green paint accented the stainless steel appliances. The countertop full of baby bottles, some empty and some full, a Batman thermos and four covered containers of different sizes kept the country chic design from looking staged.

"My granny loves to cook," Morgan said as she sat across the island from Ava. "The entire time I was pregnant, she talked about all the things she was going to make so that Gray and the kids would have good home-cooked meals while I was recuperating. Whereas my sister Wendy was all set to hit every fast-food and delivery spot in the vicinity to make sure we were fed. The babies are a month old now, and Granny's still sending food over here as if I'm bedridden."

She laughed and Ava smiled. Morgan Taylor was friendly and easy to talk to. She was also observant, Ava thought while finishing the last bite of the fresh-sliced country ham sandwich she'd had for lunch. The invitation from Morgan had come three days after her swim lesson with Gage, and the morning after her second run-in with Millie. The older woman had been with her girlfriends this time, coming out of the library as Morgan walked by. As Otis had already heard about the scene by the time she'd returned to the B and B, Ava figured the lunch invitation was for Morgan to find out firsthand what had happened.

"I never knew my grandparents," Ava replied and used a napkin to wipe her mouth and fingers. "My father's parents did not care for my mother, and by relation, never wanted to see me. And my mother's parents were deceased before I was born."

"Oh, that's sad. I'm sorry," Morgan said. She reached a hand across the table to touch Ava's.

The diamond ring on Morgan's left hand was more like a blinding rock of ice glittering up at her. It should have been too opulent for Morgan's small hand and wholesome personality, but it wasn't. Instead, Ava looked down at the ring and then up to Morgan and saw the love this woman had for her family. In turn, Gray Taylor had shown his love for his wife with this extravagant ring and the loving renovations to this house. It was sweet and on a level of emotion that Ava couldn't really understand.

"Thank you, but it worked out. I kind of liked being an only child, as well, and not having to attend any of the family functions my classmates always complained about," Ava told her.

There'd always been a fear of more people sharing her mother's thoughts and narrow-minded nature. With that in mind, Ava had been totally fine with not having any relatives to deal with.

"Well, we're all about functions here in Temptation. And everyone around town is just like family. Or they like to think they are," Morgan said.

"You're talking about what happened with me and Millie," Ava said when Morgan had pulled her hand away and settled back on the stool. "I'm not sure how all that came about."

Morgan waved a hand. "Millie planned it, that's how. That's what she does. You've been in town for two weeks and everyone's been buzzing about the TV producer who knows the Taylors. It's a wonder she hadn't gotten to you before now."

That made sense. When Millie had approached Ava at her car, it had been with a sugary sweet smile and wintry cool eyes.

"I did get the impression that she'd been waiting to speak to me again," Ava added. "The first words out of her mouth were 'So you're the one who works with Gage Taylor. What else are you two cooking up?' If I wasn't already used to dealing with the press on occasion, I might not have been prepared for the unannounced verbal assault."

Morgan chuckled. "I'm sure that's exactly what it

was, a verbal assault. Millie has a mouth on her, and she doesn't care what anyone else has to say, she's going to speak her piece every time."

"That's fine, but I hope she hears as well as she talks. I made it clear to her once more that Gage and I worked on *Doctor's Orders* together and that I was just here on a writing retreat."

"Oh, I'm sure you did," Morgan said. "That's just not what Millie wants to hear. But it seems like you have the right attitude where Millie's concerned."

"She can think what she wants," Ava told her. "People always do."

"That is certainly true."

Water boiled on the stove, and Morgan slipped off the stool to tend to it. Ava watched as she poured the boiled water into a plastic jug and then put those lidded containers into a shopping bag. Probably to go back to her Granny.

"I don't care what these new formulas call for, I still do it the old-fashioned way—boiling my water first." She smiled. "Never could manage breast-feeding, especially not with twins."

Ava smiled in return and continued to watch curiously until Morgan returned to her seat and picked up her glass.

"Does Gray want more children?"

Morgan choked on the water she'd just sipped.

"Not now," Ava said, reaching to hand Morgan a napkin. "I'm sorry, I should have been clearer. I just mean overall, does he want a big family like his parents had?"

"No," Morgan said, shaking her head. "Gray doesn't

want any of the things his parents had. Neither does Gage or their youngest sister, Gia. Garrek, Gemma and Gen think differently about what happened."

"That's Genevieve, right?"

Morgan nodded. "They used to call her Vivi when they were younger, but after their mother passed, Gray said she wanted to be called Gen. It was too hard to hear the nickname her mother had given her, I suppose."

From all her research, Ava had surmised that the Taylor children suffered traumatically from the early events of their lives. A part of her ached for them.

"When Theodor left, the siblings were emotionally split down the middle. Three of them sided with Olivia, while the other three held back from taking a side at all. Gage and Gia stuck close as the two youngest, but from what Gray has told me, they were adamant that their father never be forgiven for what he did to their family."

"That must have been hard," Ava said, thinking of Gage.

"You know about the Taylors of Temptation, don't you? You would have looked into Gage's past before you hired him. Isn't that how it works?"

Morgan was a schoolteacher, but she asked questions like a trained investigator. Not overtly like a police interrogation, but with an easy flow that garnered the information she wanted. Ava had only to decide whether Morgan's inquisitiveness meant she was a friend or foe in the quest to get the contract signed.

"I did," Ava replied. Again, she was telling a partial truth. She'd only looked into Gage's past a few weeks ago. "But nothing told of the emotion. I mean, there's the story of what happened and that's it. The allegiances, the toll this entire situation took on this family was not easily surmised in any of the stories I read."

"It can't be," Morgan said with a shake of her head. "Their grief is real and raw, and it lives inside them every day. Not just with the death of their parents, but also with reliving the demise of their family. That's what hurt them most. And at the same time, it's what holds them together."

"I understand," Ava said.

"Do you? Because if you do, you'll know that falling in love is not going to be easy for Gage. But when he does, he's going to fall with all his heart. Are you ready for that?"

"What? Why are you asking me that? I'm just here for a—"

"For a writing retreat, I know," Morgan said with a knowing look. "Of all the places in the world, you picked this town. And you picked it after you'd been working with Gage. I've seen how the two of you look at each other. At dinner on my deck that first night, and again at the wine festival when we finally showed up."

"Morgan, I think you're mistaken."

Morgan shook her head. "I don't think I am. But, to be fair, I hope you're getting lots of writing done while you're here."

The sound of crying poured into the room, and both women stared at the baby monitor sitting on the counter near the refrigerator.

"Duty calls," Morgan said cheerily. "I'll be right back."

Ava nodded, and the moment she was alone she let her head fall forward to rest on the cool surface of the island. She groaned with her eyes closed as she replayed the conversation. Morgan wasn't buying her being here for a writer's retreat. Was that good or bad? Was she going to tell Gray? And if she did, how was Gage going to react when he found out she'd been lying to him and his family?

"Well, look who stepped out of her writing lair."

Ava wanted to groan again. She wanted to slink out of this kitchen and take herself back to LA as quickly as possible.

"Hi!" she said instead, in a voice that was way too happy for the way she was actually feeling.

"Haven't seen you out and about in a few days," Gage said while walking farther into the kitchen.

"Ah, no. I mean, I've been out. Just trying to get some writing done. But I do come out and walk around town. I like seeing the sights and the people."

She was babbling, so she snapped her lips closed and stared at him instead. He looked good. Of course he did. Gage always looked good. Jeans and polo shirts had never actually appealed to her before, but on him, they were hot.

"That's great. I've been sort of busy, too."

"Oh, really?"

"Yes. Don't sound so surprised." He chuckled as he took a bottled water out of the refrigerator and opened it.

"Well, you are on vacation, right? And your fast *Playboy* car has been heard zooming on the streets around town. Otis told me that." Ava smiled at the recollection.

Otis had come to her room with a tray of lemonade and Nana Lou's sugar cookies that day. He made a point of visiting her while she was writing, always bringing snacks and tidbits of town gossip. He was a thoughtful but nosy man, and she liked him.

"Fast *Playboy* car, huh? For the record, it's a Jaguar XE, and she is pretty sweet when she gets going," he said before taking a drink.

Ava could watch him for days. Whether he was falling on his butt during a volleyball game, or lounging on a blanket in a park, he was very easy on the eyes. And she liked the way he looked back at her.

"You and your women," she said with a smirk.

"Hey, Gage," Morgan said, returning to the kitchen with an adorable bundle of baby wrapped in a blue Baby Mickey blanket. "Where's Gray? He said you two were meeting with a new doctor at the hospital and then he was coming home to relieve me."

Gage set the bottle on the counter and went to Morgan, gingerly taking the baby from her arms.

"That's why I'm here. To deliver a message. Gray's tied up with an overseas conference call. He'd planned to take it here at the house, but his assistant confused the times, and he had to get on the call in one of the offices at the hospital."

"But I have a meeting with Mrs. Camby about the Fall Festival. She's been the chair of this festival for the last fifty years and never leaves her house for a meeting. I don't really want to take the twins over there."

Gage had been smiling down at baby Ryan, rubbing a finger over the child's small hand. "JoEllen Camby?"

"Yes," Morgan replied. She picked her cell phone up off the counter and started scrolling on it. "Wendy's doing a double shift at the hospital today, and Granny has the food drive at the church. You remember Mrs. Camby?"

"Not really," Gage answered. "She and my mother kept in touch after we left. I remember seeing cards come in the mail from her."

"Oh," Morgan said. "Well, you two are in luck because I need a babysitter."

"A babysitter?" Ava asked.

Morgan nodded. "Yes. Two babies and two of you. I should only be gone an hour. Nana Lou is picking Jack and Lily up after school to take them to Movies and Games Day at the community center. So you won't have to worry about them."

Ava looked over at the baby Gage was holding. He looked pretty comfortable with the little boy in his arms. Ava, on the other hand, felt a wave of panic. "I've never watched a baby before."

She'd never even held one.

"I'll teach you." Gage winked at her.

Morgan looked from him to Ava with a raised brow. "Uh-huh, right. Okay. So it's time for them to be fed. Their next bottles are ready and on the counter over there. I'll finish the new formula when I get back. Ryan always wants to go first. I've already changed him. Emma's going to be up in a few minutes because she doesn't let Ryan get too much of a head start. When she wakes up, just change her diaper. Gage, give Ava my cell number. Call me if there's an emergency, and thank you both so much!"

Morgan was out of the kitchen in a blur of blue sweatpants and hoop earrings. Ava didn't know what to say.

Gage came to stand in front of her. He was so close she could smell the baby scent of Ryan, even though she resisted the urge to look down at what she knew was a bundle of cuteness.

"First things first," he said. "I don't have women. My car is *Jezebel*, and my yacht is *Seraphine*. Those are the only ladies in my life."

"Oh," was all Ava could manage as a reply.

Then her cell phone rang, and Emma's cry blasted through the intercom. Pulling the phone out of her back pants pocket, she frowned when she saw Jenner's name on the screen.

"Okay, well, I guess I'd better get…ah, both of these," she said and then repeated Morgan's previous quick exit.

She needed to get away from the extremely comfortable-looking scene of Gage holding a baby and still looking sexy. And also of Gage telling her that he didn't have a woman…so what was she?

Had she been jealous?

Gage walked to the counter and picked up one of the bottles. He removed the top and placed the nipple between Ryan's small lips. This was his nephew, a new generation of Taylor children. That made Gage smile.

Even while his mind circled back to the way Ava had said "you and your women."

He'd felt the need to clarify the women in his life, and in doing so he realized how lonely it sounded. So he didn't have a significant other. Was that such a big deal? She didn't either—or did she? It occurred to him that between their sexual tête-à-têtes and declaring that there was nothing serious between them, they had never verified that they were each available for such dalliances.

They were adults; that's what mattered. Any agreements they made were mature and thought out. There was nothing to regret.

Then why had he felt like a complete ass when she mentioned his women?

"What do I do now?" he asked, looking down into the innocent eyes of his nephew.

Of course Ryan didn't answer, and after a few seconds Gage wondered why he was even asking. Not his nephew, but himself. There was nothing between him and Ava that he should be wondering about. Hadn't he told himself that in the last few days when he'd been so immersed in the work at the hospital?

"What are you doing staying here so late? Shouldn't you be out with Ava?" Gray had asked last night when they'd both been working late.

"No. I'm not the married one, big brother," Gage had replied.

"Nope, your situation is worse," Gray had stated. "It's the dating phase. You have to work much harder on that part of a relationship."

Gage had shaken his head so hard, his neck had ached. "Not in a relationship either."

Gray's head had tilted back as he'd laughed. "Come on, Gage. You're smarter than that. Why else do you think she followed you here?"

"She didn't follow me and we're not dating," he'd replied.

"If you say so. But you've been seen at the wine festival together and then again at the community center. We can call those outings, but that's just a soft word for dates."

"She's…we…it's not serious." That was all that Gage had managed to come up with.

"Yet," Gray had stated. "And don't tell me you're not the marrying kind because I know better. There's no such thing. A man can commit when he wants to."

"I'm perfectly capable of committing, Gray. I've been committed to my career for the last ten years. That's not where Ava and I are headed," he'd said with finality because he desperately needed to believe it.

Now, Gage wasn't so sure.

When Ryan finished with his bottle and burped like a sixteen-year-old kid, Gage grabbed the second bottle and went upstairs to check on Ava.

Her cell phone was lying in the crib beside a pink Baby Minnie Mouse blanket that resembled the one wrapped around Ryan. She was leaning into the crib grumbling something as she pulled light green pants onto Emma. His niece gave a little cry, and Ava froze momentarily. He watched the rise and fall of her shoulders as she looked down at the baby and finally reached for the blanket. She wrapped her gently and then scooped her up into her arms.

"I don't know what I'm doing, so I'm gonna need you to take it easy on me," Ava whispered to Emma. "Now, we're gonna forget about the mean man on the phone and go downstairs to get your bottle. How do you like that?"

Emma made a gurgling sound and Ava chuckled. "I figured you'd agree with that part. Okay, let's go."

"Who was the mean man on the phone?" he asked before he could consider whether or not he should.

"Oh." She looked startled to see him.

She was holding Emma in one arm as she reached for the cell phone and slowly stuffed it into her back pocket.

"It was nobody," she said with a slight shake of her head. "I mean, nobody important. Just work."

Gage nodded, even while churning over the realization that he didn't like the thought of some guy being mean to her. Add that to his great dislike of other guys holding Ava's hand and Gage knew he was in trouble. He cleared his throat before speaking again.

"Well, I guess I won't have to teach you how to change a diaper after all."

"I figured it out," she told him with a slight chuckle.

Gage held up the bottle he was holding.

"You brought her bottle?" Ava asked.

"I did," he said. "Let's sit here."

The nursery was painted a very pale green with bold white stripes on one side, and pastel-colored balloons on the other. All the furniture in the room was white, including the matching gliders that faced a bay window, which opened to the front of the house.

He waited for Ava to sit before handing her the bottle. Then Gage took the seat next to her.

And there they sat for Gage didn't know how long, rocking the babies and looking out the window.

She didn't say a word and neither did he. Ryan was warm as Gage cuddled him in his arms. Beside him he could hear Ava making cooing sounds at Emma. It struck him then that this was a cozy scene. A scene he'd held in his mind for longer than he cared to admit.

His parents probably sat in this same room looking out the window all those years ago. And now, something clicked inside of Gage. It slipped into a place in his chest as if it had been the missing piece to a puzzle, and he almost sighed because it was finally where it belonged.

Just the way Theodor and Olivia probably had thirty years ago.

Chapter 7

"It's just a leave of absence, Mortimer," Gage said into the phone as he sat in the room he'd been occupying at Harper and Garrek's house. "I'll be back the first of the year."

"I thought this was just a three-week vacation," Mortimer Gogenheim replied. "What about your research? The grant?"

Gage had thought this all through after he'd left Gray's house last night and returned to this room. He'd stayed up half the night thinking of nothing else.

"I'll have weekly Skype calls with the research assistants. In addition, they'll send me weekly reports. I'll review everything, do my own analysis and decide what steps need to be taken next. We're not close to any clinical testing, so me being out of the lab for another two months isn't going to harm the research at all," Gage assured his boss.

"My last day is the end of this week," Mortimer said. "I believe Ed planned to meet with all department staff before then. I told him you would be back because that's what you told me when you left."

Gage kept his gaze on the huge trees swaying with the wind just a few feet away from the window. Leaves drifted in the air before circling down to rest on the grass.

"There have been some new developments." Gage cleared his throat. "Things relating to my father's estate. I have to take care of them before I can return. If it's necessary, I can call and speak with Rodenstein myself."

Mortimer didn't immediately respond.

"If there's something else going on, you can tell me, Gage. Is this about Ed getting the chief position instead of you?"

"I'm not that petty, Mortimer. I'm a professional, always. And I'm committed to my job. I have been for the last ten years. Which is why requesting a leave of absence to deal with my father's estate should not be an issue. But if it is, please let me know and I will deal with it accordingly."

"This just isn't like you," Mortimer said before agreeing to let Dr. Rodenstein and the rest of the staff know that Gage was officially taking a leave of absence.

For the next few hours, Gage thought about Mortimer's words. This *wasn't* like him. Since the day he'd decided to become a doctor, Gage had put nothing else before achieving that goal. And really, he told himself, he wasn't actually pushing his career aside this time. Designing and staffing the obstetrics and infertility research sections of the new Taylor Generational Wing at All Saints Hospital was an extension of his career. It was in his field and correlated perfectly with his work in New York. As such, in the last weeks, Gage had thrown himself wholeheartedly into the project.

He'd also spent more time with Ava Cannon than he had with any other woman, ever.

That thought reminded him of the text message he'd sent to her this morning, inviting her to dinner tonight. It also meant he had a lot to do before the time for said dinner arrived.

After packing the last of his clothes in the leather duffel bag he'd brought with him when he arrived in Temptation, Gage took the bag off the bed and stood in the room, looking around. It was a nice room in the old antebellum home that his father had left to Garrek, and that Harper was now restoring. The stately structure sat on multiple acres of luxurious land, and when finished, would be grand and gorgeous. Harper was really good at her job, even if Gage wasn't a fan of the ornate antique furniture in this particular room.

"Oh, are you leaving?" Harper asked when Gage was headed to the front door.

There was noise, as always here, with work being done on some part of the house every day. So he hadn't heard her approach.

"Hey, Harper. I thought you'd already be out on some other job by now," Gage said as he set his bag on the floor and faced his soon-to-be sister-in-law.

"I'm working here today," she told him. "Have to find some time to put into my own house. Especially if I want to have it finished by the time Garrek comes home."

"He's anxious to return," Gage said. He'd spoken to Garrek a couple days ago when his brother had called to ask why he was in Temptation.

His sisters had also called him because nothing was ever a secret between the Taylor siblings. What one knew, they all knew.

Harper beamed at his words. "But you're leaving? Your vacation is over."

"Actually, I'm not leaving Temptation just yet. I've decided to stay here awhile longer to help Gray at the hospital."

"Yes, with the generational wing. That's fabulous. So why are you packed like you're leaving town?"

"Since I drove my car down, I had to have my yacht shipped here. It's arrived, and I'm just going to stay there for the duration of the trip. As I'm sure you're aware, it gets kind of loud here sometimes, and it's easier for me to work where it's quiet."

Harper chuckled. "That's putting it politely. I know it's loud all the time, and I apologize."

"No need for an apology. It was generous of you to let me stay here, and this was better than intruding on Gray and Morgan with the kids and their schedules. I'll just be down at the dock, but still in town for family dinners and things like that."

"Good, I know that Gray seems really happy you're

here. And Garrek is, too. He only wishes he could be here with all of us."

Gage wished that, too. Quite a few times this week, he'd wondered how it would feel for all of them to be back here in Temptation.

"In due time," he told Harper. "We'll all be together in due time."

The words had reminded him of his mother. Once the siblings had entered high school, they'd often asked Olivia when she was going to do something for herself. They'd all agreed they wanted to see their mother happy, even if they couldn't agree on who or what would get her to that point. Olivia had only smiled and told them, "All in due time."

Now, hours later, Gage was on the luxury super yacht he was currently leasing. The *Seraphine* looked big and a bit ostentatious anchored along Temptation's weathered dock, but Gage didn't care. He loved nice things. They were the one indulgence he afforded himself as a reward for all his hard work. His condo, car and the yacht were like Gage's children, he thought dismally.

It was just about five thirty, and he'd already showered and changed into smoke-gray slacks and a lighter gray button-front shirt. He kept clothes on the yacht, so his decision to stay here longer wouldn't call for a trip to the mall.

"Helloooo down there! I say helloooo!"

Gage smiled at the sound of her voice. Ms. Pearl Brimley was a lovely woman with a wide, friendly smile and deep dimples in each mocha-hued cheek. Gage had stopped at Ms. Pearl's Diner on his way to the yacht and put in an order for dinner to be delivered here for tonight.

"Hellooooo!"

"Coming, Ms. Pearl," Gage answered as he stepped up onto the deck.

Ms. Pearl was standing on the dock, a large square-shaped warming bag in each hand. She wore a blue-and-white-striped skirt that stopped at her ankles and swayed in the breeze.

"Here, let me help you down," he told her as he went to the edge of the deck.

He unhitched the latch that kept the swinging door closed and reached up to take the bags from Ms. Pearl's hands.

"Gail and Meg are right behind me with the rest of the stuff. We'll get you all set up here," she said when Gage turned back to offer her a hand down.

"You said six o'clock, so we'll have to move quickly. But we'll get it all done."

In seconds Ms. Pearl's daughter, Gail, and her niece, Meg, came on board carrying more packages.

"This is so nice," Meg crooned. "I've never seen a boat like this before."

"That's because it's a yacht," Gail replied with a shake of her head.

"Just like the one in the pictures of Jay-Z and Beyoncé on vacation," Meg continued as she unpacked utensils and napkins from the bags she'd carried on deck.

Gage smiled and explained to Meg what type of yacht this was, and that, no, he was not as rich as Jay-Z and Beyoncé. Ms. Pearl beckoned them both back to work, and by five minutes to six, the three ladies were gone and the small bronze pedestal table at the far end of the boat was decorated beautifully.

At three minutes after six, Gage was standing at the door of the deck once more, smiling up at Ava as she stepped slowly onto the yacht.

"You look beautiful," he said, taking her hand to help her on board. "I'm so glad you're here."

And he was, Gage thought as he looked down into her deep brown eyes. He was glad to see her in the short blue dress that might have seemed plain on anyone else but her. She wore a blue-and-beige scarf draped around her neck and black boots to her calf. Her hair was free and flowing so that she had a fresh and innocently enticing look. Yes, he was glad she was here.

"I almost didn't come," she said and then shook her head as if trying to dismiss the words. "I meant to say, thank you. I'm looking forward to a great evening."

He heard the words and saw the small smile she offered, but Gage wasn't buying it. Her eyes and the slight slump in her shoulders said differently.

"Is something wrong, Ava? Did something happen to you today?"

"No," she said and waved her hand over her face like she needed to wipe away whatever was bothering her. "I'm fine. It's nothing. Let's just have dinner."

"Sure. Everything's ready," Gage told her.

He led her to the table and pulled out the matching bronzed iron chair, all the while thinking that she was a horrible liar. Something was definitely wrong with her, and he was determined to find out what.

So he could fix it. Gage knew in that instant that he would do anything to take that look off her face. Anything at all.

She was being ridiculous.

It was unlike her and she hated it.

No, it was just like her after speaking to her mother. That's what she hated more.

Ava took a deep breath, smelled the crisp evening air and looked out to the glistening surface of the water.

"It's nice here," she said quietly. "Who goes on vacation and has their yacht shipped to them?"

The last was said with a wry chuckle as she tried to shake the anger and sadness she'd carried with her for the last hour since her mother's call.

"I wanted to be comfortable since I plan to stay a little longer."

He had just slid onto the chair across from her. For too many torturous moments, he'd stood staring at her, waiting for her to tell him what was going on. Or waiting to figure it out for himself.

Ava turned slightly, hanging her purse on the side of the chair, and then turned back to face him. "How long are you staying now?"

"Through the holidays."

She folded her hands in her lap. "So you'll be here for Morgan's big Christmas dinner. Are the rest of your siblings coming?"

"Yes," he replied. "Morgan, apparently, is very persuasive."

"That should be nice. A family holiday." Ava couldn't help it.

She had decided that she wanted to be in Temptation for Christmas, as well. She wanted to attend the Harvest Brunch and then the Thanksgiving parade in November. And Morgan had told her about her annual class play at the community center. They hadn't chosen which Christmas story they would do this year yet, but Lily and Jack had been so animated last night, when they'd reenacted parts of last year's *A Christmas Carol*, that Ava knew she wanted to see anything those two acted in this year. And all of the Taylors had agreed to come back to Temptation for Christmas. Ava did not want to miss that.

She looked out to the water then and sighed heavily, recalling the earlier conversation with her mother.

"I mean, really, Ava, how long are you going to continue playing at this? May I remind you that you are not getting any younger? When I was your age, I was already married to your father and trying to get pregnant."

"I'm not thinking about marriage and children right now, Mother," she'd said through clenched teeth.

The fact that she'd thought of nothing else but the sweet smell of Emma and Ryan in her arms last night was something she'd keep to herself.

"That's my point exactly. You should be. It's time to stop wasting time with this writing thing and get on with your life."

"This writing thing has resulted in the number one

rated procedural drama last season. It's making a name for me within the industry and opening new doors for my career." At least she hoped what she was doing here in Temptation would do just that.

"Richard is preparing for a third run to keep his Senate seat. He needs your help on the campaign. Now, how soon can you get back to LA? I've already set up some meetings with my committees. They'll support as always, but I need you to get to the young people."

Richard McClain had been the Cannon family lawyer for as long as Ava could remember. Five years ago he had decided to run for Congress and had been elected in a surprise landslide. After Ava's father's death, Richard had been there offering his support to the family, which Ava had appreciated, so she did feel a bit of loyalty to him.

"I'm working and will not be finished with this until at least the first of the year," Ava had said.

"That's just not acceptable, Ava. Not at all. I want you to stop this foolishness right now. I've put too much time and energy into raising you right for you to wander off into some la-la land now."

Ava hadn't been aware that a successful producing career was considered la-la land.

"Look, Mom, I have to go. I have a da…I mean, a meeting tonight. So I'm going to have to call you in the morning."

"Ava, you will not keep putting me off. Now, I told Richard you would be back to help him, and I expect you to honor that agreement."

"I didn't agree to that," she'd replied.

"Do not disrespect me!" Eleanor had yelled.

The sound of her mother taking a deep breath and releasing it very slowly had echoed through the phone, and Ava rolled her eyes. Her mother had perfected the wounded woman act over the years, but this time Ava was prepared.

"I would never disrespect you, Mother. But I really do have to get to this meeting. We can talk more in the morning, I promise. Have a good night," she'd said before clicking off the call.

It wasn't hanging up if she said goodbye, or goodnight. Her father had told her that. It was a long time before Ava suspected it was because he'd hung up on Eleanor plenty of times in his life.

"Ava?"

It was his hand resting on her shoulder more so than the sound of his voice that jolted Ava from her memory and almost out of the chair.

"Are you all right?" Gage asked as he stooped down beside her.

He took her hands then, holding them between his as he stared up at her.

"Whatever it is, you can tell me, Ava. Tell me, so I can help."

She tilted her head, the corner of her mouth moving upward slightly. "You would try, wouldn't you? For as much as you like to give the impression that you're all about your professional life, there's a softer side to you, Gage. A side that wants to make things right for everybody."

"I just don't like the look in your eyes or the tone of your voice right now. Whatever I can do to help, I will."

"You came to work on the set of my show to help," she said. "Even when you wanted nothing more to do with TV networks. And you came back here to help your brother at the hospital. You're always helping."

"Fine. I'm always helping. So let me help you."

She shook her head. "It's nothing," Ava said.

"You're a terrible liar."

Those words were like icicles gliding over her skin. Gage had no idea how good a liar she actually was.

"It's childish and pointless," she said and then sighed because her head was starting to throb. "Just a silly argument with my mother. You know, like everyone has with their parents at some point."

His gaze remained steady. "Not me."

Great, now she really felt like an idiot. Here she was complaining about her mother when both Gage's parents were gone.

"I'm sorry. Let's just forget I even said anything." She tried for a genuine smile. "Guess I'm ruining our date. Is this a date?"

He grinned. "Let's dance."

"What? There's no music."

Gage was already tugging her from the chair. He slipped his arm around her waist and stepped closer, until their bodies were touching. Ava lifted her arms to lock around his neck and joined him when he began to sway. He smelled so good, like very expensive cologne and sexy man. And even though he wasn't holding her too tightly, she felt safe in his arms. Protected. Comforted.

Guilty.

"My mother used to say that dancing cures everything. The movement chases away old ghosts and prevents worries from piling up in your mind."

Ava sighed and let herself focus solely on moving.

"I'm just trying to do my job," she said softly. "All I've ever wanted to do is write. Not be some twenty-first-century debutante in search of a rich husband to continue some society circle nonsense."

His fingers splayed over her lower back, rubbing lightly as he stepped and moved, turning them in a small circle.

"She hates everything about me. Always has," Ava continued. She didn't know why. The words just tumbled free. "Nothing I've ever done has been good enough for her. Probably because I'm not like her. I prefer to drive an economical hybrid car instead of the expensive vehicles she travels in. I live in a reasonably priced condo and not a mansion, which, thanks to my inheritance from my father, I could absolutely afford. I'm not really into flashy things or people with titles and prestige. I just want to write my stories and live a normal life. Is that so much to ask?"

He kissed the top of her head and then waited until she lifted her chin to stare up at him.

"No. It's not," he told her. "You should be able to be whoever and whatever you want to be. That's what my mother used to tell us. It's why she wanted out of the television show. Because she thought it was creating a persona for us that we had no say in. We were stars before we even knew what that meant, or if it was something we wanted in our lives."

"You were doing what they wanted you to do because at the time you didn't have a choice," she said.

She wanted Gage and his siblings to have a choice this time. The same way she had made a choice to write instead of following her mother's plans for her life.

"Your mother did the right thing," she said.

"And your mother thinks she's doing the right thing, too," he replied. "You just have to stand your ground so that she knows her idea of what's right for you is not in your plan."

"I did," she told him. "I have so many times before. She just refuses to listen."

"Then that's her problem, Ava. It's not yours, so don't beat yourself up about it. You have a right to try this your way."

He looked so good staring back at her with his neatly trimmed goatee, thick brows and mesmerizing gaze. She couldn't have written a better scene where a declaration of love would come and happy-ever-after would ensue. Her heart tripped at the thought.

"If this were a date, I'd suggest we skip the meal and head straight to the bedroom," she said nervously.

Yes, she was nervous. Which was ridiculous, because she'd had sex with Gage before.

"Or it might be the part where I whisk you into my arms and carry you to the bed. I'd lay you down and peel your clothes from you slowly, taking the time to touch every part of your naked body, watching your reaction as I did."

She licked her lips and swallowed hard. "Oh, really? And then what would you do? If this were a date, I mean?"

They were still dancing, swaying in the cool evening breeze on the deck of his yacht. That's why she felt dizzy. No other reason.

"After touching every part of your body with my fingers, I would switch places. Using my tongue to taste you." His voice had lowered to a deep timbre.

"I would watch you ride high on the wave of pleasure, then crest and fall with your climax."

Her body tingled all over, her breasts swelling as she pressed closer to him. He was hard. She could feel his erection as surely as she felt the rise and fall of his chest.

"And...then," she whispered, the words trailing off as he'd begun to lower his face to hers.

"Then I would slip inside you, filling you, taking you," he said before brushing his lips over hers.

"Yes," she replied and kissed him back, dragging her tongue over his bottom lip.

Gage chuckled. "Yes what?"

She nipped his lip with her teeth and then sucked it into her mouth, before thrusting her tongue inside to dance along with his.

"Yes, this is a date," she said when they finally broke for air.

He nodded and then bent to pick her up. When she

was in his arms, Gage leaned in, brushing his lips over hers again. "Good. Because I'm ready for the touching and tasting to begin."

Chapter 8

He did just what he said he would, and Ava was profoundly grateful.

She was also more aroused than she'd ever been before.

Gage had carried her across the deck and down a spiral set of stairs. The bed was huge on this luxurious vessel. She hadn't expected anything less. From the moment she'd received his message to meet him at the docks and then stepped out of her car at the parking lot across the street, she'd known the *Seraphine* was going to be like nothing she'd ever experienced. She'd never been on a yacht before, the whole not-knowing-how-to-swim thing holding her back from cruises of any sort. Tonight, she was glad she'd pushed that anxiety aside.

He gently laid her on the king-size bed and first removed her boots. Propped up on her elbows now, Ava looked around briefly. The walls were dark, a mixture of blue and gray in a textured paper that reminded her of a deep blue sea. A crystal-covered lamp was on each nightstand, and beige carpet covered the floor. Gage's hands moved slowly up her bare calves and farther, until his fingers grazed the sensitive skin between her thighs.

Her attention solely on him now, she watched with anticipation as he pushed at the material of her tunic dress. He looked up at her and winked just before hooking his fingers in the band of her panties and tugging. Ava lifted her hips, allowing him to remove the white silk underwear she'd worn without question. Her scarf went next, and then he was pulling the dress up and over her head.

She was sitting up now, Gage kneeling with one knee between her spread legs, the other on the opposite side of her thigh. He leaned in, reached around her back and unsnapped her matching bra. Cool air hit her nipples, and they hardened seconds before his fingers brushed over them. She sucked in a breath and thought he may have done the same, before he pulled his hands away.

Backing off the bed now, Gage began to undress. She'd seen him naked before so that wasn't the reason for the immediate pounding of her heart. They'd had sex before, so the anticipation of that act was not making her anxious. It was the slowness with which he moved that had her skin tingling. Her eyes were riveted to his every move.

His long fingers moved precisely over each button on his shirt and continued to work steadily to undo his belt and then the snap and zipper of his pants. The shirt and the undershirt he'd worn beneath were removed first, so that when he bent down to tend to his shoes, Ava saw the muscles of his shoulders leading down to his back. He stood when his shoes were off and pushed his pants and boxer briefs down his muscled legs. Ava didn't move, even though a wicked storm of desire was brewing inside her.

"I want to touch you," Gage said as he kneeled on the bed once more. "Lie back and let me touch you, Ava."

She did as he said, hadn't even thought of not complying. His voice was low, so much so that she almost strained over the pounding of her heart to hear him.

He lifted each of her feet, kissing the arch and then the tips of her toes. He rubbed her calves once again, taking each leg in his hands and kissing behind her knee. Her fingers clenched the duvet beneath her as prickles of pleasure soared from each spot he touched throughout her body. When he came to her thighs, they'd begun to shake. She couldn't help the movement, nor could she contain the moan when his lips touched her inner thigh.

"So soft," he whispered.

Ava closed her eyes as her entire body began to tremble.

He kissed up the inside of one thigh, stopping just shy of her juncture before pulling away. She wanted to scream, but instead bit her bottom lip.

"Sexy Ava," he said as he went to the other thigh. "You've been tempting me since day one with your voice, your scent, your body."

She was going to explode. She wasn't going to be able to stop it. He was licking little circles over the skin of her inner thigh, moving upward once more until she wanted to lift her hips off the bed and offer herself to him.

"Gage," she whimpered, when he was just inches away from the plump folds of her center. "Please."

He did not oblige. Damn him.

Instead he blew his warm breath over her bare mound, causing her to shiver and groan.

"You're going to be sweet and warm," he grumbled. "I know it before I even taste you. My sweet and sexy Ava."

Oh no, this was taking too long. Ava released the duvet from her death grip and clapped her hands to the back of Gage's head.

He chuckled as he held back from her. "I'm hungry for you, too," he told her. "But we've got all night."

Ava didn't think she was going to last that long.

And she didn't.

The second Gage touched her tender folds, she almost bolted up off the bed. He placed one hand on her hip and used the other to spread her open before licking her up and down. Ava moaned deep and long, her thighs shaking around his head. Gage continued, licking, sucking and praising her sweetness until seconds later her release tore through her body like an earthquake, and she screamed his name.

He only gave her a minute to recuperate before he was moving upward, kissing her abdomen, licking up her torso and then covering one nipple with his mouth, holding the other breast in his hand. Ava arched her back and felt herself climbing steadily toward another climax.

The moment he pulled away to get a condom, she seriously considered screaming for him to come back immediately. That should have been the second clue that she was sinking fast where Gage Taylor was concerned. She never thought about dismissing safe sex.

Sheathed and coming over her like a gorgeous African god, Gage lifted Ava's legs, propped her ankles on his shoulders and speared into her with one swift motion. His name tumbled from her lips again and again as he moved expertly in and out of her. She felt like she was drowning. The pleasure was so deep, going far beyond anything in her wildest imagination, touching a part of her she'd thought did not exist.

"Look at me, Ava," he said.

She thought she'd opened her eyes, but he was asking her again, "Ava, sweetness, please look at me."

Her lids fluttered open. He released her legs, but stayed buried deep inside her, his elbows coming to rest on either side of her head as his thumbs caressed her cheeks.

"You are beautiful and you are enough," he whispered as he began to move inside her once more. "You are more than enough for me."

She wrapped her legs around his waist, her arms around his back, and moved with him.

"Gage," she whispered. "More. More than I ever expected."

"Yes," he replied. "So much more."

He was moving too slowly, going too deep, hitting her every spot just right and then some. He was too much. This was too much. But when they both trembled and fell together, Ava realized with startling clarity that it wasn't enough. Nothing she'd had with Gage so far was enough.

And wanting more was going to crush her.

"I didn't think I was going to like it here in Temptation," Gage told her as they lay in his bed once more.

After making love, they'd showered and had the dinner Ms. Pearl prepared for them while sitting in the center of the bed. It had felt like those nights when the boys and girls in his house would meet up in the kitchen for a late-night snack. Olivia did not like them eating upstairs in their room, so the siblings had to sneak and decided it was safer if they went into one room. Those were some of the best nights of Gage's life.

Now he could add tonight to that list.

"Then why'd you come back?" Ava asked.

They'd enjoyed the delicious, if a bit cold, food and cleaned up, only to lie back in the bed as if they did not have this spacious yacht to lounge upon.

"Responsibilities that I'd put off for way too long. And to see Gray and meet his new family," he said.

"Your brother has a beautiful family," she replied.

They were both lying on their sides, facing each other. Her arm was tucked under her head and her knees pulled up so that she looked almost like a child. Except Gage knew that beneath his New York Yankees T-shirt she now wore, Ava was all woman.

"I didn't think he would get that chance," Gage admitted. "Truth be told, I wasn't sure any of us would want to start a family after what we'd been through."

"Was it really that bad?" Ava asked. "I know your parents split up, but listening to you and Gray talk about your mother, it sounds like she loved each of you with all her heart. And that she gave you a good life."

"She was a great mother. A wonderful woman who deserved more than to end up raising six children on her own."

"Your father didn't help?"

"He sent money and gifts, if that's what you mean by help." Gage grit his teeth and then thought of his conversation with Gray at the hospital. He took a deep breath and released it. "I guess he did what he could. A person can only be who they are, not who or what someone else wants them to be."

She nodded at his words, and Gage hoped that she was retaining them for her own use, as well.

"My mother was the nurturer. She was meant to be a mother. Gemma is that way, too. I hope she finds love and builds a family of her own one day. Gen is tough, so for any man to crack her shell he might need to be a magician." He chuckled at the thought of his older sister.

"Gia has a soft heart. She trusts and sees the best in everyone. Too soon and usually to her detriment, but I think she'll be a great mother one day, too."

"What about you?"

"What about me?"

"Will you be a good father one day?"

Gage let the uneasy feeling that immediately filled his chest settle before replying.

"My father left his children everything he had. His company, real estate and money. I wasn't shocked by how much his estate had been worth or how quickly Gray managed to divide everything up equally amongst us. Gray has always been a good leader. The other money that Gray found did surprise me a bit, and then the pictures. I'm still trying to figure out why he left them for me."

When he caught her looking a little confused, Gage realized what he'd just told her. He couldn't take it back, and he didn't really want to. He hadn't planned on sharing his thoughts and feelings about his father with anyone, but he had. With Ava.

She reached her free hand across the bed to take his. "What were the pictures of?"

"Us," he replied after lacing his fingers through hers. "A four-month sonogram photo of each of us, and one of us after we were born with my parents."

"Maybe he wanted to show you that he'd always loved you. Regardless of what happened, he'd never stopped loving his children or his wife."

"He cheated on her," Gage snapped. "He had an affair with a production assistant and then decided he'd rather be with her than with his family."

His words were cold and stung as he spoke them. He hadn't realized how much animosity he still held inside because of them.

"My father didn't leave us for another woman. He drank," Ava said. "So much that sometimes I don't even think he saw me. He was a partner at a prestigious law firm in LA. He represented so many stars, and sometimes a studio would call on him for contractual work. He had money, houses, cars, everything, and he drank so much that one day he drove his car right off a cliff and into the ocean."

"Dammit, Ava. I'm sorry," Gage said, immediately feeling like scum as he complained about his father.

She smiled. "Don't be. He lived the life he wanted to live, and he drank because of some problem he couldn't figure out how to solve. I wish he had been able to overcome his issues, but I don't hate him for how it ended. And you shouldn't hate your father for things that, in the end, he could not change."

She was right. Gage knew that. And so did Gray. It was time to move past all that hurt he'd clung to, which was why he'd told Gray he didn't think they should continue to pay those investigators to try to figure out where the Grand Cayman money had come from. The money was divided between the children just like everything else Theodor Taylor owned, and that was that.

"Thank you for saying that," he told her. "And for joining me tonight. I know you came here to write. That's why I try not to bother you every second of every day."

But he'd wanted to. He could admit that to himself. During the hours he spent at the hospital, or when he was walking through town or having dinner at some restaurant, he thought about her.

"Oh, it wouldn't be a bother," she said. "I write better in the early-morning hours anyway. By midday I'm already beginning to fade, unless it's crunch time."

"So you're writing new scripts for the next season of the show?"

"Actually, no, I'm writing something new and totally different."

He brought her hand up to his lips and kissed her fingers. "Well, it'll be great whatever it is."

"Yes," she said after a few minutes. "I think it will be great. But right now—"

She paused and leaned over until she could reach the nightstand drawer. She'd seen him retrieve a condom from there earlier, and she pulled a packet from the box now. When she returned to him, it was to push him over onto his back.

"Now it's my turn to touch and taste," she told him as she grabbed his shirt and lifted it up and over his head.

When Gage lay back on the pillow, she straddled him. And when her warm tongue touched his pectoral muscle, he groaned.

She could take her turn…as many times as she wanted.

"Is that how you Hollywood people do the walk of shame?" Millie said the moment Ava stepped off the dock and onto the cement walkway.

The sun was barely up, shimmering over the water in hazy orange-and-red rays when she'd crept off the yacht. Seagulls flew low, bellowing a choking call to whoever else was up this early.

"Good morning, Ms. Millie," she said in as cheerful a voice as she could muster.

The woman had stepped right up to her so that Ava struggled to keep from telling her that she was invading her personal space. Millie's hair was perfectly styled as it had been on each occasion that Ava had seen her. Her makeup was likewise flawless, Millie's red-painted lips drawn in a thin line.

"I was coming to tell Gage Taylor he needs to take this monstrosity back to wherever it was before now. It's bringing unwanted attention down here to the docks where simple folk are trying to make a living."

Ava looked around, even though she was certain there was no one out here right now but her and Millie. To the woman's credit, there were a couple of smaller boats already out to sail not too far from the dock with what Ava guessed were fishermen on board.

"I don't think the yacht is a disturbance," Ava said, taking a chance at responding. "It seems the people who need to go to work are doing just that."

Except for busybody Millie, that was.

"Don't get sassy with me. You're not in California with your snooty friends," Millie snapped.

Ava was certain she didn't have snooty friends. In fact, she could count on one hand how many actual friends she had.

"Well, it was nice seeing you, Ms. Millie, but I have to get going."

"Where to at this time of morning? Because I know you didn't spend the evening on that boat with Gage Taylor writing. I want to know why you're really here,

Ms. Cannon. If it has something to do with this town, I have a right to know."

"My work is my business," Ava said, squaring her shoulders. She had been trying to be polite, but she wasn't going to be bullied by this woman a second time.

"Not if it's taking place in my town. I don't believe for one minute you're just on a writing retreat. Seems too fishy that you and Gage show up at the same time. And you're in the TV business, too. Oh, no, too suspicious." Millie was shaking her head.

Ava smiled. "Ma'am, you can make what you want out of it, but I've told you all that I plan to. Now, you can have a nice day."

Ava skirted around the primly dressed woman and did everything short of breaking out into a run to get to her car. Once behind the wheel and pulling out of the parking lot, Ava thought the first call she was going to make when she returned to the B and B was to Jenner.

The Taylor Reunion reality show was not going to come to fruition, at least not the way he wanted it to.

Chapter 9

Two weeks later
Santa Monica, California

Were they really ready for this?

As the limo rode through the streets, taking them to this year's location for the Critics' Choice Awards, Ava thought over the last six weeks of her life. She was in a different place now, somewhere she'd never thought she would be.

"Nervous?" Gage asked.

He was sitting beside her, holding her hand. Dressed in a black Tom Ford suit, his shirt and pocket square crisp white, and sporting shined Ferragamo oxford cap-toe shoes, he looked stylish and delicious even without the help of a stylist. But when they'd arrived at her

LA condo two days ago, Saraya had already called on Ava's friend Landry Norris to get her and Gage ready for the awards show. Now married to the Crown Prince Kristian DeSaunters of Grand Serenity Island, Landry's family still lived in California, and she frequently came home for visits.

"A little," Ava admitted to Gage.

She tightened her fingers around his, seeking and receiving the comfort she'd become slightly addicted to in the past weeks. He was like the rock she hadn't realized she needed in her life. After all these years of depending on herself, relying on her own instincts and discipline to get where she was in life, Ava had never imagined being able to lean on anyone else. Which made what she planned to do in the coming days so much harder.

"Don't be," he told her. "You look stunning and smell amazing. And regardless of what happens tonight, you'll still be the youngest African American writer and producer with a number one rated show on network television right now. Nothing else matters."

Ava inhaled deeply and felt the breath releasing slowly, calmly as she looked into his deep brown eyes. He'd commented on the scent of her perfume the second he'd entered the bedroom after he'd finished dressing. Landry had still been putting finishing touches on Ava—diamond stud earrings and matching cuff bracelet. The Tony Chaaya mermaid-cut black gown Ava wore was gorgeous and made her feel sexy and confident. The messy bun with loose curls around her face was elegant, her makeup flawless, and still her stomach would not settle.

"Thank you," she whispered. "For saying that and agreeing to come here with me. I know you've been really busy with your work at the hospital, and this was sort of last-minute."

He shrugged and smiled. "My schedule's a little flexible at the moment. Besides, this is an important moment for you. I'm honored that you asked me to share it with you."

She had asked him as they'd sat on the steps at Harper's father's farm after a seafood feast. Her agent, Marcelle, had called her that morning to tell her that she'd been nominated. Since she'd been in Temptation, Ava had been basically off the grid, so the news of the nominations hadn't immediately gotten to her.

Now, the night was here and she was nervous about possibly winning in the Best Drama Series category. Corbin Yancy and Miranda Martinez were also nominated in the Best Actor and Best Actress in a Drama Series categories. That gave *Doctor's Orders* a total of three nominations for their first season. It was an amazing accomplishment, one that Ava did not take lightly.

"I especially want to thank you because I know you do not like being in the spotlight," she told him as the car had begun to slow down. "I want you to know that I do respect your feelings about things that happened in your past. I was just thinking that having the experience as an adult may be totally different. But I would have understood if you'd turned me down."

He leaned in and kissed her lips quickly. Just a peck because Landry had warned him about messing up her makeup when they were at the hotel and she'd mentioned how Gage was staring hungrily at Ava.

"I'm here because I want to be here with you. That's it. We're not bringing anything else into this. Got it?"

Ava smiled because if she'd had any doubts or reservations before, she knew now with absolute certainty that she was in danger of falling in love with Gage Taylor. And that was not a good thing; at least it wouldn't be if she continued to put off telling him the truth.

"Got it," she replied just as the car stopped.

They would be walking the red carpet, posing for pictures and talking to reporters. She was ready for this. It was her dream, right? Yes, it was, and she had the best guy here with her, to share her perfect moment. She could do this. She was ready to do this.

And apparently, so was Gage.

He was magnificent, holding her hand as they first stepped onto the red carpet, smiling and posing when cameras were aimed at them. Joking and being cordial with reporters who tossed out questions like, "How long have you two been dating?" and, "Are there wedding bells in the future?" Ava had no idea how they'd even known who Gage was, but when the first reporter had approached them asking, "Mr. Taylor, how does it feel to return to the spotlight after your family's retreat thirty years ago?" Ava had thought Gage would turn back and go to the limo. But he hadn't. He'd answered every question with brutal honesty, cutting the reporters short when their questions became too pushy with a stern, but polite, reply. He was perfect.

And later that evening when they opened the envelope and called Ava's name, her perfect guy had stood and hugged her, whispering, "I am so proud of you," in her ear.

Following the show, they headed to one of the two after-parties Ava was scheduled to attend. Saraya had handled everything from securing their tickets, arranging transportation and even sending Ava and Gage the entire night's itinerary in a detailed text. The first party was at the Viceroy, where Ava and Gage mingled with guests and posed for yet more pictures. Her cheeks had already grown sore from smiling, but adrenaline continued to rush through her each time she was approached by someone else.

Until those someones were Jenner and Carroll, both beaming as they strode toward her. Gage had stepped away to find them something to drink. There was no shortage of champagne and other mixed drinks being floated around by resort staff, but they both wanted water, which was obviously too simple a drink to be offered to guests at this party. She immediately clutched her purse tightly in her hands and straightened her back. There was no doubt Jenner would want to talk to her about their last phone conversation. He hadn't been thrilled with Ava's progress, and she hadn't cared. That bravado seemed a bit easier over the phone; still she was determined not to falter.

"Congratulations, Ava! We did it!" Carroll said before pulling her into a tight hug.

"Yes, we did!" she replied and genuinely returned

his hug because Carroll had taken a chance on her, and she respected and appreciated him for that.

Jenner's hug and congratulations were just a little less exuberant.

"With this feather in our cap, our new project is guaranteed to be a hit," Jenner immediately said.

Carroll was nodding so intently that his jowls shook with the motion. "And you brought him with you. That was a great PR idea! Wish we had come up with it."

Jenner clapped his hands together and smiled gleefully. "It's perfect! The press is loving it. Sending your itinerary for the night and the name of your date to a few key members of the press was a brilliant idea. The buzz is already starting about the Taylors. So we'll be all set to announce the show just before Christmas."

Ava shook her head. "You sent my itinerary to reporters?" she asked. "Are you crazy?"

"No," Jenner said, sobering just a bit. "On the contrary, I count myself as being quite smart. I knew you'd be great for this project."

"I told you it wasn't going to go down the way you planned," Ava said through clenched teeth. They were in a crowded room full of people either trying to get the next big Hollywood scoop, or trying to get a part in the next winning movie or show. None of whom she wanted to overhear this conversation.

"My proposal is going to outline the show, leaving lots of leeway for the siblings to determine the content. My pitch to them is contingent upon their having control over how their lives are presented to the world," she told Jenner. "We discussed this already."

"And I told you we would see about that. As for now, we're starting the beginning publicity rounds. You and Gage embracing when you won that award only adds another layer to the project. We'll get to cover the love interest of one of the siblings, with our very own producer. It'll be like déjà vu," Jenner said, his eyes gleaming with his excitement.

Ava couldn't believe it—he was actually becoming happy about exploiting Theodor Taylor's infidelity, thirty years later, on television.

"That's not the outline I'm going to write," she said adamantly.

Jenner took a step closer to her then, taking her arm and pulling her to him. "You are going to do what I tell you to do. I got stiffed once by Theodor Taylor dying after he'd already signed on for this show, and dammit, I won't get shafted again. Now, you have that proposal to me next week or your career will spiral to an end as quickly as you've soared to the top."

"Is there a problem here?" Gage asked as he joined them.

He was holding two water bottles, but he stuck them in his jacket pockets as he placed a hand on Jenner's shoulder, pushing him away from Ava. He reached behind with his other hand and found Ava's, twining his fingers tightly with hers.

She cleared her throat and made the introductions, to which Gage remained unfazed.

"It's a pleasure to meet you, Dr. Taylor," Jenner said, his boisterous smile in place once again.

Jenner extended his hand to Gage, but Gage made no move to return the shake.

"Yes, it is," Carroll chimed in. "We hope you're enjoying your stay here in Santa Monica. If there's anything we can get you, please do not hesitate to let us know."

"I don't need anything," Gage told them and then looked to Ava. "Are you ready to go?"

"Yes," she replied immediately, not bothering to look at Jenner or Carroll again before walking away.

Gage thought he'd been doing well. But five hours into this glamorous evening full of celebrities, producers, agents and groupies, he'd started to reach his limits. The final push could have been when he'd been in search of their drinks and he'd bumped into a familiar face.

"Dr. Gage Taylor, what a surprise it is to see you out here," Miranda Martinez had said as she'd stepped right up to him.

Her long red-painted nails were a bright contrast to his dark suit jacket as she rubbed her hand down the lapel. Lips painted the same vibrant glossy hue and hair black as night falling in fluffy curls past her shoulders weren't as alluring as they should have been for some reason. She wore a purple gown that left more of her skin exposed than was necessary, and her perfume stung Gage's nostrils.

"Hello, Miranda," he'd said reluctantly. "Congratulations on your nomination."

She pouted, an effort that came across as foolish and almost cartoonish, with her full red lips.

"What do the critics know anyway?" she said. "I mean, they did say we were the best drama series, but that's only because of me."

Right. Gage stepped away from her. "Well, if you'll excuse me—"

She'd cut him off by lifting her hand to cup the back of his neck. "Not so fast. We hardly ever had a chance to really talk while on set. And now you're here. How about we ditch this party and go somewhere a little quieter?"

"No," had been Gage's immediate response. And since she didn't take the response to mean he didn't want her touching him, Gage clasped her wrist and eased her hand away. "I'm going to get Ava something to drink."

"Oh, she looks like she's well taken care of at the moment," Miranda had said before nodding her head in the direction across the room.

That's when Gage had seen the two men boxing Ava in. He'd been instantly irritated. He'd abandoned plans of searching for the water and moved in that direction. One of the staffers stopped him before he could get there, thrusting two water bottles and another beaming smile his way. With a curt "thank you," Gage had taken the water and then went directly to Ava. It was as he'd come closer that he'd seen the man's hand on Ava's arm. Rage as he'd never experienced boiled inside of him, and he'd gone into action.

Now he was holding her hand tightly, moving them

through the crowd as quickly as possible. He wanted to get out of here, away from all these unscrupulous and mean-spirited people. So being stopped again irritated the hell out of him; still, for Ava's sake, he managed another smile.

"Ava Cannon," the man, wearing a navy blue jacket and wide smile standing in front of them, stated.

He was quickly joined by another man of the same stature, but dressed in a dove-gray suit.

"Yes," Ava said, bringing back the smile she'd also kept close this evening. "Hello."

"Hello," the man continued and extended his hand to her. "My name is Parker Donovan, from Donovan Network Television. Let me congratulate you on the big win for *Doctor's Orders* tonight."

"Oh, well, thank you, Mr. Donovan," she replied and eased her hand out of Gage's to shake Parker Donovan's.

"This is my brother, Savian," Parker said, signaling the man beside him.

"Congratulations," Savian said. "My wife watches your show faithfully."

"Oh really? Well, tell her I said thank you."

"I will. She's a lawyer and says it's easier to sit back and watch a show about another profession and their drama than her own," Savian continued with a chuckle.

"Well, my wife might be reading for a spot on your show soon, she's such a fan," Parker added.

"Your wife...wait a minute, Adriana Bennett-Donovan? Is she your wife?" Ava asked. "I've seen her work. She's very talented."

"She is on both counts," Parker replied with a smile

that could only come from a man who really loved his woman.

Gage relaxed at that thought and extended his hand to them. "Hello, I'm Dr. Gage Taylor."

Parker and Savian shook his hand and spoke with a genuine sincerity that Gage hadn't seen much of tonight.

"Were you heading out?" Savian asked.

Ava looked to Gage. He didn't speak, but let her make the decision on her own. This was her night, after all.

"Ah, yes, we are. But I'm so glad we met up with you before doing so," she said warmly.

"I am, too," Parker told her.

"We won't hold you up," Savian said. "But we would be interested in meeting with you."

"Definitely," Parker added. "We're always interested in adding new and innovative shows to our schedule, and you definitely have your finger on the pulse of what viewers want."

Gage saw the surprise on Ava's face and once again took her hand in his, pride swelling in his chest.

"I…I would love the chance to talk further with you," she said. "Ah, I'm heading back to Virginia tomorrow morning, but if you get in contact with my agent, we can definitely set up a mutually convenient time to chat."

Parker nodded. "We'll do that very soon," he said. "Now, you two have a good night."

"Thanks," Gage said with a nod to both men.

"Take care, Ava," Savian said. "We'll speak soon."

"Thank you both. Good night."

They were in the limo when Gage finally pulled

those bottles of water out of his pockets and set them on the bar.

"Well," he said when he sat back against the seat. "You've had a pretty cool night."

"Yeah," she said, still smiling. "I have. And you know what?"

"What?" he asked.

She lifted her hands to cup his face. "It's all because of you."

He tried to shake his head. "No. This has been all about you. I didn't do a thing."

"You were here when I needed you. I'll never forget that, Gage," she said, her voice soft.

He brushed a hand over her hair and leaned in closer. "There's no place I'd rather have been, Ava."

When his lips touched hers, Gage realized how much he meant those words. He wanted to be with Ava. In the morning, on his yacht, in Gray's backyard, on the set in New York and the red carpet in California.

He wanted to be with her. It was that simple and that terrifying at the same time.

Chapter 10

Temptation, Virginia

Four days later, Ava had just finished her final draft of the outline for *The Taylors of Temptation: A Whole New World.* She'd renamed the show and changed it from a full season to a two-hour feature with a focus on each sibling and their reflection on how the original show shaped their current lives.

She'd read it over twice, making sure that she hit each emotional beat possible. In her mind, and after being in Temptation for almost two months now, this was the key to this family. While she hadn't spoken to Gen, Gemma and Gia personally, she'd learned a lot from talking with Morgan and Harper about the sisters. Gray and Gage spent a lot of time at the hospital, but on the nights she was with Gage on the yacht, his memories of his sisters and all the torturous things the brothers did to them during their years in Pensacola were unforgettable. They were the years that the Taylor sextuplets formed their bond. The bond that remained steadfast and unbreakable now, all these years later. That's what she wanted the world to see and to remember this town and these people by.

And she hoped with everything in her that the Taylor sextuplets would go along with her plan. It was the twenty-ninth of October. The Fall Festival was tomorrow. She and Gage were slated to judge the pumpkin-carving contest, and Craig—who insisted that Ava had broken his heart—had selected a perfectly gruesome movie for everyone to watch on the night before Halloween. It was going to be a great time. So she would wait until the family dinner scheduled for the day after the festival at Morgan and Gray's to propose her idea to them. Their agreement was important to her, regardless of what Jenner said. If he wanted the Taylors on television as badly as he said he did, then he would accept any changes the sextuplets wanted to make. And if not...

A brisk knock on her door had Ava almost jumping off the bed where she'd been sitting cross-legged staring at her laptop. She wasn't expecting anyone, and as such, was dressed in old gray leggings and a peach tank top that had certainly seen better days. Before she could get to the door, there was another knock and then a familiar voice.

"Ava Marie Cannon, if you do not open this door

right now, I'll have this man break it down. Although I'm not sure he could as he looks a bit frail."

Ava groaned as she reached for the knob and pulled the door open.

"What are you doing here, Mother?"

"Yes, hello to you, too," Eleanor said.

She'd been holding a handkerchief that she now placed in the palm of her hand. She then used that palm to push the door open farther and enter the room.

Ava sighed and tried counting to ten. Otis stood in the hallway, his baseball cap balled up in one hand, while the other hand scratched the tight graying curls on his head.

"You can go now," Eleanor said to him from behind Ava. "Close the door, Ava."

Ava felt awful. "I'm sorry," she said to Otis.

The man simply shook his head, his leathery almond-toned skin lifting on one cheek as he resisted a smile. "No problem. Was nice meeting you, Mizzus Eleanor Cannon," Otis said as he looked past Ava to her mother.

Ava looked back to find her mother had gone deeper into the room and was now running her handkerchief-covered finger over the top of the dark oak armoire.

"You let me know if you need anything, Miss Ava. I'll be right downstairs," Otis said with a nod to her.

"Thanks, Otis. We should be fine. Have a good night," she told him and waited while he waved and attempted to look farther inside the room once more before closing the door.

Flattening her back against the door, Ava glared at where her mother now stood near the bed.

"Does this place really not have any good hotels? I mean, this is ridiculous, Ava," Eleanor said. But before Ava could answer, she continued. "Well, I guess it is what it is. And that means it's a good thing I'm here. Let's get you packed. I have a driver waiting downstairs to take us to the nearest city with suitable accommodations. Then we can fly out of here as soon as possible."

"I'm not leaving," Ava said almost to herself.

"Where are your suitcases? Come, Ava, don't procrastinate." Eleanor continued to move throughout the room, stopping at the floral-printed couch in the sitting area of the room and scrunching her twenty-five-thousand-dollar nose at it.

"I don't need a suitcase, Mother," Ava said, pushing herself away from the door and walking toward Eleanor. "Because I'm not ready to leave Temptation."

"Well, I certainly am," Eleanor told her as she set her large Givenchy Atigona tote on the coffee table.

For a moment Ava could only stare at the woman who had not only raised her, but had also given birth to her. How could they have been any more different? Was it truly possible that people who shared the same DNA could be any less alike? The answer to that was obvious as she watched Eleanor Germaine Stanley Cannon smooth down the skirt of her winter-white Chanel suit and sit ever so gingerly on the edge of the couch. She was a very fair-skinned woman with auburn-colored hair that dared not ever show a speck of gray, or she would personally choke her hair stylist. Diamonds glittered from the ring fingers on both hands, at her ears and in the choker at her neck. Her pumps were Louboutin, her nails long and perfectly manicured, makeup light but efficient. She was beautiful and cold and the only family Ava had.

"When my work is finished I'll return to LA, then probably back to New York for site-scouting on the show."

"Nonsense, you pay people for that, and I told you Richard is expecting you."

Counting hadn't worked, and deep breaths weren't helping. Words were failing miserably. So that was three for three. Maybe food and a public place would be better.

"I'm hungry," Ava said quickly. "How about we go get dinner and discuss something else. Like, I don't know, maybe how I just received a prestigious award for my show almost a week ago."

She didn't wait for Eleanor's answer, but walked back toward the bed and slipped her feet into the flats she had there. She grabbed a jacket and her purse from the chair on her way to the door, and then turned back to see her mother still sitting with her hands folded primly in her lap.

"Are you coming, or do you want to stay here and have dinner with Mr. Otis?"

"I don't see why we couldn't have the driver bring us," Eleanor complained when she climbed out of the passenger side of the hybrid vehicle. "This...car, or whatever, is horrible. And where are we? Does this place even serve Troubadour Pinot Noir? I need a drink and a medium rare steak."

And Ava needed a tranquilizer and a six-pack. Or maybe a one-way ticket to Budapest, a place she was almost positive her mother wouldn't follow her to.

"It's a nice Italian restaurant, Mother. They have wine and pasta. You like pasta," she said as they walked up to the doors of the Temptation Trattoria.

"Well, hello, Ava. Nice seeing you this evening. I heard about your award. You go, girl!" Niecy Monroe, a tall, slim nineteen-year-old saving money to move to Hollywood to chase her own dreams, worked as a hostess at the restaurant. She and Ava had become fast friends since Niecy admired everything about Ava's life—except Eleanor, Ava was certain.

"Thanks, Niecy. Can we get a booth in the back, please?"

"Sure, sure," Niecy replied and then leaned over the podium and iPad they used to keep their seating chart to whisper, "Is she an exec from Hollywood?"

Ava almost laughed. "No. This is my mother, Eleanor Cannon."

"Oh my, well, hello Mrs. Cannon," Niecy said as she grabbed two menus and led the way to their booth.

"I'll bet you're brimming with pride for Ava. She's so talented and nice. I heard stories about those Hollywood producers being stuck up or mean. Ava's nice and friendly. She's fit right in here in Temptation. Almost like she was born here," Niecy continued as they walked through to the back of the restaurant.

"Well, she was not born here, thank the heavens," Eleanor snapped.

"Oh, well," Niecy said when they were both seated and she attempted to hand Eleanor the laminated menu.

When Eleanor only looked at the girl with a weary expression, Ava accepted the menus, and gave Niecy an apologetic smile.

"Right, so Raquel's your waitress, and she'll be over soon to take your drink order."

"Please tell her that I'd like a glass of Troubadour Pinot Noir. As a matter of fact, just bring us the bottle. We can take it back to that shack where my daughter is staying," Eleanor said without bothering to look at Niecy, who was now frowning.

"Thanks, Niecy," Ava said and waited until the girl was gone before chastising her mother.

"You really don't have to treat them like this. They're nice people here."

Eleanor sighed and reluctantly sat back against the seat. "I'm sure they are, Ava. But this is not what I'm used to. It's not what you were raised to accept. Why you refuse to take advantage of all the things available to you, I have no idea."

"I like doing things my way, Mother. It has nothing to do with you."

"That's what I'm sensing," her mother replied. "That you don't want to have anything to do with me."

"That's not what I meant," Ava said. "I'm just tired of trying to make you see me for who I am. I am not, nor will I ever be, the daughter you planned for. I'm me, and I love and respect you as my mother, but if you don't stop criticizing me and ignoring my accomplishments, our relationship is going to take a bad turn."

There. She'd said it. She'd kept her cool, and she'd maintained a respectful tone, all while telling her mother in no uncertain terms to cut this crap out.

"Well," Eleanor said before clapping her thin lips shut.

She blinked at her daughter as if just seeing her for the first time in forever, and then shook her head.

"I don't know where I went wrong—" she started and then held up a hand when Ava would have said something else. "But you are my only child, and I love you. So I guess we'll work this out. But if you think I'm going to eat from Styrofoam containers, as you just said, our relationship is going to take a bad turn."

Ava grinned. "They have real dishes here, Mother."

Working things out still meant that Eleanor had definite opinions about Ava's life and her career, and it was going to take a little more than delicious lasagna, buttery garlic bread and a great red wine to change that.

"You can still afford a better car than this." Eleanor was fussing as they drove onto the road heading back to the B and B.

The trattoria was located about twenty minutes outside the main part of town, but Ava loved their food, so she made the drive frequently. Only, her trips were usually during daylight hours. As it was a little before nine, it had grown pretty dark, and there weren't any streetlights on dirt roads. She switched on her high beams and tried to tune her mother out.

"And why television? If you're going to be in entertainment, why not go for movies? You'll certainly make more money there. I believe there was a studio executive who hired your father's firm at one point. I can probably look him up when I get home to civilization," Eleanor was saying.

"I don't need you to help me get into movies, Mother. I'm doing exactly what I want to do right now."

If that included holding the steering wheel with a death grip as a crack of thunder sounded and the skies opened up, dropping buckets of rain down around them, then so be it.

"Crap!" she said and switched the windshield wipers on.

"It's awfully dark out here, Ava. I don't like it."

"I know you don't like it, Mother. You've spent the three hours you've been in town telling me how much you don't like it here."

"Well, I don't. And that rude woman who came over to our table. What was her name? Millie something? I mean, really, who names their child Millie, nowadays? And she had on too much lipstick, looking at me as if I had offended her in some way," Eleanor continued.

Her mother had definitely offended Millie, considering she'd told her that she could purchase better wigs at professional salons instead of online. In response, Millie had run her fingers through her natural, but permed, hair as she stood over Eleanor and made a snide remark about Ava and Eleanor being suspicious characters in town. After that, and considering the other times Millie had pushed Ava's buttons, Ava hadn't even bothered to apologize for Eleanor's comments.

"Millie Randall is a special character," Ava was saying before something hit the car's fender.

She kept her grip on the steering wheel, but the car had already spun around and was now going down a slight embankment.

Eleanor screamed from the passenger seat, holding her chest and mumbling something about a heart attack, while Ava tried desperately to press on the brakes and keep them from crashing into the trees ahead. The sounds of her heart thumping wildly and her mother's screeching didn't help, so when the car slammed into something hard and the airbags exploded, knocking Ava back against the seat, she sank blissfully into the darkness.

Gage laughed like he hadn't since he was younger. Since he and his siblings were all together in Pensacola.

They were seated in the room that, according to Harper, would eventually become their formal living room. Right now there were two couches and two recliners positioned on an Aubusson rug around a long coffee table that Harper's cousin Craig had made.

Gray and Morgan sat on one couch, while Gage and Harper had pulled the recliners close to each side of the couch. Gray held his phone out with Gen on FaceTime. Gage had his phone with Gia, Harper had hers with Garrek, and Morgan, who had become fast friends with Gemma, had hers out, as well. This was how they'd had a family get-together after dinner.

"I'd forgotten all about that," Gage said after he'd laughed until his sides hurt.

"Well, I didn't," Gia replied. "All of our dolls were floating in the ocean after you and Garrek decided they could take a cruise on the raft you'd built out of branches and old shoeboxes."

"Gia cried for days," Gemma recalled with a chuckle.

"And Mom punished us for a week because we didn't ask permission to use your dolls on the virgin voyage," Garrek added.

Gray laughed. "I warned you two not to go in their bedroom, but you wouldn't listen."

"Gage was a master manipulator back then," Gen said. "He'd convince you that anything was a good idea. Remember he got Mom to let us open a gift not only on Christmas Eve, but on the day before Christmas Eve, too. Telling her it was a shame that only those two days out of the month got all the attention."

"And I used to cry about being an only child," Harper said, shaking her head.

"Those were good times," Gemma said. "I miss us all being together."

"I've missed it, too," Gage admitted. "But Gray's kids have reminded me of all that."

"Oh yes, I'm sure Jack and Lily have reminded you of how much mischief youngsters can get into," Morgan chimed in.

"More like reminding all of us how important family is," Gray said soberly.

"Speaking of which," Garrek announced and cleared his throat. "The last time we all met, Gray informed us that he'd narrowed down where the money that was deposited into the Grand Cayman account had come from."

"Someone who lived in a group home on Broad Street," Gage added.

He didn't really want to talk about this, but figured it was probably best for them all to decide to leave it alone.

"I've driven past there a few times, and I have to say, I really don't care who lived in that house or who followed Dad's instructions and deposited that money in the account. I've decided to use some of my share to start my own research foundation," Gage said.

He hadn't planned to announce this just yet, but since they were all here—so to speak—now was as good a time as any.

"Really?" Gray asked. "When did you decide this?"

"I've been thinking about it since I arrived in Temptation. My career didn't exactly work out the way I had planned, so I figured it was time for me to regroup and start again," he told them.

He left out the part that included Ava being a big influence on his decision. She'd always known what she wanted to do in life, and she'd even gone against her mother's wishes to achieve her goals. Gage had even told her she was doing the right thing, that she had a right to live the life she wanted. Well, he was making plans to live the life he wanted, with or without Mortimer Gogenheim and the chief of obstetrics position at Nancy Links Medical Center.

"I'm going to use my money to open my own restaurant," Gia announced.

"And I've been thinking about teaching and expanding my company to offer design grants in some of the colleges," Gen added.

"Onward and upward," Gemma told them. "Just like Daddy used to say."

There was a moment of silence, and then Gray spoke.

"I'll dismiss the private investigators, and we'll all accept that Dad left us this additional money because he loved us."

Morgan touched her husband's knee and smiled up at him.

"I agree," Garrek said. "We'll finally begin to focus on our future instead of being bogged down by our past."

"That's a great idea," Harper told her fiancé.

The Taylor sextuplets agreed.

"Now, with that said," Garrek began again, "I hear Gage is settling in to Temptation with a certain young lady who's been visiting, as well."

Oh no, Gage thought as all eyes, even the ones via FaceTime, zeroed in on him.

"Yes!" Morgan exclaimed. "You should see them together. They're so cute. Especially when they babysit the babies. I've used them as sitters twice now, and I would definitely recommend them."

His sister-in-law happily grinned at him, and Gage could only shake his head. He'd grown to love her and the stability and happiness she'd provided for his older brother.

"Ooooh, tell us more," Gia prodded.

Gage dragged his free hand down his face and groaned. "It's no big deal. Her name's Ava, and we worked together on her television show earlier this year. She's in Temptation for a writing retreat."

"Uh-huh, during the same time that Gage decided to come back for a visit and has since decided to stay on longer," Harper added.

"Yes, I came back to see Gray and his family. And I started working on the project Dad wanted at the hospital, so I don't want to leave until it's up and running smoothly," Gage said.

"And she just showed up? At the same time?" Gen asked. "Hmm."

"Right. Hmm," Morgan added.

"It was a coincidence," Gage said, but had to admit the words didn't sound accurate even to his mind.

"A coincidence that one of the famous Taylor sextuplets would be selected to work on another television show. And then that the producer from that show would arrive in our hometown at the exact same time that you did?" Gen asked.

"That's a pretty big coincidence," Gray said.

"Ava didn't know I was coming here," Gage replied calmly. But he was feeling anything but calm at the moment.

Why had they brought this up, and why were they questioning what had been just a chance happening? He had nothing to do with Ava showing up here and neither did his family.

Another phone ringing interrupted the conference, and Harper handed Morgan her cell phone as she stood and crossed the room to answer the landline.

"Morgan, it's Wendy for you," Harper said.

Morgan gave her cell phone to Gray and took the cordless phone from Harper.

"So we're all set for Christmas?" Gemma asked. "Everyone's coming back to Temptation for dinner in the Victorian on Peach Tree Lane?"

She sounded wistful as she smiled, and Gage wanted nothing more than to reach out and hug her. Gemma was the closest to their mother, and Olivia's love and caring nature radiated through his sister. He hadn't realized how much he missed being close to her until this very moment.

"Ava's been in an accident," Morgan said, her words effectively ending the good mood of their family conference.

"What?" Gage asked as he stood, immediately dropping his phone onto the couch.

"Wendy's on duty tonight, and she said they were just brought in by ambulance. A trucker was driving down Chambray Road and saw her car in a ditch," Morgan announced.

"I'm going now," Gage announced and had taken only a couple of steps toward the door before Gray came up behind him.

"I'll go with you. Here, take this," he said and handed Gage his phone that he'd dropped.

Gage didn't know when his other siblings were disconnected from their call, but he was on his way out the door in the next few seconds and heading to his car. All he could think about was Ava at this moment. Was she hurt? What had happened? Would he ever see her again?

Chapter 11

"Is there a possibility that you could be pregnant?"

Gage felt the world around him shift as he paused outside the curtain in the emergency room. It was only partially closed, and he'd been directed this way after he'd asked for Ava. He could see her lying on the bed, the doctor who had just asked the question holding her hand, checking her pulse.

"No," she replied. "I'm on birth control."

And he'd used protection. Each and every time they were together, Gage had dutifully donned a condom. So why had his heart rate significantly increased the moment he heard that question? More importantly, why was he feeling a sting of disappointment at her answer?

"Okay, good. We'll note that on your chart in case

we need to send you for an MRI or CT scan," the doctor continued.

He reached forward and grabbed an otoscope from the shelf on the wall, then proceeded to check Ava's eyes. When he was finished, he used his fingers to check down her neck and her limbs. She lay on the bed, staring up at the ceiling as the exam continued, and Gage resisted the urge to immediately go to her. As a doctor, he knew it was imperative for this physical exam to occur without interruption or distraction. So he remained where he stood, watching every part of the exam and breathing a sigh of relief when the doctor finally said, "I think you have a mild concussion."

"That means I can go home, right?" Ava asked. "I mean, I don't have to be admitted?"

"No. But I'd like someone to be there for you in case your symptoms change. You're just visiting us in Temptation, is that correct?"

"Yes. I'm staying at the Sunnydale Bed-and-Breakfast."

The doctor nodded. "Louisa Reed's place. She's a great innkeeper and would probably watch after you, but I don't think she lives on the property anymore. Moved into a smaller house near her daughter after her son, Harry, went to jail."

"She can come home with me," Gage said, finally entering the room completely. "I'll be able to keep a close eye on her in case her symptoms worsen."

"And you are?" the doctor asked when he spun around to see Gage approaching.

Gage extended his hand and said, "Dr. Gage Taylor."

With a smile and a curt nod, the doctor shook Gage's

hand. "Yes. Talk around the hospital is you were here and taking charge of the new wing your brother just finished building."

"That's correct. I'm in obstetrics and gynecology," Gage told him. "I'll take Ava home when you discharge her."

She'd started to sit up then, and Gage moved closer to the bed, taking her hand.

"And you're staying in that nice pretty yacht down at the dock. She's a beauty. I'm Dr. Ralston Hackney. My wife owns the ice-cream parlor at the end of the dock. She can't stop talking about that yacht. Think I may have to look into buying a boat or something just to keep her quiet."

Gage smiled. "Let me know when you're ready, I've got a great agent who can work wonders with the financing."

"I'll keep that in mind."

"Um, excuse me? Can I go now? I'd like to check on my mother."

"Oh, yes, Ms. Cannon. Sorry about that. I'll get started on your discharge papers. Dr. Taylor here will know what to watch for, but the nurse will go over everything when she comes in with the paperwork. Also, your mother's been taken down to X-ray. Dr. Leon Schilling in orthopedics examined her and thinks she broke her ankle. He's not talking about surgery, so she may be put in a cast and ready to leave in a few hours."

Ava sighed. "Just great."

"You're both very lucky the airbags deployed, Ms. Cannon. From what the paramedics said when they brought you in, that little compact car of yours is a total loss," Dr. Hackney said.

"It was a rental," Ava said and closed her eyes.

"Well, then, that's the rental company's problem," Dr. Hackney continued with a grin. "I'll go get your paperwork started. Take care of her, Dr. Taylor."

"Please, call me Gage, and yes, I will take care of her," Gage said and waited until Hackney was out of the room before he turned his attention back to Ava.

Her hair was splayed over the pillow behind her. The T-shirt she wore was wrinkled but not torn or splotched with any blood. Her legs looked good, ankles straight, feet still wearing flat shoes. Everything looked just fine, he concluded after he completed his own visual assessment. Everything except her eyes were closed tight and her fingers trembled in his.

For the first time since Morgan told him about the accident, Gage breathed in slow, measured intervals. Relief eased over him, and he leaned down, kissing Ava's forehead.

"You scared the life out of me," he whispered. "I didn't know what I was going to find once I got here. And I'm pretty sure at least six people are going to report me to the sheriff for speeding through town."

"It was a deer," she said quietly, her eyes opening as he pulled back slightly. "It was so dark and then it started to rain. My mother was complaining, and I just wanted to hurry up and get back to the B and B so I could get her a room of her own and I could find some peace and quiet."

Her voice cracked at the end.

"I wanted her to shut up. She hates it here, and Millie didn't make that situation any better. But I just wanted her to be quiet, or to not be here and now…" Her words trailed off.

"Now, she's going to get her ankle fixed up and spend a few more days here with you," he said and squeezed her hand. "She's fine, Ava. She's going to recover just like you will."

"The car."

"It's a rental. They're insured. And if they're not, I'll pay for the damn car," he said.

She started to shake her head, and Gage saw the moment pain radiated through her with the action.

"Shhhh, baby. Don't move. Don't think about any of this right now. I'm gonna take you home and get you into bed. You'll feel better after you get some rest."

"Home," she said when she opened her eyes again and stared up at him. "Everybody keeps saying 'when I go home.' But I live in LA."

"Logistics," Gage said. "I own a condo in New York, so that's technically my home. But for the last couple of weeks, since we've been staying on my yacht, that's felt more like a home to me than any place I've been since I was a child."

It was true, as the warmth spreading throughout his body and the intense weight he felt in his chest at this very moment indicated. Gage lifted her hand up to his lips and kissed her fingers. He closed his eyes, and words he'd been thinking the last couple of days came tumbling out.

"I haven't trusted any relationship since I was kid,

Ava. Once my dad left, I started to feel like a relationship between a man and woman could never work. Someone was bound to stop caring, or loving enough, and then it would be over."

He stared down at her, into her brown eyes. With his free hand he traced the line of her jaw, before brushing his knuckles over her cheek.

"Then when I was in the sixth grade and had just started middle school, I met these two guys, Fredro and Kelvin." He gave a wry chuckle. "I thought I was finally going to have friends who weren't my brothers. Gray was on the basketball team and Garrek had joined the Boy Scouts. I hadn't yet found my niche, that's what my mom said. Fredro and Kelvin just seemed to have so much fun. Laughing and joking all the time in the cafeteria, in class and on the bus. So when they invited me to go to the park with them one day I thought, This is great! I'll be doing something without my siblings. Because, you know it's hard sometimes being part of a group."

Gage took another deep breath.

"It was a cool friendship for about a week, and then Fredro asked if they could come to my house. I asked my mom and she said it was fine. That Saturday afternoon they came over. The next thing I know they're in my room, going through my stuff saying what they'd like to have. Fredro wanted my baseball bat and glove because it was signed by Eddie Murray. My dad had given it to me for my last birthday. Kelvin wanted the Lakers jersey my mom had given me for Christmas. I told them they couldn't have it. And Fredro looked me right in the eye and said, 'You think you're too good to share your stuff. Just because your family's famous doesn't make you better than us.' I couldn't believe it."

"Gage," she whispered.

He shook his head.

"I told them to put my stuff down and leave, but Fredro refused. So I punched him, and when he fell back on the bed, I took my stuff from him. He charged me and we fought. Kelvin would have jumped in, but Gray heard the noise and he came into the room. Kelvin didn't move and Gray let us fight. At least until my mom came in. Fredro's and Kelvin's mothers called our house later that day, and I heard my mother telling them to teach their kids some manners and they wouldn't end up in fights. Gray and Garrek told me not to worry about it. And on Monday when I went to school, I was prepared for round two. What I wasn't prepared for was the way everybody stared at me in class that day. Nobody talked to me or even wanted to look at me. Not that day or the days that followed. I was an outcast, again. Just because I was born a Taylor sextuplet.

"I vowed to never trust any type of relationship—"

Gage paused, trying to process the things going through his mind at this moment, the memories and the pain.

He lowered his forehead to rest on hers and closed his eyes. "I could have lost you tonight."

"I'm fine, Gage. Really I am," she whispered.

"But it could have been different. Without those airbags…if you hadn't been able to slow your descent…it could have ended differently."

She'd lifted her other hand to rub down the back of his head. "But it didn't and I'm going to be fine. I'm still right here with you."

His eyes opened at her words, and he pulled back just a little until he could hold her gaze once more.

"With me," he said. "That's where I want you to be. Stay on the yacht with me."

Gage didn't know what he expected, but tears definitely weren't on the list. Of course, he'd never done this before, but he didn't think that asking a woman that he was sleeping with to stay with him on his yacht, instead of at a B and B, was such a bad idea.

"What's the matter, sweetness? Are you in pain?"

She shook her head quickly, an act that Gage knew had to cause her some pain, if she wasn't already experiencing it. He immediately cupped her face with his hands to keep her still, the warmth of her tears touching his palms.

"No. I mean, a little. But I just… I should say so many things to you first, Gage."

"Nonsense," he said. "All you need to say is yes, and I'll take care of everything else."

She waited for what felt like the longest moment in his life before blinking more tears, and replying, "Yes."

"This isn't a hotel, but the decor is impeccable," Eleanor said after Morgan and Harper had gotten her situated on the half tester bed.

"Thank you so much for letting her stay here," Ava said as she came to stand beside Harper. "I'll hire a full-time nurse to look after her until she's well enough to travel. And I'll come by every day to make sure she's not harassing you or any of your staff."

Harper touched Ava's shoulder. "It's fine, Ava. Dr. Schilling gave us plenty of pain meds. Not that we plan to overdose her or anything."

Ava shook her head and managed a smile. "Believe me, you're gonna want to."

"We'll all pitch in and help keep watch over her. They said it was a clean break, but Wendy said with her age, any number of complications could arise if she doesn't heal properly," Morgan told her.

Ava sighed. "I don't know how to thank you two. I mean, you hardly know me and you all showed up at the hospital, and you're so willing to help."

"That's what families do," Morgan said as she moved to put an arm around Ava's shoulders.

"She's right," Harper added. "Now, you should really get some rest yourself. A mild concussion is nothing to play with."

Ava did have a headache, but she feared it had nothing to do with the car accident. She wasn't in a hurry to go back to the yacht with Gage. He was going to undress her and put her to bed, and then he was going to lie beside her and cuddle her in his arms.

And while all that sounded just fine, the real reason for her headache was because she was a big liar, and she had been deceiving him and his family for two months.

"Yes," she admitted. "I am really tired."

They left her alone with her mother, who was already dozing off as a result of the strong pain medication Dr. Schilling had prescribed for her. Ava took a moment to look down at her mother and then to think on everything Gage had said to her just a few hours ago.

It was time to stop letting the past dictate her future. If her mother couldn't do that, it was her decision. Ava was only going to focus on moving forward.

"Good night, Mother," Ava said as she leaned over and kissed Eleanor's cheek. "I'll see you in the morning."

With that she left the room, walking down the grand staircase in Harper's gorgeous home. It was another one of those movie-like romance scenes as she descended the stairs and Gage stood at the bottom looking up at her, waiting for her.

Each step Ava took grew heavier as she realized what she now stood to lose because of the sacrifice she'd decided to make for her career.

"Ready to go?" Gage asked her.

Ava nodded, words clogged in her throat because she knew which ones she needed to speak, but couldn't bring herself to do it. Not yet. Not tonight. Her head was still throbbing, and her body had begun to ache. Gage had asked her to stay with him, which was a huge step for both of them. It had been an eventful enough night. Waiting a few more hours to tell Gage about her plans wasn't too much to ask.

Still, by the time they'd arrived at the yacht, the weight on her chest had become too much to bear, and as soon as they'd entered his bedroom she opened her mouth to speak. Gage, however, lifted a finger to touch her lips.

"A warm shower, a pain pill and rest. That's what I'm prescribing for you," he said.

"Gage, I need to tell you—" she tried to say.

"Not tonight," he interrupted. "Let me just take care of you tonight."

It was so easy to give him what he wanted. So blissfully intimate standing in the shower stall while Gage lathered the sponge and bathed her. So peaceful lying in the bed cuddled in his arms.

"I can't wait for you to meet my sisters," he whispered as Ava began to doze off. "I hope you'll be able to arrange your schedule to be here for Christmas."

"I want to be here for Christmas," Ava said, her eyelids too heavy to hold open any longer.

She'd been chilly once she stepped out of the shower, but now, with his arm wrapped around her and his body cocooning hers, she felt warm and safe. And loved. She really liked those feelings.

"And I've decided to resign from the hospital in New York. I'm going to open my own clinic and research foundation. All Saints cannot provide funding for parents who cannot afford fertility treatments, or certain aspects of taking care of multiple infants. I want to start some programs that will help," he was saying.

Ava's lips lifted in a smile. Gage had stopped her from talking, but he clearly had lots to say tonight. She snuggled closer to him, loving the sound of his voice and thinking of how it would be to do this every night with him. To lie in bed and discuss their goals and dreams, the future they would share. She wanted that. Ava wanted it so very much.

So before she drifted off and while Gage was still talking, she said a little prayer, asking a big favor.

Please let him understand.

Chapter 12

Ava rolled over and reached for him, but felt the cool sheets instead. Cracking an eye open, she saw the pillows still indented from where he'd laid his head throughout the night. She rolled over again, this time plopping onto her back and then groaning at the slight thumping in her temples.

Dropping an arm over her forehead, she sighed and thought about Gage holding her in his arms last night. It was a magical feeling, one she knew now that she wanted to feel every night of her life. With that thought, Ava sat up slowly. There was no nausea and no dizziness, just the mild headache. Encouraged by the minimal symptoms, she got out of the bed and headed toward the bathroom. The note was taped to the door, and she smiled as she read his words.

I knew you wouldn't stay in bed as per doctor's orders. Gray needed my help with festival setup so Morgan's taking the morning shift with you while Harper stays with your mom. In the afternoon, Harper's going to come over. If you're doing well, Harper will bring you to the festival in time for the pumpkin-carving contest. If you have any symptoms you are to stay in bed, or at the very least, on the yacht and I'll hurry with the contest and come back to you. Gage

After a warm shower, Ava dressed in jeans and a button-front plaid shirt and slipped her feet into slippers that she knew had been at the B and B. Someone must have gone there and brought her things here because as she looked around the room, she also saw her bag, laptop and the toiletries she'd had on the dresser there, now sitting on top of the second dresser here.

It was different seeing her perfume bottles sitting next to Gage's cologne, her laptop on the table near the door with his right across from it. She turned back and looked again at the rumpled bed where they'd slept and sighed. If she wanted this lovely scene to be a part of her future, she had to set things in motion.

Morgan was on morning duty, so that meant she was probably above deck in one of the lavish rooms up there, waiting for Ava to emerge. Finding her phone on the charger sitting on the nightstand, she picked it up and moved to the table. Taking a seat, she booted up her laptop and called Marcelle.

"Hi there! I know it's early, but I really need to talk

to you about something," Ava began the moment she heard the groggy "hello" on the other end.

Marcelle was not a morning person, so calling her at seven thirty LA time would normally be a no-no. In this case, it was urgent, so Ava ignored the time.

"This better be good, Ava," Marcelle replied.

"I think it is," she said. "I'm sending you an email right now. I need you to review the two attachments. There's a synopsis of the two-night miniseries featuring the Taylors of Temptation and notes on how this deal has to be brokered."

"Has to be?" Marcelle asked, her voice a little clearer now.

Ava had known that business would wake Marcelle up completely. It always did.

"Yes," Ava told her. "Because this is how I'm going to pitch the story to the Taylors, and I'm pretty certain if I pitch it this way, and they agree, they're not going to take kindly to any abrupt changes."

"I take it this is different from what Jenner and Carroll told me about when they called me last week."

Ava's fingers stilled over the keyboard, and she had to readjust the phone she'd tucked between her ear and shoulder. She probably should have hunted through her purse to find her Bluetooth, but she hadn't wanted to waste any more time.

"They called you? Why?" she asked Marcelle.

There was some rattling in the phone's background, and Ava figured Marcelle had climbed out of bed and was now heading toward her home office so she could boot up her computer and read the email while they talked.

"They were pretty excited about this show and wanted to get started on getting you signed on officially."

"Well, you might want to hold off on that," Ava told her. "Because if they don't agree, I'm walking."

"Really?" Marcelle asked, her voice clear and questioning. "What about your new show idea?"

"I'm not going to be bullied by them," Ava said, wondering why she hadn't taken this stance from the start.

Fear. That was the clear-cut reason. She was afraid that going against top network executives would get her blackballed in the industry. And there was still a chance of that happening. Only now, she didn't give a damn. If she had to use her trust fund money to make her own movies, or buy a network where she could decide which shows would make it and which ones wouldn't, that's what she planned to do. Asking for and waiting for permission or validation from pompous men in this industry was over.

Gage had told her that. He'd said she shouldn't apologize for who and what she was to her mother and that she was enough on her own. Ava believed him because he believed in her.

Marcelle gave a whoop and said, "That's what I've been waiting to hear from you. Okay, let me look at the notes first because I already know your pitch is awesome."

"I don't want their lives intruded upon for months on end. The four-hour series can be taped in a month, edited the next month, advertised and shown in the same timespan they already have mapped out. But making this a full thirteen-week series is out of the question. They have lives and families and it's just too much to ask them to go through all of this again," Ava said.

"Okay, this all looks good. I'll work on your numbers. You're doing them a huge favor, and in return they're going to pay you a big damn chunk of money. And I want a clause in this contract that guarantees your next two shows. And...hmm, wait a minute," Marcelle said.

Ava was going through her email inbox seeing what she needed to read and what could be trashed, so she didn't speak while Marcelle paused.

"Well, this is very interesting indeed," Marcelle said after another minute or so.

"What's that?" Ava asked, just as she was about to close her email in-box. She needed to get topside to let Morgan know she was all right; otherwise Morgan might come down to check on her. Ava didn't want to be seen working when she was supposed to be recuperating.

"Apparently I need to check my office voice mail quicker. Parker Donovan sent an email to follow up to the message he left for me yesterday. He's very interested in meeting with you and discussing creative opportunities for you at Donovan Network Television," Marcelle told her.

Ava sat back in the chair and smiled. She couldn't help it—a fist bump in the air also came as she did everything she could to withhold the squeal of excitement that bubbled inside her.

"Yes!" she exclaimed. "So Jenner and Carroll can definitely take this deal for the Taylors or kick rocks!"

"You're damn right!" Marcelle yipped, excitement clear in her voice, as well. "Okay, since they're on the East Coast like you right now, I'll give them a call to let them know that I've received the message and I'm checking your availability. I'll also get a preliminary idea of what these Donovans are possibly talking about offering you to come to their network."

"Great. Keep me posted," Ava said. "Now, I've gotta go. Today's the Fall Festival."

Marcelle chuckled. "You're really settling into that little town, aren't you?"

Ava shrugged even though she knew Marcelle couldn't see her. "It happened so naturally. I mean, one minute I'll be sitting in my room writing and the next Otis is knocking on my door with the best home-made lemonade I've ever had and some sort of snack. While I eat, he tells me whatever is going on in town for that day. Then I go outside and people stop me on the street to talk about this or that. And the Taylors, they're super nice and very involved and—I guess I am getting caught up, huh?"

Marcelle chuckled. "Definitely. But Gage Taylor is scrumptious enough to have any woman moving to a small town and going to fall festivals, whatever those are."

Ava agreed and ended the call with Marcelle. She had just stood from the desk when she heard the door to the room open and Morgan come down. Just in time, she thought and then fixed a smile on her face to greet one of the nicest women she'd ever known. A woman who she could easily picture as a sister-in-law someday.

Gage could not ignore the instant swell of happiness that spread throughout his chest the moment he saw Ava come through the double doors of the old Hatlenbinger horse barn. It was chilly today, so she wore jeans, those sexy brown boots that tied up the back of her legs and a brown leather jacket. Her hair was styled in two braids, each hanging over one shoulder so that she looked younger and prettier. She stood still for a few moments, looking around the large structure similar to the way Gage had when he'd first entered a few hours ago to help Gray and the others set up.

The barn used to house Hatlenbinger's prized stallions and foaling mares when Gage had been younger. But, as told to him earlier by Fred Randall, Tom Hatlenbinger died of a massive heart attack ten years ago. After an argument with his two daughters prior to his death, he'd left everything he had to his second wife, who in turn sold the horses within the same month that Tom had passed away. The land had been bought by the town for taxes a few years prior to Tom's death, so his wife couldn't sell that, and the town decided to use the barn space to host the weekly farmer's market. The house had been renovated and was being used as a horse museum thanks to one of Hatlenbinger's daughters, who had returned to town.

Today it was filled with booths showcasing home-made items for sale. They had everything from jams to baskets to knitted sweaters. There were also tables crowded with cakes and pies, cookies and smoked meats for tasting and sale. In one of the far corners were bales of hay and a tractor for picture-taking and playing, as some children were already doing. Next to that section were five tables and an insane amount of pumpkins all ready for the contest.

"You just gonna stare at her for the rest of the day?" Gray asked.

Gage hadn't heard his brother approach and didn't bother to look over at him because he knew the smirk that would be on his face.

"She's mingling," he replied.

Two women Gage did not know had just stopped to speak to Ava, and he watched the exchange in awe of how quickly she'd made friends in this town.

"And you're ogling," Gray said. "You're so pitiful."

"Hey," Gage replied and then tore his gaze away from Ava long enough to glare at Gray. "No name-calling is allowed when you came here to sell three pieces of property and ended up marrying a woman, getting her pregnant and adopting her children."

Gray didn't look the least bit bothered by Gage's words, but instead shook his head. "You're not me," he said with a slow grin.

"Whatever, man. I'm not ashamed to admit that I came here for a visit and ended up falling in love."

"That's cool, because denying it would have been foolish. It's written all over your face," Gray said. "And truthfully, it looks good on you. I'm happy for you, especially considering how you both came to be here."

Gage did not want to hear about that coincidence again. He'd been thinking about it off and on since his siblings brought it up last night. It wasn't on purpose, he'd told himself finally, and that was that.

"To be fair, we hooked up after the end of shooting the first season of the show," he told Gray.

It wasn't something Gage would have normally told anyone, but he was tired of them acting as if he and Ava were only connected because they ended up in Temptation together.

"Really? Sleeping with the boss?" Gray said and folded his arms over his chest.

"Nah, it wasn't like that. There was this chemistry between us from day one. We fought it the whole time we were working, but then once the shooting was over, I guess we just figured it was fair to proceed." Gage thought back fondly on that night in Ava's trailer. "It was only supposed to be one time."

"But then she showed up here," Gray said.

Gage nodded. "And we were at it again. But this time it was different. I knew one more time wasn't going to be enough."

"It never is when you find the one." Gray clapped Gage on the shoulder. "Like I said, I'm happy for you. Ava's a good woman. Morgan and Harper love her, so all you have to do is get Gen's, Gemma's and Gia's approval, and you can go ahead and propose to her."

"Propose? I don't know if I'm ready to start thinking about marriage."

Gray chuckled. "Yeah, you keep right on telling yourself that."

"Really, I wasn't."

"Uh-huh. Well, if you aren't thinking about putting a ring on it, you probably should," Gray told him and then pointed toward the door once more.

Gage followed his brother's direction and saw Ava laughing at something Craig Presley was saying. More importantly, he saw how close Ava and Craig were standing to each other and how Ava easily rested her hand on Craig's arm.

He took a step in their direction and heard Gray laugh.

"Yeah, that's what I thought," his brother was saying, but Gage kept walking, until he came up behind Ava and Craig.

It was just in time to hear Ava say, "I'm sorry I never followed through on the rain check for dinner. I had work and then things just started happening."

Craig smiled down at her. "Yeah, things like you and Gage hooking up. I get it, and there are no worries. I was just offering to show you around."

"And I appreciate it," Ava said. "You were very friendly and helpful when I first arrived."

"Hey there," Gage said when he finally stepped up to them. "You look like you're feeling better."

"Hey. I am," she said and then looked up at him as if nobody else in that barn even existed.

"How's it going, Craig?" Gage spoke and extended his hand to shake the younger man's.

"Hey, Gage. Going great. Been pretty busy with projects, but Harper said we'll slow down for the holidays. We're still waiting on Ava to decide when and where she wants to build her tiny house, though," Craig said.

"I haven't even had a moment to think about that lately," Ava said.

"Well, you should," Craig continued. "Temptation's a great place to have a small getaway home."

Gage agreed. "You don't have much time to think about it now either. We're up," he told her. "The contest is about to start."

"Oh, right. See ya later, Craig," Ava said as Gage took her hand.

"What do you mean, 'see ya later'? I'm entered in the contest, so be prepared to be wowed by my creation!"

As they walked across the barn to the area set up for the contest, Gage couldn't help but think about Craig's words to Ava. Temptation was a great place to build a house. But what else? A family? A home?

An hour and a half later, Ava hugged Craig and placed the goofy jack-o'-lantern sponge hat on his head. He was the winner of the pumpkin-carving contest, and as such had won the lovely hat and a fifty-dollar coupon to O'Reiley's Pumpkin Patch. His pumpkin-turned-Darth-Vader was the best carving Ava and Gage had ever seen.

Gray, Jack and Lily came in second place and had posed happily with their creation—a crooked but valiant attempt at the Grinch. The contest had been a blast. The hot cider and sugar cookies being passed around were even better. But overall, it was just the people,

Ava thought, that made this a fantastic event. She'd been to who knew how many Hollywood parties and corporate functions with her mother, but none of them compared to this.

"It's movie time!" Jack yelled excitedly.

Morgan was there shaking her head. "I don't know. I heard Craig telling Harper that he picked something extra scary for tonight's movie. I don't think you and your sister will be able to watch."

Harper waved a hand. "My aunt Laura quickly put the kibosh on that," she said. "We're watching *It's The Great Pumpkin, Charlie Brown* first, and then Craig's allowed to show *Poltergeist*, but not the other horribly gruesome movie he was planning on."

"Charlie Brown! I love Charlie Brown!" Lily announced.

"Okay, then let's head on out so we can get a good seat in front of the screen," Morgan told them.

"We're just going to clean up here a little. Save us a seat," Ava told Morgan and Gray.

"Oh no, you're not," Gage warned. "You're going to go on and sit down. I'll clean up, and then I'll join you. So you can save me a seat."

When Ava opened her mouth to argue, Wendy, Morgan's sister, touched her shoulder. "Don't even bother. Take the offer of help 'cause who knows when you'll get another one."

Ava liked Wendy because she reminded her so much of Marcelle. She agreed with her, and they all walked outside to where chairs had been set up in rows on the grass like they were at a real movie theatre. A large screen had been rented and placed up front for the movie viewing. They found seats in the fourth row, and Ava eased down the aisle to sit alongside the Taylor family.

It felt perfect sitting here, waiting for the movie to begin, talking to Lily, stopping Jack from climbing over the chairs in the next row and laughing with Wendy and Harper. She'd never had moments like this with her mother, or even with both her parents when her father was alive. This was what it was like to belong to a real family. She smiled to herself and thanked every deity possible for her good fortune.

"Attention! Attention!" A woman stood in front of the screen with a microphone.

Ava recalled meeting her before. She was one of the women who had been with Millie the second time the brash woman had approached her. Her name was Shirley Hampstead, and she was the town comptroller. Ava loved putting names with faces and job titles. It was a lot better than putting names with the last movie someone had done, or the last scandal they'd been involved in. She put a finger up to her lips and gave Jack a stern look before returning her attention to Shirley.

"We'd like to thank everyone for coming out to this year's festival. It's been a wonderful day, and we owe it all to the Magnolia Guild for their fund-raisers throughout the year that help us pay for events like this." Shirley gave a nod to someone in the audience, and there was applause.

"Also, on behalf of Mayor Pullum, who's still recovering from knee surgery, we want to thank all of this year's volunteers. Without you we wouldn't have been set up on time." With that, Shirley and a few other people in the audience laughed and clapped.

"As always, a very special thanks goes to JoEllen Camby for planning this function—from her house—every single year. JoEllen does a magnificent job," Shirley told the crowd, who clapped in response.

Wendy leaned over to whisper to Ava. "And that, my dear, is how you serve sarcasm here in Temptation."

Ava laughed and shook her head.

Then her smile faltered slightly as a familiar face joined Shirley. Millie wore a burnt-orange pantsuit with a white blouse and a large pumpkin pendant on the lapel of her jacket.

"Now, I've saved the best for last," Shirley said, "I'm so excited about this announcement, I could just bust."

Shirley did a little shake that may have been meant to accompany her words about busting, but actually made her look a little insane, as she wore a tight green dress that surely would not support her body parts in the event any busting were to actually take place. Millie snatched the microphone from Shirley before anything like that could happen.

"As the chairperson of Temptation's chamber of commerce, I'll be making the next announcement," Millie started to say.

Ava looked around for Gage at that moment because she really didn't want to hear anything that Millie had to say. The woman was a troublemaker, and she was rude and annoying.

"This time last year, we welcomed back to town a

member of one of our most esteemed families. I'd like to ask Grayson Taylor and his wife and children to stand," Millie said.

Harper leaned over in her seat, looking past Ava to where Wendy sat. Wendy shrugged and Harper shook her head. Ava watched as Gray stood with Jack on his shoulders and Morgan stood with Lily standing in the seat beside her. The audience clapped once again.

"Yes, welcome back to the Taylors," Millie continued. "I'm saying that with a plural because Garrek Taylor was back with us for a few months this year. Just long enough to snag the heart of our very own Harper Presley. Harper, you come on and stand, too."

Harper groaned as she got to her feet, and Ava gave her a conciliatory pat on her back when she sat down again.

"It seems like all the Taylors are coming home," Millie went on to say. "And with that comes our big announcement. As you all know, once upon a time *The Taylors of Temptation* was a reality show. And this show brought lots of revenue to our fair town. Now, thirty years later when reality television is still going strong, the Taylors are going to help our town out once again by filming an all-new reality show."

Ava's heart sank, and her throat went dry as whispers began to sound in the audience.

"That's right, the new show is going to be called *The Taylors of Temptation: Remember the Times.* And it's all set to air this time next year. Filming will start soon after the first of the year, so in addition to welcoming the rest of the Taylor sextuplets home, we'll also be preparing for visitors. The crew and all those Hollywood folk will be staying here in town and eating and shopping. We'll make enough money to fix the bridge down by the stream and make necessary improvements to the dock, as well as help some of the local businesses refresh their storefronts. We want to look our best, of course."

All of a sudden Ava didn't know what to do with her hands. They'd been resting in her lap, but now she was wringing them, and when she realized what she was doing she hurriedly dropped them to her sides. She didn't want to look to her left or to her right, because Wendy and Harper were most likely staring at her in question. Instead she looked over the heads of the audience toward the barn, where Gage now stood, his gaze zeroing in on her.

"So let's give a great big round of applause to the Hollywood producer Ava Cannon, who has been staying with us these past couple of months. Ava's been here scouting locations and getting the Taylor family ready to be in the spotlight once again. Come on and stand up so we can all see you, Ava."

Ava didn't stand. She didn't need to. All eyes were immediately on her. But the only ones she gave a damn about were his.

Chapter 13

Gage gripped the steering wheel as he drove them toward the dock. So many things had been flowing through his mind since they'd left the festival, but he knew he'd needed to take a moment to get his thoughts together.

"Is that what this has been about?" Gage asked when he stopped his car.

After Millie's announcement he'd stood still, unable to move a muscle as he watched Ava moving through the crowd toward him. She was trying to get out of the row where she'd been sitting, but people kept congratulating her, or simply standing just to shake her hand. To shake the hand of the producer of the new Taylors of Temptation reality show.

"No," she immediately replied. "We... What we have is separate."

"Separate from you brokering a deal for a show that was never going to happen," he replied.

His hands slipped slowly off the steering wheel to rest in his lap. He felt calm, dangerously so.

"The deal happened before us, or rather, before this 'us' began," she said and then turned sideways in the seat to look at him. "Let me just explain from the beginning."

Gage shook his head. "You followed me here and weaseled your way into my family, so that you could film us again. You knew how I felt about that show and being in the spotlight from day one, and you stayed, you continued. You lied to me. You used me and my family."

"That's not entirely true," she continued. "When I was approached about this deal, all I knew was that your family had stayed out of the limelight for the last thirty years. I didn't know why."

"And you didn't bother to ask," he responded and felt his entire body begin to shake.

"I wanted a chance to get to know you and the family first, and then I was going to—"

"You were going to what, Ava? Would you have married me if I asked? Had my kids maybe? All to get your precious show. What's the matter, one successful show wasn't enough? Or was it that you couldn't stand your own dysfunctional family so you decided to squirm your way into another one to see if you could destroy it, too?"

She jerked as if he'd physically assaulted her, and Gage frowned.

"I can explain," she said slowly. "I can tell you exactly how this came about and the terms I've requested for you and your family."

"I don't give a damn about any terms," he said, this time through clenched teeth because the calm he'd possessed was slowly slipping. "I don't care about your explanations. This business ruined my family once, there's no way I'm going to let that happen again."

"Gage—" she started.

"No!" he yelled. "I drove you back here so you can get your things. I'll call you a cab while you pack."

He opened the door and stepped out of the car. He closed the door but still stood beside it waiting…for what, he had no idea. To wake up possibly, from this horrid dream. For her to tell him that Millie had lied and none of this was happening. That the woman he'd fallen in love with hadn't screwed him just to see her name roll in the credits of another television show.

He heard the passenger side door open and close softly.

"I apologize for not telling you sooner," she said. "I should have. I knew it all along, and I didn't say anything. I guess I didn't want to destroy the perfect moments we were having."

"They weren't perfect," he replied and gazed at her over the top of the car. "They were lies. All of this was a lie. Just like the show that was on television thirty years ago. We were never that happy family enjoying the limelight. My father was never the happily married man madly in love with his wife. We're not on television right now, so if in your mind this was going to end with a big wedding, a house and kids, you were wrong."

"If you would just let me explain," she tried once more.

"Explain what? That you were just fine sleeping with me and dragging me to parties, but when it really came down to it, you didn't give a damn about me or my feelings."

He took a breath, but more words came, and Gage was helpless to stop them.

"You want to explain why you lay in bed with me every night and never once bothered to tell me you were having my baby? Why did I have to find out the day after you aborted my child when the clinic called to check on you because your blood pressure was running high when you were discharged? Why are you constantly lying and deceiving me when I've told you how hard it was for me to trust anyone?"

Silence fell between them after those last words. Ava stared at him with tears and confusion in her eyes.

Gage cursed.

He ran his hands down his face and cursed again.

"Gage," she gasped.

"No," he said. "Just no. It's enough."

"I didn't know. I'm not like whoever she was. Let me—"

"No!" he yelled. And then sighed. "Just stay the hell away from me."

When she didn't move or speak, he walked around the car to stand directly in front of her.

"I mean it. Get yourself another consultant for your

show and find another family to exploit, because it won't be me or the Taylors. Stay away from me and my family."

He walked away then, letting himself onto the yacht but going straight back to the lounge room, where there was a bar. He needed a drink. And he needed her off his boat and out of his life…before he could deal with the fact that his heart was breaking once again—and this time it had nothing to do with a television show.

It was her fault.

She shouldn't be irritated as hell with Gage. But she was.

How dare he order her to get her stuff off his yacht and then call her a cab to get her away from him as fast as possible? And on top of all that, he'd warned her to stay away from him and his family, as if she had no choice but to listen to him on this matter. There were five other adults involved in this situation—whether she'd talked to all of them directly or not—and they each deserved the opportunity to listen to her proposal and provide an answer. She should just set up a meeting with them and see what happened.

But doing so would hurt him more.

More than what this woman had apparently done to him. He'd had a child, and she took it from him without even telling him. It was no wonder Gage didn't trust people. And Ava had lied to him, as well. She couldn't deny that fact.

Pressing this issue, forcing his family into the spotlight—with or without him—would seal Gage's distrust box closed tightly forever. And even if he couldn't bring himself to stay with her, he deserved love and happiness with someone.

By the time Ava climbed out of the cab, it was almost midnight.

She walked around to the trunk, where the driver was removing her bags. "Here you go." She extended the twenty dollars to him and bent down to pick up the duffel bag he'd placed on the curb.

"Fare's already taken care of," he told her. "I'll carry these others to the door for you."

Ava frowned. What kind of guy put a woman out and paid for her cab fare?

The kind she was desperately in love with

She knocked on the door, the last bits of her pride in her back pocket, and waited. Harper opened the door and offered her a small smile. A genuine smile.

Once she and all her stuff were in Harper's foyer, Ava cleared her throat and said, "I apologize. I should have been up-front with everyone the moment I interrupted the volleyball game that day."

"You could have done that," Harper said as she folded her arms over her chest. "But then you wouldn't have learned all you did about the Taylor family, and you wouldn't have had the chance to fall in love with Temptation and Gage."

Ava ran her hands through her hair and sighed. "I don't know how any of that happened. I was just trying to do my job."

"But something else occurred," Harper said with a nod. "Been there. Done that."

"You deceived and alienated a family that you not only needed for work, but loved and admired, as well?" Ava asked and chuckled to keep from crying.

"Not exactly," Harper replied. "But it took me a minute to accept the love that had blossomed because of my independence and everything I'd built my life to be."

"There's nothing to accept now," Ava said quietly. "Absolutely nothing."

She walked away from Harper and up that gorgeous romantic stairway with heavy steps. It was all over. Tomorrow she would arrange for her and her mother to go back to LA.

"Oh, Ava. Darling, I wasn't expecting you," Eleanor said and then giggled.

Yes, Ava thought with a start as her eyes widened and her mouth gaped, her mother was giggling. And she was sitting up in the bed accepting grapes from Otis, who sat on the side of the bed, also giggling.

"Ah, hiya, Miss Ava," Otis said before popping another fat grape into her mother's mouth.

"What. Is. Going on here?" Ava asked. She couldn't stop her feet from leading her deeper into the room. Even though her eyes were burning at the sight of her mother in such an—for lack of a better word—intimate position with a man.

"Otis took off work today. He's been here taking care of me since this afternoon when Harper left to go see about you," Eleanor said. "Did you have fun at the festival?"

"No," Ava replied instantly. "That's what I came to talk to you about."

"Well, go ahead and talk," Eleanor told her. "Otis has been such a doll, making sure I had everything I need while recuperating."

"Right," Otis said. He looked from Ava to Eleanor and then back to Ava. "But I think I'll be going now."

"Thank you," Ava said. Since her mother apparently wasn't getting the hint that she needed to talk.

"I'll come check on you tomorrow," Otis said as he stood. He set the bowl of grapes on the nightstand and was about to walk away when Eleanor reached for his hand.

"That's very nice of you, Otis."

"We won't be here tomorrow," Ava said. "I mean, I'll be making arrangements for us to fly out tomorrow."

"We are?" Eleanor asked, the surprised look on her face real and perplexing.

"Oh. Well, yeah, I'll just be going. I, um, guess I'll give you a call or something sometime, Ellie."

Ellie?

Otis touched her mother's hand, and the two shared a look. It wasn't a look that Ava wanted to explore, and so she glanced away from them. Seconds later Otis was touching her shoulder lightly as he walked past.

"It was a pleasure, Miss Ava," he mumbled before leaving the room.

Once the door was closed, Ava moved closer to the bed. "What was that?"

"That was me having the most fun I've had in the last ten years," Eleanor quipped.

Her words, in addition to the situation, once again startled Ava, who sighed and sat on the end of the bed.

"Well, I messed up big-time. So the fun for both of us is over," she said.

"You? The one who has her life together, who knows what she wants and is going to go get it with or without her mother's approval. *You* messed up?"

Her mother was a lot of things, and condescending was one of her specialties. Ava very rarely admitted that Eleanor was right.

"I thought I was doing the right thing," Ava said after recounting the whole story for her mother. "I figured if I could just rework the deal, the Taylors would definitely go for it. And I was going to tell them everything tomorrow night at dinner. I had it all planned out."

"Yes, you seem to plan things out very well," Eleanor said. "The problem is, you don't account for life happening throughout your plan."

Ava kicked off her shoes and turned around, pulling her legs up onto the bed. "What are you talking about?"

Eleanor waved her hand and then fluffed the pillows behind her before settling back again. "Life, Ava. It happens to all of us. Do you think I wanted my successful and handsome husband to turn into an alcoholic? Did I want to have the managing partner of the firm call me and tell me that if my husband didn't get himself together, he would be fired and we would be thrust into the poorhouse?"

The last was a bit dramatic considering Eleanor and Ava had huge trust funds courtesy of Eleanor's godfather, who died six months after Ava was born. In addition, Ava's father had made millions at the firm. He was a shrewd investor and doubled his yearly earnings consistently. So when he died he left a pretty hefty estate, with enough to take care of his wife and daughter comfortably for the rest of their lives.

"I wanted my fairy tale," Eleanor continued. "I'd fallen madly in love with Haywood Cannon, and on our first date had pictured our lavish lives together. We would have a magnificent house full of beautiful children and want for absolutely nothing. I had to have an emergency hysterectomy after giving birth to you. Fifteen years later Haywood found out he was adopted. His birth brother killed four people before taking his own life. And when Haywood traced the rest of his family, he found out his parents were also criminals and had died in jail.

"He was devastated, and a glass of wine in the evenings turned into a bottle of scotch hidden in his office drawer, our bathroom and his home office. I thought if I continued on with our lives, proving to Haywood that I would stand by him no matter what his birthright, that things would eventually return to normal. The phone call in the middle of the night informing me that my husband was dead was a cruel wake-up call."

Eleanor blinked. Her eyes shone with tears. Ava couldn't speak—she didn't know what to say because she'd never heard this story before.

"Life happens, Ava. There's no way to plan for it, and no amount of running away from it will fix problems. It just happens."

"I could have told him," Ava said quietly and looked down at her hands. "I could have just told Gage the truth."

"And I could have insisted your father get help."

"It's not the same," Ava argued.

"The circumstances aren't, no. But the concept is. Look at me, Ava."

At the sharp tone, Ava's head shot up, and she stared back at her mother to see tears streaming down Eleanor's face.

"If I had told Haywood to get help, if I had insisted and then worked with him to get through the disillusionment he'd suffered, maybe he wouldn't have thought driving off that cliff was the only answer. I had the love of my life, and I didn't do enough to hold on to it."

When Ava opened her mouth to speak, her mother held up one elegant hand.

"If you had told Gage about the show for his family from day one, he might have said no and sent you away. Or he might have listened to you and let you speak to his family, and they might have all made a decision. But that time has passed. You cannot determine what the outcome would have been at this point any more than I can. But you still have the opportunity that I missed."

Ava shook her head. "I don't know what to do now. I mean, I do. I should just go. I betrayed him, all of them."

"You were doing your job and you fell in love. That's life. But you are no quitter," Eleanor told her. "You're not like me. Don't miss the opportunity to say something, do something, that might change the course of these events. If you really love this man, you need to grab hold of that love and don't let go."

She heard what her mother was saying, and she knew what she meant, but Ava was tired, and she was certain that she never wanted to see Gage looking at her the way he had just a short while ago again. Her heart couldn't take it.

"We're going home tomorrow, Mother," Ava said and crawled to the head of the bed to sit next to her mother. She took her hand and laid her head on Eleanor's shoulder. "Thank you for talking to me about Dad and what really happened. I'm sorry it didn't turn out better."

"Not as sorry as I am, my baby. Every day I wonder and I hurt. Well, every day until I met Otis."

That made Ava smile. "Wow. You and Otis."

Eleanor chuckled. "I know. There's just something about this town."

That was something else Ava and Eleanor could agree on. There was something about Temptation and the people here. Especially the Taylors. But that something would soon be in Ava's past. It had to be.

Chapter 14

Two weeks later

Gemma Taylor sat at the head of the formal dining room table in Gray's house. She was a tall woman, at five feet ten inches, with a heavily creamed coffee complexion and ink-black hair that fell in perfect soft waves past her shoulders. She sat with her shoulders squared, brown eyes searching and assessing everyone in the room with her. She looked, to Gage, just like their mother.

"This is ridiculous," Gage said. "There's nothing to discuss."

"That's not your call," Gemma told him calmly. "This involved all of us, so we should have all been consulted."

"I agree," Gray, who was sitting across the table from Gage, said. "This is how it should have happened from the start. All of us here, listening to what the network has to say and then deciding how to proceed."

"I don't want to be on a television show," Gage insisted.

"And neither do I," Garrek chimed in from the Skype call he'd been connected through. "But I don't think I can make that call for anyone else."

"He can't," Gia replied.

She and Gen had once again been connected to the meeting via FaceTime calls, with Harper and Morgan sitting at the table holding the phones.

"And you're certain Ava never mentioned this to you, Gage?" Gemma asked. "You could have simply dismissed it because you're so firm in your answer."

Gage stared at her blankly for a moment, and then he fumed. This was all Ava's fault. Now she was pitting them against each other.

"I definitely would have remembered her telling me that she was here to spy on my family for the sake of a new show," he said.

"It could have been after those steamy bouts of sex on your lovely yacht," Morgan said and then looked across the room as if she hadn't just aimed those words at him.

The doorbell rang, and Harper set her phone on the table, saying, "I'll get it."

Gage could have sworn he heard her chuckle as she walked out of the room and headed to the door. He wisely remained silent and sat back in the chair. He rested his hands on his thighs and decided to play this as cool as he possibly could. It wasn't going to be easy. Not like handing in his resignation to the hospital and packing up his condo had been. That was a surprise to him, because he'd spent his entire life striving to get to those places. It shouldn't have been so easy to walk away. But he hadn't wanted to examine the reasons for that. He'd just wanted to get back to Temptation and to get started on his new dream, even if a huge part of it had fallen through.

"Everyone, this is Ava Cannon. She's here on behalf of Donovan Network Television and would like to present a business opportunity to the family," Harper said.

Gage heard his siblings speaking to Ava and thanking her for coming. He did not turn around to look at her, nor did he say a word to her. He couldn't. There were no words to describe what these last two weeks had been like for him. And heaven help him, he couldn't figure out the words to make things better.

"Thank you for inviting me," Ava said.

From the sound of her voice, and because he could see her movement out of his peripheral vision, he could tell she'd entered the dining room and followed Harper to stand at the other end of the table.

"It's a pleasure to meet you all. I've heard a lot about you from…your family, and then I've done some research," Ava said.

"You should probably focus more on what the family says," Gemma joked. "Even though they can embellish a bit, too."

Everyone around the table laughed. Except Gage.

"Well, I'll get right to it," Ava said. She pulled out a laptop and placed it on the table. After tapping some keys, she turned it to face everyone.

Gage couldn't help but look. On the screen was a purple-and-gold logo that read The Taylors of Temptation. In seconds, that screen dissolved and in its place was Lemil Mountain Lake, the words "A Whole New World" appearing in shimmering letters over the water.

"Awww, it's the lake," Gia said. "You remember playing softball there, Gage? You were always begging Mom and Dad to take us there on pretty summer days."

"I hated swimming," Gen said. "But Gage loved the water."

"He still does," Gray said frankly.

Ava cleared her throat.

"I was first approached by producers at my former network to create a show surrounding the Taylors. It would have been a thirteen-episode reality show following each of you and your new life around Temptation. Marketing and scheduling were already in place. I didn't ask why in the beginning, but I should have. As it turns out, the producers had already worked out a deal for this show with Theodor Taylor. They'd even paid him an advance in the amount of seven million dollars."

Silence filled the room.

"I've since gathered additional information," Ava continued. "The advance money was wired to an account in the name of S. Frank Brewster. He was a carpenter who worked on the houses on Bond Street. S. Frank Brewster died last month, and his son, Tobias Brewster, has a Christmas tree farm just south of Temptation.

Tobias was kind enough to let me go through some of his father's papers, and I found email receipts of when Frank set up an account in Grand Cayman Island with 6.8 million dollars. The remaining money was reported as a fee to Frank from Theodor, and Tobias inherited it upon his father's death."

"I'll be damned," Gemma said, resting her elbows on the table and staring at the laptop screen.

"So Dad decided we were doing this show without conferring with us either," Gia said. "Ain't that something."

Gray shook his head. "It's something, all right."

Gage remained speechless. He'd said he didn't care about where the money had come from, but it was nice to finally hear about the money trail and receive the full story.

"When the executives came to me about the show, it was because upon Theodor's death, the signed contract they had became null and void. But they were out seven million dollars," Ava told them.

"So they needed you to come here and make it happen. They needed you to get the show on air because you'd done such a great job with *Doctor's Orders*," Morgan stated.

"And they knew that Gage had been working on the show with me," Ava said.

This time her voice—which Gage had been trying to convince himself he hadn't missed hearing—cracked a bit, and guilt settled into his chest like a pile of hot rocks.

"All of this was happening in LA," Harper said. "How did Millie find out?"

"I can explain that, too," Ava said. "My agent found out that Miranda Martinez, one of the actresses from *Doctor's Orders*, was sleeping with one of the execs at the network. She wanted to be involved in the reality show as a possible love interest."

Gage frowned at those words. He recalled Miranda's not-so-subtle advances when they'd been at the awards show.

Ava continued. "When they turned her down, Miranda threatened to leak the show idea to another network. To counter her threat, the execs hurried to release a preliminary announcement about the show to a few key press contacts. We assume someone from the press contacted Millie in the hopes of a background story about the town."

Gemma shook her head. "This is unbelievable," she said. "The things that go on in the world of television and celebrities."

Which was exactly why Gage had wanted nothing to do with this world. But hadn't he already been involved in the world? He was working on a television show, even as a consultant, and he'd been sleeping with a writer/producer.

"So what happens now?" Gen asked.

"I am no longer working with that network," Ava told them. "Their idea for the show and what I was willing to present to you were different. They weren't open to a compromise, and neither was I."

Gemma leaned over and pinched Gage's knee.

"Soon after I severed ties with the station, I went to Miami and met with Parker and Savian Donovan from Donovan Network Television. They asked about you, Gage," she said.

When all eyes fell on him, Gage looked down the table to Ava. She looked amazing in a black pantsuit and teal blouse. Her hair was pulled over to rest on one shoulder, and that spot he loved to kiss—the hollow of her neck—beckoned him. He cleared his throat.

"Why would they ask about me?"

"You met them when we were at the awards show, and they remembered," she replied.

"Oh, yeah. Right," Gage said, and after a pause continued. "What happened at the meeting?"

"I'm not sure if any of you have heard of them, but the Donovans are a very large and prestigious African American family. They have their hand in just about everything, from oil to television to casinos. Anyway, the Donovans are all about family first. So when Parker and Savian asked about Gage, I took that as a sign, and I pitched my revised idea for the Taylors of Temptation show. And they loved it!"

Gia squealed. "What's the revised idea?"

Ava explained the four-hour, two-night special and that they could decide which siblings appeared and how their story would be told. She talked about payment and contracts and negotiable points. She suggested, if they were considering it, that they should each get an agent or a lawyer to look over their contracts and advise them further of their rights before they commit.

And then she said, "I never meant to exploit any of

you, or what your parents went through. I was reluctant about even taking the job at first. But then I came to Temptation, and I saw Gray and Morgan and the kids. I met Harper and I listened to how she talked about Garrek and falling in love with him. I listened to Gage talk about your childhood and the things you lost because of the show. And I changed my mind. I didn't want to do anything that would hurt any of you. I should have told you all from the start, but I didn't know how."

She shook her head. "No. That's not true. I didn't want to. I didn't want my time with this family and with…" She paused, her gaze resting on Gage. "I didn't want any of it to end. So I pushed it off, and I worked on an idea that I thought would suit you better. But believe me, I understand completely if you don't want to take it. If you want to remain a family outside of the spotlight, I get it. I do, and I envy you for it."

"I'm in!" Gia yelled. "It'll be great exposure for my new restaurant."

"I think you're right," Gen added. "We could get some great advertising for our businesses out of this."

"I'm not sure what my schedule will be like," Garrek said. "But if you want to get in on the advertising possibilities, Harper, I'm okay with it."

Gage looked across the table to see Gray staring at him.

"Morgan and I have to talk about this," Gray said. "We're the only ones who have children involved, and I don't want to risk them in any way," he said.

Morgan reached out to take his hand. "We'll talk about it and figure out what works best for us."

Gemma smiled. "Well, I don't know. I've got a lot going on right now and...I just don't know."

Gage looked at his sister. He'd been wondering why she'd shown up in Temptation six weeks before their scheduled Christmas dinner, but he hadn't found a moment to ask her about it.

Conversation about the show and questions for Ava continued, but Gage didn't want to hear any of it. He'd heard enough and now...well, now he was right back to being unsure of what he should do or say. So he opted to leave instead.

He couldn't help it; he looked at Ava as he stood. She was in her element, talking about shows and episodes and advertising blocks. She was great at her job; that had never been a question to him. It was everything else. How she felt in his arms. How it felt to have her sleeping next to him, writhing beneath him, laughing beside him. All of that had been amazing and he'd fallen for it. Hard.

Now, he needed to figure out how to pick himself up again.

An hour later, Gage stepped out of the First Unity of Temptation Bank and looked up to the sky. That's where his mother was, and he wondered if she were looking down on him, curious as to what his next step would be. And if his father were in heaven, too, was he standing beside his wife—the woman Gage had once heard Theodor say was the love of his life—watching to see what their fifth-born child would do about his future at this moment?

Gage held the key his father had left for him in one hand, his cell phone in the other, and stood in the middle of the sidewalk on Crane Street for another few minutes. He looked up and down the street to the people moving about. The two male tourists who walked hand in hand looking into the window of a gift shop specializing in Lemil Mountain Lake memorabilia, and the grandfather across the street holding his young granddaughter's hand while they waited for the traffic light to change. Cars drove past, at a much slower speed than they traveled in New York, and the coffee shop just a few blocks down served coffee, sticky buns and much better conversation than the coffee place on the main level of Nancy Links Medical Center.

He smiled as he turned to walk toward where his car was parked, because in this moment Gage knew that he'd made the right decision. Although none of this had been part of his original plan, he felt with every fiber of his being that this was what his life was meant to be.

He drove for almost half an hour before parking his car on a grassy spot. He reached into his back pocket and pulled out the papers he'd retrieved from the safe-deposit box in the bank—the one that his special key had opened. He checked the address on the papers and then looked at his GPS. He had arrived at his destination, but there was nothing here.

Gage stepped out of the car and stuffed his keys into his pocket. He kept the papers in his hand, but rolled them up as he walked across the grass. There were acres of grass to one side, and to his delight, mountains on the other side. He continued to walk because he heard a familiar sound—the rustling of water over rocks and sand. The lake was about twenty miles ahead. Folding his arms over his chest, Gage stood and simply stared, enjoying the sight before him.

"Patsy and Jebediah Johnson built a house here sixty-two years ago," a woman said from behind.

Gage turned abruptly to see her standing there, wearing a long purple dress fringed in lace that looked as old as the years of which she'd spoken. Her gray hair was pulled up in a neat stack, pearl earrings at her ears that perfectly matched the color of the wool coat she wore. Her gloved hands were clasped in front of her while gray eyes stared directly at him.

"You don't remember me," she continued. "I'm JoEllen Camby, and I remember you very well. Patsy was beside herself with joy the moment she found out her daughter, Olivia, was pregnant. Teddy and Olivia had tried for so long, Jeb had begun to believe he'd never get grandchildren. But Patsy, oh, she was a praying woman. Yes indeed. She and I used to stay at the church long after Sunday service was over, and we'd go down to the altar and get on our knees. We prayed until times got better, yes, we did."

The woman talked with the old lyrical voice of someone who had seen and experienced a myriad of events, and nothing but her faith had brought her through. Her honey-brown skin was wrinkled and sagged a bit at the cheeks, but she stood straight and strong. She sounded wise and knowledgeable, and Gage was instantly captivated by her words.

"You and my grandmother prayed for the in vitro treatments to work," he stated.

"Yes, we sure did. Some silly folk in the church thought it wasn't godly, but we knew that the good Lord made a way for his faithful children. And if the only way Olivia and Teddy were going to have a baby was with the help of science, then so be it," Mrs. Camby said with a swift nod. "And, oh, when Teddy announced it at the town council meeting he was attending one night, we all cheered. We couldn't wait until the babies were born. Then those TV people came, and the devil went to work."

She shook her head then. "Olivia was unhappy after the first two years of the show. She wanted desperately to have her husband and her babies to herself. She cried to Patsy many a day, and Patsy walked up on my back porch or we came right out here to look at the water and talk about how such a happy time had gone sour so quickly. I thank the good Lord for taking Patsy and Jeb away from here in that fire, three years before their only daughter packed up her children and left town. But I still come out here from time to time."

Gage remembered his mother telling them about her parents and how they'd died. He also remembered talk of his great-grandfather, Patsy's father, who had offered his vacation home in Pensacola to Olivia and the children when she'd left. He'd lived until Gage and his siblings were fifteen.

"This is the land their house was on," he said after thinking on Mrs. Camby's words for a few seconds.

She nodded. "Yes. Right here. It was a great big ol'

house because Patsy had wanted more children, but that wasn't meant to be. The remnants of the house and the land fell to your mother after her parents died. So she could have repaired the house and moved you children here after what Teddy did to her. But I understand why she had to get away. Gossip can be unrelenting, especially in a town like Temptation."

"People have a hard time minding their own business," Gage said, thinking about Miranda and Millie.

"Ain't that the truth," Mrs. Camby said with a smile. "But this is your mother's land, free and clear."

Gage shook his head. "It's my land now," he said with a glib smile. "My mother apparently missed a tax payment at some point, and when the town would have foreclosed on it, my father bought it. And when he died," Gage said, holding up the hand with the rolled-up papers in it, "he left the land to me."

Mrs. Camby nodded and smiled. "Teddy loved himself some Olivia. I never believed he stopped loving her or his children."

"He just couldn't do right by her or us," Gage said drily.

"Every man can't make the right decision all the time. It's not natural," she told Gage. "You should know that for yourself. But if it's your land, you do with it as you please. Just don't forget the love that was here. That's what happens too many times to count—people forget about the love."

Gage didn't. He couldn't. And that's why he'd sent the text message to Ava before he'd left the bank.

For what seemed like a long stretch of time after Mrs.

Camby left him alone on the property, Gage heard a car stop and park. He looked out at the water, holding his breath and rehearsing the words in his head. He needed them to come out right, and he needed her to listen and to accept his apology, his heart and his soul.

Ava stepped out of the rental car and looked straight ahead to where Gage stood. His back was to her, but she had a feeling he knew she was there. Of course he should, since his text message had said for her to meet him here. She had only planned to stay in Temptation overnight, making herself available in case the Taylors had immediate questions about her offer. But she hadn't wanted to chance being here any longer because the memories were just too tough to ignore.

In the two weeks they'd been apart, Ava had used every ounce of strength she had to hold her head up and forge forward with her work. But there wasn't a moment in each day that she didn't think about him, about the brief time she'd been allowed the dream of what they could be together.

Seeing Gage earlier today had proven to her that the dream had fizzled and burned. He hadn't even wanted to look at her as she'd stood in his brother's house, and a part of her couldn't blame him. Another part was pissed with him for not at least hearing her out and then making an informed decision. And for not telling her about the woman who had broken his heart and his spirit. But that was beyond her control.

Walking toward him now was a bad idea—she sensed it, and yet she didn't pause.

"Thank you for coming," he said, when she finally stopped and stood silently beside him.

"You asked me to come because you had something to say. I wanted to give you the chance, even though you denied me the same," she said in a tone that she knew was frosty, but she couldn't help it.

He surprised her by replying, "I know. That's what I wanted to tell you, that I was an idiot."

"Oh," was all she could manage to say. "Well. Okay. Then I guess I'll get going."

Ava didn't know why exactly, but she hurriedly turned away to leave. Gage's hand on her arm stopped her.

"Don't," he said.

She glanced down to his hand and then up to him. He looked as good as she recalled. Not that it was logical to think that in fourteen days he would age fifty years, grow a potbelly and regret ever letting her go. That had been one of her thoughts when she was lying awake at night, cursing him for making her fall in love with him.

"Do you have something else to say?"

"I do," he told her. "But first, I've been thinking about this for the past two weeks."

"Thinking about wh—"

Her words were cut off when Gage pulled her to him, wrapping an arm tightly around her back to hold her there, and his lips crashed down over hers. The kiss was hot and rough, rugged and delicious. His tongue worked masterfully over hers, his hands moving over her back, down her arms and to cup her hips. She wrapped her arms around his neck because there was nothing else she'd rather do with them. Her palms flattened on the back of his head as she leaned into him and they took the kiss deeper.

"One perfect moment," Gage whispered when they finally broke apart.

He was breathing fast, and so was she.

"What?"

"This was the one perfect moment. Right here, in this place and at this time. It was the perfect moment to kiss you and to tell you that I'm madly in love with you. I want to spend the rest of my life with you," he said.

He was staring down at her so intently, and Ava was still trying to catch her breath. "Wait a minute. You told me to stay away from you and your family."

"And you didn't listen," he replied.

She nodded. "Yes. But you acted as if you wanted nothing else to do with me. And I kind of understood, because I lied."

"You should have trusted me enough to tell me what you were doing," he said.

She opened her mouth to speak again, but Gage kissed her once more. A slower kiss, but potent nonetheless.

"And I should have trusted you enough not to accuse you of being like Bethany. She's the woman I was involved with for two months, three years ago. I let her in and she lied and betrayed me. She killed my child, and while I get that it was her body and her decision, it was my child. I deserved to know."

"Yes," she said, her heart breaking at the memory of seeing him with Ryan, Emma, Jack and Lily. He was going to be a terrific father.

"You deserved to know," she continued.

"But you're nothing like her. And I should have trusted you enough to at least let you explain why you did what you did."

He took a breath and let it out quickly. "But it was easier and more familiar not to believe there was something good between us."

Ava sighed, because all the wind had been taken out of her sail. All the life that she'd thought she'd had in her had been washed away by this new feeling, this new opportunity for a life with Gage.

"I meant what I said, Gage. I never meant to hurt your or your family. I was just so focused on my work and proving myself to everyone. I love you and your family too much to ever intentionally hurt any of you," she said.

"Me," he said, lifting his fingers to run along the line of her jaw. "Right now, I just need you to say that you love me."

Her heart was thumping wildly in her chest. "I love you, Gage."

His smile and the warm hug that followed brought tears to her eyes as she thought about the fact that she never imagined she'd get to say those words to him.

"I want to build your tiny home right here in this spot so that when we're in Temptation we can look out at the lake, just like my grandparents used to do," he was saying.

Ava had pulled away from him and was now looking at him through eyes swimming in tears. "What did you just say?"

"We can set up a time to meet with Harper and her crew in the next few days, but I want to get started on the house relatively soon. And I want to marry you, Ava," Gage said.

"Wait, you're talking too fast and I can't keep up."

He chuckled. "Well, get out your notepad so you can take notes. I want to marry you. Not next year, but next month. All my family will be here for Christmas. What better time to start a new life with my beautiful new wife?"

"I don't know what to say," Ava managed as she used her hand to wipe away the tears.

Happy tears that she felt deep down in her soul. Tears that she shed for the love her parents had lost somewhere along the way, and for Theodor and Olivia Taylor, who had gotten swept away in the limelight and forfeited their love as a result. Between her and Gage, she felt all that love, all that hope, and wanted to reach out and grab it and hold on tight, just as her mother had advised.

"Say yes," he told her. "Say you'll marry me and we'll build this house and we'll live happily ever after, no matter what."

She was shaking her head as she cupped his face in her hands. "No matter what, Gage," she whispered. "I will love you and I will marry you and we will be happy together, no matter what."

* * * * *

BIDDING ON THE BACHELOR

KERRI CARPENTER

For my fabulous agent and wonderful friend, Nic.
I seriously could not do this without you.

Chapter One

Carissa could not believe this was her life.

She glanced around the nearly empty apartment—excuse her, the *luxury condo* that until recently she'd shared with her husband. Now the condo was on the market, her marriage was over, and she was left standing in a deserted room, with stacks of boxes the only thing to keep her company.

Of course, most of those boxes didn't even belong to her. As she'd packed up almost a decade of her life, she realized that she had very few belongings. Strange, since she'd been surrounded by mountains of items before she and Preston signed on the dotted line.

Even now, she took a moment to peruse the neatly packed and labeled cartons.

China—Preston's grandmother's.

Jewelry—Preston's mother's.

Antique desk—Preston's father's.

Only the kitchen gadgets and appliances, clothes, and some old high school yearbooks belonged to her now. And she didn't even want the yearbooks. She ran a hand over the maroon cover from her senior year. Good old Bayside, Virginia. Maybe she should move back home.

Carissa snorted. Yeah, right. She'd vowed to never return to Bayside, a promise easily kept after her parents moved away while she was in college. Except for her aunt Val, she hadn't stayed in touch with anyone from the town where she went to high school. Not her group of girlfriends, not her favorite teachers, not even…

"Jasper Dumont," she said aloud, and then sighed.

Her fingers itched to open the yearbook and search for his picture. She knew what she would see. His blond hair and dazzling blue eyes. That handsome face and devastating grin. They'd known each other most of their lives but for one spectacular year, they'd dated. Their relationship had been amazing and fun and passionate and…she'd gone and ruined it.

Carissa put the yearbook down. "That was a long time ago," she whispered. Ten years. A whole decade. She hadn't communicated with him since, but she did hope his life was going better than hers. She'd broken up with him and headed straight for college. Then she'd married Preston right after graduation and they'd made their life in Chicago.

We made his *life*, she thought with another glance around the room.

Even so, she did need to move somewhere. Chicago was far too expensive. As she'd quickly learned after they announced their separation, most of "their" friends turned out to really be "his" friends.

Carissa wasn't much of a crier, nor was she someone who gave in to sulking or whining. But after everything that had happened over the last year, she needed a moment. Just one moment to grieve the loss of her marriage and her life.

Maybe the problem had been marrying so young. She'd only been twenty-two when they got engaged and twenty-three when she walked down the aisle. But in her defense, she'd dated Preston all through college at Northwestern. His family had been nice and welcoming to her, and Preston graduated with an offer to work at his father's media company. That made him steady, reliable and stable.

Three traits missing from her own father, who'd barely worked a day in his life, choosing to live off her mother's inheritance instead. Well, trust funds dry up, and so did all of the promises people make to each other when they stand at the altar.

She'd worked in the beginning. Nothing fancy and not directly tied to her business degree. But she'd put in a couple years at an event-planning firm. While Carissa thought she'd done a pretty good job, her heart hadn't been in it completely. When Preston suggested she quit so she could help him entertain colleagues and clients, she'd jumped at his suggestion. She'd wanted to make him happy, and besides, she'd always loved planning meals, searching different grocery and specialty stores, puttering away in the kitchen. Watching a handful of ingredients turn into scrumptious meals with amazing aromas made her happy.

In fact, she'd enjoyed planning and hosting dinner parties so much that she'd taken countless cooking classes. Moroccan dinners, making pies from scratch, holiday baking, Italian basics…any time she got wind of any type of lesson involving food, she made sure to be the first one in line.

From Preston to his parents to all of the clients and friends they entertained, everyone raved about her cooking. Soon, she found herself enjoying the kitchen of their luxury condo much more than any other room. Including the bedroom.

Especially the bedroom.

Of course, Preston continued to adore that room. Why

wouldn't he, when he was bringing so many different women there to receive a very personal tour?

Carissa sighed and kicked one of the boxes, cringing when she heard the indelible sound of breaking glass. She checked the label and winced. Figures she'd picked one of the few boxes that held her stuff instead of the mountains of Preston's belongings.

She'd signed a prenup, which entitled her to a tiny bit of money. Apparently, the fact that Preston broke their marriage vows did nothing in the way of changing the terms. Oh well. She wouldn't want someone else's money anyway. Carissa knew she needed to move on. Now she had to figure out how, why and where.

She'd already decided that there was only one job she was qualified for. Caterer. Only, that seemed crazy. Who was she to start her own business? Sure, she'd cooked for two to fifty people multiple times a week over the last couple of years. And she did have her business degree. But she didn't have any practical experience. Not to mention references. It wasn't like she could go to Preston's clients or family and ask for their testimonials.

She also didn't have a home. She had to be out of the condo by the end of the week. It was going to be tough to cook for anyone when she didn't even have a kitchen to use.

She took another glance around the beautiful space and let out another sigh. Preston had surprised her by buying this place. At the time, she'd thought it was romantic, that Preston was taking care of her. Now those idyllic shades from her early twenties had been lifted. Her husband's buying a condo without so much as consulting with her on any aspect was controlling. Her opinion on the neighborhood had never been sought. Her name had never been added to the mortgage. The moment she'd taken the spare key from

Preston's hand had been the moment she'd lost the first part of her independence.

She heard a little chirp. Her cell phone. Someone must have left a message. She'd been so engrossed in her thoughts that she hadn't heard the phone ring.

Digging her phone out from under a mass of Bubble Wrap, packing tape and newspapers, she saw her aunt Val's name and number on the display. Carissa quickly held the phone to her ear to listen to the familiar and comforting sound of her favorite aunt's raspy voice.

Hey, gorgeous. You better not be moping in that monstrosity you call a condo. Never did like that place. Who puts marble in their bathrooms? And why do two people need four bathrooms? Anyhoo, I'm taking a little trip over the next couple of months. So if you need a place to stay, my cottage will be free.

Carissa always thought she got her strength and her levelheadedness from Aunt Val. She wasn't one for mushy scenes or histrionics and neither was her aunt. So she was surprised to hear her aunt's voice soften.

I know you have your reasons for staying away from Bayside all these years. Hell, I even understand some of them. But honey, sometimes when life kicks you in the hooha, there's no place to go but home.

Carissa didn't know whether to laugh or cry. Since she wasn't a crier and she didn't feel like laughing at the moment, she put on her thinking cap.

Never in her wildest dreams would she have imagined herself returning to Bayside. Back in high school, she'd told everyone who could listen that she was meant for bigger and better things. And those things did not include the tiny Mayberry-esque town situated on the Chesapeake Bay in Virginia. To return now, divorced, humiliated, broke, lost…well, that wasn't exactly appealing.

She crossed the room and entered the kitchen. After pouring a rather large glass of wine, she leaned back against the quartz counter she'd always loved and considered the kitchen tools she still needed to pack.

At almost twenty-nine years old, she'd been both married and divorced. She'd heeded her husband's bad advice and stopped working. She may have a college diploma, but she had no professional experience or useful contacts.

She eyed her beloved KitchenAid mixer. Cooking was the one thing she was good at. But starting a catering company in Chicago was damn near impossible on a financial level.

Bayside, on the other hand, could be doable. Many people considered Bayside to be the Hamptons of the South. The town boasted both a healthy working class and an old-school elite who lived in sprawling mansions with immaculate lawns. And the latter group loved throwing parties.

And people at those parties liked to eat.

She'd grown up as part of that upper class. The money ran out just as she reached the end of high school thanks to her deadbeat and financially challenged dad. Thank God she'd been able to keep that little secret. Small towns always seemed to have the longest memories when it came to scandals. And Bayside was a town that loved its gossip.

Carissa's heart began beating faster. She had a free place to stay, which meant she could put what little money she had into her business. If she did well, she could acquire some much-needed references. Then, if she wanted to branch out and go to DC or down into North Carolina, she could.

She took a big gulp of wine and then rubbed her hands together. Her aunt's message was exactly what she needed to hear.

Carissa still might not know the how or the why. But she finally knew the where.

Bayside, Virginia, here I come.

Here I come, Jasper thought.

After months of proposals, number-crunching, presentations, research, wining and dining, not to mention good old-fashioned face-to-face meetings, Jasper was going in for the kill. He needed Arthur Morris to agree to his terms. Since Jasper had taken over Dumont Incorporated, he'd done well. Numbers were up in all divisions, but a deal like this would really go far in persuading the board that he was the right man for the job.

He rolled his shoulders. The fact that he still had to prove his worth stuck in his craw. But Jasper wasn't one to dwell on the negative. The board wanted him to bring in more big deals. Game on.

He'd come so far. Especially considering that he wasn't supposed to be here at all. His older brother, Cam, should have been heading up the family company, but Cam had decided to buck tradition and started a construction company instead. That opened the door for Dumont child Numero Dos and Jasper had barged right through. He'd always wanted to head up the company. Unfortunately, most of his life he'd been under the impression that he would never get the chance.

He thanked Cam every day for following his heart. His brother was happy, which made Jasper extremely happy. Because he was now at the helm of Dumont Incorporated and ready to impress everyone.

"As you can see, Mr. Morris, Bayside would offer you everything you're looking for." As they walked around the waterfront, Jasper pointed out landmarks to Arthur Morris. "There's a lot of tradition in this town. When it's not the height of tourist season, there are still festivals, charity events and a lot of other town activities. We've recently built up the area to the west of the bay and put in a great park. They hold farmers' markets on Sunday and an artisan and craft fair every Saturday that brings in people from all over the state."

He noticed Arthur working his jaw and jumped in before he could object. "At the same time, Bayside is an up-and-coming hot spot according to *Virginia Magazine*. Also, the *Washington Post* recently named the town one of Virginia's best-kept secrets."

Jasper fanned his hands out in front of him and made a box to highlight the site. "Putting the apartments here is a prime location, central to the town square, shopping, nightlife. Not to mention, it's an easy jaunt to both the elementary and high school for anyone with kids." He turned and put an arm around Arthur's shoulders. "And then there's this."

Arthur nodded. "It is one hell of a view. I'll give you that."

And Jasper had timed it to make sure they got the peak sunset with its array of colors blending into the water of the bay. The docked boats were bobbing along as tourists and citizens strolled along the man-made walkway that circled a good portion of the water.

Jasper was an expert negotiator and he knew he'd made his case. Still, after he'd learned of Arthur Morris's love of crabs, shrimp and lobster, he added one last detail. "And the seafood is pretty out of this world, if I do say so myself."

Arthur turned to face him. "After the dinner we had last night, I'll agree with that." He patted his round belly. "Still full from it, but don't think that will stop me from getting more before I head out of town later tonight."

Jasper smiled, but on the inside his emotions were having a dance party. "I thought you'd like that restaurant." He'd also managed to arrange the best table, with the best view, and had the chef prepare a special menu just for them. That was a definite perk that came with the Dumont name.

"Listen, kid," Arthur began, and Jasper folded his arms in front of him, intent on the next couple of sentences. "This has been a great pitch. But honestly, it comes down to the other numbers you put together for me. After that amazing dinner, I studied every sheet cover to cover. The prices you're offering go a long way and I think the return on investment is worth the risk."

Jasper nodded, reining in his excitement. He'd been working on this deal for two years and he wasn't going to rush now.

"So I'm saying yes," Arthur finished after what felt like ten minutes of silence.

"Great to hear it, sir." Jasper shook his hand and continued to play it cool. "We're thrilled to welcome a Morris complex to Bayside."

They spoke about a couple other details for the next several minutes as they walked toward Mr. Morris's rented car. Before he could drive away, Jasper had to know one thing.

"One last question. What made you say yes?"

Mr. Morris nodded as if he'd been expecting this very question. "Your father met with me regularly over the years. He gave me some great pitches."

"And yet you never said yes."

"He nagged me the same way you did, that's for sure." His smile came fast and brief. If Jasper had blinked, he'd have missed it. "But you went the extra mile."

"By plying you with the best seafood on the East Coast."

"By showing me the town. Really showing me. You love Bayside. That came across clear as day. I feel like I know the people who live here. They're not just numbers and stats in a spreadsheet. That made my decision easy."

Now it was Jasper's turn to smile. Only he held it in. He kept his usual calm business face.

"I have to say, though, I used to hear stories about you. Heard you were quite the little party kid back in the day. Weren't we all as teenagers? Happy to see you've grown out of it." Then he shook Jasper's hand, got in the car and drove away.

Only when he knew he was completely alone did Jasper let the grin out. And a fist pump for good measure.

Today is a good day. Jasper could feel the spring in his step as he made his way toward the center of the town and The Brewside Café, the addictive coffeehouse he frequented on a daily basis. While he walked, he took in the town he'd lived in for most of his life.

He'd always loved Bayside. He'd only left for college, business school and a couple years of working for another company to gain credentials. All that time, he'd missed the large bay with boats of varying sizes going in and out, the picturesque town square with the identical white siding and inviting blue awnings and shutters.

He reached for his phone and quickly scrolled through some text messages before seeing Simone's name. He grinned. Simone Graves was a feisty little redhead he'd been noticing at the gym for the last couple of months. She liked to go to Zumba classes and Jasper enjoyed seeing her shimmy around the room in her tight-fitting clothing. He'd finally asked her out, but they hadn't set a date and time yet.

Up for a drink tonight? he wrote to her.

It only took a minute for her to write back.

Wish I could. Stuck at work. This was accompanied by multiple sad emoji. But she proposed a different night to meet and Jasper accepted.

Whistling, he continued toward The Brewside. But before he entered the coffeehouse he decided to take a moment. So he changed course and headed toward the water, Mr. Morris's parting words ringing through his head.

I used to hear stories about you. Heard you were quite the little party kid back in the day. Happy to see you've grown out of it.

Well, he had been a lover of parties and the original good-time boy. But he'd also been just that—a boy. A kid. A teenager who'd been told from birth that his older brother would take over the family business. Sure, he'd been expected to work for Dumont Incorporated but he'd never been groomed to be in charge.

After all, he was the "second" son, after Cam. Overlooked and undervalued at every turn. His mother had always said he was the most good-natured child she'd ever seen. Jasper liked to think he'd held on to that his whole life. He enjoyed seeing the glass as half-full, excelled at finding the positive. He'd never harbored jealousy toward his big brother. In fact, he'd worshipped Cam. Still, being the younger child had hurt. So he'd lived it up in high school. Why wouldn't he? He knew he'd get into a good college thanks to his parents' connections. Likewise, he knew he'd be employed after college.

But as Mr. Morris said, he'd grown out of it. He'd been forced out of it, really.

Thanks to Carissa.

At the mere thought of her name, Jasper halted. Standing on the dock, he looked out at the bay, gripping the railing hard.

When was the last time he'd allowed himself to think about Carissa Blackwell? He shook his head.

Oh please. You think about her all the damn time.

Of course he did. She'd been the single most beautiful female he'd ever laid eyes on. She'd also been his first love. And with one cutting remark after graduation, she'd changed the course of his life.

Like most of the kids from his graduating class, they'd all known one another since birth. Bayside was a small town. About 90 percent of the classmates he walked with to "Pomp and Circumstance" at eighteen had been in his nursery school class, too. Carissa was no exception.

They'd continued to run in the same crowd throughout high school. They had both been popular. They were both involved in sports—he in baseball and she in cheerleading. Their parents had been friends and enjoyed the same kind of lavish lifestyles. They'd even lived on the same street.

But they hadn't crossed that line of romance until the summer before senior year.

Jasper turned and gazed toward the beach. It had happened over there. Down on the sand after one of the town's big festivals. A bunch of kids had built a bonfire. They'd both been hanging out, having some beers. Carissa used to drink wine coolers, he thought with a laugh.

Jasper started walking toward that spot on the beach. He'd always thought she was gorgeous. Who hadn't? She was like the quintessential California girl come to the East Coast with her long legs, golden skin, perfect pink lips and full blond hair that fell halfway down her back. Plus, she had those really intriguing gray eyes. To this day, he'd never seen eyes quite like hers.

That night she'd been wearing sexy jean shorts and a little red tank top. They'd shared a glance, then a head nod. Next thing he knew he was sitting next to her on a log sharing her s'more. Didn't take long for them to move their party of two farther down the beach where they'd shared one hell of a make-out session.

Just like that, they'd become hot and heavy and completely inseparable during senior year. Until about a month after graduation. Carissa had been accepted to Northwestern and he was going to UPenn, just like his father. He could never think of Carissa without his mind going to that last fateful conversation.

"Jasper, you aren't serious about anything."

"What are you talking about? I'm serious about you."

She shook her head. "That's not enough. You party all the time with your friends."

"So what? And anyway, they're your friends, too."

"I know. But I'm just saying that there's more to life than keg parties in the woods and making out in someone's basement."

"I think we did a little more than make out."

She pointed at him. "See, you can't even be serious now. Just like my dad," she said under her breath.

"I know you're upset because your parents want to move away from Bayside..."

"That doesn't bother me. I want them to move away, actually."

"Why?"

"Never mind, that's not the point." She flung her long hair over her shoulder.

"Okaaaayyyy." He would never understand girls. "Then, what is the point?"

"You are relying on your parents' money and connections to get you through life. You have no ambition and no drive. Do you think I want to be with someone like that? I don't." She looked at the ground.

He felt like someone had slapped him across the face. "What are you saying?"

"I don't want to ever come back to Bayside. I'm so done with this town. I want someone who has goals and like, initiative and stuff," She bit her lip. Even as she insulted

him, there was sadness in her eyes. "I'm sorry, Jasper. You just don't."

With that, she'd walked away with his heart.

He'd tried to call her but she'd never answered. Her parents said she went to a prefreshman-year program at Northwestern. She'd wanted to get a jump on classes. Then her parents had moved away later in the year and she didn't have a reason to return to Bayside anymore. He never saw her again.

It was Jasper's nature to find a bright side. But in truth, Carissa's words stung. Not only did she break up with him, but she insulted his very character.

It had taken some time. A lot of time. But eventually, the memory of Carissa's words had kicked his butt into gear. She wanted someone with ambition and that's what he'd decided to give her. Even if they weren't actually together.

His father's name may have gotten him into college, but he worked his butt off once he got there. He joined a fraternity but when it was time for midterms or finals, he'd camp out at the library to make sure he kept his GPA up, finally graduating with honors. He never told his parents about applying to grad schools so they couldn't influence the process.

He'd come a long way from the irresponsible, somewhat reckless, carefree kid who was always the life of the party. Some people had called him foolish, but in Jasper's mind he'd always been underestimated.

At some point, though, all the hard work stopped being just for her. He'd become obsessed with doing the very best he could and in the process he'd become the head of Dumont Incorporated. If Carissa were here maybe he'd thank her. Especially after his victory tonight. But the odds of ever seeing Carissa Blackwell in Bayside again were slim to none.

His phone made a little ding alerting him to a text message. He looked down to see his brother's name. How'd it go with Morris?

Jasper began texting back but something caught his attention. Out of the corner of his eye he saw a woman standing at the same location where he'd been before his little walk down memory lane. Fingers still poised over the keypad on his phone, he didn't have time to text Cam back before his brother added, Either way, come over tonight. Let's hang out and watch the game.

Again, he began typing a reply but the woman reached her arms above her head and stretched. She was really beautiful. He peered closer and got a chill up the back of his neck.

She looked familiar. Too familiar. Jasper gripped his cell harder and began walking faster. Closer. But as he rounded the corner, she was heading away from the dock toward a black car.

He would know that sashay of hips anywhere. After all, the last time he'd seen a movement like that had been her swaying body walking away from him.

No way. No freaking way.

"Carissa?" he said into the silence around him. Luckily, no one was there to hear him talking to himself. Likewise, no one was there to see him step to the side to ensure he was actually seeing his first love and not some late-summer apparition brought on by too much work. In any case, he slipped, hit the railing with too much momentum, and before he could say *Carissa is back in Bayside*, he'd fallen over the metal divider and into the bay.

Chapter Two

Greetings, dear readers! After a brief hiatus, your ever-faithful Bayside Blogger is back from a much-needed summer vacay! And color me shocked, surprised and downright confused. Carissa Blackwell, former Bayside High A-list superstar, has also returned to our fair shores! And just why is little-miss-too-good-for-good-ole-Bayside back in town?

Let's get down to it, folks—the far more interesting question is…how does Jasper Dumont feel? Well, I understand he took a late-evening swim in the bay after catching a glimpse of his long-lost prom queen. And let's just say that the swim wasn't exactly planned…

Jasper needed some liquor.

Once he was home, freshly showered and in dry clothes, he crossed the room to the wall that held a floor-to-ceiling bookshelf. He scanned the bottom shelf until he found what he was searching for. His high school yearbook. Jasper grabbed it from the shelf, made a cup of coffee and started riffling through the pages until he got to the B names.

There she was. Carissa Blackwell. Jasper didn't need to ogle the photo to recall that long golden hair, legs that went on for miles and flawless skin that always looked like it was kissed by the sun.

Flipping more pages, he eyed the photos of the cheerleaders. There she was again, all decked out in that appealing little uniform. His lips quirked. Damn, he'd loved watching her cheer at football games. He'd loved making out with her under the bleachers after the game even more.

They'd done everything together senior year. Until she'd broken up with him. Jasper could feel his eyebrows growing close together just as something fell out from between the pages of the yearbook. A picture of the two of them at prom. He couldn't remember who had snapped it. But in the photo they were dancing; Carissa was staring up at him adoringly as he had his arms wrapped tightly around her.

To this day, Jasper still wondered what had changed. Prom had been one month before she'd dumped him. When had she stopped looking at him like that and decided he hadn't been good enough for her?

His phone—which luckily had fallen from his hand and landed safely on the dock—rang.

"Hey, Cam," he greeted his big brother.

"So?"

Jasper shifted in his seat. So what?"

"So what have you been doing?"

Jasper eyed the garbage can, where he'd decided to throw his clothes out after he climbed out of the bay. As he'd hoisted himself back onto the wooden dock, he'd snagged his pants. The quick jaunt from the water to his new condo in the center of town had been interesting. Wet and interesting. If his brother found out about it, he'd never hear the end of it.

So he decided to play it cool. "I haven't been doing anything," he lied. He paced the length of the living room. He loved this condo with its exposed beamed ceiling, brick walls and amazing view of the bay. Although, the sight of the water at the moment made him cringe.

"What do you mean you haven't been doing anything? Wasn't your huge meeting with Mr. Morris today? I've been texting you for the last hour."

Jasper snapped out of his Carissa-focused stupor. "Right. Sorry." He proceeded to tell Cam all about the meeting. His brother seemed ecstatic for him.

"That's amazing, Jasp. Congratulations."

"Thanks, Cam." And he meant it. He'd always idolized his older brother and Cam's approval meant the world to him.

"Now, what about after the meeting?"

"What do you mean?" Jasper asked hesitantly.

"I heard you celebrated by going for a little swim in the bay."

Jasper ground his teeth together. "How did you…" He trailed off. Of course, he already knew the answer to that question. How did anyone in Bayside know anything? The ever-loving, always-gossipy Bayside Blogger, of course.

The Bayside Blogger wrote for the *Bayside Bugle*'s Style & Entertainment section. No one knew her identity, or how she always—and it truly felt like always—found out the gossip before anyone else. She also utilized a daily blog, Twitter, Facebook, Instagram and just about every other form of communication in existence.

"And the Blogger said that Carissa Blackwell is back in town," Cam was saying. "She alluded to your little dip in the water having something to do with a Carissa spotting."

Spotting? When had his brother become TMZ? Time to call him out. "I thought you didn't read that…what did you used to call it? Trash, I believe," Jasper said.

Cam coughed. "Uh, Elle reads it. I just happen to catch snippets here and there."

"Sure, sure. *Elle* reads it. Doesn't explain how you would know about me falling into the bay today, though, since your beloved is out of town checking out that up-and-coming artist for the gallery. You must be losing your mind without your better half around." Got him.

Since Elle returned from living in Italy last spring, she and his brother had been practically attached at the hip. Jasper was happy for his brother. And jealous, if he was being honest. The guy was head over heels in love. And Elle looked at him the way Carissa gazed at him in that old prom photo.

"She'll be back tomorrow afternoon. Listen, Jasp," Cam said, his voice growing serious.

Here we go, Jasper thought. He knew exactly where this was heading. This was so not going to be fun.

"Yes?"

"Carissa." Cam said her name the way one might say *cancer* or *terrorist*.

"Was my high school girlfriend."

"She was way more than that and we both know it. And she's back in town."

Jasper ran a hand through his hair in frustration. "We don't know that."

"The Bayside Blogger said—"

"So what? Just because the Bayside Blogger—"

This time Cam cut him off. "Hate to admit it but the Bayside Blogger—whoever he or she may be—does tend to be right."

"It doesn't matter." Cam started to say something so

Jasper quickly beat him to the punch. "We dated a million years ago. I heard she got married and was living in the Midwest somewhere. I, on the other hand, have a date lined up with a certain hottie from the gym."

There was a long pause. "Do you want to come over?" Cam finally asked.

What he wanted was to forget that he'd seen Carissa Blackwell. He wanted to have a couple beers, be alone with his thoughts, and not hear about the damn Bayside Blogger.

Luckily, he knew just where to accomplish everything he needed. The Rusty Keg, an old dive bar, sat on the outskirts of town. People would recognize him there but they'd also give him room and leave him alone.

"No, I'm good. Honestly," he assured his brother.

And he would be. So long as he didn't see Carissa Blackwell again.

And he stayed away from water.

Carissa was not a suspicious person. She was rooted in the here and now and considered herself rational and practical. And yet she couldn't shake the feeling she was being watched.

She'd left Chicago yesterday, stayed overnight in Ohio, driven all day, hit some nasty traffic, and drunk about fifteen coffees before finally arriving in Bayside. Needing a moment to stretch—not to mention, take in the town she hadn't laid eyes on in over a decade—she'd pulled over at the dock before she made her way to her aunt's cottage.

It was while she was there, taking a moment to refamiliarize herself with Bayside, stretching and getting the kinks out of her tired muscles, when she started to get that spooky feeling. First, goose bumps broke out on her skin. Then she thought she saw someone out of the corner of her eye, over to her right. Fed up, she'd left the dock and returned to her car. That's when she'd received full confirmation that she was indeed being watched. About five people stood outside the town's popular square, staring and pointing at her while they whispered to each other and tapped away on their phones.

Great. Back in Bayside for five minutes and the welcome committee was already starting with the gossip. She wondered how long it would take for the whole town to know she'd returned. They wouldn't know she'd come home with her tail between her legs. Not as long as she could help it.

She hightailed it to her aunt's cottage in record time.

She found the key where Aunt Val had instructed her to look, in the flowerpot around back. She peered closer. A flowerpot that appeared to be holding a weed plant if she wasn't mistaken. Given that, she wasn't sure if she was excited or nervous about what she might find inside.

Carissa let herself into the two-bedroom cottage, flicked the light switch and smiled. It was the same cozy and eccentric home she remembered from high school, maybe with a few more knickknacks collected over the years. Every room was painted a different pastel color. The kitchen wasn't the most updated she'd ever seen but it was definitely workable. And bonus, it overlooked the deck, the small backyard and the bay beyond that. The view was probably worth more than the entire rest of the house.

The decor was beachy and comfortable, the exact opposite of the modern high-rise she'd shared with Preston in Chicago. Perfect. Two minutes in this place and she already felt more at ease than she had in six years in her condo. This place screamed for you to kick off your shoes, whip up a margarita and blast some Jimmy Buffett from the radio.

Carissa nodded definitely. "This will do just fine," she murmured to herself. She saw a long note on the counter and quickly scanned it. Her aunt explained the AC system, which apparently went on the fritz from time to time. Great—since it was the last week of August, the temperature in Virginia was sweltering.

She also left instructions for watering her eclectic—and hopefully legal—garden out back. There were notes about the proper remote for the television, what days the trash was picked up, and a large warning for her *not* to enjoy the absinthe in the liquor cabinet. But everything else was hers to use, borrow and enjoy.

Carissa spent the next hour hauling her boxes from the car and getting settled. Her suitcases went into the guest bedroom she would be using. A bedroom, she noted, that was decorated in an explosion of peach paint and shell tchotchkes. It was kind of like sleeping in *The Golden Girls* house but Carissa couldn't complain. The rent was free and she would be able to catch her breath.

Her parents had never liked this house. They'd claimed her aunt had too much crap and the interior decorating was childlike and outdated. But Carissa had always loved coming over to visit Aunt Val. She didn't have to worry if she spilled crumbs on the floor or made her bed. Living in her childhood home had been like growing up in a museum. The floors had been hard and the furniture uncomfortable. Forget eating anywhere but the kitchen or dining room. And a cleaning lady came through twice a week.

How'd that work out for you, Mom and Dad? Carissa shook her head. Her parents had lost all of their money and most of their stuff. Her dad had lost the money, she corrected. Not that it had been his to begin with. Her mother had come from a wealthy family with old money, which her dad had misspent, mismanaged and eventually blown through.

She didn't quite feel like unpacking yet so she meandered into the kitchen for a snack. Aunt Val said she would provide some munchies to get her started. Carissa eyed the weed plant out the sliding glass door as she recalled the use of the word *munchies*. But when she started hunting through the cabinets and fridge, there wasn't so much as a bag of chips to be found. There was another note attached to the fridge with a magnet shaped like a starfish.

Didn't have time to go to store. Sorry, Dollface.

Well, that explained that. There was a calendar hanging on the wall next to the fridge. She sighed. Just what she needed to see. A visual reminder of what today was.

Happy birthday to me.

Happy birthday to me.

Happy birthday dear recently divorced, almost completely broke twenty-nine-year-old meeeeeee.

Happy freaking birthday to me.

As part of her practical nature, Carissa never needed or wanted a big party, lots of presents or any kind of fuss made over her birthday. But even she hated the fact that she'd spent the first day of the last year of her twenties driving hundreds of miles because she'd just gotten divorced. Twenty-nine years old and already she'd been both married and divorced. Not exactly the path she'd envisioned for her life.

Snagging her car keys and shaking off the morbid mood, Carissa headed out the door toward the grocery store for a few essentials: coffee, milk, bread, peanut butter and alcohol. Lots and lots of alcohol. But since there was a nice breeze, she decided to forgo the car and walk to the store instead. After the long drive, she could use the exercise.

Once at the store, she steered her shopping cart down one aisle after another, unsure of what she was in the mood for. She grabbed cereal and some snacks, a couple bags of fruit and the ingredients for chocolate chip cookies. A little birthday present to herself. But as she perused the different brands of coffee, she couldn't help but tune in to someone else's conversation. In fact, a couple different snippets of conversations. All about her.

I'm not making this up. It was her. *Carissa Blackwell.*

Didn't you read the Bayside Blogger's tweets today? She already knows about this.

…can't believe she's back here! Didn't she swear off Bayside back in high school?

Strange that no one ever heard from her parents again. It's like they disappeared into thin air.

Carissa checked the time on her phone. Two hours. That was all it had taken for her to become the topic of hot gossip. And who was this Bayside Blogger who seemed to know her every move?

Didn't matter. Enough of this. She needed to get outside, stat. She pushed her cart to the side, items completely forgotten, and exited the store.

All she wanted was to escape the gossips and get some air.

As she walked along the back streets of the neighborhood back toward the cottage, she remembered something. There was a dive bar that used to sit back this way. She could go for a drink. Or two.

While she headed in the direction of the bar, one of the gossipers' words reverberated through her head. *Can't believe she's back here.*

Carissa kicked at an imaginary stone. "Yeah, that makes two of us," she muttered.

Then, like a beacon calling her home, she saw the old bar at the end of the street, surrounded by a small parking lot full of stones and overgrown trees. Score. She definitely wouldn't be recognized here. Double score. Carissa knew if she filled in the gaps on the half-burned out neon sign hanging above the door, she'd read the name, The Rusty Keg.

True, she'd come out for a snack. But bars had snacks. Even more importantly, bars had alcohol. And nothing was going to make this nightmare of a day better than some good old-fashioned liquor.

She pushed open the creaky door and was immediately assaulted by a musky smell of cheap beer, fried food and sweat. The place was dark, dank and completely off the beaten path.

In other words, it was perfect.

Carissa strolled up to the bar, noticing the scratched-up wood just waiting to give someone a splinter. She reached under the bar, feeling around for a purse hook, then immediately snatched her hand back. Had she just touched someone's used wad of gum? *Yuck.* She shook her head. An establishment with a half-lit, crooked sign above the door outside and a rotting bar with mismatched bar stools that probably hadn't been cleaned since the nineties was definitely not going to have purse hooks. They probably didn't even have pinot noir. She slid a glance toward the single-stall bathroom and scrunched her nose. Forget about toilet seat covers. That was probably a mere pipe dream.

"What can I get you?" a burly man with a full *Duck Dynasty*–worthy beard bellowed from behind the bar.

"Shot of tequila and the local beer on tap."

He nodded, pulled her beer, poured the shot, but otherwise stayed silent. Carissa didn't waste any time. "Happy birthday to me," she said to no one in particular before throwing the shot back. The liquid burned her throat and made her eyes water. She turned her head and let out an exasperated "wowza" just in time to see none other than Jasper Dumont sitting right next to her, an unreadable expression on his face.

"Oh." It was all she could think to say aloud. On the inside, however, there was a whole vocal party happening. *No-freaking-way-it's-your-ex-boyfriend!*

No, not just an ex-boyfriend. Jasper Dumont was so much more than a simple ex. With some age and perspective, she realized their one-year relationship was such a short period of time in the grand scheme of life. But damn, that one year had been nothing short of amazing. Making out, dances, football games, making out, skipping school occasionally, making out, one epic prom, passing notes in calculus class, wanton looks by the lockers and even more making out. Well, making out that quickly led to much-less-PG versions of mere kissing.

Now this boy—er, man—whom she hadn't seen in a decade, but whom, if she was being brutally honest and the tequila was already loosening her up on that score, she'd never stopped thinking about was sitting right next to her. At a dive bar in her hometown.

"Carissa Blackwell," he said, his voice smooth and cutting. "Pigs must be flying because here you are. Back in Bayside."

Despite the coldness coming off him in waves, he looked amazing. Same blond hair and striking blue eyes. But that lanky boy she used to kiss under the bleachers was now all filled out with broad shoulders and from what she could see, an impressive chest. She leaned back in her chair and took a sip of her beer. More to give herself a moment and to slow down the pulse that Jasper had sent soaring.

"Miracles can happen," she said, raising her mug of beer in a toast.

"Apparently." His gaze drank her in from the top of her head over her navy blue tank top and down her capri jeans to the toes that desperately needed a pedicure. Toes that curled as he gave an appreciative nod.

"It's, um, nice to see you, Jasper." She pushed her hair over her shoulder. "I wouldn't expect to find you in a bar like this."

"Likewise," he quickly said. "Actually I wouldn't expect to find you anywhere in the city limits."

She nodded. She probably should have expected that from him. But what was she supposed to say? The truth? *I got divorced. I have no money or career and this was the only place I had to go.*

"Touché," she said instead. "But I'm back in town."

"For how long?" he asked quickly, too quickly. In fact, if she wasn't mistaken, anger laced his question. She must have reacted to it because his features softened. "Sorry, it's none of my business. And I do remember that today is your birthday. So happy birthday, Carissa."

"Thanks," she said, and meant it. She decided to offer an olive branch because the truth was that she'd dumped him and she hadn't been kind about it. This icy reception she was receiving was well deserved. While she knew the reasons behind her decision, she'd never let Jasper in on it. She'd been a bratty, selfish teenager, not capable of understanding her emotions. Unwilling to admit that Jasper had always reminded her of her father and that summer her dad had dropped a bombshell on her.

"I don't know how long I'll be in town. I'm sort of in a transition period right now." He waited patiently. After another long drink of beer, she finished. "I just got divorced." Saying the words out loud left an awful taste in her mouth. An acidic aftertaste of yuckiness.

First, shock flashed on his face. Then true concern shone in his eyes. "I'm sorry," he said.

And that might have been her undoing. Because he had every reason to be stiff and awkward with her. Instead, any kind of compassion from him loosened her lips.

"Today is my twenty-ninth birthday. I'm having a beer next to my ex-boyfriend, who hates my guts, in a dive bar in the town I swore I would never step foot in again. An ex-boyfriend I should really apologize to because I was an evil witch to him." The words were flying now. She gripped her hand tightly around her glass. "I'm not even thirty and already I've been married and divorced. And I got divorced because he freaking cheated on me."

She couldn't miss the way Jasper's eyes narrowed, his hands curled into fists, and there was a definite tic in his clenched jaw. "He cheated on you?"

"Yep. Apparently, the fact that I was homecoming queen, prom queen and head cheerleader did nothing to impress him. Or keep his pants zipped up when anyone wearing a skirt in the Central Time Zone walked by. That probably makes your whole day, doesn't it?"

He slammed his hand on the bar and she jumped. But she just as quickly composed herself. "What? You have every right to revel in my misery after the way I broke up with you. I got divorced. You win."

His eyes narrowed. "I don't want to win at that game. And I certainly don't want to hear that some idiot cheated on you. I'm sorry you're getting divorced."

"That makes one of us." With that she chugged the rest of her beer and let her head drop onto the bar. Then she remembered the threat of splinters and lifted her face back up, the tequila and beer rushing to her head.

"Water over here, please," Jasper called to the bartender. "Two waters, a basket of mozzarella sticks, and..." He looked to her.

"More alcohol," she called out weakly.

He chuckled but also reached for her hand. As he squeezed her fingers a jolt of awareness traveled up her arm. It was a sensation she hadn't felt in years. In fact, she'd never felt it with her ex-husband. Not once. Only Jasper made her toes curl, sent electric shocks to the system, and caused her stomach to flip over.

Jasper leaned back. "I don't want to talk about our past. Not tonight."

"But you're still mad."

He nodded. "Wouldn't you be?"

She couldn't argue with that.

He seemed to be considering something. Finally, he said, "I have a better idea. Like I said, I don't want to talk about our history right now. Instead, let's call a truce and be friends for the night."

Chapter Three

"Feeling better?"

She turned to Jasper. The fried cheese sticks and water went a long way to making her feel better. So did the friendship, even if it was only temporary. Jasper listened as she mumbled into her breaded mozzarella.

"Much. Thank you."

He was looking at her with an expression that she couldn't decipher. "What?" she asked.

"I'm not gonna lie," he said with total confidence in his voice. "I've thought about seeing you again since that summer. But never in my wildest dreams would I have imagined I'd run into you at a hole-in-the-wall bar of all places."

"Would it have made it any less awkward if we'd met behind the library? I seem to remember spending a lot of time with you there." Her traitorous eyes flickered down to his lips.

"Well, I remember spending a lot of time with you in my car, in my basement…"

"All those times you sneaked into my room after my parents went to sleep," she added.

"And one epic moment in the middle of the football field."

She covered her face with her hands. "Ohmigod! I can't believe we did that. What were we thinking?"

He let out a sound that was purely male. "I know what I was thinking." He wiggled his eyebrows. She wondered how one man could manage to look both adorable and sexy at the same time.

She leaned forward. "I was never thinking. Not when you were around." And wasn't that the problem? No one else in her life had been able to make her lose her train of thought. Even now, she could get lost in those mesmerizing baby blues. Which was why she needed to take a step back. But with their closeness it was hard. So she sat back in her chair, flung her hand in the air to signal the bartender.

Jasper's brow shot up. "Another one?"

"I'm twenty-nine. I'm divorced. And I'm thirsty."

His gaze roamed over her again and his eyes darkened. "Yeah, I'm thirsty, too."

God, she wanted to kiss him. Luckily, she was saved by the bell when George, otherwise known as the burly, bearded bartender, strolled over. "Still dating that little brunette from the next town over?" he asked Jasper.

"Maria? From the ice-cream place?" Jasper asked.

"No, the other one. The one who always has part of her hair in a braid," George said, pointing to the braid in his own long hair that was tied back with a red bandanna.

"Oh, you mean Julie." Jasper shook his head. "No, that's over."

Carissa raised her eyebrow. She couldn't help it. Same old Jasper apparently. Except for the year they'd dated, he'd always been a ladies' man. Not that she could blame him now. After all, he was gorgeous, young, successful. Why wouldn't he be the toast of the town? And yet this conversation was leaving a very unsettled feeling in the pit of her stomach.

George placed a large mug of beer in front of Jasper, who offered a questioning look. "It's on the house," George said. "Despite your active and envious dating life, thought you could use a pick-me-up after your little spill into the bay earlier today." With that, he turned and headed toward two older men, more than likely local fishermen if she had to guess, sitting at the end of the bar. They nodded at Jasper and started snickering.

"You fell into the bay?" she asked Jasper.

"It was nothing."

"Not what the Bayside Blogger is saying," one of the men at the end of the bar offered.

"Bayside Blogger said you saw your high school girl-friend and fell into the bay," added the other man.

Carissa's mouth dropped open. She'd thought someone had been around her when she'd stopped to look out over the water. Jasper had been at the dock when she pulled up a couple hours ago? He'd fallen into the bay? Because of her?

"Jasp…"

"Don't say anything."

She didn't know whether to laugh or cry. But she decided to give him a break since he looked so uncomfortable. "Who is this Bayside Blogger I keep hearing about?"

He looked relieved at the change in topic and proceeded to tell her all about the town's biggest gossip columnist as they enjoyed their drinks.

"So, Carissa…" He trailed off and his eyes met hers. A shadow fell over his face. "What happened, Car? I mean, what really happened between you and the man you married?"

Car. No one had called her that in ten years. Such a simple little nickname, and yet it had a huge effect on softening her heart.

She didn't know if it was the use of *Car* or the alcohol or the stress of the last couple of months. But something had her turning toward her first love and spilling everything.

"We met in college. We got married shortly after that. We lived in Chicago."

He waited. "And?"

"And what?"

He chuckled. "Come on, Car. That's nothing. I could have found out more information from Twitter."

She relented. "Fine. Our marriage was good. At first." She twisted her empty shot glass around in circles. "But Preston started working longer hours, taking more business trips."

"Uh-oh," Jasper said.

"I knew he was cheating on me. I don't know how long I knew. Only that I didn't really want to admit it. But when I found him in our newly purchased California king bed with someone, I knew keeping up the pretense of a perfect marriage wasn't going to be possible." And still, she hadn't been the one to file for divorce. Pathetic. But she kept that to herself.

"Why did you marry him in the first place?"

Because he was an escape. Because he was ambitious and driven. In other words, because he was the polar opposite of her father. Of course, she didn't dare tell Jasper that, either.

"It's a long story," she said, in lieu of the truth.

"Okay, then let me ask a simpler question. Where did you work?"

She took a long pull of her beer and wished like hell that was a simple question. "Nope." He raised a brow. "I didn't work."

His mouth fell open. "You? You didn't work. You, the queen of 'have ambition, get some drive and determination.' Little Miss 'why don't you have goals, Jasper?' did not actually have a job?"

When he put it like that…

"You've gotta be kidding me." Jasper ran a hand through his thick hair, clearly exasperated.

Her cheeks were heating up and she knew it had nothing to do with the alcohol or the stuffy bar. She didn't mean to get defensive when she said, "I mean, I did work at an event-planning firm. For a few years."

"Before you quit to be a stay-at-home wife?" He held up his hands in surrender. "I'm not judging you or anyone else for staying at home. I'm just completely confused given the last conversation we had before you left Bayside."

God, she'd been such a brat to him that day. Briefly, she considered telling him about her parents. Revealing why she'd acted so drastically and broken up with him. But he jumped in with a question.

"What are you going to do now?"

She paused for a long moment before answering. "Become a caterer. At least, I hope so."

"Seriously?"

Was it just her or had he moved closer? She could smell his cologne, a clean, crisp scent that wrapped itself around her, making the dirty bar and stale alcohol smell slide away into the background.

"Sure," she said, her voice breathy. "I love to cook, and I was the queen of the dinner party back in Chicago."

"You have experience as a caterer?" His arm was mere centimeters from hers. Although they weren't touching, her body was tensed in anticipation.

"I do." She would have crossed her fingers at the lie if Jasper wasn't sitting so close. She did have *some* experience. Informal experience, but that was a start. Maybe she didn't technically know how to run a business, but she could cook. In that area, she was confident. And she'd decided back in Chicago that she would cling to that confidence.

"So really you moved back here to start your business." Jasper's finger finally made its way to her skin, traveling from her wrist slowly over her forearm and up toward her elbow, leaving a trail of tingles in its wake.

"Yep." Damn, she couldn't concentrate.

He turned, angling himself. His gaze flickered down to take in her lips, which she conveniently pursed for him.

What in the hell was she doing? She couldn't do *that*. Not with *him*. Could she? She supposed she was officially divorced now. Yes, she was a free agent. She could do anything—or, um, anyone—she wanted.

And maybe tonight, she wanted Jasper. Maybe she needed the connection with him because it had never felt so easy with anyone else. It wasn't like they hadn't slept together a million times already.

Confused, she threw back the final shot of tequila. Then she nodded to indicate his finger, which was still gently caressing her skin. "Jasper, what are you doing?"

His grin spread slowly but assuredly. "What do you think I'm doing?"

Even as the words left his mouth, she was moving closer to him. His eyes flickered down to take in her mouth, and she responded by biting her lip. She opened her mouth to say something seductive, something sexy. In a practiced move she used to perform all the time when she was younger, Carissa flipped her hair and placed her elbow up on the bar. Only, she missed the bar and nearly nose-dived into his lap, and she let out a very loud belch.

Embarrassed beyond belief, she shook her head.

Jasper grinned. "Yep, I think we may be done here for

the night." He pushed the mug with her remaining beer away from her.

"I'm not ready to leave." But even as the words left her mouth she let out a hiccup. When had she become buzzed?

"Last call," George bellowed out from the end of the bar to groans around the room.

Jasper nodded. "See, time for everyone to go. Not just you."

Carissa rose from the bar stool and almost toppled over. Whoa. Maybe she was a little more than merely buzzed. She had to grasp the edge of the sticky bar to keep from falling. "Gotta pay," she informed Jasper, who had already handed his credit card to George.

"I got it," he said.

"No!" she said defiantly.

"Consider it a welcome-back present."

"No," she repeated, trying to untangle the straps of her purse. "Gotta be independent. Can't rely on a man."

Jasper scribbled his signature on the check and turned to her. "You can't even get into your purse. Come on."

Suddenly, this seemed like a bad idea. She couldn't leave with Jasper, her ex-boyfriend. "Nope," she told him. "You hate me. Can't go with you."

"You have to go with me. I'm going to walk you to your aunt's house."

She swayed and tried to right herself, but Jasper had to reach out and steady her. "What will the peoples think?"

"I don't think 'the peoples' in this bar really care too much about anything except getting in one last drink order before George shuts down. Now, shall we?" He nodded toward the door.

Her head felt fuzzy. Thick and fuzzy. And she was very tired.

"Carissa Blackwell," Jasper said. "Get your hot butt out the door."

"You think my butt is hot?"

He made a show of looking around her back and then considering. "Yep. That is one fine behind. Now let me get a better view by walking to the door."

"Okay, but you're not the boss of me. I can get to the door by myself."

And with that she took two steps forward before tripping and ending up on the floor.

"Everything okay?" George asked, an amused expression visible, even under the depths of his beard.

"Yeah, I got this." Jasper turned to take in Carissa, who was currently in a pile on the floor laughing her head off. He sighed. He probably should have cut her off earlier.

After helping her up, Jasper waved good-night to George and the other patrons who were busy settling their bills. Then he ushered Carissa out the door and into the dimly lit gravel parking lot.

Even as he concentrated on getting her across the lot, he couldn't help but think about the night.

Carissa Blackwell was back in Bayside. Carissa Blackwell was divorced. Carissa Blackwell was incredibly drunk.

He didn't want to admit to himself that he'd been flirting with her. He'd looked into her eyes and gotten lost in old memories. Something he'd been adamant about *not* doing. Seeing her walk into The Rusty Keg had his insides all twisted up. The anger and hurt he'd felt all those years ago had bubbled up to the surface.

Then she'd admitted her husband cheated on her and something changed. Maybe because of the embarrassment that emanated from her when she told him. Perhaps it was the way her gaze flicked downward every time she said the word *divorce.*

Jasper wasn't entirely sure. All he knew was that the resentment took a back seat to caring.

Didn't take much to move closer and eye that tempting mouth. He shook his head. Everyone knew he was a big flirt. That's how he liked to communicate. And he hadn't seen Carissa in ten years, so they had a lot of communicating to catch up on. That's all.

They walked to the end of the parking lot. She was swaying and stumbling a little more than he would like to see. But cabs weren't abundant at this hour in Bayside, and he needed to get her home. She stopped in front of him, her long hair settling around her heart-shaped face.

"It was weird to see you tonight."

He didn't know what to say. That may be the truth, but still.

"But I'm glad I did," she continued. "You still make me feel tingly."

Tingly? Was that good or bad? "Really?"

"Yep," she said. "You were my best friend and my boy-friend. And you know what else? You were my first love."

Something softened inside him. "And you were mine."

"But now you hate me. Except for tonight when we're playing nice-nice."

He sighed long and loud, a decade's worth of angst spilling out. "I don't hate you."

"You're not happy with me," she said.

He shook his head. "No. Hey, it's your birthday though."

"Not anymore. Past midnight." She ran a hand down her side, highlighting her killer body. "Mmm-hmm." She licked her lips and those mysterious gray eyes met his and he lost all train of thought. He placed one hand at the back of her neck, pulling her toward him. With the other hand, he pushed a strand of hair behind her ear.

He shouldn't kiss her. He really, really shouldn't kiss her. And yet he was tilting his head.

Walk away, Dumont. But he couldn't get his feet to work. It was Carissa who finally broke the spell. She tilted her head up, lips pursed, eyes fluttering closed. Jasper met her halfway, pressing his lips to hers.

Instantly, he felt a spark. That feeling he only got with her. But it had been such a long time since he'd experienced it, he almost dropped to his knees.

Instead, he brought her closer and devoured her lips. She wound both arms around his neck, holding tight as she met his lips with equal desire.

The sound of a car starting snapped him out of the moment. "Damn," he said, looking around the parking lot, hoping whoever just got in their car hadn't seen anything.

When he turned back to her, he saw that her lips were swollen and her eyes hazy. He wanted to kiss her again right there and then.

"That didn't feel like hate to me," she said, her voice husky and appealing.

"Carissa…" he began.

"I broke up with you."

"I remember," he said.

She scrunched up her nose. "That was mean."

"Little bit," he admitted, and took a breath. "Why did you break up with me?"

"I can't tell you."

Amused by her, or maybe by the whole situation, he grinned. "Oh yeah? Why not?"

"Because there are three of you and um, uh, I'm dizzy."

Oh crap. He directed her to a tree stump on the road that

would lead back to town. "Do you need water?" he asked. "I can go back to the bar and grab a bottle."

She was taking long, deep breaths, focusing on the ground. She held a hand out. "No, just give me a minute."

He gave her ten. Once she appeared to get herself under control, she met his eyes. If he had any doubt about her being drunk, it was cleared up when she tried to stand and wavered. Decision made, Jasper put her arm around his shoulders and anchored her with an arm around her waist. Then they started walking slowly back to town.

"Where are we going?" she asked.

"To my place. It's closer," he said before she could argue.

"In Chicago, we can call cabs and Uber."

"Yeah, well, you're not in Chicago anymore."

"Nope." She looked up at him. "I'm here in Bayside, with you." Then she tapped a finger to the tip of his nose. "Boop."

Despite everything else, he laughed. "Okay, Boopy, let's keep walking. Maybe we can get to my condo by sunrise."

In the end it didn't take that long. Although it felt pretty onerous when Carissa launched into a rendition of her favorite Lady Gaga song, followed by some old-school Britney Spears. Carissa had many talents, but singing had never been one of them. He thought he heard some dogs wailing off in the distance and wondered if he would ever regain the hearing from the ear she sang/screamed in. In any case, he'd never been so happy to reach the center of town. Although if he was being honest, it was pretty nice to hear the sound of her voice again. Even her off-key voice.

Jasper simply pointed at the building that housed his condo across the street. "I'm going to take care of you for the night. I live there."

Carissa looked up. "I don't. Where's my house? Oh yeah, I lost it in the divorce."

He wasn't sure what she was babbling about but it didn't matter. They were in the homestretch. Just needed to cross the street.

And that's when Carissa let out a long, loud yawn and slumped against him. She was out.

"You are lucky you're not going to remember this because it would really piss you off." With that, he repositioned her body, took a deep breath and flung her over his shoulder, caveman-style.

He put all of his effort into carrying her, concentrating so hard that he almost missed when she murmured, "I really missed you."

Almost.

Chapter Four

Bayside Blogger @BSBlogger

Spotted at the Rusty Keg last night: Carissa Blackwell & Jasper Dumont. Reconciliation? Mayhaps. A better question would be, where did they end the night?

There were three things that Carissa did not need to open her eyes to know. First, the sun was streaming through a window, making her feel like a vampire being burned at the end of the long, dark night.

Next, she was fully aware that she'd had too much to drink the night before. Her head was pounding and her mouth was dry and gritty. She'd definitely consumed one tequila shot too many.

But most importantly, even with her eyes held firmly shut, she knew without a doubt that she wasn't alone. Someone was watching her.

"Morning, sunshine." Jasper's cool, calm voice rang out with a touch of humor to it from across the room.

"Hmphhjmelskjk," she mumbled incoherently as a reply.

"I thought you might say something like that." The mattress shifted and the rocking motion did nothing to appease her headache. "I'm going to grab you a bottle of water and some aspirin."

"Thanks," she ground out even as she buried her head further in the pillow.

But once Jasper was gone, she did finally peek out from her childish hiding spot. The events of the night before came crashing back. The evening had started off innocently enough with a trip to the grocery store. Then she'd ended up at the Rusty Keg with Jasper, where it was possible she'd drunk all of the alcohol in the whole world.

She searched her fuzzy brain and tried to remember all the particulars, but the details were slow to return. She knew she'd talked to Jasper for hours. She'd told him about her divorce and wanting to start her business. Then they'd flirted and she'd fallen on her face on the dirty bar floor, and then they'd gone outside and...

Her eyes widened and she shook her head back and forth, which only served to exacerbate her already-throbbing head. "No, no, no," she said aloud. They'd kissed. No, worse, they'd made out like they were still teenagers in the damn parking lot.

What had she been thinking? Well, nothing, duh. Thanks to the tequila. And the small part of her brain not coerced by alcohol had succumbed to the power of Jasper's clever lips. He'd always been an amazing kisser. She touched a finger to her lips now and that's when she remembered she was in a bed.

Carissa looked around. She saw her jeans on the dresser on the other side of the room. She flew out of the bed. She still had her tank top and bra on, but other than that, she was in her underwear.

At least this is a pair of my sexiest underwear. She be-rated herself. That wasn't the point. The point was that—

"You." She pointed at Jasper as he came back through the door, carrying a tray. "I don't have any pants on."

He grinned, his eyes roaming down her body. "I can see that."

"You took my pants off. You…you…"

"U, v, w, x, y, z."

She stared at him, mouth hanging open. "This isn't the time for jokes. Did we…"

Tray still in hand, he leaned back against the doorjamb, an amused expression on his face. "Did we what?"

She pointed at the bed and then at him and then back to herself. "Did we sleep together?" she whispered.

His face fell. "You were pretty drunk, Carissa. Give me some credit."

Immediately, she felt like a fool. Of course, he'd never do something like that. "Ohmigod, Jasper. I'm sorry."

"It's okay," he said.

She wrapped her arms around herself, suddenly aware that she must look absolutely disgusting. She was sure her hair went beyond a messy bird's nest. It was probably a whole bird mansion.

"I bring peace offerings." He held the tray up. "You look like you need these." He handed over a couple of aspirin, a plate with two pieces of freshly buttered toast, and a glass of water. "You shouldn't take those on an empty stomach."

She sank back onto the bed. "You brought me home and took care of me?"

"I didn't do much. You were out, um, pretty fast." He said that comment strangely and it had her head tilting. Then he quickly followed up with, "I slept in the guest room."

Damn, why did he have to be so nice? His sudden kindness—so different from the teenager she remembered—made her feel...things. A blush crept into her cheeks, and desperate to hide her reaction, she turned to take a moment and admire his place.

His king-size bed was certainly comfy, decorated with a fluffy, light blue duvet cover and matching pillows. The furniture was all wood, very masculine. But the room was tidy and there were amazingly tall windows, almost the entire height of the wall, that let in the light she'd been cursing a few minutes ago. If her head wasn't throbbing she would be loving all that natural light and the view of the water beyond.

She could see through the open door into the living space. It was an open concept with brick walls, except for one, which housed floor-to-ceiling bookcases. She shifted on the bed, craning her neck to take in the kitchen, too. But all she could make out from this angle was a large island.

Jasper chuckled. "I can give you a tour, you know."

Her face grew hot. "Sorry. I don't mean to be nosy. Just curious."

"I understand." He pointed to his dresser where her capri jeans were neatly folded; her shoes sat on the floor nearby. He nodded toward the left. "Bathroom's over there. Why don't you take a moment and then meet me in the other room?"

It was only then that she noticed he was dressed in workout clothes. "Please do not tell me you've been to the gym." She jumped up. "What time is it?"

He chuckled again but also held his hands out in a soothing gesture. "Don't worry, it's still really early. I never sleep late."

She tilted her head in consideration. That was different from high school, when she'd always wait until at least eleven to call him on the weekends.

"I have some exercise equipment in one of the spare bedrooms. Helps me clear my head."

One of the spare rooms? "Exactly how big is this place?"

He grinned. "Three bedrooms, two and a half baths, a nice loft over the living room, and killer views."

A large, most likely expensive, condo. Just like she'd had with her husband in Chicago. Although her condo with Preston had been done in all beige and neutral tones, looking more like the model home real estate agents showed prospective clients than someone's living quarters. Jasper's place, on the other hand, had more of an edgy, urban vibe. Plus, she kinda wanted to marry these amazing wood floors.

"I'll go make us some coffee."

With that, he left the room and Carissa quickly chomped down the toast and swallowed the aspirin. Then she jumped from the bed, grabbed her jeans off the dresser and ran into the bathroom. Of course, she stopped to admire his killer walk-in closet on the way. The bathroom was just as nice and tastefully done as the rest of the place. Double vanity, separate soaker tub, and a shower that looked like it had no less than a hundred showerheads.

She stopped gawking at everything and she was very proud to say that she did not give in to the temptation to go through his medicine cabinet. Instead, Carissa quickly dressed, splashed some water on her face, did her best job of brushing her teeth with her finger, and ran a comb through her hair. Not a massive improvement, but definitely better than a couple minutes ago.

The aroma of coffee reached her nose and she followed it out to the kitchen. And if she thought she coveted the wood floors or the orgasmic shower, that was nothing compared to his kitchen. New stainless steel appliances, a farmhouse sink, and a gorgeous island that looked to be made out of reclaimed wood on the bottom and marble counter on top. She ran her hands along the cool stone and tried to keep from drooling.

"You like?"

"It kind of makes my aunt's tiny kitchen seem like an anthill."

"Is that where you plan to start your business from?"

"Of course." As he handed her a mug of steaming hot coffee, it occurred to her that he didn't realize her full situation. Jasper had no way of knowing that she was broke and desperate.

"You should consider renting out a space for a year or so. That would give you some separation. Plus, it would be better for meeting with clients. I could show you some places, give you a couple recommendations."

She sipped the coffee. "I thought we called a truce only for last night."

He considered. "Showing you real estate would be business."

Oh. Not really the answer she'd wanted. Then again, what did she expect? He'd been kinder to her than she deserved.

She ran a hand through her hair. "This coffee's good."

"Thanks. It's from The Brewside. A coffeehouse in the town square," he finished, clearly realizing she wouldn't be familiar with the changes in Bayside.

She put the mug down on the counter. "No, thank you. For getting me here last night, the coffee, for picking my clothes up, the toast. You didn't have to do all of that."

"I would have done it for anyone."

Again, not the response she'd expected. The sides of her mouth turned down in a frown.

"I would have let you sleep longer," he said, "but I have to get to work shortly and I didn't want you to wake up in a strange environment."

She eyed the clock above the stove. "It's still really early."

"I like to get into the office early."

"Of course," she said, and pointed toward the door. "I'll just get out of your hair."

"No, Car, I didn't mean you had to leave. Stay as long as you want."

She shook her head. "I'm sure you don't want some hungover girl lolling around in your place."

"I've had plenty of girls, hungover and stone-cold sober, loll around here." He snapped his mouth shut.

Plenty of girls. She looked away. What did she think? Jasper hadn't been dating for the last ten years? He became some kind of monk or something? Look at him. He was probably fending off women left and right.

"That didn't come out right," he said sheepishly.

Carissa held up a hand. "It's fine, Jasp. Don't worry about it." He seemed uncomfortable still. "What? Is there something else?"

He eyed his coffee mug. "Just something that happened last night. You probably don't remember but we…"

"Kissed," she finished. And what a kiss it had been. But after his "plenty of women" comment, she decided to keep that to herself. "I do remember."

"I'm really sorry about that."

He was? Because despite everything else, she wasn't sure that she was sorry. In fact, she kind of liked it. "Why in the world would you be sorry?"

He ran a hand through his hair. "You were drunk, Carissa. I took advantage of you."

She let out a relieved breath. "Jasp, we've kissed each other a million times before."

"I know, but…" He trailed off and she wondered what he wanted to say. Finally, he said, "More coffee?"

She shook her head. When he turned and crossed to the opposite counter to refill his own mug, his phone vibrated, dancing across the surface of the island. She tried not to look but couldn't help it. It was too close. Close enough to see a text message from someone named Simone Graves.

Morning, cutie. Sorry I missed having drinks w/u last nite. I'll make up for it. Promise. This was punctuated by a kissy-face emoji.

Wasn't it a tad bit early for emojis of any kind? Carissa couldn't contain the sigh.

"What was that for?" Jasper asked from across the room.

"Uh, nothing. Just exhausted." She was being ridiculous. Of course Jasper had women texting him. Was he serious about this one? Did he have a girlfriend? She searched her hungover brain. Did she even ask him last night?

"I'll bet." He crossed to the pantry and reached for a new box of sweetener.

She crossed the room and studied his very large collection of books on the floor-to-ceiling bookcases. Two entire shelves were devoted to graphic novels. She tapped them with a finger and let out a small laugh.

Then she returned to the island just as his phone lit up again. Someone named Sherry popped up on the screen this time. Me, you, our usual time and place. Don't be late.

Our usual time and place? Carissa gnawed on her lip as she considered. Just how many girlfriends did he have? She blew an errant hair out of her face. None of her business. Jasper had always been a flirt. Apparently nothing had changed.

Suddenly she felt nauseous and it had nothing to do with the copious amount of alcohol she'd consumed the night before. She pushed her coffee mug away and when she did, she noticed one last text message from someone named Elle.

4 calls in 1 day. All-time record, Jasp. Be back in town later today. Promise.

Simone, Sherry, Elle. Who were all these women? More importantly, why was she experiencing a sinking feeling in her stomach?

Because no matter what, and in spite of everything they'd been through, she would always harbor a very soft spot for Jasper Dumont. Always.

Admitting that was the first step. Now she needed to refocus. Worrying about Jasper and his apparently very active love life was futile. She had more important things to think of now, like her business. Because the one thing she knew was that no matter what, she needed time right now to concentrate on this business venture. No way would she end up like her father, relying on someone else for money and security.

An image of her Chicago condo all packed up with Preston's name scribbled on the majority of the boxes flashed into her mind. She wouldn't do that again. No, she was going to put everything she had into this business and it was going to succeed. And she simply couldn't get bogged down by a drunken night with her ex-boyfriend, no matter how nice he was the morning after and how many pieces of toast he made her.

She pushed back from the counter abruptly. "I, uh, should really get going."

Surprise shone in his eyes, but he quickly added a playful, "Worried you'll be spotted leaving my place the morning after?"

"Not particularly. Besides, nothing happened between us."

A shadow passed over his face. "Right."

"Right," she repeated.

A long moment stretched between them. Neither moved, neither spoke. Finally, Carissa backed up toward the door. "Listen, Jasp, don't worry about that kiss. In fact, don't even think about it. It was nothing."

"Really?"

Was it just her or did his expression darken? Maybe it was the light from the windows. "Yes. Like you said last night. We called a truce. Just...pretend it never happened."

"That's really what you want?"

It had to be. She nodded enthusiastically. "Yes. Absolutely. Go about your life. Continue dating, or seeing, or spending time with, whoever you might be doing those things with." She coughed. Why was she rambling? "Seriously," she finished when he opened his mouth to speak. "We are just old friends now." She ran a hand through her hair before taking the final step to the door. "Thanks again for everything. I guess I'll see you around."

With that, she made a hasty retreat from his beautiful loft, acting very much like she was worried she would be spotted the morning after.

The morning after a night like last night was enough to have Jasper dragging. He hadn't been drunk, but taking care of a drunk ex-girlfriend whom he'd securely placed in the "I'm definitely never seeing this person again" folder had been a bit much.

He ran a hand through his hair and then quickly cursed himself for messing it up while he was at work. See, one day in town and Carissa was already messing with his hair, not to mention with his lonely night out to drink away his thoughts.

He straightened in the leather chair behind his large oak desk at the Dumont Incorporated headquarters. If he was being truthful with himself, he hadn't actually minded taking care of Carissa last night. And he definitely hadn't minded that kiss. But wasn't that the problem? He should mind it.

He was going to have to chalk it up to nostalgia. He didn't harbor feelings for her any longer. In fact, he was positive they could exist in the same town without any emotional strife to speak of.

Besides, even if he was interested, which he clearly wasn't, she'd just gotten divorced. Although what moron divorced an amazing woman like Carissa was beyond him. Even more preposterous was the idea that anyone would cheat on her. That fact still set his blood boiling.

At least she'd decided to come back home instead of staying in Chicago. And now she was going to start a business, too. Maybe he could throw some contacts her way. After all, he was forever being invited to one party or another.

Leaning onto his desk, he nodded. He could definitely help her out. Not because she was an ex-girlfriend, though. He'd help anyone out.

"Right," he said aloud for emphasis.

"Everything okay, Mr. Dumont?"

Jasper practically jumped out of his seat at the sound

of his assistant's voice. "Yes, everything's fine, Sherry. Didn't I ask you to call me Jasper? Mr. Dumont is my dad."

The young woman smiled. Jasper had taken a chance hiring Sherry. Straight out of college with little experience. But he knew her family and Sherry had needed a job desperately. Luckily, she'd turned out to be one of the hardest workers on his team.

"Sorry, Jasper," she said. "Now on to our usual time and place."

"My favorite date with my favorite person," he said, referring to their usual morning rundown of his schedule and events.

"Yeah, yeah, I bet you say that to all the girls. Your two o'clock meeting switched to three," she said, beginning to go through her usual morning checklist. "I scheduled your dentist appointment for next week. Don't look at me like that. Even millionaires need to go to the dentist." She grinned. "I sent out those contracts first thing. Oh, and your brother called. Twice," she said, her smile fading. "I hope Elle is coming back soon."

Apparently, Jasper wasn't the only one Cam pestered when his better half was away. "This afternoon." They high-fived. "Anything else?"

"Nope, that's about it. Will you be heading to The Brewside for your usual morning pick-me-up?"

"Yep, about to leave. I'll bring you back a..." He waited.

"You know, my boss pays me quite well. He doesn't always have to treat me to coffee."

"Let me buy you a drink or you're fired."

She rolled her eyes, completely unaffected by him. "Fine. I'd like a medium chai. And thank you." She walked toward the door but stopped and turned back to him before she walked out. "Oh, and um, you might want to check out the Bayside Blogger's column this morning. Okay, bye."

With that, Sherry flew out of the room, returning to her workstation on the other side of the wall. Jasper sighed but quickly pulled up the *Bayside Bugle*'s site, found the link to the blog and started reading.

Well, damn.

The headline on this morning's blog was Homecoming Queen Returns to Bayside & Jasper Dumont's Condo.

It went on to detail how Carissa had been "spotted" fleeing Jasper's place that morning. He hadn't seen anyone around. He wondered how Carissa would take this. It had been a couple of months since he'd been featured on the blog. Typically, he always accepted the Bayside Blogger's attention with humility. But in this case, he knew he was about to start receiving calls and texts from his mom, his dad, his brother, and the list would go on and on. In an attempt to stave off the unwanted attention and questions, he grabbed his wallet, left his phone and headed out toward the coffee shop.

He was taking a risk showing his face there. The Brewside Café was the center of the Bayside universe, where citizens young and old gathered to gossip. Still, when a man needed coffee, a man needed coffee.

Gathering his energy, he hustled out of the building that housed Dumont Incorporated and walked the three blocks to the coffeehouse, which was situated right in the center of the town square between a shoe store and a clothing boutique. The Brewside, along with all of the establishments in the square, was painted a bright white and accented with blue shutters. There were two large flowerpots flanking the entrance. The flowers had seen better days, Jasper thought. Not unexpected, given the hot and humid summer they'd had. But he knew Tony, the owner, would soon change out the wilted flowers for something more representative of fall.

Jasper typically stopped by the café every day. Sometimes more than once. It was cozy inside with its old wood floors, rustic feel and arched ceilings with exposed beams. Wooden barrels served as table bases, and Tony had put either old doors or sheets of glass on top. An antique brass cash register sat on the large bar area, across from a glass display case holding every pastry under the sun.

Ordinarily, Jasper would take his time perusing the goodies before he ordered his usual large coffee. But today, as soon as he pushed through the door, every patron in the joint turned in his direction. He couldn't help but spot several copies of the *Bayside Bugle* throughout the place. Not to mention all the laptops and iPads littering the tables. Yep, the Bayside Blogger had reached her target audience.

Why fight it, Jasper thought. He gave a wave and continued to the bar to order.

He handed over his money and his "frequent buyer" card to Tony, who wore an amused expression.

"You're famous again, my friend," Tony said.

"Hey, I thought I was always famous in Bayside," Jasper replied with mock indignation.

Tony chuckled. "I suppose you are." He leaned forward, lowering his voice. "Is it true? Is Carissa Blackwell really back in town?"

Jasper wasn't sure how to answer but luckily he was saved by the bell as the chimes dangling on the inside of the door marked the arrival of a new patron. He turned to see a showered and changed Carissa stroll into the place. She looked as if she'd spent the night before getting a restful eight hours of shut-eye. No easy feat given her long drive the day before and her even longer alcohol-fueled night with him.

"Let me guess," Tony said. "That's Carissa Blackwell. I've heard stories about her." Tony didn't grow up in Bayside. He'd moved to town when he'd married a local and started The Brewside. The marriage didn't last, but Tony was considered a son of Bayside as much as Jasper was. Anyone plying the town with that amount of caffeine and baked goods would be. "She's as pretty as I've been told."

"That she is," Jasper agreed.

Tony handed Jasper his coffee and went off to help Carissa. Jasper noticed that everyone in the place was doing that thing where they tried to seem like they weren't ogling Carissa, only it made it that much more obvious that they were all staring at her.

She made some small talk with Tony, who, by all appearances, was eating out of the palm of her hand. She'd always been a charmer.

Then she turned and met his gaze. She looked amazing. Her hair was fluffy, her face scrubbed free of makeup, her eyes alert and completely the opposite of what they should be considering how much she'd drunk the night before.

She walked toward him, the flowy pants she had on billowing around her legs. She had on another tight tank top. This one was a deep aquamarine color that accentuated everything about her: her eyes, her skin tone, her body.

"Hey, Jasp," she said casually.

"Hey back," he returned. He tried to keep his voice calm even though the sight of her took his breath away.

"Here's your bagel with extra cream cheese and double-shot cappuccino, Carissa." Tony handed over a bag and cup.

She thanked him, then turned back to Jasper. Her eyes were taking him in the way a person on a diet viewed a double-chocolate brownie. He couldn't say he minded. The most beautiful woman he ever saw gawking at him? All was right in the world. Although after a few moments, he did have to ask. "Excuse me?" he said.

She coughed quickly and jumped back. "Huh?"

He chuckled and stepped closer. "Not that I mind, but you happen to be staring at me."

"No, I'm not," she said faster than Tony had called out his coffee order.

He took another step toward her. "Darling, I hate to argue, but you most certainly were staring."

A little crease formed as she drew her eyes together and Jasper thought it was the cutest thing ever.

"Do you always wear a suit to work?"

Her voice came out quiet but breathy as hell. Jasper had to take a moment to collect himself. Hearing her like that did things to his insides that no amount of coffee could cause.

"No, sometimes I go a bit more casual. But I have a couple meetings lined up for today."

"Oh. Well, you look…nice."

He tilted his head for her to follow him away from the counter. They set up camp at one of the high tables off to the side of the space. "Just as I suspected. You were undressing me with your eyes."

The shocked look on her face was priceless. "I absolutely, categorically was not undressing you or anyone else with my eyes. Or any other part of my body," she added quickly.

"As someone who could teach a class on how to undress people with their eyes, trust me, I have your number. But what I don't get is why. You, more than anyone, know exactly what's under here."

She gasped and swatted at him. "Oh shut up. It's been a long time since I've seen you naked." She took a long sip of her strong coffee, her eyes drifting closed in contentment. When she opened them, a small smile played over her lips.

"Better?" he asked.

"So much better. This will definitely help get me

through grocery shopping and unpacking." She frowned when she caught sight of a newspaper on the table next to them. She pointed at it. "Then there's that."

"You read it?"

"My aunt Val, who is currently across the ocean in Mo-freaking-rocco, called me an hour ago. Apparently there's an online site for this blogger person, too."

Jasper nodded. "I told you last night. She has a blog, a column, Twitter, Instagram, Facebook, Snapchat, you name it."

"Oh goody." She removed the bagel from its bag and began smearing it with a large amount of cream cheese.

He'd always envied her metabolism. "I can't believe you can still eat like that."

"There's always a silver lining, isn't there." She leaned forward and whispered, "Got divorced but I can still scarf down some yummy carbs without doing too much damage."

He covered her hand with his. "Things are going to get better, Car."

Jasper didn't have to turn toward the rest of the coffee-house to know that they were being watched. "Sorry," he said, pulling his hand away.

"I imagine that's going to end up on one of the Bayside Blogger's many social media channels?"

"Does it upset you?"

She broke off a piece of the bagel and popped it in her mouth. Chewing, she seemed thoughtful. "Not really. I don't particularly like that someone knew I was leaving your place this morning, but it's not the worst thing that's happened to me this year. Still, I'd prefer it if from now on my business stayed simply that. Mine."

He agreed and was about to say so when the door opened, the chimes gave out their welcoming jingle, and someone walked inside. "Well, looks like we've got bigger problems than the Bayside Blogger right now."

She cocked her head. "We do?"

"Hi, Mom," he called over Carissa's head.

Carissa coughed, spitting the piece of bagel out of her mouth. She quickly wiped her mouth and hands and bolted out of her seat.

"Jasper, my handsome son." Lilah Dumont knew how to make an entrance. She breezed past the other patrons, doing her best Queen Elizabeth wave. She nodded at Tony behind the bar, who immediately started whipping up whatever drink she usually ordered. Then she turned back to the room as if to say, "please, be seated."

Jasper kissed her cheek. "You're looking lovely this morning."

She pinched his cheek. "Aren't you sweet." Then she turned her gaze to Carissa. "Well, well, the rumors are true. Carissa Blackwell has come home. You're looking as beautiful as I remember."

They hugged and Carissa said, "Thank you, Mrs. Dumont. It's great to see you."

"And you. Tony," she called. "Can you bring my smoothie and yogurt over here? Thanks, hon." She made herself at home by sitting right in between Jasper and Carissa. "I hope your parents are well. No one's seen or heard from them for years."

"Ma, don't start badgering her with questions."

"Oh hush," Lilah said. "I've known Carissa her whole life. So it's not badgering. It's simply being nosy," she finished with a smile.

"It's okay in any case," Carissa said. "Actually, I'm staying at my aunt Val's cottage while she's off traveling the world."

Jasper noticed the smooth transition. Also, the avoidance of discussing her parents. Interesting. He wondered what Mr. and Mrs. Blackwell had been up to for the last decade.

The two women talked about Val and her world exploits for a while. Tony brought his mother's food and smoothie to their table.

"So what brought you back to town?" Lilah asked.

Carissa shifted uncomfortably in her chair. Jasper quickly answered, "Carissa is starting a catering business here in Bayside."

"Really?" Lilah asked, delight in her voice. "What a wonderful idea. The closest caterer is a couple towns over and not always the most reliable. Have you been working in the catering field since college?"

"Well, um, actually…"

She was cut off by Jessica Monrow, an old family friend of the Dumonts. "Sorry to interrupt, Lilah, but I wanted to tell you that Edward will be able to make it to the party tomorrow night after all."

"Oh good, that's great news. Actually…" She turned toward Carissa and then back to Jasper. "Jasper, darling, have you invited Carissa to tomorrow night's event?"

He'd actually forgotten all about it. "Um, no, not yet."

"Oh right, you've probably only just run into each other." She arched her brow with that look she used to give him back in high school whenever he would come in from a make-out session with Carissa and she would pretend not to know.

Great, so his mother had read the paper and was aware that Carissa had spent the night. He felt his cheeks redden.

"Well, invite her now. I'm off with Jess to shop for a new dress. Carissa, lovely to see you. I'll look forward to catching up more tomorrow night. Jasper, clean this up for me, will you," she indicated the trash.

With that, Lilah Dumont made her grand exit.

"Well then," Carissa said. "Same old Mrs. Dumont."

"Quite the same," Jasper agreed. He checked his watch. "I hate to leave you, too, but I really should be getting back to the office. But why don't you come to the party tomorrow night?"

She shifted in her seat again. "Oh, Jasp, I really shouldn't go to that."

"Why not?"

She looked around the coffeehouse. "I mean, I've only just gotten back and I have so much to do. Plus, seeing half the town all in one place..."

"Trust me, if you can walk in here with your head held high after a Bayside Blogger article, you can do anything in this town."

She smiled but it didn't reach her eyes. He felt for her. She'd been through so much.

"You know, even though I've taken over Dumont Incorporated, my parents still have all those connections."

Clearly intrigued, she leaned forward.

"And all of those connections have connections. And collectively all of these people throw parties and luncheons and host events." He moved closer. "Parties and luncheons and events that require a caterer in order to be successful."

He saw it almost instantly. That small spark in her eyes that said he'd piqued her interest.

"You're saying that I should come to your parents' party for contacts?"

A new idea formed. But he quickly decided to keep it to himself. Instead, he changed his tone, challenging her. "I'm saying you would be a fool not to. And if I were you, I'd make sure to get there early."

She deliberated, taking another sip of her coffee. Finally, she gave a firm head nod. "Fine, I'll go." A sexy little smile spread on her face. "If this Bayside Blogger is going to write about me anyway, I might as well give her something to write about." She winked at him.

Jasper gulped. Somehow he had a feeling that today's article was not the only one that would feature the two of them.

Chapter Five

I don't want to start rumors. *Snort* But everyone is abuzz with the news that Carissa Blackwell will be attending tonight's Dumont soiree. Is it too early to come up with their couple name? I'm thinking either Jarissa or Casper? Let me know on Twitter by using the hashtag #ShesBack.

Carissa stalked around her aunt's cottage, doing the same thing she'd been doing the entire day. Admonishing herself over her behavior with Jasper the other night, dreading going to the Dumont party tonight and clearly avoiding unpacking.

She was an idiot. She had no business getting that drunk the other night. She'd been back in town for a whopping thirty seconds before she doused herself in tequila and cheap beer. Not the best way to start off her twenty-ninth year.

She slumped down at the kitchen table. Okay, so it hadn't exactly gone down like that. Jasper had been there for her that night. He'd listened to her sob story. Well, the parts that she'd actually shared with him. Worrying her lip, she debated whether or not to reveal to Jasper the real reason she'd broken up with him all those years ago. On the one hand, it would feel good to get that off her chest. But Jasper seemed so…well-adjusted now. Why bring up old hurts?

Besides, he'd moved on if all those text messages from other women meant anything. He probably never even thought about their breakup.

Damn, he'd looked amazing in his suit the other morning. Now, that was a great way to start the day.

"Stop it," she said abruptly. She needed to get her head out of the clouds and out of Jasper's suit and back into reality. She was back in this town so she could make something of herself. So she could be a caterer. So she didn't have to rely on anyone but herself. And so far, "herself" wasn't doing her any favors.

She rose from the table with a renewed sense of purpose. Everything was going to change tonight. She would slip on one of the fancy dresses she'd brought from Chicago and head to the Dumont mansion. She would wine and dine with Bayside elite, making contacts for her business, and hopefully get a lead on one single event she could cater.

If it came to it, she would beg.

"You can do this," she said out loud.

With that, she headed back to her bedroom and looked through her clothing options for the night. She remembered the Dumont parties from her teenage years. The Dumonts always went all out. Their parties were the social events of the year.

Her parents had always been invited, of course. Even before she and Jasper dated and were simply friends, they used to slink around the outskirts of the party, snagging hors d'oeuvres and dancing to the music. When they got older, they used to also steal a glass of champagne or two.

The first time Jasper told her he loved her had been on the beach at the bottom of the Dumont property. They could hear the music lingering from the band set up on the patio. They had toasted, completely unappreciative of what had no doubt been incredibly expensive champagne. The water was lapping at their feet. He kissed her, then he stared into her eyes, pushed her hair behind her ear and said *I love you*.

She'd been so dazzled, so mesmerized by him, that she'd simply said the same words back to him before falling into his arms.

But those memories were from a million years ago. Things were different now and she wasn't attending this party as a moony-eyed, boy-crazy teenager. She needed to establish herself. "Purpose, purpose, purpose," she said to her reflection in the mirror. Once again, she eyed her dress options. Finally, she chose one of her favorites. It was a sparkly, strapless number in a pale baby blue that brought out her light eyes. The dress skimmed the middle of her thighs, making her long legs appear even longer, especially when she paired it with her favorite pair of sinful silver stilettos.

After she added a pair of long dangly earrings, she swept her thick blond hair up on top of her head, leaving a few strands down to frame her face.

She put time into applying her makeup so it appeared as natural as possible. Then she double-checked her appearance in the mirror. Satisfied, she grabbed her clutch purse and headed out the door.

When she arrived at the Dumont mansion, it was still relatively early. In fact, the party hadn't started yet. She might have taken Jasper's advice to arrive early a little too literally. She could see servants putting the finishing touches on decorations and placing chairs on the tiered patios, and she heard the band warming up on the stage that had been set up for them.

As she walked through the impressive foyer and out the French doors that led to the backyard, the sounds of the instruments faded away. She didn't notice the mounds of beautiful flowers or the fact that the sun was setting over the bay in tones of red, orange, pink and yellow. Everything melted away as Jasper, dressed in a tuxedo with black pants, white jacket and black tie, turned from admiring the water to spot her. She froze, her mouth going dry as she inhaled sharply. Damn, he could give Chris Pine, Ryan Reynolds, or any other Hollywood leading man, a run for his money.

A slow, sinfully sexy smile blossomed over his face, making her fight to keep her knees from going out. Then he walked toward her with that confident gait.

"Hello, gorgeous," he said, his gaze raking over her.

"Hello yourself. Don't you look dapper." She had to stop from reaching up and fiddling with his tie. Or better yet, slipping her fingers underneath that crisp white shirt...

"Apparently, this is the final Dumont soiree of the summer season. I had to break out all the stops. But my tux is nothing compared to this little number." He wiggled his finger at her dress.

"Oh, this old thing?" she said coyly as if she wore short sparkly dresses on a daily basis.

He took another step toward her, his eyes darkening to a deeper shade of blue. He opened his mouth but before he could say whatever was on his mind, Mrs. Dumont darted out of the house. Even in the stunning yellow designer gown, with tasteful diamonds twinkling from her earlobes, Carissa could tell she was agitated.

"Jasper," she yelled across the patio in a very un-Lilah-like manner. "Oh, hi, Carissa. Don't you look lovely. Jasper, have you seen your father?"

"What's wrong, Mom?"

"Our caterer had a family emergency and she had to leave. I have no idea what I am going to do now."

"What about Joanna? My parents' chef," he explained to Carissa.

"She's on maternity leave. I knew we should have hired a backup chef. I told your father. But does he listen to me?"

"Can you run to the store and get some snacks?"

Carissa and Mrs. Dumont turned to him at the same time and both shouted, "No!"

"Go to the store for five hundred people?" Mrs. Dumont said at the same time Carissa said, "That's completely impractical, Jasper."

Mrs. Dumont turned to her. "Exactly. Not to mention that people expect a certain culinary experience when they come here The menu has been set for weeks and the oysters arrived not long ago."

Guests were starting to arrive. Carissa noticed a congregation at one of the bars. "That's horrible," she said to Mrs. Dumont.

"I just can't believe this happened. I always have a plan A, B and C. I guess I've gotten lax in my retirement."

"I have an idea," Jasper said. "Why don't you fill in?" He turned his attention to Carissa.

Her? Fill in for someone who was no doubt a world-class chef with decades of experience? After all, this was a Dumont event, not some little dinner party she was throwing for friends.

"Jasp, you're nuts."

"And you're a caterer," he countered. Then he leaned in and whispered, "This could be your big chance."

"Do you think you could handle it?" Lilah asked, hope filling her eyes.

Carissa glanced around as even more people streamed onto the terrace. "I've never catered an event this big." She realized that didn't sound like the best review and quickly amended her statement. "I meant to say, I usually work at much more intimate affairs. I'm not exactly used to an entire kitchen staff."

"Mom does have some great people back there though. I'm sure they could help you with any questions or concerns."

She bit her lip. Carissa understood what Jasper was saying. Catering an entire Dumont party would go a long way to helping her start her business. Then again, if she messed up, her business was dead on arrival.

A man around her father's age, with similar features, walked past them. Carissa thought about her dad. How he always took the easy way out. He would go into business, only to be derailed when the going got tough. Instead of fighting his way through it, he'd bail.

Sometimes, he wouldn't even start. If a project seemed like it was going to take up too much time or be too hard, he would pass.

Even as a teenager, she knew his attitude was all wrong. She knew she never wanted to be like that.

With renewed determination and a confidence she didn't quite feel, she lifted her chin. "Mrs. Dumont, I can help."

It took a lot to impress Jasper, but Carissa had managed to do it.

He peeked in the kitchen and couldn't suppress a grin when he found her still wearing that wickedly seductive dress with all that luscious hair piled atop her head. Someone had lent her a pair of sneakers, but even without those tempting strappy heels, her legs still managed to look amazing. Her dress was partially covered by an apron and the steam from the various pots on the stove gave her skin a dewy look.

Anyone could tell she was in her element. As soon as his mom had let her take a look at the catering menus, she'd gone into a no-nonsense business mode. She'd reviewed the menus, spoken briefly with the staff, washed her hands and immediately dived into work. Before Jasper or his mom could even say thank you, the appetizers had begun to appear.

He snagged a mushroom bruschetta from the counter now and almost had to close his eyes as the succulent flavor took hold. The woman could cook.

He reached for another and got his hand smacked for his efforts.

"Jasper Dumont," Carissa said, pinning him with a stare. "Those are for the guests."

"I'm a guest," he countered.

She pointed at the door. "Out!"

"Yes, ma'am." He wanted to tell her that her bossiness was turning him on but didn't think that would go over well with her Gordon Ramsay persona. Instead, he slunk outside, but not before quickly grabbing a carrot stick from one of the crudités platters. He retreated from the kitchen to the sound of Carissa's swearing.

The party was in full swing. Like most of his parents' events, it felt like the entire town had come out. His mother did usually invite everyone. Plus, there were plenty of colleagues, business associates and future business prospects. Jasper worked the party for a while, making small talk and promising follow-up emails and meetings. Then he skirted a table of desserts to avoid a woman he'd dated for a few weeks and firmly broken up with, but who didn't want to accept that. He spotted Simone in the crowd but was stopped by Aly, an incredibly intelligent brunette he'd spent an amazing ski weekend with in Aspen last year.

"Hey, Jasp," she cooed, happiness radiating out of her pores.

He tapped the large rock on her ring finger and grinned. "I hear congrats are in order."

She beamed. "Sorry you didn't snap me up when you had the chance?" she teased.

He put on his best mock-sad face. "I will forever regret it."

"I'll just bet." She laughed and wagged her finger at him. "I'm telling you, one of these days you're going to meet a woman who will bring you to your knees."

"Doubtful. Now that you're taken," he quickly added. He enjoyed hearing her laugh as she walked away to join her fiancé.

He chatted with his father, making plans for a round of golf in the following week. His dad wasted no time getting into full retirement mode. After seeing his dad work in some regard almost every day of his life, this change in behavior was a shock to Jasper. He had been sure he'd have to drag his father away from the office kicking and screaming. Still, his dad did manage to get in the usual fatherly concerns.

"Heard about the deal with Morris. Well done."

"Thanks, Dad."

"Now, remember, you can't just jump into that project with your usual gusto. Morris requires finessing."

"I know, Dad."

"You don't want to make one of your usual mistakes. That's all I'm saying."

Jasper held in a sigh, all of the positive vibes he'd been experiencing quickly draining out of his body. When was he going to be good enough? Even at his age, his dad could make him feel like that second son all over again. The kid that was not meant to take over the company. The one who couldn't possibly have the ideas and drive to run Dumont Incorporated.

"What are you doing with the waterfront property on Oak Avenue?" his dad asked.

Jasper shrugged. "Haven't decided yet."

"You know what I think."

Of course he did. His dad, as well as other members of the board, was intent to see him make a deal with the city over a prime piece of real estate. Jasper wasn't so sure that was a great idea. But this wasn't the time or place to get into that same old argument.

"Let's talk about that next week when we golf."

With that, Jasper made his way across the patio and took a moment for himself. He'd always loved his parents' house and particularly the expansive grounds. The back side of the house faced the bay with an abundance of French doors and windows to allow in the light and the stunning view. A large patio opened to a terrace, which cascaded down into more terraces—a scalloped effect that made for an amazing party setup. Guests could mingle in a variety of areas. Or they could chat around the large swimming pool or take a walk through his mother's gardens and end up at the tennis courts.

Naturally, his mother had several bars set up throughout the backyard, even though the drink of choice at a Dumont party tended to be the champagne passed on trays by waiters wearing white gloves. A little much in Jasper's opinion, but he did love that his mother never changed. She continued to throw these lavish parties with an overabundance of colorful flowers, mountains of food and the occasional fireworks display. In fact, he wondered if there would be one tonight.

On the main terrace he met up with his mother and brother, who were busy sampling some of Carissa's appetizers.

"How'd she do?" he asked his mother, referring to Carissa.

"I'm impressed. I'm happy. The guests are satisfied. And I want her to make whatever this is every single day for the rest of my life," Lilah said, acknowledging a cracker with some sort of pâté spread on it. "Thank God she returned to Bayside. I don't know what we would have done."

"I'm sure you would have figured something out," his brother Cam said around a mouthful of shrimp.

"Ohmigod, have you tried this?"

Jasper turned to see Cam's girlfriend, Elle Owens, and her best friend, Riley Hudson, strolling toward them.

"That's what I just said," his mother agreed.

Cam immediately snaked his arm around Elle, pulling her close to his side. Jasper was bemused to see big bad Cameron Dumont turn to goo every time little Ellie Owens was in his presence. The way Cam was lovingly watching her now, Jasper had a feeling it wouldn't be long until Elle was a permanent part of the Dumont family. Personally, he was thrilled at the prospect of a sister-in-law as amazing as Elle.

"Everyone's raving about the food," Riley added.

They really were, Jasper thought. He'd overheard his mother say that Carissa had mostly stuck to the menu but she did add a few twists of her own. Apparently those twists had everyone's taste buds singing her praises.

While Elle, Cam and his mom talked more appetizers, Jasper nodded at Riley. "Hey Ri, how's it going in the newspaper business?"

"No complaints. Did you read my latest column?"

"Would I ever miss a soon-to-be-Pulitzer-Prize-winning article on the importance of taking a proper selfie?" He winked at her and Riley laughed. She currently wrote for the *Bayside Bugle* in the Style & Entertainment section. Riley kept the town up to date on all the latest fashion trends, celebrity canoodlings, best restaurants in the area and all things related to the Real Housewives.

He sidled up to her. "I know I've asked before…"

"Jasperrrrr," she moaned. Elle and Cam tuned in.

"Come on, tell me. Who's the Bayside Blogger? I know you know."

Riley rolled her eyes. "You know I don't know. Just because I work at the *Bugle* does not mean that I know that one closely guarded secret. Only our editor, the workaholic Sawyer Wallace, knows that info. And he's not budging. Not even after what she wrote about me last week."

Elle scrunched up her nose. "That was kind of harsh. Everyone has a bad date from time to time."

"Exactly," Riley said. "There was no need to out me like that. Just because I spilled red wine on the poor guy."

"And had toilet paper attached to your shoe after you went to the bathroom," Cam said, trying to suppress a smile.

"And got sick in the parking lot," Jasper added, unable to control his grin.

"Hey." Riley poked him in the chest with her index finger. "That was not my fault. And I wasn't drunk. It was the clams. I'm telling you. Just wait until I have to do a review of that restaurant. Karma's a bitch."

"So is the Bayside Blogger," Elle put in. "I wish Sawyer was here. We could tie him up and force him to reveal her identity."

"Sawyer Wallace is not at my end-of-summer party?"

Mrs. Dumont looked quite offended. "He was invited, of course."

"He's working. Finishing up the weekend edition," Riley explained. "But he said he would be here a little later."

Jasper's mom gave a firm head nod. "Good. After all, Dumont Incorporated does enough advertising to keep that paper afloat." As she strolled away, Carissa emerged from the house. The apron and sneakers were gone, but she was still flushed from her exertion in the kitchen. When she reached the center of the terrace, people began to clap and his mother engulfed her in a big hug. As they chatted, with his mother clearly imparting her pleasure, Jasper was helpless to do anything but watch Carissa. Okay, maybe blatantly stare was a more apt description.

"Careful," Cam whispered in his ear low enough that neither Elle nor Riley could hear.

"What?" Jasper asked.

"Come on. If you were ogling her any harder your eyes would pop out."

Jasper took a swig of his champagne. "Hey, it's not my fault that a beautiful woman is standing right over there. Any man not staring at her is either dumb or blind."

Cam took a moment to look him over. Jasper almost started squirming under the scrutiny. Finally, Cam said, "You know what I mean. Just be careful."

"Careful with what?" Elle asked, sauntering up to them. Her hand found Cam's, and completely in sync, their fingers intertwined.

"Please don't tell me I made the firecracker shrimp too spicy. I really try to find a good balance." Carissa had appeared next to them.

Jasper couldn't help but notice Cam's smile fade. He did, however, compliment Carissa on her cooking. "It's all amazing and the shrimp were fantastic."

She smiled, an air of relief taking over. "Thanks. But if I had a kitchen like that and a staff of that many sous chefs, trust me, I'd never stop cooking. Good to see you again, Cam. I don't remember the last time I saw you without a full beard."

His brother was one of those kids who'd been able to grow facial hair earlier than most. In both high school and college, he'd donned a whole lumberjack appearance that had intimidated most people. Jasper would have laughed at Carissa's comment but he saw the way Cam was eyeing her.

"Welcome back," Cam said through gritted teeth. "Seems like just yesterday that you broke up with Jasper and left Bayside forever."

"Cam," Elle said in a very low, warning tone. "Welcome home, Carissa. Here you go." She offered a champagne flute, which Carissa accepted very tentatively. Despite the kind gesture, Jasper did notice a certain standoffishness with Elle, too.

Interesting, he thought. Carissa, Elle, Riley and he had all been in the same class in high school. He didn't remember any bad blood between the girls. Nor did he remember Elle and Carissa really being friends, either. Elle had been the smartest person in their class but her chief of police father had been really strict so Elle didn't tend to show up at the many parties he and Carissa went to. Riley, on the other hand, had been friends with literally everyone. Still was. She proudly held the title of social butterfly of Bayside.

Carissa took a deep breath, presumably centering herself. "Ellie...Elle—oh," she said, looking like she was putting something together. She shook her head. "Ellie, you look absolutely stunning. I'd heard that you'd moved to Italy." She gestured between Elle and Cam. "But it looks like you may have found a reason to come back."

Elle blushed. "Well, this burly man was not the reason I got on that flight home. But I'm certainly glad that he turned out to be my welcoming committee."

Carissa smiled and turned to Riley. "Ri, it's so good to see you."

Riley offered a hug. "You, too. Even though you never accepted my friend request on Facebook." She waved an accusatory finger but was smiling as she did so. "What's up with that?"

"Sorry. I'm not really on Facebook much, to be honest. Or any social media really. I just started that Facebook page because my husband wanted me to."

At the word *husband*, everyone seemed to freeze.

"Er, ex-husband, I mean." Carissa cast her eyes down.

Jasper wanted to jump in, save the day. But Elle and Riley exchanged a glance and quickly changed the subject. Before he realized what had happened the three of them were thick as thieves and had headed off to the dance floor. He wouldn't have minded joining them, but his mother returned.

"She is a beauty," his mother commented as she settled next to him.

He couldn't agree more. He didn't have to glance in her direction to feel that his mother was pinning him with a hard stare. "Watch yourself, Jasper," she said in a serious tone.

He let out a long exhale. First Cam and now his mom. His family was acting like he was some innocent little girl with a red cape and basket and Carissa was the big bad wolf waiting to pounce. "You have nothing to worry about, Mom."

"Don't I? My youngest child is staring at someone like she's the only woman on the planet."

"She's gorgeous. You said so yourself."

"She's also the only woman who's ever broken your heart." At the sharp edge in her voice, he finally met her stare. "Remember, I was the one who saw you after she hightailed it out of Bayside without stopping to look back."

"She just saved your party."

"And I'm grateful for that. I plan on recommending her to anyone who will listen." She grabbed a flute of champagne from a passing waiter, took a delicate sip, then returned her attention to him. "Don't think that I don't like Carissa. That's not what this is about."

"Then, what's it about? That she broke up with me when she was eighteen years old?"

Her lips quirked. "Well, no mother likes when someone dumps their child. But no, that's not it. I like her. But I love you. You know what comes with loving a person?" He shrugged. "Worrying about them."

He draped his arm around her shoulder. "You don't have to worry about me. I'm a big boy."

She nodded in Carissa's direction. "Not where she's concerned. I just don't want to see you get hurt again."

Neither did he.

He'd always had an open, honest relationship with his mom, so Jasper didn't have any trouble being truthful now. "I don't know that I could ever forget the hurt she caused me. I don't know that I want to." He paused, collecting himself. "Doesn't mean I can't be friendly. Or admire that dress." He wiggled his eyebrows.

Lilah batted his arm. "Behave."

"Never." He pointed out Simone Graves. "See that woman over there? We're going out soon. In fact, I'm going to go check in with her now." He started to walk away but turned back. "You really have nothing to worry about." With that, he continued toward Simone.

But if Jasper had turned back again, he would have seen

his mother shaking her head, a knowing and doubtful expression on her face.

Simone seemed ecstatic when Jasper made his way to her. He produced a champagne flute from behind his back.

"Jasper Dumont, aren't you sweet." She stepped closer and whispered in his ear. "I'm excited for our date."

"Me, too," he replied, but a movement to his right caught his eye. The dance floor was getting busy and Carissa had just thrown her head back and laughed, her husky voice floating over the other noises of the party and hitting him right in the gut.

"Don't you think?" Simone was asking.

What? "Oh yeah, right."

Jasper and Simone made more small talk. Ordinarily, Jasper loved nothing more than enjoying champagne and flirting with a beautiful woman at one of these parties. And Simone was fun, sweet and bubbly. Some of his favorite qualities in a woman. But tonight, he couldn't seem to keep his gaze from the dance floor.

He noticed Robbie Hartwell, a guy he employed at Dumont Incorporated, move toward Carissa. He sucked in a breath. Robbie was a great addition to a poker game, but he was a player away from the card table, as well.

"Why are you frowning?" Simone asked, oblivious to his inner thoughts.

"Uh…because you're already out of champagne," he covered smoothly. "Would you like another?"

"I think I'm okay. There's an early-morning Zumba class I want to hit at the gym tomorrow."

"Uh-huh," Jasper said absentmindedly as he continued to eye the dance floor. He let out a breath when he saw Carissa shake her head and Robbie walk away.

He continued talking to Simone.

"Right now, I teach dance to little kids part-time. But I'd love to open my own studio."

Jasper tried to concentrate on Simone's words, but it was hard when Carissa was right across the patio shimmying around the dance floor with Elle and Riley. Her short sparkly dress hugged every curve and seemed to be getting even snugger in the late-summer humidity. His mouth went dry.

"So what is it you do?" Jasper asked.

"Um, I just told you."

He snapped to attention and took in Simone's confused face. "Uh, sorry. It's been a long week." He couldn't stop himself from glancing toward the dance floor one last time.

"Hey, are you looking at..." Simone trailed off as she also took in the dance floor. "Is that Carissa Blackwell?" She peered closer.

"Do you know her?"

"Not really. I was a freshman when you guys were seniors. Every girl in my class wanted to be her. She was the captain of the cheerleading squad, she lived in that amazing house by the water and she was so, so beautiful."

Still is. Jasper shook his head and tried to focus.

"There was this rumor that an agent had spotted her at the mall and wanted to take her back to Hollywood to be in movies. And that's why she and her parents disappeared from Bayside."

Jasper chuckled. He wondered what Carissa would think about that. "Never happened to my knowledge, and I knew her pretty well."

Simone turned back to him. "Of course. I'm an idiot. You guys dated. Hey, didn't she, like, break up with you after graduation? There was another rumor that she was into a college guy."

"Not to my knowledge," he repeated. "I mean, we did

break up. It's great to see her again," he added as flippantly as he could manage.

Simone ran a hand over his chest and leaned in to whisper in his ear. "And it will be more than great to see you without all these people around."

He couldn't help it. He slid one last glance in Carissa's direction. *Be careful.* Both his mother and his brother had uttered those ominous words. But there was nothing to be careful over. Carissa was back in town. That didn't mean anything. He'd helped her the other night when she'd been drunk. He would have done that for anyone.

And the kiss they'd shared? Ordinarily, Jasper wasn't one for kissing more than one woman at a time. He liked to date. Some even called him a perpetual dater. He didn't mind that, because whoever had his attention at the time was the only one who had it. He had a firm rule of one woman at a time. Even if he only dated a woman for two weeks, he was completely monogamous for those two weeks.

True, he hadn't gone out with Simone yet, so kissing Carissa the other night didn't break his rule. Still, he'd prefer to keep things as uncomplicated as possible. That's why he'd have to rule their kiss the other night as nothing more than a little slip into the past.

Besides, Carissa had been adamant about the kiss meaning nothing. What had she said before she made her quick escape that morning? Something about how he should continue with his life. Couldn't get clearer than that in Jasper's opinion.

He took in Simone's big chocolate eyes, waiting for his answer. He would go out with Simone and that would show everyone that he was no longer stuck on Carissa Blackwell.

"Sounds perfect," he said, and gave her a quick peck on the cheek.

As he pulled Simone into his arms for a dance, though, he couldn't help but notice that he wasn't alone in staring. Across the dance floor, Carissa was watching him, as well.

Chapter Six

What a night! Who else was impressed by a stunning Carissa Blackwell saving the party by filling in for the runaway caterer? Not everyone, apparently. My sources tell me that Jasper's big brother is anything but happy to see Carissa back in Bayside. Will Cam's long memory ruin any chances for a Jasper-Carissa reunion? We'll have to wait and see…

Carissa made her way to The Brewside the morning after the party. She'd walked over from her aunt's cottage, excited to continue her high from the night before. But as she neared the coffeehouse, her anxiety level started rising. Now she stood right outside the door, taking a moment before she entered.

While they'd been dancing together the night before, Elle and Riley had invited her to meet up in the morning to dissect the night's events. Well, Riley had invited her anyway. Carissa hadn't missed the look Elle had slid in Riley's direction when she'd extended the offer.

Not that Carissa could blame her. Carissa had never been a mean girl. But with some age and perspective, she had to admit that she'd hung out with a couple of mean girls. And those mean girls had given their best to Elle back in high school. Just because Carissa hadn't been the one doling out the insults and snickering behind Elle's back, she'd known it was going on. And then, of course, there was that video they'd made of her that had completely humiliated the poor girl and maybe even driven her from town altogether.

Carissa stepped back from the door. What was she thinking? She couldn't go in there and pretend that video had never been made. She needed to hightail it back to the cottage. Mind made up, she took another step backward and ran directly into someone.

"Hey, girl, great timing." Despite how late the party went last night and how early it was now, Riley looked fresh and comfortable in linen pants and a flowy tank top. "Elle just texted me. She'll be here in five minutes."

"Listen, Ri, I really don't think I should…" But she couldn't finish her thought because Riley had linked arms with her and was pulling her inside the coffeehouse. Her unease abated slightly when the enticing aroma of ground coffee beans and freshly baked goodies made its way to her nose.

"I'm dying for coffee. What can I get you?" Riley asked.

"What? Oh, you don't have to do that."

"No problem. Think of it as your welcome-home coffee."

Carissa ran a hand through her hair. "Um, thanks, but I'm not sure everyone is as excited I'm back as you."

Riley simply waved a hand through the air as if Carissa was speaking nonsense. "Go grab us a table."

Resigned, Carissa did as instructed, and soon she was joined by Riley, two lattes and a bundle of nerves in her stomach. The best thing to do was to lay it out on the table and apologize for the past. But when Elle walked through the door, her confidence faltered.

Elle waved at them and then headed for the counter, placing her order.

"Are you okay?" Riley asked. "You seem tense."

Carissa didn't have time to answer.

"I need caffeine and carbs," Elle announced as she slunk down in her chair with her coffee and a large bag. She pulled half a dozen bagels out of the bag. "I bought a variety. I knew you would go for the blueberry bagel. You are so predictable, Riley Hudson."

Riley smiled as she immediately started applying strawberry cream cheese. "Sorry if you wanted the blueberry, Carissa, but it's mine. All mine!"

Carissa ignored the amazing-smelling bagels and took a deep breath. "Elle, I'm really, really sorry if I was a bitch to you." Both Elle and Riley froze. "In high school, I mean."

Riley still had half a bagel in one hand and a knife loaded with cream cheese in the other. Elle was holding two sugar packets over her coffee. Neither of them had blinked since she started rambling.

"Er," Elle finally mumbled in confusion.

"I know, this is completely random. But I sort of sensed last night… I was grateful for the two of you dancing with me and inviting me to breakfast this morning. I suspect you didn't really want me to be here, though. I mean, it makes perfect sense for you to give me the cold shoulder."

"Huh?" Riley asked.

Carissa couldn't stop herself. She wasn't the best apologizer. "To be honest, I knew you had a crush on Jasper back in high school, Elle. I think everyone did. I wasn't threatened by it. And I don't really get jealous. Not over stuff like that. I mean, I just felt really secure in my relationship with him. You know? Oh God, does that make me snotty?"

"You need to breathe, girl," Riley said.

"I want you to know that I had nothing to do with that video my friends made of you."

Something passed over Elle's face. She lowered her eyes and pursed her lips. Then she finished fixing her coffee, took a sip and locked eyes with Carissa.

"I know you didn't have anything to do with that video."

Back in high school, Elle had been as shy as she was smart. She'd worked hard to become the valedictorian. And, yes, she'd also had a hopeless and passionate crush on Jasper. Toward the end of senior year, Carissa's friends had invited Elle to a sleepover. They'd spiked her drink and taped her professing her love for Jasper. They didn't leave it there, though. They played it during senior prom in front of everyone. Elle was humiliated and had her valedictorian status stripped from her after she'd been shown drinking.

Carissa heard that Elle went to college and then off to Florence, Italy. Gone from Bayside for a decade because she felt she'd embarrassed her father, who had lost his election to become county sheriff due to the scandal. Carissa knew all about leaving Bayside and embarrassments behind. But while she'd left willingly, Elle had not.

Elle took a deep breath. "Your friends were mean, Carissa. But you never were. At least, not to me. I mean, we didn't speak all that much. If I was weird or cold or distant last night it's because I was the one who professed my love for *your* boyfriend. I should be apologizing to you. Not the other way around."

Carissa couldn't believe what she was hearing. "No, no, no, I really am sorry."

"So am I," Elle countered.

Riley snickered. "How about we call it a truce and say you're both sorry? We're all adults now. Can we eat these bagels and gossip yet or what?"

All three of them laughed. With the past settled, they enjoyed their breakfast and chatted about the party the night before. Riley and Elle filled Carissa in on the new faces in town and refreshed her memory on some of the people from high school.

When their bagels were consumed, Riley leaned forward. "Well, I'm glad the past is in the past and we can all move forward as friends."

"I do have to ask, though. Is that the reason why Cam was giving me the cold shoulder and a bunch of not-so-friendly stares last night?"

Elle bit her lip. "I'm sorry he was being that way. Unfortunately, I think it's only part of the reason."

Carissa waited for a moment before she realized. Idiot. "And the other part would be that I dumped Jasper after graduation."

Elle nodded but Riley snorted. "Yeah, the dumping sucked. But I think it's also the fact that you never contacted him again. Like, not ever. In fact, you never contacted anyone from Bayside after you left," Riley finished. "What was up with that?"

Carissa could feel her cheeks heating up. "I wanted a clean break." She sat back in her chair and took a long, deep breath. Then she met her friends' eyes again. "The day that Jasper and I broke up, well, I said some things to him that I'm not proud of. I told him he had no ambition, no drive. I didn't want to be with someone without any goals."

Little did Jasper, or anyone else for that matter, know that she'd found out that very morning that her parents had run out of money. Her father had blown through her mother's very large trust fund. Since he was always in and out of jobs, he had no real experience to fall back on. Parties and socializing had been more important to him than ensuring that his wife and daughter were taken care of.

She'd been eighteen years old and the proverbial rug

had been yanked out from under her. The fact that her relationship with her father had always been on the rocky side didn't help matters. She might react differently today, but back then she'd been embarrassed. And angry. And scared.

Carissa had to spend the summer figuring out how to pay for college, which she had done with the help of her aunt Val. But those four years at Northwestern had been tough. She'd studied her butt off while holding down three different jobs.

Fearing that all their important friends in Bayside would find out that they were now poor as church mice, her parents had moved to New England where her mother had taken job after job to make ends meet. When Carissa found out that her dad still wasn't pulling his weight, she'd been furious.

Jasper reminded her of her father. They were both so handsome and the life of every party. All charm and no ambition. At least, that's how he'd been in high school. Spent his parents' money and partied with his friends. Not a care in the world. Not a mention of a future. He slept until noon on weekends and never really cared about college or anything beyond that.

She remembered walking to meet Jasper the day she'd broken it off with him. All she could think about was if Jasper was so content to breeze through life at that point, what would he be like when they became adults? Would he repeat her father's behavior? Would she then go through another period of embarrassment? Of anger? Of fear?

Carissa shook her head and continued. "Although what I said to Jasper back then doesn't seem to have stopped him. He's doing amazingly well now. Even with everything I said to him that day."

"Maybe he's doing so well *because* of everything you said to him," Elle said.

She cocked her head to the side. "What do you mean?" Elle and Riley exchanged a look.

"Come on, spill," Carissa said.

"Cam told me that after you left Bayside and after Jasper got over his initial shock at the breakup, he turned his life around."

"Well, that's good."

"It is, in the end."

Carissa couldn't miss another look between Elle and Riley. "There's more."

Elle nodded. "He threw himself into studying. He took job after job to learn as much as possible about business from the ground up."

Riley sat forward. "He became…obsessed."

In Carissa's experience, the word *obsessed* was generally not a good thing. It was usually a drastic reaction to something.

To hear that her words caused Jasper to alter his life— even if his life ended up better because of it—made a pit form in the bottom of her stomach. Maybe she was more of a mean girl than she realized.

"Hey, don't worry about it." Riley shook her arm. "Jasper's right where he was meant to be. And so are you."

Carissa let out a tiny laugh. "Where's that exactly? Living in my eccentric aunt's cottage because I got a divorce?"

"Basically." Riley toasted her with her coffee. "You're with us and I think the three of us are going to be really good friends."

She hoped so because Carissa could certainly use friends. Not to mention, she could use money if she ever wanted to get out of her aunt's place.

"So now that we're all friends and sharing secrets," Elle began. "I have to ask. You're completely over Jasper?"

"Of course," Carissa said quickly. Maybe a bit too quickly. "I just got divorced like five minutes ago."

"That's not really an answer," Elle said.

"Besides," Carissa continued, "I saw Jasper with that redhead last night." And that had stung a little. She hated to admit it. Jasper was at liberty to date whoever he wanted. But at the same time, they had kissed the other night. When she saw him pull that pretty woman into his arms, she'd almost tripped on the dance floor. Wasn't that just silly?

"That's not an answer, either," Riley countered.

Carissa sighed. "Okay, then let me be clear. I do not have any romantic feelings for Jasper Dumont. Or anyone else, for that matter. I am here to start my catering company. I just need some business."

Just like that, the front door of The Brewside opened and in waltzed Jasper's mother. Once again, she didn't have to give her order. Tony had it ready for her in a minute. She scanned the room, saying hello and accepting compliments on last night's party. Finally, her gaze fell on Carissa, who had to wonder if she shared Cam's judgment of her. But her lips quirked, turning into a beautiful smile. A smile that definitely reached her eyes. Carissa's stomach settled.

"Carissa, I'm so glad to run into you here. Hello, Riley, Elle—darling." She gave a quick hug to Elle, who would more than likely be calling Lilah Dumont mother-in-law soon. "I was going to stop by your aunt's cottage."

"You were?" She couldn't keep the surprise out of her voice.

"I wanted to thank you again for saving the party last night."

Carissa smiled. "I don't know if I saved anything, but I'm glad I could help out."

"So am I." Relief washed over her face. "I also wanted to give you this." She handed over an envelope.

Curious, Carissa opened the flap and took a peek. It was a check made out to her, and the amount almost had her falling off her chair.

"I didn't know your catering company's name so I just made it out to you. I hope that's okay."

"It's fine. I don't actually have a name yet. But I wasn't expecting any payment."

Lilah waved a hand. "Nonsense. You did a job, completed a service. Of course you should be paid. You saved the day."

Carissa was about to protest again, even as she tightly clutched the check in her hand. But Riley piped up. "That's it. Why don't you call your company Save the Day Catering?"

Elle's eyes lit up at the name. "Great idea."

Carissa mulled it over. Save the day. And she really would love to save someone's day with her cooking. No one needed to know that starting this business would also be saving her. "You know, that's not bad. Save the Day. I like it."

"It's settled. A very productive morning," Mrs. Dumont said. "And I think I can add to it. Carissa, I'm hosting a ladies' tea and I would like you to cater it. It's on Wednesday, so short notice."

"Not as short as the five minutes she had last night," Elle said kindly.

"I think it was more like two minutes, actually," Mrs. Dumont said. "If you are willing, I'd like basic tea party food. Sandwiches, scones, tea cakes, that sort of thing. What do you say?"

Carissa was floored by the generous check first and now by the opportunity for more business. Mrs. Dumont's offer was more than she could have expected. What a great way to start her business.

"That would be amazing. Thank you so much. Why don't we set up a call for later this afternoon to go over the logistics?"

"Perfect," Lilah said.

Carissa was so busy reveling in her thoughts and good fortune that she'd tuned out of Elle and Mrs. Dumont's chitchat. Tuned out, that is, until she heard Elle ask what Jasper was up to today.

"He has a date with some new girl." She waved her hand in a flippant manner.

Riley rolled her eyes. "There's always some new girl. Good luck to this one, too." Mrs. Dumont laughed with Riley. But Elle reached over and patted Carissa's hand.

"It's fine," Carissa whispered so only Elle could hear. "I told you I'm not interested in him like that."

"I know." Elle squeezed her fingers. "But just in case you needed it."

What was that supposed to mean? Jasper was free to do whatever, or whomever, he wanted. She wished him well. If he wanted to spend an evening with that perky little redhead, then more power to him. Maybe they would really hit it off and get married. But she'd been down that road before. So good luck to them both.

In the meantime, she had a new purpose. She was starting a company and thanks to Mrs. Dumont, she already had her first assignment.

See, much more important things to think about than Jasper's love life. Not that she cared anyway. Not one little bit...

Jasper was at an amazing restaurant, enjoying a particularly good sauvignon blanc with a stunning woman. The food was great and the ambience was romantic. The perfect date.

Only, it wasn't, and not only because Jasper's mind was a million miles away from Simone and the Boat House.

Jasper sipped his wine and stifled a laugh as Simone regaled him with a story of her Zumba class as she simultaneously finished a third glass of wine. Deep down, he tried to figure out why he wasn't enjoying this night more. He'd been out with plenty of flirtatious women. Usually he loved hearing about their lives. But tonight, he just wasn't feeling this.

He'd had a nice Saturday. Spent some time with his brother, did a little bit of work, went to the gym. Plus, the party had been fun last night, he thought as Simone switched topics and started filling him in on the recent episode of her favorite reality show.

Carissa had seemed to enjoy herself last night. He wondered if she'd made any business contacts. Of course, she'd been in the kitchen for the first half of the night and then shimmying around the dance floor for the rest. She'd looked good out there. Reminded him of watching her cheer at football games in high school.

"Do you agree?" Simone asked, ripping him out of his thoughts.

"Uh, totally."

Simone scrunched up her nose. "You do?"

"Of course not," he said, completely confused. "I was messing with you."

Simone relaxed back against her chair. Jasper tried to clear his mind of Carissa and her dancing. Instead, he focused on the dessert menu. There was a seasonal favorite on the list, peach pie. His mouth watered at the thought.

The waiter came by and asked if they wanted dessert. Jasper opened his mouth but Simone beat him to it. "No, we're fine. Just the check please."

"Really?" he asked. "No dessert?"

Simone shook her head. "One night of dessert equals a month of gym time."

He couldn't help but think of Carissa and how she'd devoured her bagel and cream cheese the other morning. No way would she pass up dessert. But in the end, Jasper pushed his disappointment aside, especially since his mind had been wandering all night. All he could concentrate on was the image of the dress Carissa had been wearing at the party. How every time she moved on the dance floor it would inch just a tiny bit higher, revealing her long, toned legs.

The check came and Jasper reached for his wallet. After leaving the restaurant, he and Simone walked around the water hand in hand. Jasper realized he had been on this date many times over the years. Nice restaurant, pretty evening walk, and, if it was a good night, a return to his condo. But he was sure taking Simone home would not be a good idea this evening.

"And, of course, I don't see why people are down on reality shows. I'd love to be on one. Don't you think I'd be great on a reality show?" Simone didn't wait for an answer. "I mean, to be like the Kardashians. They're so amazing. And smart. People don't think they're smart, but come on. I mean, hello! What about their clothing lines?"

"I guess," Jasper added. He had no idea what she was talking about.

"Not to mention, they marry well. People can say whatever they want but I don't see a problem with a woman wanting to marry a rich man. Do I want to be poor?" She let out a little chuckle. "Um, of course not."

Red flag, red flag. If Jasper had been wearing a tie, this would have been the point when he loosened it.

"Not that I wanted to go out with you because you're

rich. Obviously, everyone knows you have money. You're a Dumont."

This conversation had gone south quickly. "Yes, I am."

"So," Simone said, turning to him and puckering her red lips.

"So," he countered lamely. Jasper repressed the urge to roll his neck. "It's getting late. We should probably get home."

She stepped closer. "What a great idea. I've been dying to see your place," she said boldly.

Ordinarily, a statement like this would have left him grinning and taking off for his condo at record speed. After all, the last woman he'd brought home had been…Carissa, he realized with a jolt.

"Actually, I was thinking I should drive you home. I'm sorry," he quickly added at her frown. "I have a really early morning tomorrow."

Simone crossed her arms over her chest. "Tomorrow is Sunday."

"Right, well, I have some work I need to catch up on and you said you have that exercise class."

She nodded slowly but didn't look at all convinced. Jasper couldn't blame her. "You know, Jasper, this has been a really great night. But I have to admit that I've had the feeling you'd rather be somewhere else. I mean, you didn't even think my story about the youngest Kardashian liking my tweet about lip gloss was interesting."

"I'm sorry, Carissa."

She let out a laugh, but the sound was harsh. "I suppose that's my answer."

"What?" he asked, confused.

"Jasper, you just called me Carissa."

He wanted to cover his face with his hands. He might not have enjoyed his date with Simone, but he was never,

ever disrespectful when it came to women. Calling her by the wrong name was unacceptable. He pulled her into a hug. "I'm really sorry about that, Simone."

"You know, the Bayside Blogger has been speculating about you two since Carissa got back to town last week. Even though I was younger, everyone in school knew how intense you guys were when you dated."

Intense? That was one way of looking at it.

"I'd wondered if you were interested in getting back together with her, but since you still wanted to go out…"

"Oh no. I don't want to get back together with Carissa and I'm sure she feels the same way about me."

Simone tilted her head. "Really? Because she kept staring at you last night at the party."

"Really?" Jasper asked quickly. Too quickly, if Simone's huff was any indication. He shrugged and tried to play off his comment. "Trust me, nothing's happening with us and nothing is going to happen. I guess I just called you by her name because this is where I saw her when she first returned to town. I hadn't seen her in over a decade." He squeezed her hand. "And I did want to go out with you."

"Really?"

"Yes, of course."

Her gaze drifted to the side as she considered. "Then, how about this. You take me home tonight. And maybe we can try another date next week?" She smiled, showing her dimple. One of the things that he'd been drawn to when he'd first talked to her. "I'd love to introduce you to my mom and sisters."

The red flag turned even redder. Meeting the family after one date? He didn't think so.

"I think we may want different things, Simone," he said honestly. "You're wonderful, but right now, I need to concentrate on my career. You should be with someone who can devote every waking hour to you."

This seemed to appease her, and they walked back to his car and Jasper held the door while she got in. Then they began driving away from the town toward Simone's place. She was renting an apartment not far from Carissa's aunt's cottage.

There he went, thinking about Carissa again. He tightened his hands around the steering wheel. Why couldn't he get her out of his mind? Wasn't it bad enough that she'd already ruined a perfectly good date?

Okay, maybe the date with Simone hadn't been the best of his life. If only he'd been more into reality television and the E! network. But she was still an attractive, fun, energetic, talkative female. Moreover, she was a female who had never ripped his heart out and fed it to him before disappearing from his life.

Jasper cursed under his breath. The first thing he was going to do after dropping Simone off was get a drink and put a concerted effort into not thinking about Carissa Blackwell.

When he reached Simone's place, he walked her to the door and gave her a quick hug. Before she inserted her key into the lock, she paused.

"If you change your mind about going out again, you know how to reach me."

"Absolutely."

At least she was being a good sport about the evening. From his obvious lack of attention to calling her the wrong name, a lot of women would have written him off immediately. In the end, he knew the two of them weren't a fit. And despite her offer, he knew she did, too.

Jasper hustled back to his car and began driving home… and continued to try and shake thoughts of Carissa from his head. Obviously, it wasn't her fault she was stuck in his head. Still, he was supposed to be over her. Isn't that what he kept telling everyone else?

He took a right, and as he went around a curve, he saw a black car on the side of the road. He slowed, and as he did, he watched a tall woman wearing jeans and a pink T-shirt yell something and kick one of the tires hard.

Carissa.

Jasper sighed. The universe was clearly enjoying messing with him tonight.

He brought the car to a stop behind her black sedan and let out a long, frustrated exhale. Then he exited the car and walked to Carissa, who was covering her face with her hands.

"Everything okay?" he called out. Clearly, she hadn't heard him pull up, because she jumped a mile.

"Jasper," she said, placing a hand over her heart. "You scared the crap out of me. What are you doing here?"

Despite their surroundings, he couldn't help but inhale her perfume, a clean scent with just a hint of flowers. "I was just driving home and saw you on the side of the road."

Carissa's eyes flickered to his car and then back to him. "Out by yourself on a Saturday night?"

There was something about the way she asked the question that had his ire rising. "What if I am?"

"None of my business." Again, she glanced over at his car as if she was searching for something. Or someone. "I just heard you had a date tonight."

"You heard… From who?"

"Your mother."

He clamped down on the urge to roll his eyes. "Well, since you're so interested in my social life, yes, I was on a date."

She tossed her hair over her shoulder. "I don't care if

you were. I have bigger things to worry about than you and your libido."

"Let's leave my libido out of it. What's going on here?"

She deflated. "My car... I can't believe... I so don't need this right now."

She was flustered, an emotion he didn't often see her exhibit. Carissa was one of the most levelheaded women he knew. At least, she used to be. Her frustration got to him.

"Don't worry. I can help you change a tire."

"I know how to change a tire." He would have been impressed but he noticed she was nailing him with a furious stare. "What I don't know is what to do when your engine overheats." She pointed at the open hood.

"Ah. Well, that's different, then." He hadn't even noticed her hood or the smoke billowing from it.

She raised an eyebrow and tapped her foot.

He relented. "Okay, I don't know what to do, either. But I have a really great mechanic."

She laughed. "Well, that's something. Can we give him a call?"

"It's Saturday night. His shop closed at five."

She shook her head. "Of course. I didn't even think about that. I guess I'll call him first thing tomorrow morning."

Jasper's turn to shake his head. "Nope. Tomorrow's Sunday. They're not open. Most things aren't."

"Seriously? Where am I? Back in 1955?"

"You're back in Bayside."

She rolled her eyes. "Goody. The joys of small town living."

"There are advantages to small towns, too. I can call my mechanic at home and let him know what's going on. He's a good guy. He'll probably come tow your car to his shop tomorrow and it will be there first thing Monday morning. I can give you a ride home now."

She emitted a half cough, half laugh.

"What?" he asked.

"You want to drive me home? I thought our truce was over."

This time he let his eyes roll dramatically. "Are you seriously bringing that up at this moment? You're stranded and your aunt's cottage is only a couple minutes' drive from here. What's the big deal? I'm not going to let you stand here by yourself, especially at night. I mean, do you want to walk home by yourself in the dark?"

She looked around at the woods lining the road. The crickets were doing their best nighttime chirping. Other than that, there wasn't a sound. It was creepy. As if reading his thoughts, Carissa shivered.

"Fine," she relented.

While she grabbed her purse from the front seat and locked her doors, Jasper called his buddy from the garage and made arrangements for him to pick up Carissa's car. Then they walked back to his car.

"Nice car," she said, pointing at the red Porsche.

"Thanks. I always wanted one."

She joined him in the front seat. "It's certainly cozy in here."

What the heck? Did she not want to sit close to him? "Like I said, it's only a couple minutes' drive."

Who knew how long a couple minutes could feel? Sitting so near to her had his pulse skyrocketing. Between her heavenly scent and the sight of those long, shapely legs, he was finding it difficult to concentrate on the road.

"I probably should have just called Elle or Riley to come get me," she said under her breath, but loud enough for Jasper to hear.

"Honestly, Car, I was already right there. Good to see you're still stubborn."

She snorted. "Oh please. You are in no position to say I'm stubborn. You don't know what I'm like. You haven't seen me in ten years."

"Exactly." He banged his hand off the steering wheel. "Ten years with no contact."

Silence fell over the car. Jasper's words hung in the air.

"See," Carissa said quietly. "I told you. Dumb idea."

He hated to admit she was probably right. Luckily, they'd reached her house and he threw the Porsche in Park. Carissa practically bounded from the car.

"Thanks for the ride and for calling your mechanic," she said quickly and slammed the door.

Was she kidding him? Jasper yanked the keys from the ignition and bounded across the driveway that led to the front porch steps. "Car," he called. The air smelled of hamburgers and charcoal. Probably a Labor Day weekend barbecue.

She spun around, confusion on her face. "What?"

"You're going to just leave like that?" he asked.

"Yes," she said adamantly. "We're not on a date. In fact, you were on a date with someone else tonight. Where is she?"

He cocked his head and studied her. Her cheeks were flushed, her eyes bright. Realization dawned. "Are you... jealous?"

If her face was flushed before his question, it was on fire now. "Jealous? Excuse me?"

"Help me out, Car. Because I've never seen you like this before."

"You haven't seen me at all in ten years."

"Yeah, we've established that. Whose fault is that? Not mine."

She threw her arms in the air. "You have no idea what you're talking about. Go home, Jasper."

"You know, Car, a little gratitude would be nice."

She ground her teeth together. "Thank you so much, savior Jasper. I so appreciate it." Sarcasm coated each word.

"You are such a spoiled brat."

She put her hands on her hips. "You're a snobby playboy."

"Oh really?"

"Yeah, really," she said.

He groaned and ran a hand over his face. "What are we doing?"

"I think we're arguing."

He didn't want to ask, but at the same time, he couldn't stop the words from leaving his mouth. "What is your issue with me?"

She walked down one step. "My issue is that you kissed me only a matter of days ago. Tonight, you went on a date with another woman. And I know that I told you to keep dating and forget about our kiss," she continued in one breath. "And I also know that you have every reason to hate the fact that I'm back in town. But...but I can't help how I feel knowing you were on a date tonight."

"How do you feel?"

She blew out a loud breath. "Well, not good."

He leveled her with a stare. "That's not fair, Carissa."

She threw her hands in the air. "You think I don't know that? Of course it's not fair. It's completely irrational."

"I date a lot."

"Of course you do."

He took a step toward her. "What is that supposed to mean?"

"It means you're the golden boy, the life of the party."

He had no idea where that comment came from but he could see the strain in her eyes. "Are those bad things?"

"You have no idea."

"I think you're the one who has no idea. What did you think, Carissa? I wouldn't have a life? You broke up with me and disappeared. Did you think I would sit around pining for you for the rest of my days?"

The tides changed. A surprised expression crossed her face. "No, of course not," she said quietly.

"You got married. Really young, too. Did you honestly think I wouldn't be with other women?"

"I didn't really think…"

"No, you didn't. You just dumped me and ran away."

"Jasper, wait."

"No." He started walking away with long, determined strides. Then he realized he needed to stop and face her. He'd waited too long, held the words back for too many years. So he turned back.

"You know, it wasn't bad enough that you broke up with me. But it came out of nowhere. We'd been to the movies the night before. Remember?" He didn't wait for her to comment. "The next day, it was over. And that wasn't the worst part. Do you know what was?"

Her eyes had widened and her arms had woven around her stomach protectively as she bit her lip. She shook her head.

"You were my friend. We'd known each other our entire lives. We'd been in the same circle since before we could even remember. And you just left. Without warning. Do you know how hard that was on me? It felt like you had died."

"Oh, Jasper."

He clenched his fingers into a tight fist as the years of pent up anger and hurt washed over him. "You told me that I wasn't good enough."

She sucked in a harsh breath and walked to him. "I never said that."

"Might as well have said it. All I did know was that I

was this eighteen-year-old kid who had been overlooked by his parents time after time. I was never good enough for them. Cam was the heir. I was just extra. But with you, I was someone. Until you took that away. Because I wasn't good enough for you, either."

She closed her eyes and a pained expression shadowed her face and those gorgeous features. He watched her take a deep breath. "You reminded me of my father and that scared the hell out of me," she said so softly he almost didn't hear.

His anger deflated. Carissa had never had a great relationship with her dad. He'd never understood all the particulars but he'd witnessed more than a fair share of fighting between the two of them. It hadn't been the usual teen versus parent butting of heads, either. There was something deeper there. Even as a kid, he'd realized that.

She closed the distance between them and took his face in her hands, forcing him to meet her gaze. "Listen to me, Jasper Dumont. I was a selfish, scared eighteen-year-old girl. And my life hasn't turned out so great. But you," she lightly shook his head. "Look at everything you've accomplished. You were always good enough. I was the one who made a mistake."

"You still left."

Sadness filled her eyes as she nodded. "It didn't have anything to do with you, Jasp. It was me. All me."

It seemed like she wanted to tell him more, say something else. While Jasper wanted to know, wanted to know everything, he also feared hearing it. Afraid that she could say something that would seep in and hurt him again. So he did the only thing he could think to do. He retreated into himself.

"Jasper, look at me." She shook him. "Dammit, don't do that. I broke up with you because of my issues, not yours."

She had no idea about his issues. About how he never allowed people to get close enough to hurt him. He was still the life of the party but from a very safe, very self-imposed distance. His manner of thinking was that you could have fun with people, but as soon as you truly let them in, you gave them the power. Once someone had power over you, they could squash you.

Just like she'd done.

Suddenly, he felt tired. The exhaustion allowed his guard to slip. Just a bit.

Carissa must have sensed this. "Jasp," she whispered. As if she desperately wanted to show him his importance, she pressed her lips to his. As soon as her lips touched his, he was helpless to do anything but kiss her back. Slowly, he felt himself coming back from the dark place he'd just been. The dark place he rarely allowed himself to go.

She nipped at his lower lip and he sucked in a breath. He pulled her closer to him, reaching for the back of her head so he could angle her better. His tongue dived into her mouth as she clutched at his shirt.

They were so in sync. Every nip, bite, kiss, tease, moan, was shared until they were both left breathing heavily, staring into each other's eyes, wondering what had just transpired between them.

Pressing his forehead to hers, he took a moment. Needed a moment. But clarity didn't come.

He didn't know how long they stood like that, heads pressed together, breath mingling, arms wound around each other. But he did know that he felt like a huge weight had been lifted from his shoulders. Carissa had admitted her fault in their breakup.

She sighed.

"What's wrong?" he asked.

"We really should stop doing this."

Jasper agreed. Wholeheartedly. Because if he kept kissing her, he didn't know if he'd ever be the same again. "You're right," he whispered.

She turned and retreated to the front door. When she reached it, she looked back, biting her lip, as she waved good-night.

Yes, they definitely had to stop kissing. And yet… Jasper wasn't sure if he could.

Chapter Seven

Quite a few people saw Jasper Dumont on a date at the Boat House with Simone Graves last Saturday night. But he somehow ended the evening in the driveway of Carissa Blackwell's cottage. My spies heard them arguing, until they didn't hear anything at all. Hmm, wonder what those two old lovebirds were doing? Leave a comment if you think "Casper" (which won by a landslide over on Twitter) is happening!

In related news, you're never going to guess what I found out about Carissa Blackwell's ex-husband...

In theory, catering Mrs. Dumont's tea party seemed like a great idea. But as Carissa glanced around her aunt's kitchen, she wasn't feeling 100 percent confident.

"You can do this," she said aloud.

And she knew she could do it. At least, she hoped so. She'd thrown dozens of parties for her husband's colleagues and friends, but nothing of this caliber. Mrs. Dumont was holding a ladies' tea for one of her charities that provided scholarships for local high school students. There was also a silent auction to raise even more money.

In Chicago, Preston had wanted her as involved with the local charities as possible. It was the perfect combination. She provided the food and he wrote a big, fat check. She'd catered teas, luncheons, brunches, costume parties, swanky dinners and more.

Then, why was she feeling so nervous? Perhaps because she'd gotten up at four in the morning to bake scones. Or maybe it was the three cups of coffee she'd consumed while the scones were in the oven and she began assembling the tea sandwiches, icing the mini cupcakes, putting the finishing touches on the fruit platters, and fixing the large containers of lemonade and iced tea.

The kitchen smelled of baking, that wonderful aroma of sugars and spices merging together. She'd put orange zest into one batch of scones, and that fresh citrus scent set her mouth to watering.

She just wanted everything to be perfect. She let out an exhausted chuckle. If someone walked into the house at this moment, *perfect* would probably not be the word that came to mind. Ingredients were spread throughout the room. Pots and pans and other kitchen utensils littered the counters. Of course, her aunt's kitchen wasn't the largest room she'd ever cooked in. But hey, it had gotten the job done. Now she just needed to load her newly fixed car and make herself a little more presentable.

Spotting her car sitting out in the driveway, she didn't even want to think about the bill she'd just received on that. But at least she wouldn't break down again on the side of the road only to be rescued by Jasper.

Jasper.

She stopped in her packing and leaned back against the counter. Absentmindedly, she tapped a finger against her lips as she remembered how it had felt to kiss him the other night.

She'd meant what she'd told him. She had been selfish when she'd broken up with him. She'd never really thought about how he took her words that day. Maybe because she didn't want to let herself think about it. Maybe now she needed to tell him the full story. Why she'd really dumped him that day.

She began stacking cupcakes in her special travel container. Still, she couldn't stop thinking about Jasper. She'd been back for a week and kissed him twice. There hadn't been any real closure the other night in her driveway and maybe that was a good thing. She needed time to think and decide what she wanted to do. Because on the one hand, she desperately craved her independence. But on the other, the feel of Jasper's mouth against hers sent waves of pleasure through her days later.

An hour later Carissa was parking in the back of the Dumont estate, near the kitchen. Some of the staff appeared to help her carry everything inside. Mrs. Dumont told her they would hold the event in the atrium, a part of the house she'd always adored back in high school. It seemed so fancy and sophisticated with its glass walls, pretty decor and dainty furniture. Who else had an atrium in their home?

The next two hours were a total blur. Between setting up the food and the arrival of Bayside's most charitable women, Carissa was too busy to be nervous.

Of course, her mother used to run with this crowd, so there were quite a few reunions and hugs. There were even more questions about her parents. She'd expected that though and did a fairly good job of evading the queries and seamlessly switching topics.

As her part of the job wound down, she did a quiet lap of the perimeter of the atrium. The women seemed to be enjoying the event. She'd displayed the food on tiered trays provided by Mrs. Dumont. One layer held the sandwiches, the next had the scones, and chocolate-covered strawberries and shortbread cookies sat on the top. Waiters served the cold beverages plus Mrs. Dumont's prized tea collection.

As Carissa reached the back of the room, she noticed that the silent auction was doing quite well. Having had to provide her own college tuition, she appreciated that the ladies of Bayside were raising money for such a worthy cause.

"Ohmigod, your scones are to die for." Carissa smiled as Riley rushed over to her. "Where did you learn to make these?"

"My aunt Val taught me when I was thirteen. The shortbread cookies are her recipe, as well."

Riley's face grew serious. "Listen, we are having a fundraiser for the high school next month. It's to raise money for the different sports teams. Cheerleading is one of them."

Carissa had been a cheerleader back in high school. She liked the idea of raising money for any sports programs.

"It's going to be a huge event," Riley continued. "There's going to be a raffle, a huge bake sale, and—wait for it," she said dramatically. "We're holding a date auction."

Carissa groaned. "Please don't ask me to go up for auction. I'm damaged goods right now. Seriously, I don't think you would get fifty cents for me."

Riley frowned. "You're not damaged goods. You got divorced. Half of the people who get married end up splitting."

Carissa relented. Riley always did have a way to cut to the chase. "I suppose you're right. But I'd still rather not have people bid on me."

"Don't worry. The auction is for the men of Bayside. So bring your wallet. Jasper's going to be up on the auction block." She wiggled her eyebrows.

Carissa almost let out a sigh at his name. Then she silently admonished herself. Since when was the mention of Jasper enough to have her stomach twisting into knots and leave her with the idea to keep sighing over and over like some Victorian-era damsel?

"I'll keep that in mind. Anyway, did you need some help with the high school fund-raiser?"

"Yes." Riley's emerald green eyes were practically sparkling. "Would you mind doing some baking? We can't pay you, of course. But I'd really appreciate it. Usually, Myrtle, who owns the bakery in town, makes hundreds and hundreds of cookies. But since the tourist season is over, she's taking a long vacation."

"No problem. I'd love to help out."

They chatted a little longer, agreeing to meet up later that night with Elle for cocktails. Then Carissa made her way back to the kitchen to begin the arduous task of cleaning up.

"A job very well done." Carissa looked up from packing the utensils she'd brought from her personal collection to see a glowing Mrs. Dumont enter the kitchen.

"Thank you."

"I had several women ask me for your information, so I suspect you'll get some jobs from this one."

Carissa crossed the room. "I can't thank you enough for trusting me, not once, but twice. I appreciate it so much."

"My pleasure." Mrs. Dumont peered deeply into her eyes. Then she pushed a strand of Carissa's hair behind her ear in a very maternal and comforting gesture before cupping her cheek. She stared into Carissa's eyes for a long time, a caring expression on her face. "You've been through a lot, haven't you?"

"No more than other people," Carissa admitted honestly, even though she wanted to scream, *yes, I'm hurting*.

She patted Carissa's cheek. "True, everyone goes

through hard times. But it's different when it happens to you. I'm always here if you need to talk."

After a long look, Mrs. Dumont started walking away and Carissa was left standing in the kitchen wondering what in the heck had just transpired between them. Without overthinking it, she called out.

"Mrs. Dumont," she waited for the woman to turn back to her. "There's a reason for it." Mrs. Dumont cocked her head to the side. "There's a reason why my parents left town. I'm sure you've been wondering. You were all so close."

Lilah seemed contemplative before speaking. "I always suspected there was."

"There's a reason why I broke up with Jasper, too."

Lilah nodded. "That's not a surprise, either. I also suspect that the two things are connected somehow." She pinned Carissa with a stare. "Am I right?"

"Yes," she whispered. "I'm not really ready to talk—"

Mrs. Dumont held her hand up. "If and when you're ready, you know where to find me."

"Thank you. I just wanted you to know that, because you've been so kind to me."

And because I kissed your son again the other night. But she didn't dare say that out loud. Instead, she accepted Mrs. Dumont's kind smile as she continued out of the room.

Carissa tried to pack up more of her things but it was tough with all the thoughts running through her head. She couldn't help but think about her parents. They had spent so much time at this house when she was growing up. She wondered what they would think about her walking these halls as the hired help instead of their privileged daughter.

When she pushed her anger aside, she felt sad for them. It must have been difficult to go from one extreme lifestyle to the other.

Then she shook her head. They'd done it to themselves. At least, her father had with his mismanagement of money and foolish investments. If that weren't bad enough, they'd practically hightailed it out of town in the middle of the night. Not a word to their friends, to good people like the Dumonts whom they'd spent so much time with.

An image of getting into her car in the wee hours of dawn and driving out of Chicago filled her mind. Carissa bit her lip. *It's not the same.* Right?

"You look like you're in deep thought."

She jumped at the sound of Riley's voice. "Hi. I didn't hear you come in." She noticed Riley's pinched expression. "What's up, Ri?"

"Um…" Riley took her hand. "I'm really sorry, Carissa."

The hairs on the back of Carissa's neck stood up at full attention. "You're sorry? What in the world for?"

Even though they were the only two people in the kitchen, Riley still glanced around the room before lowering her voice. "I didn't realize that your husband, er, your ex-husband that is—"

"What about him?" Carissa interrupted.

"You didn't tell me that he cheated on you."

All of the cakes she'd been sampling, the goodies she'd been nibbling on throughout the day, sank into one heavy stone at the bottom of her stomach. She knew she couldn't keep her divorce quiet, but dammit, she'd wanted to keep the cheating part out of the mix. Wasn't it embarrassing enough that she had to endure the end of a marriage?

"I, I…well…"

Riley kept going. "It sucks. I've had boyfriends cheat on me before. And when I lived in New York, well, let's just say that I understand how you feel."

Now she was curious about what in the hell happened when Riley lived in New York. But it was only a fleeting distraction. Carissa was still reeling that Riley knew any of this. Then something clicked. Oh no. The realization slapped her in the face. Riley wasn't the only one who knew about this.

"Riley, please tell me you didn't find out about my ex from the Bayside freaking Blogger."

"Well…"

"You've gotta be kidding me." She kicked at one of the crates she'd used to haul the food in. "She wrote a blog about my divorce? About Preston?"

"Actually, she was also tweeting about it." Riley looked contrite.

"How in the hell would she even find out?" If she thought she felt a stone sinking in her stomach before, it was like all of Stonehenge just landed hard in her midsection. There was only one time she'd spoken about the affair. Only one person she'd divulged that information to.

"Carissa, are you okay?" Riley asked. "You look a little pale."

Okay? She's wasn't okay. But at least she was no longer feeling sad. Now she was pissed at the person who had revealed her secret to the Bayside Blogger.

Jasper Dumont.

Jasper was feeling pretty damn good. He'd had a great day in the office. All of the meetings he'd attended that afternoon promised exciting opportunities for Dumont Incorporated.

He crossed to his bar and poured a glass of his favorite scotch. Taking the glass to the windows, he took a moment to soak in the scene below. The sun still shone brightly, even as it would shortly be making its descent. Soon, the sky would become a mix of brilliant colors, reflecting over the bobbing ships and boats docked in the bay.

Some high school kids were down in the square, fooling around, just being kids. He remembered those days well. School had started back up the day before and it would take a little while longer before they remembered they hated school. For now, the excitement over being reunited with friends, upcoming Friday night football games, and new school supplies was running rampant.

The kids entered The Brewside, a luxury he didn't have back in high school. Ten years ago, an old used bookstore stood in the café's spot. He'd spent a lot of time there. It was the only place in town where you could grab a coffee and hang out. No one rushed them. It was really chill.

His favorite thing to peruse were graphic novels. He gave a quick glance at the bookshelves in his condo. Carissa had noticed his collection the other day.

He could hear Carissa in his head now, as if it were a decade ago.

"I don't get it. They're just a bunch of dumb comic books. I didn't realize I was dating a comic book geek."

"No, no, no. They are graphic novels and that makes them infinitely more cool."

She, on the other hand, was forever flipping through the pages of fashion magazines and cookbooks. He should have realized back then she'd go into the cooking field.

Jasper shook the liquid around in his glass as he considered their old hangout. A bookstore. Something Bayside didn't currently have. Of course, brick-and-mortar bookstores were risky businesses these days. But he liked a challenge. He grabbed his iPad and made a few notes. Then he glanced down at the square again. Yes, definitely something to consider. If he could think of something else to pair the bookstore with, it would be easier to get the funding. Maybe a bookstore with a café inside. A café that would need catering help. Which led right back to Carissa Blackwell.

He'd managed to keep thoughts of Carissa at bay for most of the day. He'd decided to give her some space. After their kiss the other night, he thought she might need some room.

"Ah, hell," he said. He was the one who really needed space. They'd delved into very sensitive territory. After all these years, he'd never dreamed that he'd actually get to have a conversation with her about it.

The truth was, she'd really hurt him all those years ago. Getting to voice that hurt went a long way to healing an old and very potent wound.

Then they'd kissed.

He sucked in a breath at the memory of her lips on his, at the little sounds she made, at the way she felt in his arms.

Jasper wasn't an idiot. He knew the very best thing would be for him to keep his distance. Go back to his usual dating pattern. There were plenty of women out there.

But only one stunning blonde who could kiss him senseless.

A loud knock sounded at his front door, pulling him from his musings. Jasper put down his glass of scotch and crossed the room. When he opened the door, he was shocked to see the very person he'd just been thinking about. But there she was, her thick hair cascading over her shoulders, her gray eyes alert and bright. Her face was flushed.

"Carissa," he said with surprise in his voice.

Jasper was thrilled to see her at his door. But taking a long look at her gave him the feeling that this was not a happy visit. Unless the smoke coming out of her ears was actually glitter. Those red cheeks were apparently not from the exertion of walking down the hallway to his door.

Nope. She had her mad on. And he had a feeling she would be sharing that mad with him momentarily.

"Can I come in?" she asked around a clenched jaw.

"Of course." He held the door open farther and allowed her to pass into the room. "Can I get you a drink?"

He decided to make himself comfortable by sitting back in his favorite leather recliner. He gestured to the other chair and the couch but she simply moved to stand directly in front of him, arms crossed over her chest.

"What the hell, Jasper?" she said, her voice exploding into the quiet room.

Like a firework being set off into the night sky, her temper roared into the stratosphere and then quickly dissipated back down to Earth. She deflated, her shoulders collapsing and a frown appearing on her face. In a split second her anger had morphed into sadness.

He rose from his chair. "What's wrong, Car?"

Her eyes held a mix of confusion and worry. "The Bayside Blogger. Does that ring any bells?"

Not what he'd been expecting her to say. Of course, he really had no idea where she was going with this. "I haven't read her column today. What did she say?"

"That I got divorced because my husband cheated on me. That's what she said." Her voice broke on the last word.

He leaned forward. His heart went out to her. That couldn't have been easy to read. Now the entire town would realize what she'd went through, and knowing Carissa, she definitely wouldn't want any pity. Or take kindly to her very personal business being out in the public realm.

"I'm sorry, Car."

Her lip quivered. She pointed at him in question. "Jasper, did you tell her?"

He wasn't sure what she meant. "Did I tell who what?"

"Did you tell the Bayside Blogger, whoever she is, that Preston cheated on me?" The anger in her words was clear.

An icy cold feeling seeped through his body. "You're asking me if I told a gossip columnist about your ex-husband and your personal marriage problems?"

She nodded. "I'm sorry, Jasp, but I have to ask."

Was she kidding him? "Carissa Blackwell, you've known me my entire life. I can't believe you would come over here and ask me that."

Her gaze darted around the room and then she pushed her hands through her hair. "If it wasn't you, then who else? Process of elimination. You are literally the only person I told about, about…the cheating." She lowered her voice when she said the word *cheating*.

He felt for her. He did. But he was having a hard time remembering that fact when she was standing in his living room insulting him.

"For you to accuse me—"

She quickly cut him off. "I'm not accusing you, Jasper. I'm simply asking."

"It's never simple with you."

She rolled her eyes, which filled with anger once again. Fine with him. He'd rather have her mad than sad.

"And it's always so dramatic with you," she countered. "It's a logical conclusion for me to reach."

She'd hurt him that day she'd dumped him all those years ago. And she was hurting him again today. After their conversation the other night, he thought they'd at least taken a step forward. But this accusation pushed them quite a few steps back.

Jasper's temper didn't flare often. He was a master at staying calm and cool. But he was having a hell of a struggle keeping composed at the moment. He took a step toward her and she held her ground. "Listen to me. I did not tell the Bayside Blogger, or anyone else for that matter, about your marriage, your divorce, or any other details about you. No one, Carissa."

She tossed her head up, meeting his gaze. "How else do you explain it?"

"I can't. I don't know how the Blogger finds out the information she does. Or he does. But I swear on everything that I hold dear that I did not out you."

She paced a few steps toward the window and then back again. Her mouth opened and it seemed like she was about to say something. But she quickly shut it. Then she paced again before finally landing in front of him. She whispered, "My divorce is the single most embarrassing event of my life."

That comment took the wind out of his sails. "A lot of people get divorced, Car."

"Riley said the same thing. And I know it's true. A lot of people get cheated on, too," she said in a shaky voice. "I was fine knowing that everyone in Bayside would learn of my divorce. But the reason for it..."

He hated seeing her like this. She'd always been good at keeping her emotions in check. It used to impress him back in high school. She had some of the greatest control he'd ever seen. And she was much easier to deal with when she was laughing or angry or yelling at him. But as a tear formed in her eye, threatening to fall, Jasper reached for the only lifeboat he could find. Unfortunately, it wasn't to comfort, but to antagonize.

"I understand that. I do. But for you to come in here, guns blazing, and start blaming me for something that is pretty repulsive is not okay. Maybe the real problem is that you didn't really take the time to get to know me back then, because you sure as hell don't know me now."

"Jasper—"

"Before you say something else that is sure to outrage me, I suggest you go."

"But I only meant to—"

Again, he cut her off. "You walked away from me all those years ago. Maybe you should do it again right now."

He turned his back on her and walked to the kitchen. He waited until he heard his front door close. As usual, his anger dissipated quickly and he was left with a raw, hollow feeling.

He hadn't meant to bring up their past. In fact, he didn't really know where that even came from. Maybe he'd been holding it in for far too many years. Maybe it needed to be said. In any case, it hadn't helped matters. He didn't blame Carissa for being upset about the Bayside Blogger's reveal of her ex-husband's infidelity. But taking it out on him was not the answer.

Perhaps his original idea of giving her space and time hadn't been so crazy. He should probably give her even more because he sure as hell needed some himself.

Carissa was a mess. She'd been a mess since Riley first told her about the Bayside Blogger's article. She'd become even more of a mess after she got home and read the article herself. But what just happened with Jasper might have put her over the edge.

She kept racking her brain but she was positive she hadn't told anyone else about Preston's cheating. Only Jasper. But when she'd brought it to Jasper's attention—okay, accused him, because that's really what she'd done. Accused him with guns blazing. When she'd done that, the look on his face had been heartbreaking. If he'd been just plain old angry, she could have dealt with that. But it had been hurt that crossed his handsome face. Not anger.

More than that, he was clearly still holding on to their breakup. And she couldn't blame him for that. It might be time to finally reveal the whole story to him. That is, if he would ever even talk to her again.

She pushed her hand through her hair. She'd been up since four this morning. She needed a shower. A good stiff drink wouldn't hurt anything, either. And she'd definitely like to be off her feet.

Her phone alerted her to a text message from Riley.

Where are you? Cocktails with me and Elle, remember? Boat House. Now.

Damn. Well, at least she would get that stiff drink.

Carissa had been wandering around the streets of Bayside aimlessly, trying to decipher this mystery. Luckily, she wasn't far from the Boat House, the upscale restaurant right on the water. They had excellent seafood, a nice ambience, and according to Riley, a great bar and lounge area. Apparently, Riley and Elle met for cocktails there quite frequently. If she wasn't so emotionally exhausted, it would have touched her to be included.

She pushed open the door and her stomach growled at the enticing smell of salty seafood, fresh bread and melted butter. She stole a quick glance around. Looked as if they'd renovated the place from what she remembered. It looked good. The bar area was cute with high tables and tall wooden chairs. The entire restaurant seemed abuzz with activity.

She easily spotted her friends and made her way toward their table. They both waved as she approached.

"I'm sorry," Carissa said. "I lost track of time."

"No wonder. I heard you had quite the day," Elle said, pushing a glass of water toward her.

Carissa slumped in her chair. "It was awful. I went over to Jasper's and blamed him for the whole situation with the Bayside Blogger because he's the only person I told about it. But then he turned it on me somehow. I'm not even sure how. He made me feel awful and you know what? I deserved it. And then he kicked me out and now I feel doubly horrible."

Both Riley's and Elle's mouths were hanging open as they stared at her. Finally, Elle spoke. "I was actually referring to the ladies' tea you catered, which Lilah said was a huge success."

"But you were clearly busy after that," Riley added with a twinkle in her eye. "We definitely need to discuss."

A perky young waitress bounced over to their table, wearing a black skirt and a crisp white blouse. "Drinks?"

"Hells yeah," Riley said. "We've been waiting for you to order, Carissa. A round of cosmos and keep 'em coming," she said to the waitress.

Both women leaned in as Carissa spilled the whole situation.

"But you see, right? It had to be Jasper. Because he's the only person I told about Preston."

"Not necessarily," Elle said.

"What do you mean?" Carissa asked as she finished off her cosmo.

"It's crazy," Riley said. "The Bayside Blogger just knows stuff. No matter how hard you try to keep something a secret, she finds out. Last year, I was dating someone who lived about thirty minutes away. We had a horrible breakup. In his town. Not a soul from Bayside in sight. And yet the next morning, there it was splashed across her blog."

Elle nodded. "When I first returned last spring, I was in her stupid column every day. Not to mention all the Twitter discussions."

Carissa's jaw dropped. "Really?"

Riley finished her drink, as well. "Yep. It's awful. No matter what you do or where you go, there she is. She's probably in this restaurant right now."

The waitress stopped by their table. "Another round?"

"Yes," all three of them answered in unison.

The waitress widened her eyes, but replied, "Okeydokey."

"So see," Elle continued, "Jasper may very well be innocent in all of this."

"Oh God." Carissa moaned as she ran a hand over her face. "If that's true then I'm a huge witch."

The waitress, who had returned with their second round of drinks, froze, giving Carissa a wary once-over.

"Don't worry, sweetie. She won't be a witch," Riley said amiably.

"We're also very good tippers," Elle added, and the waitress seemed appeased. Still, she did ask if they wanted to order any appetizers but didn't actually wait around for their response.

"See what I mean?" Carissa pointed toward her. "I'm scaring off innocent young waitresses now."

Riley snorted. "Oh, she'll be fine."

"And Jasper will be fine, too." Elle put her drink down on the table. "I really don't think he would betray your confidence and reveal something so personal to the town gossip columnist. Besides, what would he have gained by doing something like that? Seems to me like he's trying hard to get back in your good graces."

Carissa bit her lip. "Jeez, when you put it like that it makes me feel like an idiot for even going over there."

"You shouldn't," Riley said. "He was the only one you told. Makes sense to jump to that conclusion."

Seems to me like he's trying hard to get back in your good graces. Elle's words repeated in her head. Carissa wondered if that was true. It didn't seem like it the other night when he was on a date with some other woman. Of course, he did help with her car and drive her home. And then there was the very sultry, very passionate kiss they'd shared...

"Can I ask a question?" Carissa said suddenly. "Jasper isn't married."

"That's not a question," Riley pointed out.

Carissa played with a strand of her hair, twisting it around her finger. "He's not dating anyone, either."

Riley chuckled. "Still not a question. But I think I know what you're trying to ask. You want to know about Jasper's dating history."

"I mean, not in extreme detail, but I am curious. He's gorgeous and charming. Not to mention, he's incredibly wealthy. He runs his family's freaking business. He's a catch."

"Careful," Riley said. "One might think you're still interested."

She ignored Riley's comment. "It's just, with all those qualifications, I would think a line of women would be following him everywhere."

Elle smiled. "Oh, they do. Trust me. He dated someone named Mindy for a couple months when I first got back. I thought it might be serious, but they broke up."

"Of course they did." Riley took a sip of her drink and looked pensive. "He always breaks up with them. Have you noticed?" she asked Elle.

Elle nodded. "According to Cam, Jasper never stays with the same woman for more than a few months."

Carissa was shocked. "Never?"

"Nope," Riley said.

"Not in college?"

"Not that I know of," Riley answered.

"But..." Carissa sat back in her chair, considering. "That would mean I was the last long-term girlfriend he had." She looked to her friends, who exchanged a glance and nodded. "But there must have been someone he was serious about."

Elle took a moment before answering. "I don't want to make you feel worse than you already do, but I think Jasper is afraid of getting hurt."

"So he never lets anyone get close enough to hurt him." *Except me*, Carissa thought with sadness. What did she do? Hurt him at the first chance. "I feel so stupid," she admitted.

"You shouldn't," Elle said, loyalty in her voice.

"Thanks, but I do. For so many things, so many choices I've made over the years." Carissa reached for her glass but didn't actually take a sip. "When I walked in and found Preston with that woman, I wasn't that surprised. I had a feeling he'd been cheating on me for a while. That's when I got my proof."

"Well, you divorced his sorry ass. So you win." Riley toasted her.

But Carissa shook her head. "I wish I had. But in the end, Preston was the one to request a divorce." Admitting this secret felt liberating. She'd been holding it in for far too long. "I'd become so apathetic."

"About your marriage?" Elle asked.

"About everything. About my marriage, my life, my lack of a career." Her stomach clenched. She'd become her father. Living off of someone else's money and success. She'd become the one thing she'd swore she'd never be. That was the embarrassing part. That's what she really didn't want anyone to know.

Ashamed, she glanced at her friends through her eyelashes. "Pretty pathetic, huh?"

This was the moment they could agree. What shocked her was that they didn't.

"Kind of the opposite of pathetic," Elle said. Riley agreed. "I mean, if I were in your position I would probably be hiding under a rock somewhere crying my eyes out, shoving Double Stuf Oreos in my mouth and being scared out of my mind. But you came here and you're starting your own business."

"That takes cojones." Riley lifted her drink again. "Let's toast to that. To your new life, Carissa Blackwell, and to your big ole cojones."

Overwhelmed, Carissa pushed down the ball that had formed in her throat. She raised her glass and touched it to her friends'.

Maybe it was finally time for new beginnings. Only, she had to say goodbye to her past first.

Chapter Eight

For someone with almost no experience in the catering field, Carissa Blackwell has managed to pull off two yummy events so far here in town. Too bad she can't enjoy her success with Jasper, because I've heard that our resident Ross and Rachel are taking a break...again. What could be the cause this time? Dear readers, I certainly hope it wasn't something I said!

Carissa hadn't apologized to Jasper yet. She'd thought about it. A lot. She still didn't know how the Bayside Blogger had found out her ex-husband had cheated on her. She supposed the Blogger could have just Googled her. In any case, she knew that she owed Jasper an apology for flying off the handle.

She told herself she hadn't called him because she'd been devoting every waking hour to her new business, which was true. With Elle's artistic help, she'd designed a logo for Save the Day Catering and was able to order business cards. She'd even started a website, including some sample menus and a list of the types of events she was available for. It was pretty basic as far as websites went, but it would do the trick for now. She had plans to start photographing her food and adding pictures and descriptions.

Once she had more jobs under her belt she could consider a marketing campaign. Right now, word of mouth would have to suffice, but eventually she'd like to make up flyers or postcards, offer discounts and specials, and maybe one day, hire some help.

Because of the successful ladies' tea, she'd received three more jobs. Since she now had Mrs. Dumont as a reference, she no longer had to worry on that score. Besides, no one else in Bayside realized that she hadn't been a professional caterer back in Chicago. As far as Carissa was concerned, her informal experience was helping her just fine.

She'd set up a makeshift office in the living room. Or tried to. Currently, she was sitting on the floor between the couch and the coffee table, trying to organize the files she'd recently created. Just a couple more folders and color-coded labels and she would be on her way.

She let out a long sigh of relief. She could do this. She *would* do this. She wouldn't end up like her father and she would never rely on a man—or any person—ever again. She would keep full control of her life and no one else would be able to take it away from her again.

Bayside Blogger—check now.

At the sight of Elle's text message, Carissa's heart sank. This couldn't be good news. It wasn't as if the Bayside Blogger would report something happy about her. Like, "Oh that Carissa Blackwell has amazing hair and is really killing it as a caterer."

She quickly grabbed her laptop from the couch and pulled up the—she hated to admit it—bookmarked page on the *Bugle*'s website. As her eyes quickly scanned the contents of today's blog, Carissa didn't read anything that caused alarm. It was annoying, sure.

She was about to text Elle back, but then she reread the blog. The first time, she'd concentrated on the part about her and Jasper being compared to Ross and Rachel from *Friends*. That was enough to make her snort.

But on second glance, she homed in on the opening sentence. "For someone with almost no experience in the catering field…"

Carissa felt like someone was simultaneously extracting all the air from her lungs.

Oh no. Oh no. Oh no. This could not be happening. She paced away from her computer and then promptly returned to reread the blog a third time.

She'd been outed. Again. Damn, damn and double damn. She eyed the stack of business cards she'd just ordered. What was everyone in Bayside going to think? More importantly, how did the Bayside Blogger even find out about this? She'd told no one about her lack of experience. Not Elle, not Riley. Not even…

Jasper.

She rubbed her eyes as a tension headache began. Elle and Riley had been right the other night. They'd said that the Bayside Blogger just knew things. Things that no one else was privy to. Carissa hadn't told Jasper about her lack of experience in catering and yet, here it was in the gossip column anyway.

Carissa pulled up Twitter and started reading through the Bayside Blogger's recent tweets and replies.

Bayside Blogger @BSBlogger

My latest column's up at the @BSBugle site.

Judy Fashley @jdmfash
OMG! Jasper & Carissa broke up AGAIN?!?! @BSBlogger

Harry P. Belding @bocceball
RT @tdmfash They broke up? Didn't know they were dating. The real scoop is that C doesn't have much catering experience.

Reva Lewis @RLLight
Just read @BSBlogger's column. I wouldn't give C.B. my business, that's 4 sure.

Gertie Ward @gertieward26
Big reveal today on @BSBlogger. Although... I had her food at the Dumonts. It was yummy!

Carissa's first instinct was to scream, loud and long. Instead, she paced to the window, took a few deep breaths and then let out an oath. Why did people always make it seem like taking a couple deep inhales would change the way you feel? It never worked with her. She eyed a bottle of wine she'd picked up the other day. Now, there was a better solution for calming herself.

But in the end, Carissa filled a glass with water and sat at the small table in her aunt's kitchen. Perspective. That's what she needed. It was a stupid blog on a small town newspaper's website. How many people really read this article anyway? More importantly, how many people cared? She couldn't imagine that someone would deny her business simply because a blogger wrote an article about her. Right? Then, why was she starting to feel nauseous?

Her phone rang and she saw Elsie Reynolds's name on the display. Carissa was going to be catering her daughter's bridal shower in two weeks. If that went well, she held high hopes that she would be chosen as the caterer for the wedding reception. A wedding would be a major coup at this point.

"Carissaaaa," Mrs. Reynolds said, drawing out her name. "I just happened to be at the store shopping for favors for Bonnie's shower and someone directed me to the Bayside Blogger's website."

Of course they did. Carissa tried to remain calm. "Oh really?"

"Is it true, dear?"

Debating how she should play this, in the end, Carissa chose the truth. "It is a correct statement to say that I don't have any official training in catering. As in," she quickly continued, "I never worked for a caterer or had a business of my own."

"Now, see, dear, that is a problem. We've already invited over a hundred people to Bonnie's shower and everyone is expecting this to be an amazing event."

"Of course." Carissa was close to losing it.

"I just don't think I can continue on with you."

Mrs. Reynolds's dismissal hurt. All of Carissa's hard work and she was going to lose this important job. She was going to fail. Just like her father.

Then something snapped inside her. She wasn't like her father at all. Hadn't she already decided that? Maybe her dad would give up at this point. Cut his losses and move on. But if she truly wanted to be independent, truly make it on her own, bumps in the road were inevitable. This was her first test and she so wasn't failing this exam.

"I got this." She didn't realize she'd said the words out loud until Mrs. Reynolds questioned her.

"Excuse me?"

"Sorry," Carissa said. "Mrs. Reynolds, I completely understand your concerns about me."

"I'm glad you do."

"However, while I may not have official experience as a caterer, trust me when I say that I've been catering events for years, oftentimes at the last minute. In fact, there was a point when I was throwing at least one dinner party a week. In addition to that, I've trained with some of the best culinary instructors in Chicago."

"Yes, dear, but your references…"

"Lilah Dumont can serve as my reference. Besides, you were at both her end-of-summer party and the charity event she hosted last week. I think it's safe to say that my food spoke for itself."

"Well, of course, it was fabulous, but…"

Carissa was on a roll now. "Again, I understand and appreciate your concerns. I would feel the same way if I were in your shoes."

"You would?" Mrs. Reynolds's voice softened

"Of course. This is your daughter's bridal shower. A once-in-a-lifetime event." *Unless precious Bonnie gets divorced like me*, Carissa thought wryly. "This day needs to be special, memorable."

"Exactly."

"And I think the menu we've chosen will go beyond meeting her expectations. I dare say that Bonnie is going to love what you have planned."

Mrs. Reynolds was teetering now. Carissa could feel it. Time to go in for the kill. "However, as insurance, I'm willing to offer you a twenty percent discount off the price we discussed. Plus, if you don't like the food or you're unhappy with my services, I will give you a full refund."

Carissa's palms began to sweat while she waited for the reply. Not only because of Mrs. Reynolds's possible answer but because taking a hit on this large party would not help her very fragile bottom line.

"This all sounds very reasonable, Carissa," Mrs. Reynolds finally said. "Okay, we have a deal."

"Great. I'll email you a revised contract as soon as we get off the phone."

After they hung up and Carissa sent off the new paperwork, she sat back in her seat. The 20 percent discount hurt, but not as much as losing the business altogether. Besides, she knew Mrs. Reynolds, her daughter and all the guests at the shower would love her culinary creations.

She bit her lip as she considered what had just transpired. She'd single-handedly saved the day. More than that, she'd taken her first step toward independence. No one else got her out of that jam. She'd done that herself.

"Go me," she said into the empty kitchen, which she followed up with a happy dance.

She felt good. In fact, she felt inspired to make some other changes. Being self-sufficient meant knowing when to admit you'd been wrong and taking the extra step of apologizing.

Reaching for one of her favorite baking books, she flipped to the pie section. Up next on the plate was a huge apology to Jasper Dumont.

Jasper decided to take a risk. Two risks, actually. The first was going over to Carissa's house to begin with. The second came to him as he drove by the local pizzeria en route to her aunt's cottage. He promptly pulled a U-turn and swung back around to it. Twenty minutes later he was back on course.

When she opened the door, a surprised look crossed her face and her mouth opened into an appealing little O. "Jasper, I can't believe you're standing there. How crazy."

Intrigued with her response, he said, "Crazy good or crazy bad?"

She considered. "Crazy, crazy. I have something for you. In fact, I was just on my way to come see you."

She tugged on an apron she was wearing. Under it was a pair of comfy-looking gray pants and a turquoise T-shirt that clung to all the right places. The outfit should have been frumpy, but with her body, the sweats were as good as wearing a black-tie gown. Her hair was piled on top of her head and there was a smear of flour on one cheek. His fingers itched to reach out and brush it away.

Instead, he produced the large pizza box from behind his back. The smell of the cheese and tomato sauce had his mouth watering on the drive over. He saw interest piqued in her eyes as she took in the pizza.

"I have something for you, too. I hope you still like your pizza the same way. Extra cheese and anchovies?" he asked.

The corners of her mouth twitched until she relented and let the smile blossom. "Still my favorite." She pointed a finger. "And the best topping of all time ever for pizza."

"So you always said. Can I come in?"

She stepped back. "What kind of idiot doesn't let a pizza in the front door?"

"Good point."

He took in the cottage as they made their way back to the kitchen. He chuckled. "I haven't been in this house in ages." He picked up a small clock nestled inside a large seashell that was bedecked with glitter and shook his head. "Same old Val."

She grinned. "It's comforting, really. She hung wallpaper in the bathroom. Peach wallpaper with flowers. Also, I think she may be growing weed in the backyard."

"No kidding?" He stopped, tilted his head up, his nose twitching. "What's that smell?"

She smiled. "It's your surprise." Moving to the left, she

revealed the source of the aroma. "I made a peach pie for you."

He grinned and pumped his fist in the air. "My favorite. But what's the occasion?"

"What was the occasion for the pizza?" She nodded at the box.

"You first," he said.

Her smile faded. "An apology. I'm so sorry for accusing you of outing me to the Bayside Blogger. Things have been so tough this year and coming back here and..."

She trailed off when he raised a hand. "You don't have to go into all of that, Car."

She removed her apron. "I hurt your feelings."

"You did," he admitted easily.

"I'm sorry."

"I accept."

She cocked her head. "Just like that?"

He nodded. "Just like that."

She threw her apron onto the table. "You are infuriating. You're not even making me work for it."

"Not my style." He leaned over and wiped the streak of flour from her skin, allowing himself to linger there a moment longer than necessary. Then he met those intoxicating gray eyes. "I care about you, Car. I always have. I always will. Your being a bit angry for one night isn't going to change that. You'd been hurt, and I get it. Even if I didn't like bearing the brunt."

He'd thrown her off balance with that. He liked puzzling her. She got the cutest little line on her forehead when she tried to figure out something that baffled her.

"You're too sweet, Jasp," she finally said.

"Sweet?" He nabbed a piece of the piecrust and popped it into his mouth. "I'm other things, too."

"Yes, you are." She batted his fingers away from the pie. "Now your turn. What's with the pizza?"

He shrugged. "Just like that night in the bar, I thought you could use a friend."

"A friend, huh? Being my friend wouldn't have anything to do with a certain blogger's recent article about me?"

He opened his mouth but quickly shut it. He coughed. "I think we need to eat this pizza before it gets cold. Plus, the sooner we eat this, the sooner we can eat that." He pointed at the pie.

Carissa offered him a knowing smile but she didn't say anything. Instead, she went to a cabinet and came back with two plates and a stack of napkins. "How about we eat this out on the deck? It's a nice night."

While he brought the pizza and plates outside, she grabbed a bottle of wine and glasses. A few moments later she emerged with an uncorked bottle of red.

"This might be the best meal ever," she said after she took her first bite. Her eyes were closed and she made the most seductive sound he'd ever heard. Jasper's mouth watered yet again, only it had nothing to do with the pizza this time.

They ate in companionable silence for a while. But after Carissa finished her second piece, she took a long pull of wine and turned to him.

"I'm catering a bridal shower. Elsie Reynolds read the Bayside Blogger's column today and tried to fire me."

He felt his eyebrow rise. "Tried to?"

"I didn't let her."

Good girl. He put his plate down and faced her. "Was the article true?"

"You mean, is it true that I don't have any catering experience?" She was staring straight ahead at the water. "Yep, pretty much."

"Car, why didn't you tell me that? You know I would have helped you."

Her head whipped around and her eyes focused on his. "That's exactly why I didn't. I spent the last decade completely out of control, dependent on someone else. Finally, I have the opportunity to gain some independence, some freedom."

And she needed to do this for herself, he realized. Jasper got that. He'd been the same way when he'd finally started applying himself in college.

"She tried to fire you and you didn't let her. Looks like you are in business for yourself." He tapped his wineglass against hers and reveled in the smile that blossomed over her face. "Carissa," he began, but she jumped up suddenly, as if sensing the mood shift between them.

"I think it's time for pie."

He decided to give her a break. "I think it's always time for pie."

A few minutes later they were both finishing up their slices of what Jasper deemed the very best peach pie he'd ever had. And that included the Dumont chef's masterpiece.

"Elsie Reynolds is very lucky she kept you. Damn, that was good," he said, dropping his fork on the plate.

She laughed. "I'm glad you like it. The rest is yours to take home and eat in the middle of the night while standing in your kitchen naked."

"Who says I stand in my kitchen naked?"

"You don't?"

"Nope, if I'm eating pie naked, it's always in the living room."

Her grin lit up the deck, which was growing dark thanks to the diminishing sun. "Oh, sorry to have mixed that up," she finished on a laugh.

He smiled, enjoying the happiness of just being with

her. "Sometimes when we joke around like this, it feels like you never left."

She nodded, but once again she let her gaze slide toward the water. "I know what you mean. It feels so easy with you." She rose and walked toward the end of the deck. When she faced him again, her eyes were clouded, her face serious. "I need to tell you something, Jasp."

"Is it something that will end with more promises of pie?"

Her chest rose and fell as if she was silently laughing. "It's something that should end with the promise of a dozen more pies."

He crossed the deck, stood beside her. "Then, I'm definitely listening."

"This isn't the easiest thing for me to talk about, but I want to tell you why I broke up with you after graduation."

He hadn't been expecting that. Part of him had wanted to know the answer to this puzzle more than he wanted to breathe. But another part felt anxious about finally understanding the answer to something that had been a deep source of hurt for over a decade. Would learning the truth make him feel better or relive the hurt?

"Okay," he said tentatively.

She bit her lip and narrowed her eyes, as if she was trying to figure out where to start. He retrieved their wineglasses, pouring more while he waited. He didn't really want any more but he needed to do something.

Carissa accepted the wine. "You know…that is, my dad…well, my dad and I didn't have the best relationship."

"I remember." He took a sip. "I never really understood why, though. Your dad was fun. He always made me laugh."

"He always made everyone laugh." She pushed a hand through her hair. "He was the life of the party. Everyone loved him. He was witty and clever and charming."

"Yes, he was," Jasper said slowly, wondering where this was going.

"He was also unreliable."

Surprised by that statement, Jasper leaned against the deck and waited for her to continue.

"I remember being in elementary school, about eight or nine. We were having a career day where our parents came in and talked about their jobs."

"I remember that," he said.

"Do you remember that my dad didn't come in to speak to the class? He couldn't, because he had nothing to talk about. He had no career. It was the first time I remember feeling disappointed by one of my parents. No—" she shook her head "—that's not quite right. I was embarrassed. I told the class that my dad had gotten sick and couldn't make it in for career day."

Jasper opened his mouth to object but no words came out. As he thought back, he quickly realized that he didn't know what either of Carissa's parents had done for work.

She laughed but the sound was metallic and humorless. "You're trying to think of what my parents did and you can't, right? Occasionally my dad would get into business with someone. Usually one of his friends. But it would never last. I honestly think he enjoyed the social aspect of working more than the actual work. Nothing ever stuck. He never had any ambition or desire to better himself.

"You're probably wondering how we lived in that big house on the water," she continued. "They lived off my mom's trust fund. A rather large trust fund from my grandparents. But even large amounts of money can be mismanaged. That brings me to you."

When her eyes met his, Jasper saw pain and anger there. Maybe some unresolved feelings, too.

"One morning after graduation, my parents sat me down

and explained that they'd run out of money. Just like that. It was all gone. Sometime during our senior year, my dad attempted one last-ditch effort with some business venture. He used the money set aside for my education. The venture never took off, just like all the others. And because of that, I had no way to pay for college."

His stomach tensed. "Oh, Car. I had no idea."

She nodded. "No one did. If I thought the humiliation of elementary career day was bad, it was nothing compared to that morning. I'd gotten into Northwestern and I'd been so excited to go there."

"But you did go there. Didn't you?" he asked.

"Yes, I did. Aunt Val helped me apply for scholarships, grants, you name it. She bought all the books and supplies I needed for the first year, too. I worked a lot during those four years. When I got married, Preston absorbed a ton of debt. For my twenty-fifth birthday he wrote a check and cleared out my loans." She snapped her fingers. "Just like that. Debt gone. Memories erased."

"But it's not that easy," Jasper said.

"No, it's not. In a strange way, the experience was good for me. I'd been a spoiled, pampered kid. I don't regret having to work hard. What I have a hard time with is my parents, particularly my dad. It felt like he had no concept of how much his actions affected others. In that case, me. Plus, they explained that they would be moving away from Bayside. They didn't want their friends to find out that they had nothing. They live in Maine now. So on top of everything else, I was losing the only home I'd ever known."

"You used to say that you hated it here and couldn't wait to get out," he reminded her.

"Oh, Jasp, I was just a kid. I didn't know what I was saying. I was a bratty girl who dreamed of the stars. And then one morning, I realized just how far away those stars were going to stay."

Jasper never imagined that she'd gone through so much with her parents. He was trying to absorb everything but it was a lot to think about. Then she threw one more bomb his way.

"I've told you that you always reminded me of my dad. I think that when all of that happened, I took it out on you. I mean, I didn't mean to do that. Not consciously anyway."

He held up a hand. She looked so young, so vulnerable. "Your dad had just hurt you and stripped away everything you had known and were counting on. You saw similarities between me and your father. So you broke up with me."

He was struggling. On the one hand, he wanted to be understanding. Carissa was opening up to him. At the same time, just talking about this was bringing up all that hurt and all that angst; as if a hand had reached into his chest and started squeezing his heart.

Her eyes welled up with tears. But he watched her take a few breaths and push those tears back down.

"When the first big betrayal of your life comes from one of your parents, it really messes with you," she said quietly.

He reached for her hand and was happy that she let him hold it. "I'm sorry, Car. Sorry you had to go through all that. I wish you would have told me back then. You know my family would have helped you."

She squeezed his fingers. "I was too mortified. I felt so ashamed. And scared."

"Where do things stand now with your parents?"

She shrugged. "Not great. I barely speak to my dad. My mom and I are okay. I guess."

"You guess?"

"I check in with her. But to be honest, I will never understand her. Why did she stay with my dad? He wasted all of her money. He had no ambition. They still live together, as if everything is fine. He didn't take care of her. Or me."

Her voice hitched on that last word. Jasper saw the emotion flooding her face.

"I was the good child. I never questioned anything. And then I got married to someone I thought I loved. I thought Preston adored me. I thought he was the opposite of my father. I thought he would do anything for me. Maybe he would have. But in the end, it didn't matter. He didn't love me, either."

And that was the heart of the mystery that was Carissa Blackwell. Jasper felt like his eyes had just been opened after a very long time of staying firmly shut. Carissa was this amazing, beautiful, smart woman with an abundance of confidence on the outside. But underneath it all, she was hurting. Her trust and her heart had been betrayed. She just wanted to be loved. That was all.

And he understood perfectly. Because under all of his flirting and bravado, Jasper craved the same thing. Love.

He ached for her. For that little girl in elementary school, for the teenager who almost had her life taken away, for the wife who'd been cheated on.

She pointed at him. "Don't do that."

"What?"

"Don't feel sorry for me. I am the one who was awful to you. I'm sorry for the way I broke up with you. I'm so sorry if I caused you any pain."

He let out a frustrated sound. "Of course you caused me pain. I loved you, you broke up with me out of the blue, and I was confused. But given everything you've said tonight, I can't help but feel for you. Not pity. I just feel *for* you."

And he did. More than that, he was suddenly seeing Carissa in a whole new light.

* * *

Carissa didn't know what to think or how to feel. She'd revealed her deepest, darkest, dirtiest secret.

She'd expected to still feel that shame, that discomfort. Surprisingly, she actually felt lighter, freer.

"I hadn't planned on spending the evening this way, but I'm really glad I told you all of this," she confessed.

He smiled. "I'm glad you told me, too. I wish I had known sooner, but I understand completely."

His eyes were so mesmerizing. She could stare at them for days at a time. The blue color was so brilliant and welcoming. When she talked to Jasper, it was as if she was the only person on the planet. More than that, it was like whatever she was talking about, big or little, was the most important thing in the universe. No wonder everyone wanted to be around him. Be with him.

She remembered something. "Um, should I ask you whatever happened to that girl from the other night? The woman you had the date with before you found me on the side of the road," she supplied.

Finally, he drank his wine. A rather large sip, she noticed. "I think you have a pretty good idea how that ended."

She raised an eyebrow in question.

"The date wasn't that great."

Yikes. "Sorry," she said.

"Are you?" he asked.

"Not really." She let out a harsh, bitter laugh. Carissa couldn't believe she'd just admitted that. "It's wrong, I know. I shouldn't wish your dating life any ill will. But I do."

His smile faded. A breeze came off the water. She'd let her hair down and she could feel the long blond strands blowing around her face. Something shifted between them. He put the wineglass down and closed the distance between them. "It's wrong. For so many reasons. But since you got back, I feel drawn to you."

She'd experienced the same sensation and yet his words had the breath leaving her body. "We've kissed a couple times."

"Yes, we have."

"I will blame the first one on alcohol. And fried cheese sticks."

"I don't get how the cheese sticks factor in but I'll agree." He tilted his head. "What about the second time?"

"Imminent danger always ups your adrenaline."

"We're now calling your overheated car imminent danger?" he asked.

"As long as you buy that."

"The kisses probably shouldn't happen again," he said, running his hands up her arms.

Her tongue darted out to wet her lips. "You're right. Definitely no more kissing."

And that's when he kissed her. His mouth met hers in a slow, sensual buildup that left her breathless. She wound her arms around his neck as he pulled her closer.

This was no ordinary kiss. This was the kiss of old-school Hollywood movies. It was like that one where... And then she couldn't think anymore. Not about movies or kisses or anything except Jasper Dumont.

After a very long time of devouring her mouth, he pulled back, running his thumbs over her cheeks and using those baby blues to dazzle her erratically beating heart even more.

"I told Riley and Elle that you were an amazing kisser," she said, her voice breathless.

Interest at this statement shone in his eyes. "Really? You talk about me with Riley and Elle?"

"Oh yeah. Girls talk about everything."

He pushed against her and she realized that he was just as aroused as she was. "Everything?"

She bit her lip. "Well, almost everything."

He grinned. "Then, let's give them something to really discuss next time you're together."

"What did you have in mind?"

He leaned in and nuzzled the side of her neck. "How about some of this?" He sucked her earlobe into his mouth, sending shivers down her spine.

"Yeah, that's, uh, good." He was scrambling her thoughts again. Any hope of stopping this evaporated.

"Maybe some of this," he said as his hand made its way up her side, grazing her breast.

Then she realized there was no reason to stop this. Why end something that felt so right?

"We could try some of this, too." She moved his hand so that it firmly settled over her breast.

"What a great idea. You are very wise." He cupped her breast, rubbing his thumb over her straining nipple.

Her head fell back as a moan sounded. "Jasp, maybe we should move this inside?"

"Why?" He kissed her again. "You have this nice big lot, protected by trees on either side and that fence over there."

"Jasp, we can't." But even as she said it, she was reaching for the waistband of his pants. She ran her fingers along his skin there, enjoying the way he sucked in a breath.

"When did you lose your sense of adventure? Remember that time on the football field?" He winked before he returned to her neck, sending delightful tremors down her spine. "I think Chicago took that bold, fearless girl away."

He was goading her and she knew it. Still, she fell for it. "Oh yeah?" With one fell swoop, she had his pants undone and yanked his shirt up and over his head.

"Impressive," he said on a strangled laugh.

So was he. Damn, she thought. Jasper was all grown up. The tall, lanky boy had definitely filled out. He was still in excellent shape but there was just more of him now. Just to make sure he was real and not some fictional daydream, she ran her hands over his chest, his broad shoulders, down his lean torso. She smiled when he jumped. "Still ticklish, I see."

"Shh, that's our secret."

"Yeah, mine and all the other women you've been with." Until the words escaped, she hadn't realized how much that thought bothered her. She frowned.

"Hey." He tilted her head up with one long finger. "You're the only one here with me now. Only you. The most beautiful woman I've ever seen." He kissed her deeply.

He still made her feel special. Even after everything she'd told him tonight. She stepped back and removed her shirt and then her lacy blue bra. His appreciative look made her feel feminine and powerful.

Before she could blink, he'd come to her and was everywhere. His fingers, his lips, his tongue. He ravished every part of her he could reach. When his mouth settled over her breast, she wound her fingers into his hair and hung on for dear life, even as the sensations threatened to break her.

After some time of being feasted on, she reached into his boxer briefs and cupped him. He groaned and then pressed his mouth to hers again. Slowly, she moved her hand over his length, listening to his accelerated breathing.

"Car, I…we need to…"

She got the message. Removing her hand, she pushed the briefs all the way off. He quickly reached down for his pants and removed a small foil packet. After that was taken care of, she plastered herself to him again.

They continued kissing and touching as they headed toward a lounge chair. In the process, they finished shedding all of their clothing.

She pushed him back and quickly straddled him. Rising above him, she took a moment to enjoy the look of pure lust in his eyes. She could only imagine that her own face would mirror the same expression of desire.

With another long kiss, she lifted her hips and took him in. They let out matching moans as she adjusted to the feel and size of him. Then he gripped her hips, urging her to move but accepting that she would set the pace. All while never taking his eyes off hers.

The moment was massively erotic. Being outside, with the wind cooling off their overheated skin, the sounds of the water lapping against the beach and the fading sunset illuminating their joined bodies, Carissa had never felt so turned on.

She began to move, slowly at first. But it wasn't long before she started needing more and more. Jasper complied by pumping his hips up to meet her beat for beat. Before she knew it, she was rising higher and higher, her moans and gasps mixing with Jasper's. She felt him tensing just as she fell off the cliff of desire. And he joined her right after.

Sated, she collapsed onto him. His arms circled her body protectively. Turning her head, she brushed a kiss over his mouth. Overwhelmed with his generosity throughout the whole night, she could think of nothing to say but "thank you."

He answered by staring deeply into her eyes for a long time. Then he kissed her and they finally rested. No more words needed.

Chapter Nine

Carissa woke first. As the sun streamed into her bedroom, she took a moment to gather her thoughts and take inventory of her body.

She quickly found that she felt amazing. Sated and content, she wanted to stretch her arms high over her head and purr like a cat. But the masculine arm draped over her side stopped her.

Slowly, she shifted so she could take in Jasper. Even in sleep, he wore a tranquil smile. His blond hair was mussed, stubble shadowed his jaw, and the sheet had draped low so his full chest with its smattering of appealing hair lay bare. In other words, he looked like sin on a stick, she thought, stifling a giggle.

He'd been amazing last night, and she wasn't even thinking about his moves in bed. Although those were quite improved from high school, and that was saying something.

Coming over here to check on her, when really, it should have been her to reach out to him. Then he'd listened so intently, without judgment, to her story.

Excluding Aunt Val, it had been the first time she'd ever

fully shared her thoughts on her parents. This morning, she had that amazing sensation of the proverbial weight being lifted from her shoulders.

He mumbled something in his sleep and that too made her smile. She wanted to do something nice for him so she quietly slipped from the bed. After a quick stop in the bathroom to freshen up—and okay, put on a quick coat of lip gloss—she entered the kitchen and started a pot of coffee.

As she waited for it to brew, she decided she was buying Aunt Val a Keurig for Christmas. But since she had a minute, she peeled an orange, arranging it on a plate. When the coffee was ready, she added mugs and the general coffee accessories to a tray and made her way back to the bedroom.

When she entered, she was greeted by Jasper's full-wattage smile. "Good morning, gorgeous," he called from the bed.

"Good morning to you."

"I thought maybe you were ashamed of me and ran out in an embarrassed huff."

She brought the tray to the bed. "I considered it. But in the end, I thought caffeine was a better and more mature option."

She handed him a mug and took her own. His eyes closed in contentment at his first sip. "This is from The Brewside," he said with certainty.

"You were right about their coffee. I'm quite addicted already."

They enjoyed the coffee and orange. Carissa ran to the door and grabbed the newspaper, which they read together in bed. It was all very comfortable and normal, until the hairs on the back of her neck stood up. Over the rim of her mug, she saw that he was watching her intently. Only, he wore an expression that she couldn't quite identify on his handsome face.

"What are you thinking?" she wondered aloud.

Without hesitation he said, "I was just thinking about how we've never done this before." He patted the bed.

She could feel her eyes widening in surprise. He'd clearly lost his mind. "Um, Jasp, we've kinda done *this*," she said, pointing toward the bed, "many, many times."

He shook his head. "I know we've slept together. I only meant we've never *slept* together. You know, woken up in each other's arms before." He ran a hand over her cheek. "I've never seen you first thing in the morning."

That statement shocked her into silence. My God, he was right. They'd been horny, hormone-driven teenagers. They'd hooked up all over Bayside in every sense of the term *hook up*. But of course, at the end of every night, they'd had to return to their respective houses.

The idea of making love, falling asleep in each other's arms, only to wake together as well, had simply never been in the cards.

This morning had been a first. A first that clearly meant the world to Jasper, if the way he was looking at her now meant anything. And it meant the world to her, too, only she found it hard to say that out loud. So she did something else.

First she placed her mug on the nightstand and then Jasper's. She pushed the newspaper off the bed and took complete advantage of his mouth. The morning make-out session was better than the coffee at waking her up.

After a long round of kissing and caressing, Jasper said, "Spend time with me."

She wiggled her hips and ran her leg up and down his. "I kinda think we're spending some time together right now."

He kissed her nose and trailed his hand up and down her arm. "And I like this kind of time. Trust me. I love it. But I was thinking about something else."

"Oh yeah?"

"Spend the day with me," he whispered against her mouth.

"I don't know, Jasp."

"Afraid people will talk about you?"

She rolled her eyes. "Not anymore. People are already talking about me. I was thinking that I should go over some recipes and think about my events for the next week. Try to drum up more business."

"There's this thing called a weekend. People who work usually enjoy them. Even CEOs. Trust me, I know."

She gazed into his eyes, realizing her mistake a moment too late. There was no way she could say no now. That blue gaze was a potent weapon.

"Fine," she relented. "I'll spend the day with you." She started untangling herself from him, but Jasper pulled her back and flipped her so he was towering over her. "What are you doing?" she asked.

"I forgot to tell you. Our day together starts right here in this bed."

She reached down and felt exactly how ready he was for the day. She grinned. "What a start."

True to Jasper's word, they started the day in bed. And then in the shower.

Once they finally left the house, with a quick stop for Jasper to grab clean clothes at his loft, they made their way to a local restaurant near the bay. They sat outside and enjoyed a long and luxurious brunch with decadent Belgian waffles, fresh fruit and sinfully rich coffee.

Then Jasper led her to the bay and his sailboat. She couldn't miss the name of the boat. *Determination.*

Coming around the dock, he noticed she was staring at the name. "I, uh, bought this little thing right after college.

Spent a lot of time fixing it up myself. Took a lot of determination to get it in working order."

She had a feeling that wasn't the only meaning of *determination* in Jasper's life. Once again, she felt ashamed at the things she'd said to him back when she'd broken up with him. She suppressed the urge to grab his face in her hands and demand that he realize how sorry she was. Instead, Carissa offered an encouraging smile. "It's a good name."

The awkwardness didn't linger once they were out on the water. It had been some time since she'd been in a boat, with the wind in her hair, the salty crispness of the water around her. She loved tilting her face to the sun and feeling its warm rays shower down on her. There wouldn't be too many more days like this. In a couple weeks, the weather would start to cool off, the leaves would begin to change colors, and summer would be nothing but a memory.

But for right now, she was enjoying watching Jasper in his element. After a couple hours, he pulled up to an older part of town. As she'd said to Jasper previously, there really weren't seedy parts of Bayside. However, this definitely wasn't a spot to send the tourists.

A large structure sat right on the water. She noticed a couple signs. Looked like a clothing boutique and a liquor store, and the rest of the doors appeared to be out of business.

Hand in hand, they walked up the dock.

"What is this place? Doesn't look too good," she said.

"Dumont Incorporated actually owns this property."

Surprised, she eyed him. "I'm shocked that you would allow such disrepair in the Dumont portfolio."

He laughed. "One step at a time. We've had a lot of offers on this place. The most persistent one from an adult entertainment store."

"A what?"

"You know, a place that sells videos and toys. Plus, you can get racy lingerie and, ahem, accessories for active adults." He accented the word *accessories*.

Whoa. "By active, I'm assuming you don't mean hiking and running."

He chuckled. "More like active in bed."

Ah, she got it now. She scrunched up her nose. "I'm not judging. To each their own. Isn't there a place like that out on the highway, right before the exit ramp?"

Jasper nodded. "There used to be. It closed not long after you left. That's the thing. The closest adult store is fifty miles from here. There's a market."

"How does the town feel about that?"

"I'm sure some of them are ecstatic on the inside. But in public, not that happy, as you can imagine. I'll admit, their bid is high. A lot higher than the others, in fact."

She meant what she'd said to Jasper. She truly wasn't judging. Besides, Carissa wasn't an idiot. Plenty of people frequented that kind of establishment.

Jasper continued. "Should I sell to one person? Should I renovate and then lease out space again? There's another possible idea, but it's out of the norm and therefore might not sit well with the board."

He looked tired just talking about it, like it was something that had been keeping him up at night. She touched his arm. "This is important to you."

"All of the deals are, but this one…let's just say that I want to make my mark with this one."

She got it. He wanted to show that he was the right man for the job. Despite his outward confidence, he was feeling insecure about heading up the family business. Carissa couldn't imagine how much pressure came with his job.

"In any case, whatever I decide to do here, it definitely needs a makeover on the outside, that's for sure. But I've heard my mom and Elle talk about this clothing boutique. I know they both do a ton of shopping here. Despite appearances, word of mouth has done wonders for this place."

"Elle does have fabulous taste in clothes, so maybe I should just peruse a little." She'd already untangled their fingers and was heading toward the door. She heard his laugh as she walked inside.

When she entered the store she was greeted by a pretty woman wearing a darling maxi dress in a fun, frisky chartreuse color.

"Welcome to Victoria's Attic. Can I help you find something today?"

"Just browsing. I've never been in here before. Are you Victoria?"

The woman smiled. "No, Victoria is the owner. I'm Leslie, the manager."

"Nice to meet you." Carissa shook her hand and they kept chatting as Carissa scanned the merchandise. There was an impressive array of flirty dresses, fabulous skirts, interesting tops and killer accessories.

She learned that Victoria, the owner, didn't come into the store much anymore. Instead, she let Leslie handle the day-to-day work.

"So you're a caterer?" Leslie asked with interest in her eyes.

"Trying to be. I'm just getting my business off the ground."

"I may be able to help with that."

Carissa dropped the silky lavender scarf she was coveting and gave Leslie her full attention.

"We hold a monthly ladies' night in the store. Nothing fancy. But everything is on sale. We have raffles and some other little games. I've been making most of the food myself. And by making it myself, I really mean that I beg every person I know to lend a hand. I'm surprised I have any friends left," she said with a wink.

"And you'd like to hire me to cater one of the ladies' nights?"

Leslie let out a relieved sigh. "Actually, I'd like to hire you to cater all of them."

"But you haven't even tasted my food or heard about what I can do," Carissa said.

"Actually, I was at the Dumont party and my best friend was at Mrs. Dumont's fund-raiser you catered. Trust me, we're both big fans already. Our ladies' nights are nothing fancy. Nothing like a Dumont party. Just appetizers and desserts."

Carissa couldn't believe her luck. Before Jasper had commandeered her weekend—and she meant that in a really good way—she'd planned on spending her time searching for more business to keep her new company afloat. Who would have thought a day of sailing would end up drumming up new business anyway?

She chatted with Leslie for a few more minutes, agreeing to send some menu options over later in the week. And because she simply couldn't resist, she bought the scarf, too. Refraining from doing a leap out the door, she clamped down on her excitement as she left the store.

But once she was outside, she practically bounced down the steps to where Jasper was standing, scrolling through his phone and waiting patiently for her. "Look at that smile."

She launched herself into his arms and hugged tight. "I'm amazing," she announced.

He leaned back and pushed a strand of her hair over her shoulder. "Yes, you are. Any particular reason why you've realized it recently?"

"Yes, I…" She trailed off when Jasper's phone began ringing. "Do you need to get that?"

He checked the display and nodded. "Just one sec. This is business."

"I thought CEOs didn't work on weekends," she called after him with a smile as he took the call and stuck his tongue out at her. When he returned, he seemed a little miffed. "What's up?" she asked, nodding toward the phone he was tucking back into his pocket.

"That adult entertainment shop again. They increased their bid. If they keep this up, it will be hard to keep the board from pressuring me to accept."

"You don't want to accept?" she asked.

"Let's just say that it would be very good business for us. But I have other plans for the space. However, if I do what the board wants on this one, I will make a lot of people very happy." He shook his head and grabbed her hand. "But enough of that. Are you hungry?"

"A little."

"Great, because I happen to know of a very romantic place with the best lobster you've ever tasted."

It was amazing how fast he could go between business and pleasure. She was fascinated watching him. On the one hand, he'd changed so much since high school. He was wheeling and dealing, running a huge and very successful business. Of course, he was still the same Jasper at heart. Still caring, still kind, still funny, and still the most handsome man she'd ever seen.

So engrossed with thoughts of him, she followed him back to the boat, her own business deal forgotten for the moment. He spoke of Dumont Incorporated a little more over dinner. Anyone could hear the pride he had in the company. But the business talk didn't last long. He quickly shifted into more casual conversation.

"So how do you like the lobster?" he asked.

Glancing around the hole-in-the-wall restaurant that sat

on the water a couple of towns over from Bayside, Carissa couldn't help but be enchanted. Small rickety tables were dressed up with old drippy candles, and twinkly lights were strung around the small patio where they sat. Stars twinkled overhead and soft music played out of speakers mounted on the walls. The smell of fresh fish wafted out of the kitchen.

She threw her napkin on the table. "You were right. This is definitely the best lobster I've ever had." And she really liked that she was having it in this small mom-and-pop restaurant rather than the fancy places Preston used to drag her to. He'd always claimed that he was a foodie, willing to try anything. In reality, he'd try whatever new restaurant opened up on Michigan Avenue. In her opinion, places like this were the real treasures of American cuisine.

"Say that again," Jasper said, reaching for her hand and entwining their fingers again.

"This lobster is amazing? I'll be saying that until my dying day."

He offered her a mischievous grin. "No, not that part. The bit where you said I was right."

She laughed and rolled her eyes at the same time. "Oh please. Such an ego on you."

"But I *was* right." He started playing footsie with her under the table.

She ignored his statement. Instead, she moved her foot far up his leg, delighting when he jumped.

"Are you trying to seduce me, Ms. Blackwell?"

"Do I need to try?" she said cockily.

"Not even a little." He yanked her over the table and kissed her.

Even such a short, spontaneous kiss left her breathless. When they separated, she licked her lips, relishing the taste of him mixed with the lobster butter on his lips. "So what's next?" She fully expected him to make a quip about his bed or some other sexual thing. But he surprised her.

"I was thinking about dancing."

Besides some fun girls' nights back in college, Carissa had never been dancing. In fact, she didn't really know anyone who went dancing and had kind of doubted that it was even a thing. Instead, she thought it was some activity that writers made up to put in books and movies.

But here she was with Jasper, having one hell of a good time at a Latin club he knew about, having caipirinhas and salsa dancing. She had no idea Jasper even knew how to do this, but he sure did. She was so mesmerized by his gyrating hips that she kept stepping on his toes.

"I'm sorry," she said for the hundredth time, even as she laughed.

He pulled her closer. "You're overthinking it. Just follow my lead."

She would follow his hips to the end of the earth. But in the meantime, she'd settle for this dance floor. They kept it up for a couple hours. Finally, they both needed a break so they grabbed water from the bar and headed outside to a quiet spot.

"Are you cold?" he asked.

The temperature had dropped a bit from when they'd been out on the water earlier that day. "No way. This air feels great on my skin." They had matching layers of sweat from their dancing.

Carissa had to admit that she'd had more fun today than she'd had in a very long time. In fact, she couldn't remember the last time she'd let her hair down. From sailing to that amazing dinner to the dancing, everything had been perfect.

Jasper had been perfect.

Careful, she cautioned herself. Preston had been perfect, too. She didn't even realize she'd frowned until Jasper gently ran a hand across her forehead where she was sure a frown line had formed.

"Where did you just go?" he asked kindly.

"Back to Chicago," she answered without thinking. She really shouldn't bring this all up again. She turned from Jasper but he gently pulled her back.

"Tell me more," he said gently.

"I was thinking about my marriage."

"Anything specific?"

He was so damn patient. It made it impossible to keep anything from him. "I was thinking about how boring it was, actually." He seemed surprised at the admission. "I mean, on paper it was… Well, let's just say that Preston would have never salsa danced. In fact, he would have never even known this place existed or had the inclination to ever find it."

"Everyone's different," Jasper said evenly. "What kind of stuff was he into? What did you guys do together?"

Not much, and wasn't that depressing. "We'd go to events for his company. Everyone spoke in hushed tones and pretended to like each other."

"Fun," Jasper said drily.

"Yeah, a real riot. He liked art. I do, too, but I tend to go for the bolder, brighter, more eclectic stuff. Preston prefers whites, beiges, very modern, very streamlined. He got me this painting for one of my birthdays and it was, well, I'm thrilled he wanted it back in the divorce. It was a white canvas with three black dots. I mean, what the hell is that?"

He chuckled. "Maybe the dots represent something."

"Yeah, like the boredom that was my marriage. Like the apathy of my husband toward me."

"What do you mean, Car? How could anyone be apathetic around you?"

She smiled even though she felt like crying on the inside. "I think that Preston chose to date me because I looked good on the outside. Because I was the perfect package of what a trophy wife should look like. To be honest, I don't think he ever really knew a damn thing about me." She was on a roll now and couldn't stop the words coming out of her mouth even if she wanted. "He didn't know my favorite band or the fact that I really like beer. And he definitely didn't know that I like extra cheese and anchovies on my pizza." She touched Jasper's chest. "One time I told him that I liked anchovies and he said we couldn't ever have them in the condo because they were too salty and we should strive to maintain a low-sodium diet."

She ran a hand through her hair. "I didn't see you for over ten years and you remembered. You remember everything about me, don't you?"

Staying silent, Jasper nodded.

"One time I tried to talk to Preston about my dad. He listened. He said he was sorry. But he never mentioned it again. My dysfunctional family would mar our perfect image. And it made me less amazing."

He kissed her then, out of the blue. Deeply, tenderly. When he pulled back, he framed her face in his hands. "Didn't he ever tell you how beautiful you are?"

"No," she whispered.

"Didn't he tell you that you are the most amazing person?"

She shook her head.

"Didn't he thank God every single day for the mere fact of getting to be with you?"

Beyond moved by his words, a single tear fell from her eye.

"Because getting to be with you, Carissa Blackwell, is the biggest gift in the world. He should have realized what he had."

She sniffled and moved her hands so they lay around his. "You see me differently than everyone else."

"Lucky me." And then he kissed her again.

Overwhelmed, Carissa hugged him tightly. Then she pulled herself together, pushed back and smiled up at him. "I'm sorry. I don't really know where all of that came from."

A crease formed on Jasper's forehead. "You don't have to apologize for feeling things. Not with me anyway. I think you needed to get that off your chest. I think you've been through a bad time and you're healing. Keeping it all bottled up will never help you."

"You know what will help me?" she asked with a sparkle in her eye.

"For me to go to Chicago and beat the snot out of your ex-husband?"

She let out a little chuckle. "Well, actually, yes. But I was thinking since the airport is closed already we could go back inside and do more salsa dancing."

He kissed her, grabbed her hand, and together they returned to the dance floor.

Jasper had learned to salsa dance from a girlfriend back in college, but he'd never enjoyed it as much as he had tonight. Even though Carissa was not the world's greatest dancer, she did try. And watching her eyes lock onto his lower region was definitely a turn-on.

Who wouldn't be turned on by her, though? Well, apparently her husband. What an asshat, he thought. But it wasn't the first time he'd thought it. After what she'd shared tonight, Jasper was truly shocked. He was also saddened. To know that she'd been disappointed first by her father and then by her husband made his blood boil. Especially when he knew how amazing she was.

Growing up together, he'd always gravitated toward her. And not only because of her looks. Even before they'd dated, he'd call her up when he wanted to do something fun. She'd always been up to try something new. Kayaking, fishing, laser tag, you name it. So it was interesting to learn that her husband hadn't been on the daring side.

Although after everything he'd learned this weekend, he got why she'd married him. Her father had been unreliable, and even though Preston sounded dull as hell, at least he'd been consistent and dependable. Maybe a little too consistently boring, but still.

He returned his attention to his dancing partner, who was laughing and throwing her hair back and finally getting the hang of the dance. They weren't out on the dance floor for too long before the sensual movements and close proximity of their moving bodies started to remind him of another intimate act.

When the music slowed down and they were swaying together, he saw the same look in her eyes as he was feeling. "Do you want to get out of here?" he asked softly, lingering a moment to nip at her earlobe.

"You have no idea," she said back, trailing her hand just a little too low to be appropriate in public.

Jasper settled their bar tab and they made their way to his car and then back to Bayside. Driving was difficult, though, as Carissa was dancing her fingers up his thigh. At every stoplight, he'd lean over and take her mouth until some driver laid on their horn.

As they neared his condo, Carissa leaned toward her window. "I'm still surprised they put apartments in Bayside."

"They're condos, actually, and my company did them.

We're really trying to revitalize Bayside. It's not a very large building. I actually just made a deal with someone for more apartments, retail space—"

"Jasper, that's great and I totally want to hear all about it. But um, right now…" She nodded toward the condos and squeezed his leg. "I really want you to take me inside."

He looked down at her hand. He had to hold back a growl from escaping. "Yes, ma'am."

Jasper had never parked his car so fast. After they left the underground garage, Jasper punched in a code on a keypad to let them into the elevator, which was thankfully empty at this hour because he couldn't hold himself back from attacking her. She plastered herself to his strong body as his arms went around her and his lips feasted on hers.

He didn't even remember the elevator stopping or walking to his condo at the end of the hallway. But clearly they must have made it because the next thing he knew, the door to his condo was flung open, banging against the wall, as their mouths stayed fused together.

"Before I forget, I had so much fun today," she said, ripping her mouth from his. But the rise and fall of her full chest, along with the pure lust shining in her eyes, told him she wasn't in for a long conversation.

Suddenly, their hands were everywhere at once. He kicked the door shut and felt her fingers running along the waistband of his pants. He couldn't stop his intake of breath at the feel of her fingers grazing along the sensitive skin of his stomach.

The moonlight was streaming through the large picture window, shining on her thick hair. He ran his hands through her locks, which allowed him to angle her head just where he wanted it. He plunged his tongue inside her mouth. She met him kiss for kiss, nip for nip, touch for touch.

He took her mouth again as she tugged at his pants.

While the kiss started off as steamy as the thing she was doing with her fingers, it soon turned soft and lingering. When he was done feasting on her lips—although, he didn't think he would ever really be done—he trailed his lips down the long column of her throat. She gasped, wrapping her arms tightly around him. Ah, still responsive there.

She pulled his shirt and he helped by reaching his arms over his head. With his shirt removed, her gaze swept over the length of him and she let out an appreciative sound.

It dawned on him that they were barely inside his condo. But the way her hands were all over his chest, igniting the skin everywhere she touched, made it abundantly clear they weren't going to make it all the way back to his bedroom. "Couch?" he asked with a strangled voice.

"Sure," she said, nipping at his bottom lip. But then she pulled him toward her roughly. Jasper lost his balance and they both fell to the hard floor. Luckily, he broke her fall, landing on his back with Carissa plastered on top of him.

She didn't waste any time. Her mouth was greedy as it devoured every inch of skin she could reach. Jasper felt helpless in the best possible way. He simply ran his hands over her curvy body as she had her way with him. When she pushed back and removed both her lacy top and the equally lacy red bra she wore underneath, Jasper's mouth went dry.

Damn, how could she be even more beautiful now than when they were teenagers?

"You're—" he began to say, but stopped when she put a finger to his lips.

"Shhh. Don't talk. Just touch me. Touch me everywhere."

Jasper was fine taking orders. Especially sexy orders that came from a half-naked woman straddling him.

They continued kissing, touching, caressing each other as the light from the moon made its way to their spot on the floor. Somehow she managed to shuck out of her jeans. He took advantage of the time to remove his own pants and boxer briefs. When she turned back and saw that he was completely undressed, a slow, seductive smile spread over her face. A strand of hair fell over her eye and she pushed all of it back. Then she leaned down, positioning her body flush with his. The feel of skin on skin was beyond heady. She kissed him deeply, their tongues mingling.

Everything felt so damn good. She was moving her body over his, teasing him with a preview of what was about to happen. He could feel the warmth at her center, a reminder that he needed to take care of safety first.

Flinging his arm out to the side, he quickly located his pants. It took another minute to work his wallet out of the pocket and retrieve the condom he'd just replaced that morning.

"Thanks," she said.

"Of course." And then he took her lips again.

"Carissa," he moaned as he flipped their positions. Looking down at her, he almost chuckled. Jasper would have never guessed the weekend was going to be like this back on Friday afternoon. But what an amazing surprise.

She reached between his legs, wrapping her fingers around his length. The gesture made him buck up in surprise. She offered him a cocky smile. But he got the advantage back when he took her breast in his mouth, sucking and licking her swollen nipple. By the time he moved to the other breast, offering the same attention, Carissa was moaning. He knew neither of them could wait another minute longer.

Positioning himself between her legs, Jasper took one more long look at her before entering her, filling her completely. Matching gasps escaped their mouths and Jasper leaned forward to catch her moan. Her nails sank into his back and she brought her knees up, urging him to move.

Jasper tried to stay slow, tried to use long, languid thrusts. But it didn't take long for him to become intoxicated by the feel of her. Surrounded by her sweet scent, the soft touch of her skin and the sensation of her limbs firmly locked around him, he was helpless to do anything but give in.

He pushed them harder and higher. Their voices rose together as they both panted out their pleasure. Before long, he began to see stars. Jasper knew the moment she came and pressed his mouth to hers. With three final strokes, he joined her on the other side of ecstasy.

Jasper wasn't sure how long they lay there together, their limbs a tangled mass on the cold, unyielding floor. Their rough inhalations eventually died down and the room was filled with the contented sound of deep, heavy breathing.

When he knew he could move again, he began running his hands up and down her arms. She let out a pleased murmur. Opening her eyes, she met his stare with those penetrating gray eyes.

Jasper knew he could get lost in her eyes. Knew he could, and probably would, spend hours obsessing over this night. That's why he decided to keep it light.

"So welcome back to my place."

She laughed. "Nice to be here sober this time. Impressive entryway. Nice floor." She patted the wood.

"I'm glad I went with the hardwood. Of course, I didn't exactly have *this* in mind when I picked it. Had I known you'd show up again, I might've chosen a softer material."

"Maybe next time I can see the bedroom."

"Got hardwood in there, too."

She punched his shoulder and he leaned down for another long, sultry kiss. When he lifted his head, he noticed an expression on her face he'd never seen before. "What's going on in there?" he asked, tapping a finger against her head.

"You don't want to know."

"Probably not. But tell me anyway."

She bit her lip, stalling for time. When she finally spoke, she said, "I'm happy."

Her words did more to his ego than closing any business deal ever could. His eyebrow arched. "Really?"

"It's been a long time since I've said that. So thank you."

"Come on." He reared back onto his feet, grabbed her hands, and pulled her up.

"Jasp, what are you—"

He cut her off with a long kiss. When her body went soft, he scooped her up in his arms, satisfied at the sound of a very feminine sigh.

"I think it's time for a proper tour."

She cupped his cheek in a gesture that was sweet and somewhat out of character. "I'd like that. Hopefully the tour will start with the bedroom."

"Honey, it starts, stays and ends with the bedroom."

She laughed. "My kind of tour."

With that, he walked them into the bedroom, where they remained the rest of the night. All of those questions and insecurities staying outside the partially closed door. For now.

Chapter Ten

Time is flying, my friends. It's officially autumn, a time for bonfires, football games and candy corn. Apparently, it's also a time for new relationships, because Carissa Blackwell and Jasper Dumont have become inseparable. Just like old times. Hopefully, nothing can break them up again…

Carissa wasn't superstitious, but she was cautious. And realistic. So to say that her life had been perfect lately was definitely a bit overzealous. However, even she could admit that things had been going well.

September ended and she couldn't believe it was October already. Then again, she'd been so busy it wasn't that surprising.

She'd catered the bridal shower for Mrs. Reynolds's daughter to fantastic reviews. When she was asked to cater the wedding in January, Carissa thought she would weep. But she kept it together, stayed professional.

Despite the Bayside Blogger's continued references to her in her daily column, no one in Bayside seemed to care much. And she hadn't been questioned again on her references or experience. She was actually making a name for herself.

In the meantime, she'd picked up other jobs here and there, including her first ladies' night at Victoria's Attic. It had gone well and she already had a ton of ideas for the next one. She definitely put extra energy into that event since it was still her only repeat customer. That meant a lot to her.

Other than work, she'd been hanging with Elle and Riley. It was nice to have girlfriends to go to the movies with, have drinks, share laughs. She realized that friends were another thing she'd missed during her marriage. All of her "friends" had been Preston's, and even when they did hang out it was to attend charity events and fund-raisers. Also, just like Preston, they'd been dullsville.

And then there was the opposite of dullsville. There was Jasper. Talk about excitement and fun and spontaneity. She sat back on the porch steps where she was waiting for him. He'd called earlier to say he had a big surprise for her.

She bit her lip as she considered. Two weeks ago he'd taken her to a concert where they'd danced and sung along all night. Last week he'd surprised her with a really amazing bottle of red wine. She licked her lips just remembering it.

But he wasn't the only one with the surprises. She baked for him constantly. The way to a man's heart really was through his stomach. She'd even come up with a recipe where she used The Brewside's coffee in a decadent chocolate cookie. His response to that one had been orgasmic. Literally, she thought with a grin, remembering the end of that particular night. It was safe to say their relationship was going well.

Their relationship. She sucked in a quick breath of air. When had it become a relationship? Maybe somewhere between the passionate nights they spent together and all of the places they went together.

They had a standing date every morning at The Brewside. She had to admit she looked forward to that short time with him. They'd have coffee, share a goody from the bakery display and talk about what they each had planned for the day. Then he'd buy a beverage for his assistant and they'd both go on their way.

What a simple routine. Simple, but meaningful. And exactly like a relationship. Her stomach tensed as a wave of panic hit her in the gut.

She wasn't ready for a relationship. She'd only been divorced a matter of months. She needed to wait... Carissa let that thought trail off as she chewed on a fingernail. Preston sure hadn't waited for the ink to dry. Besides, it wasn't like there was some definite amount of time set in stone that one had to wait before embarking on a new relationship again.

Relationship. There was that word again. That word that evoked feelings of trust and hope and love. All emotions that could be taken away in a flash. Isn't that what happened with Preston? Wasn't that what had happened with her father?

It seemed like every time she opened her heart to a man it was crushed. Well, except for one man. In that case, she'd done the crushing. And what if this time around, Jasper broke her heart? Being disappointed by Preston was one thing. But she didn't know if she could bounce back from Jasper.

Speak of the devil. Jasper's car came to a stop at the end of the driveway just then. He hopped out and walked to her, looking like some kind of Greek god out for a late-afternoon stroll.

"Hey, gorgeous," he called.

She stood up and closed the distance between them. "Are we in a relationship?" she blurted.

Jasper worked hard to make sure his smile didn't fade. It wasn't the words that came out of her mouth that caused it to falter, but more the emotion behind her question. The way her face tensed up and her eyes narrowed.

He'd loved getting closer to Carissa since she'd returned to town. While there were so many familiar things he remembered from high school, they'd both grown up. For better or worse, they were different people, and learning all of the new Carissa quirks was fun and exciting, too.

But in all of that time of reconnecting, Jasper had not been oblivious to the fact that she had issues to work through. He tried to give her the space to do that. Today, he wasn't sure where this question had come from, so he proceeded with caution.

"Well," he began, "we seem to spend a lot of time together."

She nodded. "True, but not all the time. I mean, we each have our own friends."

He was bemused by her statement. "Of course we do. We have some friends in common, too."

"Well, yeah. But what else?"

He considered this for a moment. "We're sleeping together."

"But that doesn't always translate to a relationship," she said.

"Maybe not, but I don't sleep with more than one person at a time."

"Me neither. So…we're sleeping together and we hang out a lot and…" She trailed off, looking down at the ground.

"Carissa," Jasper said, using his index finger to guide her head back up so she would look him in the eyes. "We're in a relationship." Then he drew her to him and kissed the living daylights out of her.

When they came up for air, he had to take a moment to collect himself. He'd kissed this woman thousands of times over the years and yet each time felt like the first.

"Car, we don't have to be in a super-serious, heading-to-the-altar kind of relationship. But to answer your initial question, yes, we are in a relationship."

"I want to build my company," she said, her lips swollen from their kiss.

Jasper raised an amused eyebrow at this statement. "Who's stopping you? And anyway, I have something to show you that might help with that company."

It was her turn to raise her brow. "Oh really, is this my surprise?"

"Yep." He leaned over and kissed her again. "Want to take a ride?"

He started walking toward the car before she could say yes. Carissa reached for his hand and tugged him back to her. Then she pressed her lips to his, gently, reverently. The softness of the kiss hit him right in the gut.

"Not that I mind," he said when they were done. "But what was that for?"

"'Cause that's what people do when they're in a relationship." He couldn't stop a grin from spreading, and then she punched him in the arm. "But not a super-serious relationship."

He wisely changed the subject as they got in his car and drove away. "How's Aunt Val?"

"Great, as usual. She's in Spain now."

Jasper drove through the center of town and out toward the outskirts. "No doubt she's drinking too much sangria and causing all kinds of raucous trouble."

"No doubt," Carissa agreed.

They listened to the radio, both singing along to a song that was popular during their senior year of high school, until Jasper turned onto a tree-lined street.

"Oak Avenue," she said. "What are we doing here? You want to go shopping at Victoria's Attic?" She wiggled her eyebrows. "Because I wouldn't mind that."

"I think I'll leave the shopping to you." Jasper threw the car into Park and hopped out. Then he came to her side and opened her door. Carissa got out, gave another look at Victoria's Attic, and then arched her eyebrow in question.

"Spill. What's going on?"

His grin was fast and devastating. "I have made one of the best deals of my career." He made a sweeping arm gesture to include the building.

Carissa waited patiently. "More details, please. Because right now I'm looking at a big building."

"A big building that won't be here next month."

Jasper could barely contain his excitement. He'd been working day and night on this deal. There were a lot of moving parts, a lot of people this affected.

The board had been putting on the pressure for him to accept the adult entertainment shop, but it had felt wrong. When he first started dropping hints he was thinking of a bookstore, he'd gotten some expected pushback.

But he'd kept working on the proposal until the board had seen the benefit to Bayside. Jasper was offering multiple businesses and more jobs to the local economy than one racy shop. His plan housed a bookstore with both the latest publications and a nod to his favorite high school hangout with a robust used section. There would be an adjacent event space. And his favorite part, a café.

All day, he'd been dying to tell Carissa. A café would offer her steady employment, yet she could still do her catering jobs. She could set her own hours, hire an employee or two.

Carissa was taking in the building. "Wh…where's it going? Oh no, the sexy adult shop?"

"No lingerie. I'm tearing down the building," he said gleefully. "Gone, kaput, dust and rubble."

"What's going to happen to the businesses here? Victoria's Attic and that liquor store," she asked in a quiet voice.

"Gone."

"Are they moving somewhere else?"

That was an odd question. "Not that I know of. Victoria's Attic is closing permanently. See?" He pointed to a sign on the door.

Carissa walked closer to read it. Final Sale, Everything Must Go, Jasper read from where he stood.

She whirled back to Jasper. "They're closing?"

"Yep," he said proudly. "You are looking at the future home of the Bookworm."

She responded with a blank expression.

He grabbed her hands and squeezed. "Car, remember that old used bookstore we used to hang out at all the time in high school? I'm going to open one just like it."

"Sure. But what do you know about running a bookstore?"

He chuckled. "Not a lot. But I won't be running it. I'll find someone to do that. I know it's risky. But I think I can make this work. New and used books, access to online sites, rooms for students to meet and study, and a whole event space next door. Plus, the best part." He paused for dramatic effect. "A café that serves killer food."

He waited, holding his breath. But she didn't say anything. Didn't jump into his arms and kiss him. Didn't say thank you.

Jasper dropped his hands. "But first we need to do a massive renovation because the structure is a mess."

She remained silent, so he started rambling. "This idea met with some resistance at first, but now it's made everyone happy."

Stepping back, she aimed him with a level gaze. "Everyone?"

He wasn't sure what was going on in her head. "What's wrong, Car?"

Shaking her head, she stepped to him, placed a palm against his cheek and offered a small smile. "I'm happy for you, Jasp. This is an interesting idea and I definitely like it more than that adult shop." She scrunched up her nose.

"But?" he guessed.

"I don't mean to rain on your parade or make this about me, but I'm just a little disappointed."

Not what he'd been expecting her to say. "Babe, why?"

She glanced back at Victoria's Attic. "They're my only regular client. I know that's small potatoes compared to what you can do here."

Ah, he understood now. Plus, he hadn't told her the best part yet. "Your work is not small potatoes in any scenario. I had thought about the ladies' nights. I offered Victoria a lease on a different location. A better location, actually."

"You did?" She reached for his hands again, hope springing up in her eyes.

He nodded. "Turns out, she's ready to retire. I'm really sorry about that, Car."

"Well, you tried, at least. I'm sure I'll find other regulars."

His heart rate picked up at the opportunity. "I know you will. In fact, I might be able to help with that."

She smiled. "You're going to throw a party every Friday and hire me to cater it?" Her smile faded. "Actually, that sounds exactly like something you would do. I think that kind of investment might be more than my non-super-serious-relationship partner should have to endure on my behalf."

"I have a better idea. I want you to run the café." He gently turned her shoulders so she was staring at the building. "You would have total control. You pick the name, set the hours, the prices, everything. Plus, there's enough room to have a full working kitchen. You can run your catering business out of this location."

She spun back to him. "Are you serious, Jasp? Like really serious?"

He held his breath. "Yep."

Carissa was quiet for a long time as myriad emotions crossed her face. Her brain looked like it was running at full capacity. Finally, a huge grin lit up her face. "Jasper, ohmigod!"

She threw herself into his arms and kissed every inch of his face she could find. "Thank you, thank you, thank you. I won't let you down. Ohmigod," she repeated. "Would I really have full control?"

"Absolutely. I know even less about catering and cafés than I know about bookstores. And I know I said you could name it yourself, but I do have an idea."

She paused. "You do?"

"Make this an extension of your catering company. I know you wanted to add photos of some of your food on your website. This would be a real-life sample of what Save the Day Catering can do. The Save the Day Café," he finished, gesturing grandly at the building.

Her lips pursed as she considered. "You know, I actually like that. And while breakfast food is always appealing, Bayside already has The Brewside—"

"Exactly," Jasper interrupted. "That's why I was thinking you should stick to the lunchtime crowd. We don't have many lunch places."

"Well, that's something to think about."

His excitement grew. "And you could even get a van and make local deliveries. I know a great company that can help with that."

She held her hands up. "Whoa there, tiger. Let's just give me a second to take this all in."

He backed off. "Of course. Sorry. So," he said, offering her his best grin. "You're not mad that I took away your regular client?"

"I think you've more than made up for it." She kissed him soundly. "Now I have so many ideas in my head. Wow, my own café."

"Let's go grab dinner and celebrate," he said.

Jasper couldn't feel any happier. Finally, he'd come up with a business deal all on his own. Something different from his parents and an out-of-the-box concept for Dumont Incorporated that would be good for the bottom line and for Bayside.

Not to mention, he was able to help Carissa in the process. Show her that he was very different from the carefree, party-loving boy from high school. Proving that he'd worked his butt off all of these years.

He was good enough.

"There are so many decisions to make," Carissa said. "I can't wait to start making lists and coming up with ideas."

As they walked back to the car, he added, "I have a ton of suggestions for you. I've already called in some favors and lined up a couple meetings for you."

Jasper was so thrilled she'd gone for this idea that he missed her frown.

* * *

Carissa stared at her laptop, mouth hanging open, as she read over the Bayside Blogger's latest column.

Golden boy Jasper Dumont is opening a bookstore with a café. And who is going to be running this café, you ask? Shocker! His girlfriend, the recently returned Carissa Blackwell. Guess Carissa has moved from one man to another in record time. Not that I blame her. I'd love to be taken care of by Jasper Dumont, too...

She shut the lid of her laptop and pursed her lips. What did the Bayside Blogger mean by that?

She wasn't moving from one man to another. Although the ink had barely dried on her divorce papers and she was in a relationship with Jasper. And now they were going to be working together, too.

But she'd work her butt off to make this business succeed. In turn, Jasper would turn a good profit. Needing a pep talk, Carissa reminded herself that she had majored in business at Northwestern. And she was already well on her way to setting up her own catering company. She could do this. Jasper or no Jasper.

Besides, she had to admit she liked having a partner. Someone to bounce thoughts and ideas off. Of course, sometimes she did wish Jasper would tone it down a tad. As she was quickly learning, he could get a little too enthusiastic at times. Maybe that eagerness manifested in a bit of a controlling way, but the café was going to be hers. Jasper was only helping.

Then, why did she get a sinking feeling in the pit of her stomach every time she thought about it?

"You look like you're deep in thought," Elle said, breaking into Carissa's thoughts as she took a seat at the table in

The Brewside where Carissa currently had papers, note-books, her computer and two empty coffee cups spread out.

"Yes, no." Carissa shook her head. "It's nothing. Just a lot of details. What's going on?"

Elle looked great. She was wearing a light green dress that brought out her equally green eyes. Her brown hair was pulled back in a neat ponytail and her skin was glowing. Ah, to be in love.

"Taking a break from the gallery. I needed caffeine." Tony called out her name. "And there it is." Elle grabbed her drink and returned to the table. "What's all this?"

"Just ideas about the Save the Day Café. I'm meeting Jasper in a little bit to go over some things."

"I do love that name." Elle smiled.

"Me, too. Although it was actually Jasper's idea."

"You two have been working hard the last two weeks."

"What can I say? Jasper works fast. Demolition on the building happens next week."

"Wow, that is fast. How is it working with him?"

"Fine, I guess."

"You guess?"

Carissa couldn't stop her thoughts from returning to the last line of the Bayside Blogger's recent column. *I'd love to be taken care of by Jasper Dumont, too.*

That's not what this was. Right? It was a business arrangement. A business arrangement that he'd given to her without so much as a second thought. A business arrangement organized by her boyfriend.

She met Elle's curious gaze. There was a twinkle in her eye that was unmistakable. Why did people in love always want everyone else to be in love, too?

"What's with you today?" Carissa asked, ignoring Elle's original question. She pointed at her instead. "I can't put my finger on it but something is definitely different."

A coy grin spread across Elle's face. "I don't know what you're talking about." She touched her cheek. "I'm exactly the same as I was yesterday." She flipped her hand around.

"You are being so weird…" Carissa trailed off when the light caught the large diamond ring on Elle's finger. As soon as Carissa realized what she was looking at, Elle's smile became even brighter. If that was possible.

"Ohmigod, Elle." Even Carissa could hear the fluttery tone of her voice. "You're engaged!"

"Cam proposed last night." Elle's dimples winked as she thrust her hand forward. Carissa got a better look at the round diamond flanked by two pear-shaped emeralds set in what appeared to be a vintage band.

"This is gorgeous," Carissa squealed.

Elle studied the ring herself. "Cam said the emeralds reminded him of my eyes."

Carissa's heart gave a little flutter. "Did you have any idea?"

"None." Elle sat back. "I mean, we'd sort of danced around the topic. We spent the weekend at his cabin. We'd just finished dinner and were watching the sun set over the lake. I didn't even realize it, but next thing I know, he's down on one knee."

"Oh, Elle, I'm so happy for you guys." And she was. Elle and Cam were the perfect couple in Carissa's opinion. After their initial rocky reunion, Carissa and Cam had spent some quality time together, thanks to Jasper and Elle. She realized Cam only wanted the best for his little brother.

"It was so romantic. He asked my dad and everything. We told his parents this morning."

"I bet Mrs. Dumont was beside herself with happiness."

Elle laughed. "I think she already has the entire wedding planned. Plus, I heard her mention grandchildren as we were leaving. So watch out."

Carissa tilted her head. "For what?"

Elle extended a finger in Carissa's direction. "You're next."

"Next for…" Oh. She finally caught on to Elle's meaning. "I just got divorced, Elle. I have no plans to remarry in the immediate future."

Elle waved a hand. "I know that. But you and Jasper are really moving forward with gusto." She indicated all the papers on the table. "You're even working together."

Carissa's pulse picked up. "We're not working together exactly. I mean, I guess we are in the beginning phase."

"Who would have imagined all of this when you returned to Bayside?"

"Right." Her palms were sweating. She wiped them on her jeans. Who would have thought that when she returned to Bayside seeking her independence she would have jumped right back into a relationship with her high school boyfriend and accepted a job from him?

"You okay, Car?" Elle's eyes held worry.

Carissa felt horrible. This was Elle's day. She didn't need to steal her thunder with the dark thoughts circulating in her head. She forced a smile. A smile she really didn't feel on the inside.

"I'm fine. Just tired. And blissfully happy for you. We should celebrate."

"I haven't told Riley yet, so no celebrations until I do. And mum's the word."

Carissa pretended to lock her lips and Elle giggled.

"I have to get back to the gallery. But I'm glad I ran into you. Cam's telling Jasper the news now so next time you see him, tell him he'll make a lovely flower girl in the wedding."

Despite the anxiety Carissa was suddenly feeling, she smiled. "Will do."

An hour later, Carissa was seated in the waiting room outside Jasper's office. His assistant, Sherry, made sure she had a bottle of water.

"He'll just be about five minutes longer. The conference call he's on ran late," Sherry said.

"No problem. I'll just play around on my phone." Carissa grabbed her cell out of her purse.

She scanned through her emails but she wasn't really giving them her undivided attention. Instead, she couldn't stop thinking about, well, everything. Elle engaged, Jasper, the café, her independence, moving to Bayside, Mrs. Dumont wanting grandkids, her ex. Everything was a huge jumble.

As she clicked from email to email, she wound up on the Bayside Blogger's site again. "Damn gossip," Carissa said under her breath.

"What was that?" Sherry asked.

"Nothing. Sorry."

Embarrassed, Carissa glued her eyes to the screen as she perused another article. No mention of Elle and Cam's engagement yet. That was good news.

There was an item about Tony from The Brewside. Apparently, he'd gone on a date last night. Carissa kept scanning until she froze. Two mentions in one day. New record. She refrained from rolling her eyes and read the item instead.

Remember when the Dumont caterer ran out of the end-of-summer party last month? Carissa Blackwell helpfully stepped in, beginning her new career as Bayside's favorite caterer. And we've all enjoyed her culinary masterpieces since. Well, I've just learned that it was no coincidence. Jasper Dumont may have had a hand in getting his high school love the gig...

Carissa stared at the screen. She had no idea what to say or even how to feel at this new development.

How did Jasper have a hand in that night? Jasper was a good guy. Maybe the best she knew. But to set up that opportunity for her, well, it did reek of control.

Carissa searched her memory. The caterer had had a family emergency that night. How in the world could Jasper have orchestrated that? It was impossible.

Only nothing was impossible for a Dumont.

If the Blogger was right and Jasper meddled in her business then everything she'd been working so hard for hadn't been her own doing. She hadn't shaped her future. Jasper had. For the second time today, her palms began to sweat.

"Carissa," Sherry called. "Mr. Dumont will see you now."

With a heavy heart, Carissa rose and walked into Jasper's office.

Jasper loosened his tie. He'd already shed his jacket. He'd been looking forward to this meeting with Carissa all day. Before he could get to it, he'd been bombarded with meetings and conference calls. And one very happy lunch with his brother.

Carissa walked in looking sinfully amazing in tight jeans, a red blouse and a black blazer. Her hair was pulled back, revealing her long neck and accentuating her big gray eyes.

He crossed to her. "Hey, babe. Have you heard the news yet?"

She glanced down at the phone she was holding in a death grip. "Uh, yeah."

"Isn't it awesome?"

She met his eyes with confusion. "Awesome?" Then her face quickly changed, softened. "Oh, do you mean the news about your future sister-in-law?" Her normal smile finally surfaced.

"I had no idea Cam was planning that. He kept it under lock and key."

"Are you happy?"

He was beyond ecstatic. It had been a big year for his brother and seeing him with Elle left no doubt that he'd found his soul mate. "More than I can say. Words are inadequate."

"I'm thrilled for them." Her smile faded. "Jasp, I have to talk to you about something." She held out her phone.

Curious, he took it from her. He quickly read over the Bayside Blogger's article, clicked the phone off and looked Carissa in the eye.

"Is this true?" she asked, taking the phone and shoving it in her purse. "Did you really have a hand in me helping at your mother's party?"

He considered for a moment. She was never supposed to find out about that. No one was. Which didn't sound great when he put it that way. But he'd only been trying to help her.

Now was the time he needed to come clean. "Yes, it's true."

She deflated, slipping into one of the chairs around a small table in the corner of his office.

"How?" she asked. "I thought there had been a family emergency."

"There had. Only not a super bad one. Jasmine, the chef, found out her daughter broke her arm. I was snagging snacks in the kitchen when she took the call. She said her husband was there and she would work the party first and then leave at the first chance."

"But you convinced her to go early."

He nodded. "Yep."

"Jasper, what were you thinking? What if I had been late to the party? What if I hadn't stepped up to fill in that night? Your mother's party would have been ruined."

He followed her example and took a seat across from her. "I had complete faith in you. I still do."

Any remaining anger drained from her face. She reached out and cupped his cheek. "Thank you for that. But Jasp, you can't keep creating opportunities for me. That's not right."

"It was nothing. Just one night."

Her hand fell. "What about this café? Be honest. Did you do all of that for me, too?"

"No," he said adamantly, and meant it. "I really think this is a good addition to the town. Maybe I bucked tradition and good business practice by going straight to you for the café." He offered his best smile. "But you're just so damn good. You deserve this."

She bit her lip. "I haven't earned it."

"You will."

He watched as she wiped her palms on her legs. "That's a lot of pressure, Jasp. Plus, you have to let me do this myself. My way."

He leaned forward. "I am. The café is yours."

She let out a small laugh. "You own it."

"But you're running it. You make all the decisions. This is your baby."

Carissa frowned. "That's all I want. To be independent. To take care of myself." She cracked her knuckles. "In fact, I was thinking that maybe I could, I don't know, invest some of my own money into the café."

He glanced up at her, surprise evident on his face. "Do you have money to invest?"

"Not much," she admitted. "But I did get a small settlement from the divorce. Because my catering business took off faster than anticipated and I'm not paying rent at my aunt's cottage, I have a little to play with."

He nodded, apparently deep in thought. "Car, I don't want you to waste your money."

"It wouldn't be a waste. It would be an investment into our joint business."

And it would give her some semblance of control. The independence she craved. Jasper got it.

"I understand that. Listen, why don't we table all of this for now and talk about the café? The lawyer will be here soon for us to fill out the paperwork."

She nodded, but Jasper sensed something was still off. He didn't understand what bothered her so much. He was only trying to take care of her.

He put everything else out of his mind as they went over some legal documents. When the official business was over, he brought the conversation back around to the café.

"I have some ideas for the logo," Carissa said. "I was going to ask Elle to work up a couple options for me."

Jasper crossed to his desk and returned with a large poster board.

"What's that?" Carissa asked.

"I had our art department come up with a couple of possibilities." He showed her the board.

She peered at them and then met his gaze. "These aren't really what I was thinking."

"That's okay. They can make more for you. Although I think this one really pops." He pointed at his favorite logo. "It would look great up on a sign. Don't you think?"

"Well, I…"

"Oh, before I forget. I found a great web designer. He can fix up what you have now."

She sat up straight. "I made that website myself. I'm proud of it."

Yikes. He needed to tread lightly. Jasper was aware that sometimes he got a little overzealous. "You did a really great job. But now that you're expanding, you need to get something a little more professional."

"I don't even know this guy."

"He's a friend of a friend, but he's worked on a ton of my clients' websites. You'll like him."

A red blush was working its way up her neck. "I'm sure I will but that's not the point."

"Oh, one more thing," Jasper continued. "I've been thinking about your menus."

She sat up straighter. "The menus for my catering business?"

He nodded. "I have some small suggestions."

Carissa rose, paced to the window and returned to the table. "You have suggestions for the menus that I created? Me, the caterer? The area where I actually know exactly what I'm doing and that has nothing to do with your café?"

He observed her for a few moments. He could see that she was agitated. But he didn't understand why. He wanted this business to succeed for her.

"Like I said, I have small, tiny, minuscule suggestions." Another thought popped into his head. "Oh, and about the hours you set—"

She slapped her hands on the table between them. "Jasper, stop it."

His attention flew to her. The blush now covered her face. Red cheeks, alert eyes that had turned a much darker shade of gray sat across the table from him. "Stop what?"

"You're trying to control me."

"No, I'm not. I'm trying to help you." Wasn't he?

"Help me? By making every single decision for me? By completely ignoring all of the things I want to do?"

"That's not what I'm doing," he said, defensiveness coating his words.

"Yes, it is, and I don't want to work this way. I don't want to live this way." Her lip trembled. "In fact, I already have lived this way. That's how I wound up back in Bayside."

Anger smacked him right in the gut at that comment. "Are you comparing me to your ex-husband?" Now he rose and met her strong gaze.

She looked away. "Yes, I am, because you're acting just like him. 'Do this, Carissa. Act this way, Carissa. Choose this logo, these hours, this menu, Carissa.'"

Jasper felt like she'd slapped him. How could she compare him to her ex? He was nothing like…

He couldn't even finish the thought. Instead, he glanced down at his notes. All of the ideas he had for the café. Maybe, well, maybe there were some controlling elements at play. But he was doing this out of the goodness of his heart. He wanted her to succeed.

He took a step toward her but she retreated farther away. "Car, don't you get why I'm doing all this?"

She shook her head slowly, her eyes darkening. "No, I don't think I do."

The intercom on his desk rang out and Sherry's voice filled the room. "Mr. Dumont, your lawyer is here."

Carissa ran her hands over her face. Jasper pressed the button on the intercom. "One minute, Sherry." He pinned her with a stare. "Why don't we just sign the papers and discuss the rest of this later?"

She stood in the middle of the room, frozen. Her beautiful face was set in a stoic expression. Jasper would give anything to read her thoughts at the moment.

"Car?" he asked.

"I can't do this, Jasp. I'm sorry."

With that, she gathered up her belongings and quickly

made her way to the door. She couldn't do what? The café or their relationship? In either case, panic rose in his chest as he watched her walk away with his heart in her hand. For the second time in his life.

Chapter Eleven

Bayside Blogger @BSBlogger
What recently reunited couple is ALREADY calling it quits?
Check my blog for the full story.

Carissa would have liked to spend the entire day in bed.
Instead, she was surrounded by copious amounts of chocolate chips, bags of flour and sugar, and more butter wrappers than one person ever needed to see in their lifetime.

Despite wanting to curl into a ball and mope for the next week—or year—she'd promised Riley she would bake cookies for the high school fund-raiser. She might have walked out on Jasper and the Save the Day Café, but she wouldn't let the kids down.

You'll just let Jasper down.

Every time she thought about Jasper, it felt like a very large, strong fist was gripping her heart and clenching it tightly. If she was honest with herself, she hadn't even felt this way at the demise of her marriage.

"It doesn't make sense," she said as she took a break from cookie-making and made a cup of tea.

She'd only been in a relationship with Jasper for a short time, and that relationship was supposed to be light and fun and not serious. She'd been with Preston for almost ten years. But when she compared the hurt from being cheated on to how she'd felt learning that Jasper had interfered in her life, the adultery took a back seat.

Because Jasper was so much more important to her than Preston had ever been. She guessed that the more you cared about someone, the harder it hurt. And it did hurt.

She knew she'd panicked. Pure and simple anxiety as she watched Jasper taking the reins of the café. Not to mention, learning that he'd interfered at his mother's party when she'd first arrived in town.

The frustrating part was that she knew it came from a good place with Jasper. Yet she still felt terrified. Carissa wanted her independence. She didn't want to rely on anyone. At some point yesterday, she'd been sitting in his office watching her life spin out of her control. Again.

It hadn't ended well the last time. As Jasper spit out names and possible vendors, she was transported back to her fancy Chicago condo with Preston.

"Of course I love it. But I just can't believe you bought an entire condo without consulting me."

"What are you talking about? I did this for you."

Hadn't Jasper said something similar yesterday? The problem was, she didn't want people to do things for her. She wanted—needed—to do them herself. Because if she didn't, she was following in her father's less-than-illustrious footsteps.

Now she'd run out on their business deal and had no idea where she stood with Jasper. She wished she could reflect on it more only... *Ding.* The oven timer reminded her why she didn't have time to dwell on the situation.

She took the sheet of chocolate chip cookies out of the

oven and shoved the next sheet in. After setting the timer, she turned back to the disaster she was currently calling a kitchen. There was no way she could get all of these cookies done in this one small kitchen, with one equally small oven, all by herself. What had she been thinking trying to open a café? Really, she was doing Jasper a favor by walking out on the contract signing.

"Stop thinking about Jasper. Focus."

Like that was going to happen. She so needed help. A knock sounded on the front door. As if on cue, Riley stood on the porch, wearing a darling outfit of skinny jeans, flats, a banana-yellow shirt, and a matching bright yellow scarf with lime-green polka dots around her neck.

"You look like something out of an old Audrey Hepburn movie," Carissa said by way of greeting.

"Why thank you." Riley beamed. "Not gonna lie. I've seen you look better." She eyed Carissa's outfit of pajama bottoms, ratty Northwestern T-shirt she'd had for a million years, and unbrushed hair piled on top of her head in a messy bun. If she had to guess, there was more than likely flour on her face and raw dough behind her ear.

Carissa let Riley inside. "Please tell me you're here to help. Please, please, please."

Riley put her hands up in front of her. "Whoa, girl. I've never seen you like this. Cool-as-a-cucumber Carissa never freaks out."

"Well, I've turned a new leaf. I'm in way over my head with these cookies."

Riley stood back and gave her a long once-over. "Cookies, I can help with. But…is there something else going on? You seem upset, and not just because of the baking."

Carissa was running her hands over her face, rubbing her tired eyes. In answer to Riley's question, she blurted,

"I think Jasper and I broke up." She hiccuped to hold in the tears that threatened.

Riley's face morphed from question to sympathy. She led Carissa to the couch and forced her to sit down. "I'm sorry. What happened? No, wait, we need Elle for both this conversation and the cookies. Give me a second." Riley whipped her phone out, then had a quick conversation with Elle. After, she brought Carissa's tea to her and made a cup for herself while they waited for Elle, who showed up fifteen minutes later.

"Good thing I just hired someone to help out at the gallery. Now, what's going on?" Elle said as she breezed in and sat on the other side of Carissa.

Flanked by her friends, Carissa sighed and then told them the entire story. She started all the way back in high school with her dad's antics and finished with her fight with Jasper in his office yesterday.

"It's like he didn't even see how controlling he was being. I know he was trying to help, but there was a point when I was sitting there that I thought about my future. And it resembled my dad's life," she finished in a quiet voice.

Riley raised a hand. "And there is the real issue."

"It really is, isn't it?" Carissa agreed. "It's not exactly the same scenario as my dad but there's this way in which I would be relying on someone else. It's Jasper's investment and it was all of his suggestions and ideas and none of mine. Plus, we're in a relationship. I would be dependent on him for everything."

Elle was tapping a finger to her lips as she considered. "On the one hand, it's kind of sweet. On the other, it's controlling and I get why you freaked."

Riley sat forward on the couch. "Where do you and Jasper stand now?"

The question set off a flurry of nerves in her stomach.

She shook her head. "I really don't know. I haven't talked to him." She clasped her hands together. "And I haven't heard from him, either. I think I really messed this up."

"You reacted honestly," Elle said. Her loyalty touched Carissa. "I'm surprised Jasper hasn't called or come over here."

"I'm not," Carissa admitted. She took a moment as her friends patiently waited for her explanation. "Jasper has always had an issue with being good enough. It started with his family and was exacerbated by our breakup after graduation. I basically rejected both the business deal he was so proud of and our relationship yesterday."

"That's not exactly what happened," Riley said.

"That's how he'll see it, though." Carissa knew him. He hadn't called because she'd hurt him.

Riley patted Carissa's hand. "I think you guys can work through this."

Could they? Carissa wasn't so sure. There was ten years of hurt and sadness and confusion between them. How could she be with someone who had the ability to get inside her so easily? Who could hurt her more than anyone else? Why would she allow that person in her life? Give them control over her emotions?

She was aware that both of her friends were eyeing her with concern. But she needed some time and space to work this out on her own. A master at changing the subject, she did just that.

"We have another problem," Carissa said. "A problem that might have a simpler solution." Elle narrowed her eyes and Riley leaned forward. "The cookies. One oven and mounds and mounds of raw dough. I need some help." She checked the clock on the TV. "With less than twenty-four hours to go."

"Oh, that," Riley said, swishing her hand through the

air as if this problem was nothing. "You got us. We can help bake."

Elle agreed. "I'll have to check in on the gallery through-out the day and go back to close up, but other than that, I'm here at your command. Put me to work."

Carissa let out a huge sigh of relief. "Thank you, thank you, thank you. And I'm sorry if I ruined whatever plans you had today."

"Don't be sorry," Riley said. "What do you say we put your independence issues and all things related to Jasper Dumont aside, and bake some damn cookies."

She couldn't help herself, Carissa grinned. "Now, that sounds like a plan."

"We are done," Riley said triumphantly.

Elle stretched her arms high over her head. "I can't be-lieve we did it. I'll be seeing flour and sugar and sprinkles in my dreams for weeks, but we did it. How many did we make total?"

"One million," Riley answered around the peanut butter cookie she had just shoved into her mouth.

"Not quite that many, but close," Carissa put in.

She looked at each of her friends. Two women who hadn't been in her life a couple months ago. Now she couldn't imagine what she'd do without them. They'd stayed up the entire night mixing recipes, laying out cookies on trays, baking, and repeating the whole process over and over again. They'd consumed a whole extra-large pizza, countless cups of coffee and more cookie dough than was probably wise.

"Thank you both so much. Literally, I couldn't have done this without you."

"You're welcome. Now we have two hours to spare before the fund-raiser begins. I'm going to go home, make out with Cam for a little bit, and then take a shower."

"Same," Riley said as she crossed to the door. "You know, except for the making out with Cam part. And I think I'm going to plan another outfit around this scarf. It's fabulous and totally got wasted being here with you two all night."

Carissa laughed as she fingered the bright yellow material. "This scarf *is* fabulous and so are you."

Riley beamed. "See you guys at the high school."

Carissa waved goodbye from the door. Exhausted, she stood there a moment, taking in the fresh air. The weather had finally cooled off and she could smell the beginnings of fall. Leaves were just beginning to turn their autumnal colors. She might even need a jacket today.

Carissa didn't know how long she stood like that, one foot on the porch. But luckily the sound of her phone pulled her back in. Then she saw the name of the caller. Mom. Carissa sighed. She was way too tired for this. But manners had her saying hello anyway.

"Carissa, sweetheart, it's so good to hear your voice." Her mother's bright, cheery voice was so familiar and comforting that it had her heart longing for a hug.

How long had it been since she'd seen her parents? Too long. But it was so hard to be around her father. Every time she was, he'd go on and on about trips he'd taken and new things he'd bought.

"It's good to hear your voice, too, Mom. What's up?" She poured herself a glass of orange juice as she listened to her mother.

There was silence on the line. Never a good thing when dealing with her mother. Finally, her mom offered that mother of a mother line that had kids shaking everywhere. "Anything you want to tell me?"

Where to start, Carissa thought.

Instead, she decided to play it cool. "What do you want to know?"

"I'd like to know why my only child moved back to Bayside and didn't so much as mention it to her loving mother?"

Carissa bit her lip. It did sound bad when it was put like that. "Who spilled the beans?"

"Aunt Val mentioned it in passing. The question is, why didn't you?"

She shrugged but then remembered her mother couldn't see her. "I don't know, Mom. I made the decision pretty fast. I had to get out of Chicago."

"Because of the divorce?"

"Because of the divorce and the fact that I didn't have anywhere to live or any money or any friends or a job."

"Oh, baby. Why didn't you come here? We would have taken care of you."

Just like you took care of me when Dad spent all your money? Like how you left me to figure out higher education on my own? Like when you ripped everything away that I'd known my entire life at a very scary time?

She didn't say any of that, though. Sometimes old wounds were better left alone. "I wanted to figure it out for myself."

She could practically hear her mother's smile. Even through the technology of cell phones, she sensed her mother relax. "You always were independent."

Not always. Not during her marriage. "Well, I'm back in Bayside, living at Aunt Val's place while she travels the globe."

"I do miss Bayside. What's it like to be back there again?"

An image of Jasper flashed into her mind. "It's kind of the same. But kind of different, too."

They talked about the town and some of her mother's old friends. Carissa tried to catch her up on everything. She also told her mom about her desire to be a caterer. But at her mom's expressed pleasure, she started fidgeting. So she changed the subject. "What's going on with you, Mom?"

"Nothing much on my end. Just working hard."

After her parents left Bayside in shame, they'd moved to Portland, Maine. Her mother had held a series of positions; most recently she was working at a day care center. Her mother's bubbly attitude and aptitude to deal with children made the job a perfect fit, in Carissa's opinion.

"Where's Dad?"

"He's playing golf with a friend of his."

Of course he was. Her mother was carrying the load and her dad was out playing eighteen holes. He'd probably also placed some friendly wager on the outcome, too. "Whose money is he using for his golf game?"

"Oh, Carissa. Stop worrying about us. You do that far too much. Your father and I, we're fine."

Fine? Fine? Carissa shook her head. How could her mother say that they were fine? Nothing about her father's spending habits and her mother's blind eye was fine.

Carissa took a deep breath. "Don't you think that Dad should pull his weight? Wouldn't it be good for him to get a job of his own and help support you?"

"Your father's a good man."

"But, but," she stuttered. "He's made so many mistakes."

"So have I," her mother replied simply. "I didn't marry your father and stay with him all of these years because he was perfect."

That comment had her freezing in place. "Why did you stay with him all this time?"

"Because I love him."

Four small words. Carissa wanted to protest. She wanted

more of an answer than that. After everything they'd been through as a couple, how could her mother love him?

"I know how it must seem to you, Carissa. Like your father constantly messed up business deals and jobs."

Uh, yeah, pretty much.

"You don't know the whole story," her mother continued. "There were times your father did mess up of his own accord. But other times, there were circumstances that were out of our control. I know you don't want to hear it, but sometimes your dad was the victim."

"But, Mom—"

"Not always," she was quick to finish. "Life isn't always black and white."

It didn't make sense and she had a feeling it never would. Like always, she dug deep within herself to separate the pain and confusion her father evoked and the love she had for her mother.

Then her mom said something that took her by complete surprise. "I'm sorry about what happened to your college money, Carissa. I'm so very sorry you had to get all of those jobs and work as hard as you did."

"I'm not." She realized for the first time she actually meant that.

There had been days where she'd worked early in the morning, gone to classes and study groups, and then finished her day at a different job. It had been hard, but it had also taught her so much.

Another realization hit. Before college, she'd been a pampered and sheltered teenager. Because of what she'd learned during that time at Northwestern, she was able to build her company today.

Her mother continued. "If it had been up to me, you would have floated into college on a cloud and lived in a protective bubble for four years." She let out a little laugh.

"I suppose all parents want that for their children. I didn't want you to want for anything."

"It was better the way it was. Trust me, Mom."

They spoke a little while longer before hanging up.

Then Carissa stood in the kitchen with half a glass of orange juice and the makings of a killer headache. She needed to take a shower and get ready for the fund-raiser. But she couldn't seem to move her feet. Somehow, she felt relieved and renewed after the conversation with her mother. Everything came back to one statement her mother had made.

Because I love him. The phrase echoed throughout her mind over and over. No qualms. No conditions. Her mother loved her father and that was it.

Carissa dropped the glass she was holding, the shards of glass raining onto the countertop she'd just cleaned. But she was too amazed at the epiphany she'd just had to worry about some broken glass.

For all of these years, Carissa had been searching for perfection. That's why she'd dated and subsequently married Preston. She'd wanted perfection and she'd gotten it. Only, life hadn't been quite so perfect. Preston had the pedigree and the manners. He was smart and handsome. They lived in the picture-perfect condo with the gorgeous view of the Chicago skyline. Their parties were attended by the best people. They drove the right cars. They belonged to the right clubs. They played the part just right.

Only it had been very, very wrong.

Her perfect-on-paper husband had been a massive disappointment off the page.

Then, there was Jasper. She always seemed to return to him. Not just her body, but her thoughts, her feelings. Even in college, he never strayed far from her musings. During her marriage, she would find Jasper creeping in to remind her of a much happier time.

She'd walked out on him and the café deal because he'd scared her. She loved him so he, and he alone, had the ability to hurt her more than anyone else. More than her dad even. And still, she wanted to be with him. He drove her crazy and she longed for him. Why?

"Because I love him," she said into the silence of the kitchen, echoing her mother's earlier statement. "I love Jasper."

She ran a hand through her hair. *Ohmigod, I love Jasper.* She started giggling uncontrollably as she wondered when it had happened. Maybe she'd never stopped loving him from back in high school. It didn't really matter because despite everything, she was in love with him now. More importantly, she realized that loving someone meant loving all of them, imperfections and all. After all, she had a lot of imperfections and Jasper seemed to look past them.

She may not understand her parents' relationship. She definitely didn't get how her mother could put up with her father's lack of ambition and general laziness. But it wasn't up to her. After that phone call, she understood that her mother loved her father anyway. In spite of everything life had thrown at them.

And she loved Jasper Dumont in the same careless, crazy, makes-no-sense kind of way. At one time, she'd thought that her ex-husband was the polar opposite of her father. But she'd been wrong. Jasper was the one who represented everything her father didn't.

Now she had to figure out how to tell him and hope that she hadn't pushed him away too much the other day.

Jasper walked through one of the side doors to his alma mater. It smelled of school—pencils, erasers, gym shoes. He glanced around the hallway. The lockers had been upgraded since his time here. But the large overhead light still flickered like it had when he'd been a student. Were they never going to fix it?

Jasper continued down the hallway. He knew it was still the same old Bayside High and yet it seemed smaller somehow. Maybe because this was no longer the center of his universe. That had been a different era where things like study hall, baseball practice and Carissa Blackwell were the most important things on his mind.

Well, maybe one of those things was still in the forefront of his mind.

He continued toward the gymnasium. The last thing he wanted to do today was show up for this date auction. He hadn't slept in two nights and felt like crap. But he'd promised Riley before Carissa had even returned to town, and he wouldn't go back on that. Even though he really didn't want to go out with anyone but Carissa. Was that ever going to happen again? Jasper still didn't get what had gone down in his office. One minute they'd been discussing the café. The next, she'd been accusing him of controlling her life and walking away from him.

And once again, he felt like he hadn't been good enough. Like all of his work and all of his planning wasn't enough.

Worse was the fact that her words had the ability to make him feel the way he used to when he'd originally walked through these hallways. Fun Jasper Dumont who everyone likes but no one takes seriously.

Cam came around the corner from the opposite direction as Jasper reached the gym. Cam's face fell instantly. "What's wrong?" he asked.

Jasper shook his head. "Nothing. Just gearing up to be a piece of meat."

Cam placed a firm hand on Jasper's shoulder and steered him away from the gym's door. "Cut the crap, Jasp. What happened?"

He shrugged first, but the next thing he knew he was spilling the entire story. "In conclusion, well, I don't really know what the conclusion is or where we stand." He let out a harsh laugh. "I wasn't ambitious enough back in high school and I guess now I'm too ambitious." He threw his hands up in the air. "Can't win. But the bookstore and café is a great idea. Now I have to figure out how to proceed." *Without Carissa.* Jasper looked down at his feet. If he hadn't, he may have anticipated the slap upside the head from his brother. "Hey, what was that?"

"Did that knock any sense into you? Because there's more where that came from. Stop feeling sorry for yourself."

"I'm not..." He trailed off. He couldn't finish the sentence because he was, in fact, feeling sorry for himself.

"Nothing to say?" Cam goaded.

"Fine, I'm being indulgent. But who cares. The woman I love didn't accept what I offered her and walked out on me."

Love? Yes, love. He still loved Carissa.

Cam's face softened. "Oh, Jasp."

Anger suddenly took over. "What? It's not like you didn't know." For extra emphasis, he gave a good hard push squarely in his brother's chest. "Tell me you didn't know."

Cam was shaking his head as he said, "Christ, Jasp, everyone knew. You love her and she loves you."

"She doesn't love—"

"Don't even finish that sentence, bro. The only two people in Bayside who are unaware of their feelings are you and Carissa."

Jasper wanted to lash out. Instead, he sank back against the lockers, exhausted. "Answer me this. If she loves me, then why did she react that way when I offered her such a great opportunity?"

Cam shook his head. "I love you, but you are incredibly stupid."

"Hey," Jasper protested. "I'm hurting here."

"You're hurting because you're an idiot. And it sounds like Carissa is screwing you again." Cam held up a restraining hand as Jasper straightened. "I'm sorry but I think she left you hanging high and dry just like she did back in high school."

"It's not like that, Cam. There are other things at play here. Issues with her parents. Her dad, in particular. And you don't even know the reason why she broke up with me after graduation."

"Do you?"

"Yes, we talked about it. It's all tied to those issues."

Cam rolled back on his heels and leveled Jasper with a firm stare.

"What?"

"Did you hear what you just said?"

Jasper replayed their conversation. He didn't detect anything special.

Cam punched him in the arm. "She has issues. Issues that made her run from you once already."

"I just told you that."

"You really are dense. If she ran from you once due to her own personal demons, might that be the same reason she's doing it again?"

"Well…huh." He hadn't thought of it that way.

"She's not rejecting you, Jasp. She's protecting herself."

"But that's what I was trying to do by setting up this café for her. By helping her get everything started."

"Helping? Or controlling?" Cam laughed. "I know you, Jasp. You run in at full speed and try to help so much that you end up taking over. Maybe that's not what she needs."

It most certainly wasn't. He was an idiot.

"Come to your senses yet?"

"Seems like it."

"Then, go get your girl." With that, he shoved his hands in his pockets and walked down the hall to the gym, whistling while he left Jasper with a lot to think about.

When had Cam become so damn wise? Had to be Elle's doing. Cam had never been in touch with his emotions— or anyone else's, for that matter—before Elle came along.

He exhaled and ran a hand over his face. But the truth was that he did love Carissa. And he hoped Cam was right and she loved him, too. He hadn't meant to force his idea on her. It really had come from a good place.

He started walking toward the gym but suddenly froze. Maybe it had been for himself a bit, too. Maybe he had come on strong. Maybe he should have listened to her more and not forced his opinions.

"Dumont, there you are."

He turned to see Riley's bubbly face bouncing toward him. "Did you just call me Dumont?"

She slapped him on the arm. "It's the gym, I'm telling you. Makes me feel all masculine."

He chuckled. "Nice scarf," he commented. Riley was always dressed to the nines. Today she wore all black with a pop of color from a bright yellow scarf with lime-green polka dots tied around her neck.

"Thanks. I'm going for dramatic effect for my emcee outfit."

"That means you didn't decide to cancel this whole date auction then?"

Riley chucked him under his chin. "And disappoint all the women of Bayside? I expect you to bring in the most money."

"That's a lot of pressure." He followed her into the gym and was immediately assaulted by the usual suspects. His mother and her friends were all dancing around him, offering advice for the auction and pledging their desire to bid on him, all while his brother and Elle stood hand in hand against the wall with identical grins as they watched him. He offered a finger of choice in his brother's direction just before Riley led him onto the stage.

"Hey, Ri, have you, um, seen Carissa lately?" he whispered so none of the other bachelors would hear.

Her eyes instantly softened as she looked his way. "As a matter of fact, I have."

He waited but Riley didn't give in. "And?" he asked.

"And I think the two of you should talk. Like, really talk."

"Apparently, that's a popular idea," he said drily. He searched the gym, hoping for a glance of Carissa. Even if he couldn't see the rows of tables in the back of the gym filled to the brim with cookies, his nose would have alerted him. This was definitely the best this gym had ever smelled. It also meant that Carissa had to be around somewhere. "Is she here?"

Riley opened her mouth but before she could say anything, her name was called. She needed to go to the podium to begin the auction. "We'll talk afterward," she promised.

He nodded because what else could he do?

The auction began but Jasper spent most of it in a blur. He knew every single bachelor up on stage. Heck, he also knew almost every single person crammed into the gym to witness this spectacle. But he kept his eyes trained on the tables of cookies in the back of the gym. Surely Carissa would show up at some point.

Riley seemed to be doing a great job as emcee, offering stats and hobbies of each of the bachelors. She had people placed around the gym to help her as arm after arm shot into the air, pledging money in exchange for a date with Bayside's finest.

One of the men to bring in the most bids was Sawyer Wallace, editor of the Bayside Bugle. Interestingly, he was promised to Simone, who seemed ecstatic she'd won. As they marched off together, Jasper noticed a rare frown on Riley's usually happy face.

But she pulled herself together quickly and announced the last bachelor of the day. Jasper didn't even realize it was his name being called until he felt someone push him from behind and he stumbled onstage.

"Ah, here's the man everyone's been waiting for. Making quite the entrance, it's Jasper Dumont."

A round of applause, along with the obligatory catcalls, sounded. Jasper took his first mark, having been trained by Riley the other day. They had three different marks to hit while Riley read out their stats. He felt like an idiot standing there as people stared at him.

"Jasper Dumont is one of Bayside's most eligible bachelors. Besides running Dumont Incorporated, Jasper enjoys coffee from The Brewside, graphic novels, baseball and long, romantic walks on the beach."

Jasper turned and shot Riley an annoyed look. He most certainly had not said that about the beach walks. She snickered and continued reading her stats, only half of which were true.

When she finished, he took center stage to thunderous applause. He noticed his mother was standing front and center.

The bidding began at twenty dollars. It quickly rose to forty.

"Forty-five," one of his mother's friends offered.

"Fifty." Jasper almost choked at his old high school English teacher's bid.

"Fifty-five." Lilah Dumont jumped up and down excitedly.

"You can't bid on me, Mom," Jasper said through clenched teeth. Everyone laughed.

Once the figure got up to one hundred dollars, a bidding war ensued. Both women were beautiful and a couple months ago, Jasper would have been glowing from the attention and the opportunity to go out with either one of them.

But at the moment, he couldn't seem to find any excitement in the idea of sharing a meal with anyone but Carissa. His gaze drifted over to the cookie tables and once again he was disappointed to see they remained Carissa-less.

"Ladies, ladies, let's keep it G-rated," Riley was saying. "There are kids here today. We're up to two hundred dollars and the fight seems to be narrowed down to Jenny Heatherlea and Trina Wingate. Do I hear two-ten?"

"Two-ten."

Everyone, including Jasper, turned to the side entrance of the gym as the new voice rang out over the crowd. He heard a few gasps at the sight of Carissa.

"Hey, that's not fair," Jenny, one of the women bidding on him, called out. "She just got here."

"And they used to date," Trina, the other woman, complained. "She has an advantage."

Riley tried to calm the crowd down from the podium. "There are no exclusions in this auction. Anyone is free to bid. Let's continue."

"I heard they're still dating." This came from Tony from The Brewside, who had donated coffee and tea for the event. "According to the Bayside Blogger."

"Thanks, man," Jasper called out.

Tony offered a grin in exchange, clearly enjoying himself.

"Nope, they broke up again. Didn't you see Facebook today?" someone else called out.

"In any case, we are going to accept Carissa's bid," Riley continued. "Even though she's starting her own business and really shouldn't be spending any extra money at the moment."

Jasper would have chuckled at Riley's commentary if he wasn't so entranced by Carissa's entrance. She looked beautiful, as always. Today she had on tight jeans, a bright red sweater and tall, sexy boots. But she also looked tired. Even from across the gym, he could see the strain on her face, the shadows under her eyes. She wove her fingers together nervously as she bit her lip.

Part of Jasper wanted to rush to her. He wanted to pull her into his arms and never let go. Another part of him felt cautious, unsure of what she was thinking. To be honest, he was still a little hurt. And yet there was a glimmer of hope. She'd shown up and bid on him.

"Last bid was two hundred and ten dollars. Do I hear two-fifteen?" Riley asked the crowd.

"Three hundred dollars," one of the women shouted. The rest of the crowd offered a collective "ooohhhh."

Riley looked toward Carissa, who was frowning. Jasper knew she didn't have the money to do this.

"Four hundred," the other bidder screamed.

Holy crap, Jasper thought.

"My, what generosity we're seeing today," Riley said. "We have an offer of four hundred dollars for Jasper Dumont."

"Five hundred," Jenny said. "I always win," she added with a determined look toward Trina, who threw her hands in the air and backed up. She was out.

So it was between Jenny, who always won, and Carissa.

When Jasper turned in Carissa's direction though, she was nowhere in sight. His heart sank.

"Okay," Riley said uncertainly, also noticing that her friend was absent. "We have five hundred dollars for Jasper Dumont. Do I hear five-ten?"

"No."

Everyone flung around to face the back of the gym where Carissa now stood. She was next to one of the cookie tables.

She'd said no. Jasper wanted to melt into the stage.

Then Carissa grabbed two of the cookies and held them high in the air. "I don't have five hundred and ten dollars. But I do have cookies. I bid all of these peanut butter cookies."

"She can't do that," Jenny said.

"I don't know. These cookies are pretty good." This was said by George from the Rusty Keg, who had cookie crumbs embedded in his beard.

"I offer my chocolate chip cookies, the oatmeal raisin, the shortbread." Carissa was walking forward as she spoke. "I give you all of my coconut bars, the white chocolate macadamia nut." She handed the two cookies she still held to Cam as she walked by, her eyes now clasped onto Jasper's.

"I give you the brownies I made, both the regular and the double-chocolate caramel ones. And…and…well, that's everything I made for today. But I will make you anything you want, Jasp."

She spread her arms wide, offering herself to him. Jasper realized how huge the gesture was for her, so he jumped off the stage and met her halfway.

"All of this for one date with me?" he asked her.

"Well," she said in a quiet voice, lowering it so only he could hear. "I was hoping for more than one date."

"The café," he began. "I'm sorry I was so controlling and that I…"

She held up a hand to stop him. "I want to do the café, Jasp. You challenge me and I know you only wanted what's best for me."

"Hey, can you guys speak up? We can't hear you," George called out. Everyone started chuckling, but Jasper softened his voice even more.

"I was trying to help you, because I love helping the people I care about."

"One of your best qualities." Red tinged her cheeks as she glanced around at all of the people watching them. "I overreacted."

"That's not true—" he began, but she cut him off.

"I was blaming you for other things in my life and… well, it doesn't matter. Because you're not my father. You're not my ex."

"What am I then?"

Her gaze drilled into his. "You're the person I want to be with."

He was having a hell of a time staying calm. "I'm not perfect, Car."

A tear spilled over onto her cheek. "Thank God." With that she launched herself into his arms and held on tight. "I want you, Jasper. Just the way you are."

"Good," he whispered into her ear. "Because I love you, Car. I did back then and I do now."

"I love you, too." She pressed her lips to his to the sound of monstrous applause.

"Well, folks, I think we have our winner for Jasper Dumont. Sorry, Jenny," Riley said from the stage, not sounding sorry at all. There were tears shining in her eyes.

The crowd kept clapping and whistling but Jasper couldn't care less. He felt like the luckiest man alive. Carissa beamed up at him even as her eyes shone with unshed tears.

He might be back in his old high school, but everything was different now. Today, he felt like a new man. A happy man, who couldn't believe how fortunate he was to have the woman of his dreams standing in his arms.

Epilogue

Life is sweet, dear Bayside.

How can you not think that after watching Carissa and Jasper in the gym earlier today? Seems like they got over their issues and let each other in. No doubt another happy ending. And too bad for Jenny and Trina, who I heard were both drowning their sorrows in the dozens of cookies they purchased after the auction...

From her seat in The Brewside, the Bayside Blogger sat back, perusing her screen and what she'd just typed. She was happy about Carissa and Jasper. And she liked to think that she had something to do with their reunion. Sometimes people just needed a little push. After all, where would Bayside be without her meddling? Some people may claim to get annoyed but honestly, she only nudged where she saw a need. And Carissa and Jasper had definitely needed a big fat shove.

Now they were together. They'd left the gym hand in hand, right behind big brother Cam and Elle. Two other people who'd needed some help to get to their happy ending.

The Bayside Blogger reread her column again, made some tweaks, and then hit Post. Now that the Dumont brothers were taken care of, perhaps it was time to focus on herself. Maybe it was her turn to find love.

Luckily she didn't do a video blog or everyone would see the frown on her face. Like most people, she'd been through her own ordeal. Did she deserve love? She wasn't sure.

Shaking her head, she tried to dispel the sudden dark mood. After all, today was a good day. She'd helped two more people get together. For now, that would have to be enough.

Her story was one for another day.

Packing up her laptop, she rose, flinging her computer bag over her shoulder and reaching for her purse. She gave a little wave to Tony, who offered a smile and wave back.

As she pushed through the door and smiled at the sound of the melodious chimes, she had no idea that she'd left her bright yellow scarf with lime-green polka dots on the table...

* * * * *

LET'S TALK

Romance

For exclusive extracts, competitions
and special offers, find us online:

Ⓕ facebook.com/millsandboon

Ⓣ @MillsandBoon

Ⓘ @MillsandBoonUK

Get in touch on 01413 063232

For all the latest titles coming soon, visit
millsandboon.co.uk/nextmonth

MILLS & BOON

THE HEART OF ROMANCE

A ROMANCE FOR EVERY KIND OF READER

MODERN

Prepare to be swept off your feet by sophisticated, sexy and seductive heroes, in some of the world's most glamourous and romantic locations, where power and passion collide.
8 stories per month.

HISTORICAL

Escape with historical heroes from time gone by. Whether your passion is for wicked Regency Rakes, muscled Vikings or rugged Highlanders, awaken the romance of the past.
6 stories per month.

MEDICAL

Set your pulse racing with dedicated, delectable doctors in the high-pressure world of medicine, where emotions run high and passion, comfort and love are the best medicine.
6 stories per month.

True Love

Celebrate true love with tender stories of heartfelt romance, from the rush of falling in love to the joy a new baby can bring, and a focus on the emotional heart of a relationship.
8 stories per month.

Desire

Indulge in secrets and scandal, intense drama and plenty of sizzling hot action with powerful and passionate heroes who have it all: wealth, status, good looks…everything but the right woman.
6 stories per month.

HEROES

Experience all the excitement of a gripping thriller, with an intense romance at its heart. Resourceful, true-to-life women and strong, fearless men face danger and desire - a killer combination!
8 stories per month.

DARE

Sensual love stories featuring smart, sassy heroines you'd want as a best friend, and compelling intense heroes who are worthy of them.
4 stories per month.

To see which titles are coming soon, please visit

millsandboon.co.uk/nextmonth